THE PENGUIN CLASSICS

FOUNDER EDITOR (1944–64): E. V. RIEU

MARY SANDBACH has known Sweden and its writers for over fifty years. After teaching translation in various language schools in Cambridge for six years, she translated her first book, Strindberg's *Inferno*, in 1962. Other works by Strindberg followed: *From an Occult Diary* in 1965, *The Cloister* in 1969 and *Getting Married* in 1972, the latter being the only annotated edition of the work in any language. She has also translated novels by modern Swedish authors and a number of films by Ingmar Bergman. She is currently working on another prose work by Strindberg, *By the Open Sea*. In 1974 she received the Swedish Order of Vasa for her services to Swedish literature.

Virtue is the key to freedom.

AUGUST STRINDBERG

INFERNO
AND
FROM AN OCCULT DIARY
(SELECTED BY TORSTEN EKLUND)

TRANSLATED
WITH AN INTRODUCTION
BY MARY SANDBACH

PENGUIN BOOKS

Penguin Books Ltd, Harmondsworth, Middlesex, England
Penguin Books, 625 Madison Avenue, New York, New York 10022, U.S.A.
Penguin Books Australia Ltd, Ringwood, Victoria, Australia
Penguin Books Canada Ltd, 2801 John Street, Markham, Ontario, Canada L3R 1B4
Penguin Books (N.Z.) Ltd, 182–190 Wairau Road, Auckland 10, New Zealand

—

This translation of *Inferno* first published by Hutchinson 1962
English translation copyright © Hutchinson & Co. (Publishers) Ltd, 1962
This translation of *From an Occult Diary* first published by
Martin Secker & Warburg Ltd, 1965
Selection copyright © Albert Bonniers Förlag AB, 1963
English translation copyright © Martin Secker & Warburg Ltd, 1965
This one-volume edition published with a new Introduction in Penguin Classics 1979
Introduction copyright © Mary Sandbach, 1979
All rights reserved

—

Made and printed in Great Britain by
C. Nicholls & Company Ltd
Set in Linotype Pilgrim

CONTENTS

INTRODUCTION

[For an explanation of all abbreviations used in
this volume see page 91.]

It is appropriate that these two translations[1] should appear
together in one volume; the most important parts of each
are based on a diary that Strindberg kept from 21 February
1896 to 11 July 1908, and which, after 1907, he called his
Occult Diary. But whereas in *Inferno* the material used was
selected by Strindberg himself and presented in the form in
which he wished it to be read, in *From an Occult Diary* the
selection has been made by the distinguished Strindberg
scholar Torsten Eklund, and the entries from the diary made
more intelligible by the addition of letters to and from
Harriet Bosse, Strindberg's third wife, and by short pass-
ages from her commentary on them.

The early entries in the diary cover a variety of subjects,
but from 1901 they are mainly about Harriet Bosse, and his
relationship with her.

Strindberg seems to have found it difficult to decide
whether the diary should ever be published. In 1904 he
told Emil Schering, his German translator and intimate
friend, that he wanted it to be bound in one volume with
his other autobiographical works. In 1907, when he was
in desperate financial straits, he saw it as a way of raising
money for his rent, and sent it to his publisher, Karl Otto
Bonnier, saying that it might be published after his death.
A year later, in January 1908, he withdrew this permission,
and in March wrote a note on the diary which said that it
should never be published.

However, shortly before his death he changed his mind

1. Previously published in separate volumes, *Inferno* by Hutchinson in 1962, *From an Occult Diary* by Secker & Warburg, 1965.

again and returned to his original idea of having the diary bound in one volume with his other autobiographical works which he listed as follows:

The Son of a Servant
(to be published in one volume under the above title
after my death)
The Son of a Servant
Time of Ferment
In the Red Room
The Son of a Servant Part IV
Le Plaidoyer d'un fou
The Collection of Letters 'He and She'
The Quarantine Officer's Second Story
Inferno
Legends
Selected Letters
The Occult Diary

Needless to say no one has attempted to produce such an unwieldy volume. In Sweden John Landquist's collected edition of his works in fifty-five volumes was published shortly after Strindberg's death, but the first volume of collected letters did not appear until 1948, and the series has not yet been completed. A facsimile edition of *The Occult Diary* (*Ockulta dagboken*) was published in Sweden in May 1977. An English translation is planned and may one day be on the market, but several of the other works he listed as autobiography have not yet been translated.

Strindberg's Fortunes 1884–97

Strindberg was forty-eight when he wrote *Inferno* in May–June 1897. It is an account of his experiences from the year 1894 to the spring of 1897, a period during which he seems to have been driven off course, unable to write either drama or other imaginative literature but beset by hallucinations and strange fancies, among which was a belief that he had a great future as an alchemist. This episode cannot be understood without some knowledge of a long series of events which preceded it. Thirteen difficult years had gone before, difficult even for one who had never known what it was to have an easy life. His finances, never good, had been in a more precarious state than ever since 1884 when, after the publication of the first part of *Getting Married* (*Giftas*), he was prosecuted for blasphemy. Although he was acquitted publishers were afraid of him; his great unpopularity in Sweden made him a bad investment. People were consequently reluctant to publish his books and only a few of his plays were put on the stage. When *The Father* was performed in 1888 the outcry from the press and the public was so vehement that it had to come off after only nine performances, and all that Strindberg received was a royalty of forty crowns. In 1890 the verse version of his play *Master Olof* was a considerable success. It was acted sixteen times, but the money it brought him, altogether 936 crowns,[2] was only enough to pay some of his worst debts and keep the family going for a few weeks. It must all have gone by May, for he wrote to his brother Axel: 'On board the steamer to Runmarö I find I've ten crowns in my purse. Can you, with your fantastic ability to chase up money, borrow a hundred crowns for a month! Try to do so even if you've sworn never to lend me anything more. In a month I shall be getting a thousand crowns from Bonnier . . .' But this was one of his typical miscalculations; he had already been paid the thousand crowns.

Lack of money was not his only source of misery. In 1891 came the breakdown of his marriage to Siri von Essen, his first wife, ending a relationship that had lasted for thirteen years and had been of the greatest importance to

2. In 1890 19 kr. was equivalent to 11 shillings in the British money of the time.

him. Siri was no angel and must share the blame for what happened, but there is no doubt that their parting was agonizingly painful to both, perhaps most of all to Strindberg because his divorce, finalized in 1892, deprived him of his three children, to whom he had always been a devoted and affectionate father.

It also made him more acutely aware of the precarious state of his finances, for he was never able to pay regularly the alimony of 150 crowns a month that the court had decreed, and this was a constant source of worry and shame. By the autumn of 1892 his position in Sweden was so desperate that a new start somewhere else seemed the only answer to his problems. Ola Hansson, a fellow writer who was already in Germany, urged Strindberg to join him there and also raised the money to enable him to do so. On 1 October 1892 he arrived in Berlin, where both he and his friends believed that his prospects were considerably brighter than in Sweden.

This was to some extent true. *The Father* had been performed in 1890, *Miss Julie* in April 1892, so his name was known, at least in literary circles. But life in Berlin was a struggle too, and on 28 December, not long after his arrival, he summed up his position in these words: 'I now have 35 pfennigs. Prospects brilliant, situation desperate as always.'

In 1893 articles were written about him, some of his works were published and one of his plays, *Comrades* (*Kamraterna*), had quite a long run. This should have brought in enough money to keep him going for a time, but an unfortunate misunderstanding with the management of the theatre meant that he got nothing and remained as impecunious as before.

Moreover, his way of life and the company he kept did not help him to live economically. In Berlin he joined a group of gifted men whose favourite haunt was a tavern nicknamed by Strindberg *Zum schwarzen Ferkel* (The Little

Black Pig). The group which met there is always known as 'the Ferkel Circle', and the story of their revels – in which Strindberg played a prominent part – he has told himself in his novel *The Cloister*.

In Berlin he met his second wife, Frida Uhl, a lively young Austrian journalist many years his junior, and on 2 May 1893 he made his second unfortunate marriage. Frida Uhl was a clever and beautiful young woman but, as her later life was to prove, an inveterate lion hunter. Strindberg was her first really important lion, and naturally she wanted him to roar. After a stormy life together, which also had its moments of pleasure and peace, they parted in 1894. The story of the ups and downs of this marriage is told in *The Cloister*, a light-hearted and at times even humorous account compared with the bitterness and vindictiveness of *A Madman's Defence* (*Le Plaidoyer d'un fou*), the story of his first marriage. But he was never as emotionally involved with Frida as he was with Siri, and moreover, while *The Cloister* was written in 1898, some years after the events it describes, *A Madman's Defence* was written while he was still married to Siri and enduring all the torments of jealousy and suspicion that their relationship provoked.

Frida was a trial to Strindberg in many ways, chiefly because she would interfere with his affairs and write behind his back to his famous friends, but she had one great advantage in that her father was rich and gave her a generous dowry. This enabled them to make their disappointing journey to England in 1893, where they totally failed to arouse any interest in his works. There is no evidence that Strindberg married Frida for her money, but this made it unnecessary for him to feel that his poverty seriously affected her. She was able to come and go as she pleased. The one thing she could not do was persuade Strindberg to write literary works.

There were two reasons for this: the practical difficulties that prevented him being printed or staged, and a temperamental difficulty of long standing. At various times in his life Strindberg became overwhelmed by a feeling that it was wrong of him to devote himself to imaginative writing in prose or verse. One such occasion was in May 1884, when his publisher, Bonnier, was urging him to give up writing essays and produce another novel: '... because a novel would sell (i.e. bring me in twice as much as the pure naked truth) ... Here is my dilemma!' he told his friend the Norwegian author Bjørnstjerne Bjørnson on 1 May 1884. 'To be useful I must be read! To be read I must write "art" but I think art is immoral. Consequently: either die with a pure soul, or continue with what is for me an immoral occupation!'

Many people have tried to unravel the complexities of Strindberg's character and various reasons for his dilemma have been advanced. Perhaps Bjørnson came closest to the truth when he declared, 'He was a pietist in the past, and in spite of having got over it many times, a pietist he still is.' Certain it is that he had a great capacity for feeling that everything he thoroughly enjoyed was sinful.

His favourite avenue of escape from his dangerous temptress literature was science. 'I probably have another thirty years to live,' he wrote to his brother Axel on 12 July 1889, 'a whole lifetime, and belles lettres is a thing one should practise in one's youth, but my youth was lost, thanks to people's cruelty, and now I've no longer the necessary illusions.

'Science stands higher, and surely we must grow, we must learn, not sink into being a literary man who has written himself dry.'

The idea of turning to science occurs in a letter written six days before the one just quoted: 'Belles lettres make me sick and by degrees I shall go over to science, the practice of which is an unparalleled delight. But bread it will not give.'

The feeling that he had written himself dry was another ingredient in his disenchantment with literature. Years of overproduction were taking their toll. Between 1885 and 1889, when he started to write *By the Open Sea* (*I havsbandet*), he had written all four parts of *The Son of a Servant* (*Tjänstekvinnans son*), *A Madman's Defence* (*Le Plaidoyer d'un fou*), *The People of Hemsö* (*Hemsöborna*), *The Father* (*Fadren*), *Miss Julie* (*Fröken Julie*), *Comrades* (*Kamraterna*), *Creditors* (*Fordringsägare*) and a host of other works. It took him nearly a year to complete *By the Open Sea*, and when it was finished in June 1890 he wrote virtually nothing more until the late summer of 1891.

In February 1891 he began to think of going to Paris, where he believed there were faint signs of interest in his work. He therefore wrote on 2 February to his friend Leopold Littmansson to ask if he could find him somewhere to live. His first object, he said, would be to promote the publication of his treatise on the relations between France and Sweden; the second, he continued,

... to find myself an unassuming position whereby I could maintain myself and my three children. Suggestions: instructor in German in a family; reader of German, English, Italian and Scandinavian newspapers for a French newspaper (something corresponding to the foreign departments in our newspapers); if necessary a porter at a big hotel, able to speak French, German, English, and Scandinavian; a porter earns a lot of money.

You will think these are wild fancies. But the fact is that I have reached a point in my career when it has become a case of saving my talent from overproduction, and my children from want.

In a word, there must be a pause in my activity as an author, otherwise I shall be finished.

At the time he wrote this letter he was clearly hoping to be given custody of his three children, but it was a vain hope. The loss of his children became an obsession, and he could neither write nor think of anything else. 'And now I'm almost mad with longing for my children,' he wrote to a friend on 5 October 1891. 'I go to the southern part of the city where they live, just to experience the pleasure of being in the same area as they . . .' It is therefore not surprising that when at last he did begin to write again, his play, The Keys of Heaven (*Himmelrikets nycklar*), was woven round the theme of a father's loss. 'My children are now my *idée fixe*, and for them I am writing a fairy-tale play,' he wrote to a friend three weeks later. But his inspiration only carried him through the first act in which the Smith, his chief character, laments the loss of his dead children. The rest of this five-act play is a confused jumble of many folk-tale motifs and, though he got it printed, no one would perform it. It occupied him on and off for several months, a clear indication of his lack of inspiration.

His experience with The Keys of Heaven and with the six one-act plays that followed it convinced him that he could not earn a living in Sweden by writing drama, and it was this conviction, quite as much as his psychological difficulties, that prevented him from writing any more plays for six years.

Of the six one-act plays written in 1892, Playing with Fire (*Leka med elden*) and The Bond (*Bandet*) were among his best, but they were not staged in Sweden until 1908, and then only at his own Intimate Theatre, opened in Stockholm in 1907. On 13 September 1892 he wrote to Ola Hansson, the friend who was urging him to go to Germany: 'I've finished six plays of which two are powerful – like The Father and Miss Julie, but without any indecencies that might hinder production – abroad. In Sweden people make the excuses of the unwilling about everything that Aug. Sg. does.'

These circumstances and the mood they generated meant that Frida had no hope of persuading him to resume his career as a dramatist. The moderate success he had in Germany in 1892–3 could not compensate for the failure of his works in Sweden, nor quench the feeling that the writing of literature was something he must give up. It is arguable that if what he produced had been received with enthusiasm he might never have been troubled by doubts about the value and rightness of his literary work, but in the autumn of 1893, when he was living with Frida in Brunn (Brno) in Austria, these doubts were heavy upon him. In *The Cloister* he wrote:

What an occupation! To sit and flay your fellow men and then offer their skins for sale and expect them to buy them. To be like a hunter, who in his need chops off his dog's tail, and after eating the flesh himself, offers the dog the bones, his own bones. To spy out people's secrets, betray your best friend's birthmark, use your wife as an experimental rabbit, behave like a Croat, chop down, defile, burn, and sell. Fie for shame!

This was his mood when he sat down to write his first large pseudo-scientific work in November 1893. He called it *Antibarbarus*, the anti-barbarian, the man against the conventional scientists of his day. In it he set out to explain the nature of sulphur, the transmutation of carbon and other elements, and the composition of water and air. He called himself a transformist like Darwin and a monist like Herbert Spencer and the German naturalist Ernst Haekel, and explained his position in these words:

In my capacity as a monist I have committed myself for the time being to the assumption that all elements and all forces are related. And *if* they derive from one source, then they sprang into existence by means of condensation and attenuation, of copulation and crossbreeding, of heredity and transformation, of selection and struggle, addition and substitution – and whatever else one cares to suggest.[3]

3. Brandell–Jacobs, p 169. (For abbreviations used in the Introduction, see pp. 91–2.)

The last vague words indicate his unscientific attitude.
The fact is that Strindberg's approach to science was philosophical and speculative rather than experimental. He wrote to his gifted young botanist friend Bengt Lidforss on 1 January 1891:

> Sometimes I doubt all experiments . . . I believe rather in the depth of my conscious thought or, more correctly, of my unconscious thought. What do you say to that? . . .
>
> I put myself into a state of unconsciousness, not with drink or anything like it, for that only awakens a host of memories and new ideas, but by distractions, games, cards, sleep, novels, and then I let my brain work freely, without bothering about results, or acceptability, and something emerges that I can believe in, just because it has grown inevitably, as my family tree has grown . . .

This is the method or, if you will, the madness of the poet, and closely resembles his answer to the question 'How do you write?' put to him by *Bonniers Månadshäften* in 1909.

> Yes, let him say who can! – It begins with fermentation or some sort of agreeable fever which passes into ecstasy or intoxication. Sometimes it is like a seed growing, attracting all attention to itself, consuming all experiences, but yet choosing and discarding. Sometimes I think I am some sort of medium, for it comes so easily, half unconsciously, hardly calculated at all! But it lasts at the most for three hours (usually from 9 to 12). And when it is over everything is as boring as ever, until the next time. But it does not come on me to order, not when *I* please. When *it* pleases it comes. But best and most when there has been a general bust up . . .[4]

This point, the resemblance in his approach to his subject, whether it was scientific or literary, was emphasized by Lidforss in his article 'Strindberg as a Natural Scientist' ('Strindberg som naturforskere'), in which he says: 'The

4. Falck, pp. 80–81.

Strindberg one encounters in *Antibarbarus* is essentially the same as the one who appears in *Tschandala* and *By the Open Sea*, but the medium in which he moves is different.'[5]

When he had finished part of *Antibarbarus* he sent it to Lidforss for an opinion. He had first met this young man in Lund in 1890 and later in Berlin. There Lidforss became one of the 'Ferkel Circle'. He had strong literary interests and greatly admired Strindberg, whom he often addressed as 'Lord and Master' and, when Strindberg begged him to desist, as 'Master'.

After a first reading of what he had been sent, he wrote to Strindberg on 20 December 1892 to say that his impression of it was 'intense and overwhelming' and added, after making a few moderately critical remarks: 'Every line so clearly bears the noble imprint of genius that the whole work, in spite of a few things that will be anathema to the professionals, must be a splendid success.' On 6 February he encouraged Strindberg still further by telling him that he was to be included in a work he was preparing on modern natural scientists. It is therefore not surprising that on 15 February Strindberg sent Lidforss the completed book and asked him to undertake the translation of it into German and to negotiate with a publisher. A few days later Lidforss was able to report that it had been accepted by the Bibliographisches Bureau and that he would do the translation.

Publishers moved rapidly in those days. On 4 April Strindberg was in Berlin and had finished reading the proofs – presumably with Lidforss – and the book was published some time in May. But before this, on 13 April, a pre-publication review appeared in the Swedish daily newspaper *Dagens Nyheter*. It was far from favourable. The writer denied that Strindberg had any ability for research

5. Brandell–Jacobs, p. 303, n.8.

and declared that *Antibarbarus* was only interesting from a psychological point of view, showing clearly the way in which its author muddled up facts, hypotheses and chimeras. He added: 'Strindberg's old opponents will no doubt take this excellent opportunity to make capital out of the many eccentricities of the book, while the trained professionals will mostly dismiss it with a shrug of the shoulders and a few words about genius and madness.'

Imagine Strindberg's dismay when he discovered that the author of this review was none other than Lidforss himself. His young friend's treachery was a bitter blow, but he eventually comforted himself by attributing it to sexual jealousy. According to him, Dagny Juel, the Norwegian girl whom Edvard Munch had introduced into the Ferkel Circle in Berlin in 1893, had accepted him as a lover but had rejected Lidforss. This explanation, which he gave in a letter of 26 June 1894 to the Danish critic Georg Brandes, served to enhance his self-esteem at a time when he badly needed reassurance.

The extent of his need can be measured by the numerous letters he wrote to scientific friends or people with influence, asking for an opinion and often begging for support. Göran Söderström believes that a quarrel about money lay at the root of Lidforss's defection, and that in his review he was revenging himself on Strindberg for the latter's failure to pay him properly for his translation. But is there not another possible explanation? Lidforss was a young man of twenty-five on the threshold of a brilliant career. He had recently become the Berlin correspondent for *Dagens Nyheter*, and he may well have realized that to give whole-hearted support in that paper to a book of doubtful scientific value would do his career no good. Whatever the motive, it was a dirty trick to play on the unsuspecting Strindberg. In time he forgave Lidforss, indeed it was from him that he borrowed Swedenborg's *Arcana*

Coelestia in December 1896. But in May 1894 such a reconciliation was unthinkable; Strindberg was deeply shaken.
He was never really confident about his scientific work,
especially *vis-à-vis* the Swedes, who were always highly
critical of it.

Fortunately the circumstances of his life at this time
were reasonably happy. Frida was expecting a child and
they were living at Dornach in Austria in a little cottage
known as 'Das Häusel', which lay beyond the garden of
her grandfather's house, from which they had been ejected
when the publication in Berlin of his book *A Madman's
Defence* had resulted in a prosecution on a charge of obscenity.

It was probably the happiest time of his second marriage.
The couple were on their own and Strindberg had a garden
to cultivate, always a source of pleasure and satisfaction to
him. He tells us in *The Cloister* that it was to decorate the
bare walls of 'Das Häusel' that he painted his seven pictures, known as 'The Dornach Paintings', but they may
have had a deeper significance. They must have been
painted between the time he discovered Lidforss's treachery at the beginning of May and the birth of his daughter,
Kerstin, on the twenty-sixth of that month, and were an
emotional outlet. Strindberg often turned to painting in
times of stress, or when other forms of creative activity
were temporarily denied him.

In his letters he says nothing about these 'Dornach'
paintings until the end of June, perhaps because he had been
so much occupied in vindicating *Antibarbarus* and in trying to establish a motive behind Lidforss's treachery. When
he did mention them it was only briefly in a letter of 26
June 1894 to Richard Bergh, himself a painter: 'Among
other things I've painted a whole roomful of large, sym-
bolist pictures, some of them excellent!!' But a month
later, when he was planning his descent on Paris, he

decided to send these pictures on in advance and wrote to Littmansson:

You see I've invented a new (?) form of art that I call L'art fortuite. I've written an essay on my method. It's the most subjective of all the arts, so that in the first place only the painter himself can rejoice (= suffer) as a result of his work, as he knows what he meant by it as do the chosen few who know a little (= much) of the painter from within (= without). That is to say each picture has a double meaning: an exoteric meaning that everyone can see, though only with an effort, and an esoteric meaning for the artist and the chosen few.

I've only used a knife to paint the pictures, and unmixed colours, whose coming together has been partially left to chance, as has the whole of the subject matter.

This letter was accompanied by notes on each picture, detailing their exoteric and esoteric meaning. The essay he mentions is 'The New Arts or the Role of Chance in Artistic Creation' (Des arts nouveaux ou le hasard dans la production artistique').[6]

Strindberg called his new art 'wood-spiritism' (skogs-snufvism), a term that he first applied to it in a letter to Richard Bergh in 1892. In this article 'The New Arts' he explained it as follows:

Gentlemen, you remember the boy going through the woods who catches sight of the wood-spirit. She is lovely as the day with emerald-green hair etc. He approaches her and she turns her back to him. It is like the trunk of a tree.

Evidently the boy has seen nothing but a tree-trunk, and his lively imagination has invented all the rest.

This is what has happened to me many times.

One lovely morning when I was walking in the woods I came upon an enclosed piece of fallow land. My thoughts were far away, but my eyes perceived a strange, odd-looking object lying on the ground.

At one moment it was a cow, then ... an instant later two

6. English version in Sprinchorn, p. 99.

peasants embracing one another; then a tree-trunk, then ...
These oscillations of my sense impressions please me ... my
will intervenes, and I want to know more ... I know that the
curtain veiling my consciousness will rise ... but that is not
what I want ... now it is a picnic in the country, people are
eating, but the figures are motionless like those of a waxwork-
show ... oh dear ... so that's all it is ... it's an abandoned
plough over which the ploughman has thrown his coat and
hung up his knapsack. There's no more to be said! Nothing
more to be seen! The fun is over!

This essay is of the greatest importance for an understanding of Strindberg's methods of creation when he came
to write *Inferno*. It is clear that he already loved to see a
dual meaning in the things that happened to him and the
things he did. A study of the 'Dornach' pictures also makes
it plain that he often strove to introduce a double meaning
when he could not find one in the original work. Göran
Söderström believes that they were by no means the spon-
taneous creations Strindberg claimed them to be, and that
several of them show clear signs of having been worked
over and touched up.[7]

But, if he was not above adapting his experiences to his
needs, he was also serious in believing that these experiences
often had a deeper meaning than was apparent. In 1894,
when he wrote his essay about art, it was chance that decided what this meaning should be. Later, when he was
actively seeking a religious anchorage, he called the inter-
vening force 'The Powers', a belief that he constantly expresses in *Inferno*. For example, when he reports that his
sculptor friend showed him a picture of a Madonna, the
model for which had been some water-weeds, he cries: 'A
new art discovered, Nature's own. A natural clairvoyance!
...', adding: 'Nothing happens in this world that has not
the approval of the Powers.'[8]

6. Söderström, p. 235.   8. *Inferno*, p. 148.

'Des arts nouveaux' was written in French, a sure sign that Strindberg was thinking of making his home in France, and by November 1894, when it was published in the *Revue des Revues*, he had been in Paris for some time.

Ever since 1885, when *Getting Married* had been printed in Switzerland as *Les Mariés*, he had been working towards making a name for himself in France and in French. In spite of the interest shown in his work in Germany and the fact that Schopenhauer, Hartmann, Max Nordau and, to some extent, Nietzsche had influenced his thought, Paris was his intellectual Mecca, the place where he believed that the touchstone was talent, not material achievement. He longed to be there 'just because Frenchmen are an aristocracy of the spirit, not of wealth', as he wrote to Littmansson on 4 August 1894, and because it was the place where 'Verlaine, a convicted criminal, who could never manage his money affairs, was famous because he had talent.'

He had a large vocabulary and had practised writing French from an early age, but his grammar always remained shaky, and his diffidence and a tendency to become tongue-tied prevented him from ever speaking it fluently in public.

By the autumn of 1894 he was justified in thinking that his name was sufficiently well known for a break-through in Paris to be a possibility. His treatise on the relations between France and Sweden (*Les Relations de la France avec la Suède*) had been published there in the summer of 1891, and had been well received. On 16 January 1893 *Miss Julie* had been performed at Antoine's Théâtre Libre. It had been a sensation rather than a success. During the performance the audience had hissed and whistled, but they did not leave the auditorium as they did during the play by Edmond de Goncourt that followed it. To Strindberg the fact that he had been performed was a triumph. On 26 January 1893 he wrote to Birger Mörner : 'For eight whole days – a lot in Paris – my play has been the subject of controversy in conversation and in the press; much enthusiasm and much hatred . . . My name is through . . .'

He was right. In November 1893 the distinguished critic Victor Cherbuliez had published a long article about him in the *Revue des Deux Mondes*, and in August 1894 he was asked by *L'Éclair* to give his views on Zola's suitability for membership of the French Academy. Finally, when *Creditors* was staged in June 1894 at Lugné-Poe's Théâtre de L'Oeuvre, the audience was enthusiastic and the critics much kinder than they had been about *Miss Julie*. At the time Strindberg was still living in Dornach, but in very changed circumstances. His reaction to the news of the success of *Creditors* is revealing. On 14 July he wrote to Littmansson :

This feeling of power, it's happiness to sit in a cottage by the Danube, among six women who think I'm a semi-idiot, and to know that in Paris, the headquarters of intelligence, 500 people are sitting dead quiet in an auditorium, and are foolish enough to expose their brains to my powers of suggestion. Some revolt, but many will go away with my spores in their grey matter; they will go home pregnant with the seed of my soul, and they will breed my brood.

His position in Dornach was now far from pleasant. The baby girl, instead of cementing the bond between her parents, looked like disrupting it, for one thing because Frida made the young mother's usual mistake of putting her child first. There were also feeding troubles, the child was fretful and sickly, wet-nurses came and went, and to make matters worse a furious quarrel over the baptism of the baby into the Catholic Church developed between Strindberg and his in-laws, on whose charity he had been living for six months and who disliked and distrusted him. Strindberg is sometimes accused of having been pathologically jealous of his small daughter, but was he not reacting normally to a not unusual phenomenon in family life?

Family discord was not his only reason for wishing to leave Dornach. Used though he was to living on charity, his absolute dependence on people who detested him was becoming intolerable. Sometimes he had to wait days to post a letter because he had not the money for a stamp. For ten months he had been unable to pay any alimony to his first family, and he was receiving distasteful begging letters from his fourteen-year-old daughter Karin, egged on no doubt by her mother, who would not write herself. He well knew that so long as he remained where he was his chances of procuring any money were slim. Paris seemed a bright prospect, yet he had reservations about going there: 'My future in Paris is on the hook,' he wrote to Richard Bergh on 9 July. 'I'm even negotiating with Chateler about *Lucky Peter* and *Sankte Per* [*The Keys of Heaven*], that is I see money in the distance. But my temperament, my habits, and my anxiety about my personality, my instinct to preserve my ego drive me away from Paris.'

This fear of losing his personality was constant. He knew his vulnerability to outside influences, and he knew the temptations life in a great city would put in his path. He cast about feverishly for alternatives. One was to return to Sweden. 'I'd rather beg in Sweden, beg for freedom for myself and my family by obtaining a sinecure that would not bind me to anything,' his letter to Bergh continues, and goes on to suggest that he might become a customs officer or a lighthouse keeper in some post that would be abolished in a year's time, when he would be retired on half pay. A longing for his own country and his own language were not the least of his causes of discontent. 'Foreign countries are enemy countries,' he wrote to Bergh, 'and not speaking your own language makes your intellect superficial.'

To Littmansson the following week he proposed yet another solution of his problem. With his friend's help he would found a monastery for intellectuals in the Ardennes, where his personality would dominate and his ideas prevail, and where the spirit could be cultivated 'by isolation and removal from expensive and futile habits, by simplicity in food and drink.'

This idea of a retreat, where he could live an ordered and disciplined life, protected from the temptations of a world he both loved and feared, appealed strongly to Strindberg and recurs several times in his writings. Needless to say it never materialized, and his only stay in a real monastery – it lasted for one night – was a disillusionment. But it would be a mistake to think that he was incapable of imposing a rigid discipline on himself. His enormous output is proof that he did.

It is clear that by July 1894 Austria from being a refuge had become a prison. Perhaps his most urgent reason for wanting to escape was the prosecution for obscenity that was taking place in Berlin. He was afraid that he might be forced to attend the trial in person, and that if judgment was given against him he would be thrown into prison. A desperate letter to Littmansson on 18 July implored him to send money to pay for his journey to Paris, where he would be safe from the arm of the German law. No doubt he exaggerated his danger – and in fact he was to be acquitted in October 1895 – but the very feeling that he could not move, that he was trapped, must have made him all the more anxious to get away. 'Believe what I say for Satan's sake!!!' he wrote. 'I don't know if I can stand being put in prison! And I've lost lawsuits in Sweden where I was not only the innocent party but the injured one!'

Littmansson sent him the money for his fare but by the time it arrived his little daughter was dangerously ill and he could not leave, 'could not be a monster'. By 1 August he

could report that the child was safe, 'Which means that
I'm the loser and must emigrate . . .' and on 4 August he
sent off his paintings, his favourite writing-paper and his
winter overcoat. It looked as if he had at last made up
his mind.

But on 14 August his doubts about Paris had returned
and he was again longing for a quiet place where he could
live in peace :

If I could turn religious I should try to enter a Catholic
monastery where the inmates are allowed to practise science.
But my past makes it impossible.

There are moments when the memory of all the terrible
things I've experienced collect in me as if I were an accumulator, and then the tension is so great that I think I must explode, but I don't. What will cure that? Discharge, say the electricians. Translated : activity.

In the same letter he told Littmansson how wearied and
frustrated he was by the struggle for recognition that would
allow him to develop his talent, and at the same time fulfil
his obligations to his family :

Never to have reached my true position — that's the tragic
part of it.

And then this fearful disparity between what I am and what
I'm thought to be by those about me : the lack of proportion
between my abilities and my activities, my shame over unfulfilled obligations; this unjust hatred of me, persecution, nagging, these everlasting annoyances, the intrusion of material
things. I'm sick, nervously sick, oscillating between epileptic
fits of furious energy and general paralysis.

But the next day he was in high spirits and wrote:
'When you get this card I shall have ceased to breathe the
air of Dornach and be sitting on the great string of easy
chairs going to Versailles. Life's an odd business. Are the
hermitage and the cabbage-patch ready for me? And the
Irish coffees? I've not been drunk for a year and a half, and

I'm longing to see what it feels like.' In the same letter he
mentioned that he had with him a hundred sheets of 'feuil-
leton in French' with which to bombard the Paris press.

On the evening of 17 August he arrived in Versailles
where he spent a few days with Litmansson, quiet days
at his own request, during which he and Littmansson planned his campaign and translated into French some of the
Swedish texts he had with him. He also wrote many letters
to Frida, whom he hoped would join him. Thus on 25
August: 'The situation changes every day for the better.
Langen is arriving on 1 September, and is eagerly looking
forward to *Le Plaidoyer*, which is revised and ready for
him.'

Albert Langen was a German with a publishing business
in Paris. He was particularly interested in Scandinavian
authors and Strindberg believed he would publish some of
his works, including *Le Plaidoyer d'un fou*. This he did,
but not until 1895.

Meanwhile another way of earning money presented
itself which seemed even more promising. At a dinner-party
Strindberg met a Danish friend of Langen's, Willy Gretor,
and two days later, on 31 August, he wrote to Frida:

From Monday I shall be the guest of a rich Danish painter
who has bought *Wonderland* and *Alpine Landscape* for 400
francs, and who has told me that I'm a painter. So, I shall send
you 200 francs and you'll come? Remember that on 15 September I shall get money for *Plaidoyer*! And I'll paint more. My
friend here tells me that I should exhibit at the Champ de Mars,
that *Alpine Landscape* is a masterpiece, but the *Meadows* picture nothing. Oh God! What is what? What?

This letter is characteristic. Strindberg always believed
that money in the offing was money in his pocket. Gretor
had not paid him the 400 francs and never did, nor did
Strindberg exhibit at the Champ de Mars. But he trusted so

implicitly in Gretor's promises that he painted ten more pictures in record time.

As well as promising him a brilliant future as a painter Gretor provided him with luxurious, rent-free accommodation for a month, and offered favourable terms if he wanted it for longer. No wonder that on 3 September he wrote jubilantly to Frida: 'We've had good luck for the first time in our married life. You can come here and bring the child.' The next day alone in the house next door to Littmansson's he was assailed by doubts. Paris was dangerous, wouldn't he be wiser to return to Sweden, or to Dornach? 'I regret the Danube in spite of everything. A Home, after all. Here the street' – his picturesque way of describing a bachelor existence, which certainly included having too much to drink.

As the days passed he grew more and more uneasy, especially after he had moved into Gretor's house in Passy. The luxury of the place disgusted him and he longed for 'Das Häusel': 'I paint better there than here.' He sensed that there was something wrong: 'All that glitters is not gold.' Moreover, though Gretor had said he would buy two pictures, Strindberg had received no money for them.

In addition to his worries about Gretor, whom he rightly suspected of being a rogue, Strindberg was also apprehensive about Frida's possible reactions to life in Paris, and he lectured her on her duties as a wife and mother. If she brought the baby she would be tied, and in any case they would be poor and not able to afford many amusements. The only entertainment he envisaged for her was visits to the theatres or to the offices of newspapers with the fifty-seven-year-old Henri Becque. He himself would stay at home and work. Finally, on 11 September, he sent her 250 francs for her journey and, undeterred by his warnings, she arrived in Paris about the middle of the month.

Her presence and her apparent determination to further his interests were a comfort to him at first : 'Here we have to beg and haggle for bread and wine,' he told Littmansson on 2 October, 'but my wife's youth and her light-heartedness give me momentary courage.' But his fears about her behaviour proved only too well founded. She does not seem to have visited any theatres with Henri Becque, but she saw a great deal of her contemporaries Langen and Gretor, and quickly became an enthusiastic member of their circle. She and Langen were soon busy planning the translation into French of the works of various German authors rather than those of Strindberg, and she even offered Langen her services as social secretary. Strindberg was understandably annoyed. Frida claims that he was jealous. Disgusted is perhaps a more appropriate word. He was always remarkably detached about this marriage and told both Bergh and Littmansson that he did not think it would last. But naturally he did not like the idea that his young wife was making him look a fool by flirting with younger men. He did not know that Gretor, not Langen, was Frida's quarry : 'I was strongly attracted to Willy Gretor ... and did all I could to win his friendship, even suggested that I should go to his studio to take lessons. But I was met by persistent and marked chilliness, so I initiated a close friendship with Frank Wedekind in order to make him jealous. In this too I failed.'[9]

However, in the German playwright Frida had found her next lion, by whom she was to have a son in 1897. Of this affair Strindberg knew nothing until long after he had written *Inferno*. In it he takes all the blame for the breach with Frida, to whom he says he wrote 'an infamous, unpardonable letter'. In this letter he accused her of the very sins of which she had been guilty, but his accusations were based on what he suspected, not on what he knew.

9. Söderström, p. 259.

To punish him Frida threatened him with divorce, but she did not attempt to implement her threat for over a year, perhaps on the principle that a bird in the hand is worth two in the bush. She and Strindberg continued to correspond until September 1896, sometimes acrimoniously, sometimes affectionately. She did not decide to bring matters to a head until February 1897, when she was already several months pregnant with Wedekind's child. Her mother, Marie Uhl, although she did not at the time know of the pregnancy, was aware that Frida was Wedekind's mistress. But she concealed the fact from Strindberg, with whom she corresponded regularly, and when the marriage was annulled she seems to have been quite ready to let him repay the 2,000 gulden of Frida's dowry that the couple had squandered together in 1893.

Strindberg was not able to raise the money to repay this large debt to Frida's rich relatives until August 1900. At that time he still believed that he was to blame for the break-up of his marriage, which was annulled because, as a Catholic, Frida could not be married to a man whose divorced wife was still living. Had he known of Frida's unfaithfulness he would not have felt morally and legally obliged to honour his debt.

Strindberg is always blamed for the failure of his marriages, but anyone who looks objectively at the characters of his three wives will see that they were all difficult women to live with. All were career women who took the view that their futures were at least as important as his. It was his tragedy that he was invariably attracted to such women and was foolish enough to believe that maternity would turn them into homemakers. Strindberg was not promiscuous, he was a marrying man, and he married because what he longed for above everything was a home, a refuge, family life as opposed to the bachelor existence that he hated and feared. He himself realized the dangers of this longing: 'The flesh was your "tragic" side,' he wrote to Littmansson on 14 July 1894, 'the family mine.'

Frida left Paris on 21 October 1894, and they never met again. After she had gone his gloomy forebodings of what he might do in Paris and what Paris might do to him proved all too correct. On 4 November he wrote to Frida:

What a miserable existence. I detest mankind but I can't be alone – consequently, bad company, alcohol, late nights, *chat noir*, despair, and all the rest of it, above all paralysis. What's the point of my being in Paris? There is none. They'll perform me whether I'm here or not, translate my novels too. The newspapers and periodicals are full already. I've no means of doing anything.

And then, after describing a *chat noir* type of night-club and shadow theatre that he and Littmansson sometimes thought of starting, at which his play *The Keys of Heaven* might be performed, he says:

There we shall be, back at Ferkel again, with chronic alcoholism and all the rest of it. I shall sink to rise, die to live. The tavern instead of the family. *La joie de vivre*. After four days alone I'm already dissipated. A lunch with Becque lasting six hours; a whole day from morning to nightfall with Littmansson. An evening and half the night with Geisebart. It's disgusting, of course, but all the same, alone in a city the tavern saves me from suicide, or sweeps me towards it, so much the better.

And two days later, still on the same theme, he wrote:

Report. General paralysis. After a dinner yesterday with Osterlind. Before that Café Napolitain with Charpentier, Catulle Mendès, Papin of the ed. board of *Des Débats*, who is asking for an interview; Desmoulin, intimate friend of Zola, has made himself responsible for an article in *Le Journal*, invites me, is going to organize a banquet for Strindberg, which I shall decline. That's the tavern for you! Without it, nothing! With it: everything.

Obviously he was finding residence in Paris useful after all. It had not proved as easy to place his articles and essays as he had hoped, but he had some successes. 'The New Arts' ('Des arts nouveaux') was published in the *Revue des Revues* on 15 November, and another essay on art, 'What Do We Mean by Modern?' ('Qu'est-ce le moderne?') appeared in *L'Echo de Paris* on 20 December. What pleased him even more was that his essay 'Césarine', about Dumas fils' play *La Femme de Claude*, was published in *Le Figaro Littéraire* on 30 September. 'To write for *Le Figaro* in French is the realization of a youthful dream,' he wrote to a friend on 17 October. 'I shall soon flood the papers with my *Vivisections* in French.'

This dream was never realized. Apart from the two essays already mentioned only one more of the *Vivisections* was printed: his essay 'Substitution Crystals' ('Cristaux de remplacement'), a curious title which gives no clue to the subject, his hypothesis about the origin of the Jews. It was published in the anti-semitic periodical *La Plume* on 15 December 1894.

Two days before that, on 13 December, Strindberg had his first real success on the Paris stage. *The Father* was performed by Lugné-Poe's Théâtre de l'Oeuvre at Nouveau Théâtre and was well received by the audience and by most of the critics. But this did not mean that his financial troubles were even temporarily at an end. The previous month he had written in bitterness to Littmansson: 'I'm performed, I'm printed, but I get no money.' And now for *The Father*, which according to him was acted ten times – a triumph after the single performances of *Miss Julie* and *Creditors* – he got a mere 300 francs. Nor was his literary future any more secure. His hopes in this respect were dashed when he heard that, far from staging more Strindberg, Lugné-Poe intended to follow up the success of *The Father* by putting on a repeat performance of Ibsen's *An Enemy of the People*.

Strindberg was terribly upset and wrote to Poe :

First of all thank you for the success you tell me of. But why am I going to be used as a gun-dog for Ibsen? I've been his victim for ten years, yet *The Father* was composed and performed four years before *Hedda Gabler*, though nowadays people are pleased to set her up as the origin of my Laura, when the opposite is the case.

I sent *The Father* to M. Antoine in 1888, and he buried it, and now that I've been resurrected I'm to be entombed again under my enemy.

But in spite of his protests Lugné-Poe continued to stage Ibsen, and despite the success of *The Father* no more of Strindberg's dramas were seen in Paris for many years. Ibsen seems to have been less adversely affected than Strindberg by the unwillingness of most Frenchmen to admit that foreign plays could have any merit or originality. Such ideas as could be found in them were not new, but only a reflection of what their authors had garnered from the French. What then was the point of performing them?

Fortunately for Strindberg, he was more versatile than Ibsen. If the French saw no more of his plays, his essays and his notoriety kept him in the public eye. He followed up *The Father* with another anti-feminist broadside, his essay 'The Inferiority of Woman to Man', which Littmansson translated into French under the title 'De l'infériorté de la femme'. It was published in *La Revue Blanche* in January 1895 and caused a tremendous stir. The subject was topical, thanks to the debate that had raged in the French press since 1892. To this debate Lombroso, Herbert Spencer and other authorities quoted by Strindberg had contributed. His essay added fuel to the fire and it blazed up afresh. 'I dare not leave Paris,' he wrote to Frida on 19 January 1895, 'for the moment I do all will be lost. So long as I am here I have a feeling of power. The spirits are on the move, mocking and blaspheming me, but that's fine. You'd never believe the extent to which they're discussing the woman question here. They used to tell me that in Paris ridicule kills. It's not true, not if you have talent.'

But neither this nor any of the other essays with which he bombarded the French press brought him any money worth mentioning. If he wrote in Swedish it had to be translated. The sums paid were always small and had to be shared with those he employed. Sometimes, especially for his pseudo-scientific articles, he was paid nothing at all.

These circumstances, combined no doubt with heavy drinking, had reduced him by January 1895 to a state of destitution, and when, in the middle of that month, he had to go into the Hospital of Saint Louis to have his hands treated for psoriasis, he could only do so because money was collected for him by friends and well-wishers. He rationalized his humiliation to Littmansson as follows: 'To spare myself the mortification of miscalculation I'm adopting the character of a mendicant friar and consigning all *remuneration* and authorization to the devil. I'm voluntarily accepting poverty, and shit on all the good things of this world that are only bad . . . I shit on gold, but I'll be damned if I won't have honour.' Brave words, but he did not always find it easy to accept the charity on which he was obliged to live for the greater part of 1895-6. He was a proud man and often felt his humiliation keenly. 'You here?' he sees in the eyes of his fellow Scandinavian at the café to which he has gone to escape the boredom and misery of Saint Louis. 'So you are not in hospital after all! Fine humbug, that appeal for help!'

'I was sure that this man must be one of my unknown benefactors.'[10]

10. *Inferno*, p. 112.

In this instance he was referring to money which had been collected and handed over with the utmost tact. When a further collection was made in March it was clumsily handled. Word of it reached the press, along with the rumour that he was to be taken back to Sweden for the sake of his mental health. Strindberg was deeply offended. 'That hateful begging appeal was not well-conceived or well-meant by any but Lie and Österlind (it concealed very mean motives),' he wrote to Mörner on 16 May, and when Knut Hamsun brought him some of the money he refused to take it.

A later collection was more tactfully handled and he had no hesitation about accepting it. 'Money came to me of itself. I was able to buy books, natural history specimens and, among other things, a microscope that unveiled for me the secrets of life.'[11]

This cheerful attitude was not constant. It simply meant that for the time being he had managed to suppress the memory of his debts and his unfulfilled obligations to his family in Finland, where Siri and his three children were now living. By October his purse had run dry and he was again in desperate straits. 'Beg those who can to save me from need, humiliation, and degradation!' he wrote to a friend on 26 October. 'Everyone has deserted me and evil-doers are persecuting me and trying to reduce me to despair, and to make me return to what was even worse.

'Seek help for me, otherwise I shall perish.'

It is impossible to overestimate the effect that financial difficulties had on Strindberg's emotional and physical health. From his schooldays he had been obliged to borrow money to make his way. He was the only member of his family to pass the matriculation examination that enabled students to enter a University, yet when he went to Uppsala he got no help from his father but had to fend for himself.

11. *Inferno*, p. 125.

No doubt one of the reasons why he was unable to complete his university course was that he could not afford it. But while it was not particularly humiliating for a young student to be forced to borrow money, it is a perpetual torment to a grown man who knows that he has made his mark and that if he got the recognition and remuneration he deserved he would be able to support himself. The fact that some of his contemporaries, whom he knew to be less able than himself, succeeded where he failed can only have made matters worse.

It may be argued that his failure in Sweden was his own fault, and that if he had been prepared to conform, and had written what his fellow-countrymen were willing to accept, all would have been well. But to speak his mind was for Strindberg a matter of conscience: 'I should like to write of things as bright and beautiful, but I may not, I cannot. I regard it as my dreadful duty to be truthful, and life is so indescribably ugly,' he wrote in his diary in April 1907.

Strindberg was often merciless when performing this duty, and it is not surprising that many Swedes hated him for his outspokenness. In these days, when Sweden is regarded as a prime example of the permissive society, it is difficult for us to imagine what the climate of opinion was like in the 1880s, when his unpopularity was at its height. During these years a wave of puritanism swept through the whole of Scandinavia, and intolerance was so violent and vindictive that only the boldest spirits dared to defy it. Strindberg was almost the only Swedish writer who did, and the enemies he made were many and powerful. Their hatred of him was so intense that they refused to read his works, they simply condemned them.

If he did find a publisher he frequently had to ask for advances on work not yet finished, sometimes not even begun. Consequently he always wrote under pressure, another cause of nervous tension. This should be borne in mind by those who complain of the uneven quality of his work. He was never in Ibsen's happy position of being able to write at a pace that enabled him to give of his best.

His poverty was a source of torment in yet another respect. His movements were often restricted by the debts he had incurred. An outstanding bill at one place had to be paid before he moved on to the next and ran up another, and this no doubt aggravated his natural restlessness. The awful feeling that he could not move was in itself enough to make him feel that it was an urgent necessity that he should. Appeals for rescue are a constant feature of the letters of this period.

Most deadly of all was the feeling of guilt provoked by his inability to provide for his dependents. Even when he had money he did not always spend it wisely, and he suffered agonies of conscience as a result. But circumstances were nearly always against him. He attempted in 1892 to re-establish himself in Sweden as an acceptable dramatist by writing seven plays; the Swedes would have none of them. He attempted to make a career as a literary man in Berlin and Paris; that he failed was not his fault. It is not surprising that he gave up the struggle and devoted himself to his pseudo-scientific work, which he knew would not earn him money, but which he had good reason to suppose would bring him honour. The price was a fearful struggle with his conscience, which in *Inferno* he calls the choice between love and knowledge.

Alchemy and the French Occultists

Strindberg does not seem to have returned to what he called his chemical experiments until after Frida left him in October 1894, and his letters suggest that he did not finally make up his mind to turn from literature to science until January 1895. Two days after he entered the Hospital of Saint Louis he was interviewed by reporters from *Le Temps* and *Le Matin*. 'The cracks and swollen blood-vessels from which I am suffering,' he told them, 'are there because I have handled poisonous substances for hours on end, and have been burnt by the heat from the ovens.'[12] This suggests that he was now anxious to represent himself as being chiefly a scientist, but he also wanted to suppress a rumour that he had injured himself by causing an explosion, a slur on his competence that he did not like. It may also be significant that he did not reveal to the reporters or to anyone else the true cause of his trouble, psoriasis, of which he had presumably been told by Professor Henri Hallopeau, the famous dermatologist at Saint Louis, who diagnosed that complaint.[13] Strindberg probably knew that some researchers believed that psoriasis was connected with venereal disease, and he may not have known that Hallopeau did not. In 1891 a doctor friend in Sweden had suggested that the cause of his trouble might be syphilis, but a thorough examination by another doctor had proved that this was not the case. Nevertheless, the idea that people might think him syphilitic continued to haunt him, and he must have feared that if the word psoriasis was mentioned in the press, people would believe that their suspicions were correct.

While in Saint Louis Strindberg was able to continue his experiments with sulphur, thanks to the kindness of the chemist there, who allowed him to use his laboratory. He took samples of his results to an analytical chemist, and on 19 January received a certificate to confirm that he had produced carbon. In *Inferno* he says that he sent an article about his experiment to *Le Temps*, and that it was printed two days later. In fact an article summarizing his research, but not written by him, appeared in *Le Petit Temps* on 30 January. This was just the sort of recognition for which he had hoped. 'The password had been given,' he writes in

12. Ahlström, p. 284.   13. Ahlström, p. 281.

Inferno. 'I had answers from various quarters, but no one denied the validity of my claims. I gained adherents. I was urged to send articles to a chemical periodical, and became involved in a correspondence that stimulated me to press on with the investigations I was pursuing.'

This was no exaggeration. In February the scientific periodical *La Science Française* published an article about his experiments, and in the same month a long and respectful article about Strindberg the scientist appeared in *Le Figaro*.

The deference paid by the French press to Strindberg's pseudo-scientific work was in marked contrast to the attitude taken in Sweden, where it was regarded as a sign of madness. Strindberg was understandably encouraged, but realized that he could make no progress unless he had access to better apparatus. He therefore applied for permission to carry out one experiment on sulphur in the research laboratory of the Sorbonne. This application was granted, but the professors at the Sorbonne were unimpressed by his work, and one even went so far as to call him an 'ignorant person'. However, he was not to be put off, especially as he felt that he had been encouraged by no less a person than the distinguished French chemist Marcellin Berthelot, to whom he had written, and from whom he had received a letter which in no way refuted his ideas. Strindberg quoted part of this letter in a communication to *Le Figaro* printed on 27 February 1895. All the same he felt comparatively isolated, as he had as yet met only one of the group of people who were to become his firm supporters. These were the French alchemists and occultists.

His one contact among them was François Jollivet-Castelot, a young man of twenty who lived at Douai in northern France, whose first book *The Life and Spirit of Matter* (*La Vie et l'âme de la matière*) Strindberg had read soon after it came out in 1894. It greatly excited him, as he found in it ideas identical with those he had himself expressed in *Antibarbarus*. 'I've just read your book,' he wrote to Castelot on 22 July 1894, 'and I'm stupefied, but at the same time comforted at finding that I'm not alone in this madness, which has cost me my family happiness, my respectability, everything.'

Castelot's book also seems to have opened his eyes to the possibilities of a successful career as an alchemist in France. 'It's odd,' he wrote to Littmansson three days later, 'that I should have sniffed out this *fin-de-siècle* main current that is running through natural science. Now I shall be the prophet (Ibsen) of the young French chemists, for they are infants in arms compared to me.' And to the Danish critic Georg Brandes the following week: 'Now I see that there is a whole literature in my genre in France.'

However, when he arrived in Paris he was temporarily diverted from his alchemic studies, first by painting, then by his efforts to establish his literary reputation. But when he became disillusioned about his prospects in these fields and returned to alchemy, he soon found many people who were receptive to his ideas.

In 1894 occultism was a fashionable movement in Paris and had many followers in the literary and artistic circles that Strindberg joined when he had shaken off Langen and Gretor. Newspapers and periodicals had contributors who specialized in occult matters – *La Plume* had no less than six. *La Paix* had estimated that in 1893 there were 50,000 alchemists in Paris alone. This may have been an exaggeration, but the Paris occultists were certainly not an obscure or uninfluential group. As well as alchemy their interests embraced such things as hypnotism and suggestion, thought transference, bewitchment, cabbalism, and magic in all its forms. Strindberg was easily able to find in Paris people who shared his views and consequently did not think him mad.

At first, though he was well aware that his researches

were alchemic in character, he wanted to win recognition for them from orthodox chemists. A letter to Georg Brandes of 28 June 1894 shows this clearly. At Strindberg's request Brandes had shown *Antibarbarus* to a Danish chemist, but the latter had been decidedly critical of it. Strindberg defended himself as follows:

If we are alive in ten years' time, we shall see if these ideas are not being used, their originator concealed, and the epigons the great men, yet all the same in a hundred years the Alchemist Strindberg will be acknowledged to have been a chemist!

In Paris, and even in Berlin, modern chemistry is tending towards Alchemy, i.e. monism (= Aristotle) ... That the Dane does not seem to know.

In France he was more successful in getting his ideas taken seriously. An early instance of this is a letter he received in February 1895 from André Dubosc, an engineer at a chemical factory in Rouen, who was also attached to the editorial board of *La Science Française*. Dubosc had read in that paper an article about Strindberg's experiments with sulphur, and also the one in *Le Figaro* about Strindberg the chemist, and on 6 March 1895 he wrote: 'If the hypothesis you have put forward is justified, it is probably the explanation of hitherto unexplained phenomena in the manufacture of sulphuric acid and sulphides.'

This was indeed a feather in Strindberg's cap. In April he went to see Dubosc in Rouen, and he corresponded actively with him until July 1896. At first Strindberg wrote to him about his experiments with iodine, sulphur and morphine, and in a letter to a friend calls him 'my first and most capable pupil'. But later, when he turned more and more to the true business of alchemy, the transmutation of baser metals into gold, Dubosc could not follow him. 'I sent a sample to a chemist in Rouen with whom I was on a friendly footing. He replied by refuting my contentions' Strindberg tells us in *Inferno*.

But if Dubosc was sceptical about his gold many other people were not, among them Jollivet-Castelot, who remained a firm friend and admirer. When he started his alchemic periodical *L'Hyperchimie* in the summer of 1896, he asked Strindberg to become a co-founder. In his letter of acceptance Strindberg was able to tell him that he knew many people who would be useful to him, including Dubosc, which suggests that the latter must have changed his mind about Strindberg's gold. He had certainly done so by July 1897, when he asked Strindberg if he might reprint his article 'The Synthesis of Gold' ('Synthèse d'or') in a Rouen newspaper.

By the spring of 1896 Strindberg was well known in occultist circles in Paris, and had met their leader, Gérard Encausse (pseudonym 'Papus'), the editor of the occultist periodical *L'Initiation*. In the May number of that paper Papus published a letter from Strindberg accompanied by the following editorial note:

Our eminent author, August Strindberg, who combines vast knowledge with his great talents as a writer, has just achieved a synthesis of gold from iron. August Strindberg has an absolute contempt for riches and has never kept any of his methods secret, consequently he immediately gave us his procedure, which confirms all the assertions of the alchemists. We are carrying out control-experiments, which are all giving us absolutely conclusive proof.

Unfortunately the voluminous correspondence between Strindberg and Papus has been lost, but Papus's admiration is confirmed by a review in the August number of *L'Initiation*, in which he says that he has become convinced of the rightness of the teachings of alchemy chiefly because of the 'tremendous experiments of August Strindberg'.

Strindberg had seldom if ever received so much praise. No wonder it went to his head, especially after he was made an honorary member and 'Master' of La Société Alchimique de France, which Jollivet-Castelot and Papus started in January 1897. When he heard in February of the same year that some of Nobel's money was to be used to establish a prize for chemistry he wrote to Jollivet-Castelot (8 February) urging that the French alchemists – himself included – should work to prepare themselves as suitable candidates, and to Marie Uhl, a week later, that his Paris friends expected him to work for the Nobel Prize for Chemistry.

Perhaps he realized himself that this could not be a serious possibility. At any rate, the following week, in another letter to Marie Uhl, he came up with a better proposition: 'What should I like best of all? To live through the spring in Klam with my child, there, in two months, to write my most beautiful book, *Inferno*, write it so beautifully that I should win the Nobel Prize for Literature. That would be 300,000 francs!'

He never won the prize, but the letter is symptomatic of a change in his circumstances and attitude. He was now living comparatively quietly in Lund, away from the heady atmosphere of Paris and his occultist friends and admirers. At times throughout his gold-making period he had doubted whether it was not forbidden by the Powers who, he believed, controlled his destiny. Now he was convinced of it, though he was not always able to resist the temptation to carry out experiments and to write articles on alchemic subjects. Nevertheless, encouraged by friends, his mind was gradually turning again to literature, and his career as an alchemist and occultist was drawing to an end. His novel *Tschandala*, written in 1888, was at last about to be printed, likewise some of the essays he had written in Austria and France, which Bonnier published under the title of *Printed and Unprinted (Tryckt och otryckt)*. Best of all, his play *Lucky Peter's Travels*, always a favourite with the public, was performed 65 times in 1896-7. His letters were no longer full of desperate appeals for help – perhaps because he was now better able to borrow money on the spot – and it is clear that he knew that he would be able to resume his career as an author in his own country, which was what, in his heart of hearts, he had always wanted to do.

On 3 May 1897 he wrote to a Swedish friend : 'Have to-day begun a new book and am shut up in myself.' This book was *Inferno*.

Strindberg's Mental Health

In his book *Strindberg's Conquest of Paris (Strindbergs erövring av Paris)*, Stellan Ahlström regards it as a misfortune for Strindberg as a writer that his chemical investigations were so well received in Paris. But, had they not been, what literary work would he have done? In 1895 the tide was turning in France against Scandinavian authors. It took Strindberg a year to get his charming essay 'In the Cemetery' (Études funèbres') published, while his alchemic articles appeared immediately. There was no prospect of the French performing any more of his plays, and the expense of getting them translated had made those that were staged unremunerative. If he had written new plays they would have had to be in Swedish, the only language in which he ever worked as a dramatist. In any case, what incentive had he to write plays? As he said himself in a letter to Richard Bergh of 9 July 1894 : 'To write plays you must see a prospect of having them performed . . .', and he knew only too well how little chance there was of that. He knew too that he could only return to Sweden on one of two conditions : either he must write what the Swedes were prepared to publish or perform, or the Swedes must be prepared to accept what he could write, and in 1895 there seemed little chance of their being so tolerant. A letter of 29 December

1895 to one of his German translators, Mathilde Prager, makes it perfectly clear that he could not accept the restrictions which remunerative writing would put upon him. 'You see,' he says, 'I have ceased to deal with literature, look for no publishers, as I don't want a master, ask for no remuneration, leave the rights of reproduction completely open, but reserve for myself the right to write what I please! Poverty and freedom.'

Poor he certainly was, but he got from his alchemy and the adulation it brought him some of the comfort and satisfaction which the pursuit of literature had denied him. His real misfortune was that none of the seven plays he had written in 1892 were performed in Sweden until 1908, and that only a fraction of what he wrote from 1892–7 was published there. Had his reception in Sweden been different, his literary career might never have been interrupted by this excursion into the strange world of alchemy and occultism.

The part which this world played in stimulating his imagination and providing him with the means of interpreting the experiences he believed himself to be having has been well set out by Gunnar Brandell in his *Strindberg in Inferno* (pp. 110–20). Brandell has also identified and dated the five longer or shorter periods of crisis through which Strindberg passed from July 1894 to December 1896. He believes that the fundamental cause of the crises was an overwhelming feeling of guilt, but he emphasizes that Strindberg had an extremely complex character and that there were certainly other contributory causes.

Opinions vary as to the nature of the illness manifested by these crises. Most of the German psychologists and psychiatrists have diagnosed some form of schizophrenia, but their analyses were based on a very imperfect knowledge of the patient and other scholars who have made more comprehensive studies do not agree with them. Yet neither side is adequately informed. Anyone who attempts to un-ravel the intricacies of Strindberg's personality is faced by an insurmountable difficulty: there is no clinical record of his mental state, he was never examined by a psychiatrist, nor was he ever a patient in a mental hospital. The only sources of information about him are his works, his letters and the records left by his friends or people who knew him well, and none of these is as reliable as a confrontation with the patient himself by a skilled observer would be.

The German writers relied almost entirely on Strindberg's so-called 'autobiographical' works, and on untrustworthy translations at that. It is therefore not surprising that they went wrong, for though Strindberg can at times be remarkably objective, he was an imaginative writer, and as such quite capable of writing fiction even about himself.

Some of the more recent writers who have analysed Strindberg's psychogenic peculiarities have realized this and allowed for it when giving their verdicts. Of these, Dr Sven Hedenberg, a Swedish psychiatrist, and Professor E. W. Anderson, an English one, have made particularly useful contributions. Dr Hedenberg was able to consult all the available material in German, French, English and Swedish. He comes to the conclusion that Strindberg's trouble was psychogenic, that the causes of his psychoses were mental trauma, severe mental conflict and complexes, and that his poverty was an important ingredient, and sometimes the immediate cause, of a nervous attack. Dr Hedenberg does not rule out the possibility that some of the worst crises may have been aggravated by heavy drinking, particularly of absinth. Professor Anderson, who learned Swedish in order to be able to study Strindberg's works and the other Swedish sources, comes to much the same conclusion, but is more inclined to accept the idea that there was a toxic element in some of the acute phases of Strindberg's illness.

It is also worth noting that two medical men who knew Strindberg personally, Dr Carl Ludwig Schleich, a friend from his Ferkel days (1892–3), and Marcel Réja, who knew him in Paris in 1897, both thought that he drank too much, but say that he was able to consume vast quantities of alcohol without its having any noticeable effect. Réja's testimony is of special interest as he was a poet and a psychiatrist as well as a doctor of medicine. He saw much of Strindberg in Paris from November 1897 to April 1898 while revising with him the French edition of *Inferno*. During this time Strindberg wrote *Legender*, the sequel to *Inferno*, and still seems to have been drinking, at times heavily. Réja has this to say of him:

The Swedish poet was shy and taciturn, and I was immediately attracted to him. He was very retiring and, with the exception of myself, Herman, and Kleen, never saw anyone. I met him three or four times a week, and we dined together . . .

Strindberg suffered in some ways from persecution mania. But I got the impression that he really was persecuted by colleagues who were his inferiors, or by people who envied him, and that his own country did not appreciate his full value.

Strindberg was certainly not schizophrenic; he was ill, over-sensitive and hysterical, though in no way what is usually meant by insane. But he abused alcohol. He was shy and did not dare to enter a café. In the middle of winter he would sit outside on the empty pavement, and consume in rapid succession one American toddy after another. Strindberg always preserved his dignity, and I cannot ever remember seeing him intoxicated. I cannot say exactly what quantity of spirits he was in the habit of consuming, but I believe that alcohol played a not inconsiderable part in his Inferno crisis.[14]

Two articles published in Sweden in the mid-seventies by Dr Bo Bäverstedt and Dr Erik Carlsson deal with this aspect of Strindberg's illness at some length. They trace the history

14. Ögonvittnen, p. 136.

of his drinking habits, which began at an early age, though only on festive occasions or during periods of stress did he indulge in greater quantities of alcohol than were normally consumed by his contemporaries. They also show that as early as 1874 he was aware of the charms of absinth, although he probably did not make a habit of drinking it until he went to live in Switzerland in 1884.

The first evidence that he appreciated its dangers is in *Inferno* where, after vividly describing the way in which he was repeatedly frustrated in his efforts to enjoy it, he says: 'I realized that the good spirits intended to help me to free myself from a vice that must inevitably lead to the madhouse.' In this the good spirits were singularly unsuccessful, and he was still wrestling with the problems in 1898. An entry in his diary on 18 September runs: 'Promised myself today never more to touch Schnaps, Cognac, or Whisky! May God help me to keep this promise! This includes Rum, Arrack, and Absinth.' In another entry he repeats the promise, but after two weeks of abstinence he resumed his drinking habits, as he found himself unable to work.

This pattern of alternating periods of licence and abstinence was maintained for the rest of his life. At times alcohol was a necessity: 'The only thing that gave me an illusion of happiness was wine,' he wrote in his diary on 13 June 1908. 'That is why I drank. It also mitigated the torment of being alive. It made my sluggish mind alert and intelligent! At times, in my youth, it stilled my hunger.'

Here 'wine' is used as a generic term for all the alcoholic drinks he consumed, of which the most dangerous was absinth because, as drunk by Strindberg and his contemporaries, it contained oil of thuja, which has strong neurotoxic and hallucinative properties. It was first manufactured in this form by Pernod in 1798, but its ill effects were not recognized until the latter part of the nineteenth century, when it had become for many people an addiction. It was not forbidden in France until 1915. Attention was drawn to its dangers by a Swedish pharmacologist in 1868–9, and a long quotation from his work in the first article by Bäverstedt and Carlsson shows that its effects were precisely those described by Strindberg in *Inferno*: a feeling of anxiety and fear, visual and aural hallucinations, loss of appetite and consequent loss of weight, difficulty in breathing, loss of muscular power, a feeling of paralysis and, finally, a conviction of being pursued. The only one of Strindberg's symptoms absent from the list is the sensation of being attacked by an electric current, but another observer cites acute cutaneous sensation (parathesia) as being a symptom of absinth poisoning.

At the same time, whatever influence alcoholic poisoning may have had on the torments which Strindberg suffered in Paris, it cannot explain the periods of crisis during which he had no access to quantities of drink, notably those which occurred in Austria in the summer of 1894 and the autumn of 1896. But the circumstances of his life in Austria on both occasions were quite enough to produce a high state of nervous tension in a hyper-sensitive man. In 1894 there were his absolute dependence on Frida's grandparents, who clearly wanted to be rid of him and with whom he had nothing in common, his fears and worries about the prosecution in Berlin, his conflicts with Frida about the child and, in addition to all this, his acute poverty and the feeling that he was trapped.

The situation in 1896 was rather different. Poverty was still a major factor, but combined with it was an acute sense of guilt because he knew that for many months he had done nothing to improve his material position. In 1894 he had painted pictures which he hoped to sell, and was planning a literary career in Paris which he hoped would make him rich and famous. In July 1896 he had for months been

content to live on charity and pursue his alchemic investigations. At the height of his crisis in July he fled from
France to his good friend Dr Eliasson in Sweden, and he
remained with him until the end of August. While there,
on 20 August, he wrote this most revealing letter to
Hedlund:

> Did I not tell you that I believed that my researches into
> hidden things were forbidden and that I had been punished for
> them? Did I not give you plainly to understand that my oc-
> cultism had cost me my health, almost cost me my personal
> freedom, and that I thought it criminal to continue? That, lost
> in the selfish pleasure of the development of my ego, I had
> neglected and withdrawn from unrewarding work, broken
> bonds that may not be broken, and that my first step towards
> reconciliation with life and the powers would be to resume
> the yoke, work for bread, and seek to procure the same for
> those I had put into the world, and who are in need.

But when in September he moved to Austria, to stay with
Frida's mother, his good resolutions came to nothing. In
Klam he found some of his chemical notes and apparatus,
and back he went to his experiments. He knew this was
a lapse from grace, for on 8 September he wrote to Eliasson:
'Found here as well as my library and apparatus 1,000 pages
of natural science, mostly chemistry, in manuscript. Just
imagine it, to encounter Scylla when I'd run away from
Charybdis!'

Nothing in his letters or in his diary suggests that the
feelings of guilt which this return to his experiments engendered resulted in fantasies as macabre and persistent as
those depicted in *Inferno*, but he certainly believed that he
was being persecuted by a host of dangerous enemies, and
this produced mounting fear and anxiety. By November
this state had become so acute that he himself recognized
that he was ill and must seek medical help in his own
country.

These two episodes show that not all the factors that combined to make him ill were necessarily present at every period of crisis. Strindberg's mental balance was so precarious and his imagination so vivid that it was perfectly possible for him to work himself up into a state of panic without the aid of drink. On the other hand, Bäverstedt and Carlsson are convinced that heavy drinking was much to blame for his most severe crisis in July 1896.

Strindberg's Attitude to His Own Experiences

Inferno has so often been accepted – particularly in England – as conclusive proof that Strindberg was clinically insane, that it seems impossible to discuss the book without saying something about his mental health. Of equal importance is his own attitude to his state of mind, and to the experiences that resulted from it.

In his book *The son of a Servant* (*Tjänstekvinnans son*), Torsten Eklund argues that Strindberg more than half enjoyed and welcomed his agonizing experiences. This is borne out by his essay 'Deranged Sense Impressions' ('Sensations détraquées', 1894,) a description of some strange delusions of sight and sound that came upon him when walking in the grounds of Versailles. He believed that he was able to experience these because the sensibility of his nervous system had been 'sharpened by physical and psychical suffering'. One of these experiences is aural. He leans against a wall and hears a multitude of sounds. Can it be that he has stumbled upon Louis XIV's 'Dionysus' ear', by which he listened to the sounds of Paris? That must be it, for it is Paris he hears:

Is it possible? I ask myself yet again. Or, born as I was in the good old days when we had oil-lamps, mail-coaches, female boatmen, and six-volume novels, am I deranged because I have been involuntarily forced to live too rapidly through this era of steam and electricity? Has the result of this been that I have lost my breath and developed bad nerves? Or is it that my nerves are evolving in the direction of hyper-refinement, that my senses are becoming all too acute. Am I casting my skin? Am I turning into a modern human being . . . ? I am as nervous as a crayfish that is casting its shell, as irritable as a silkworm during metamorphosis.[15]

The word *détraqué* needs some elucidation. As Brandell has pointed out, although it properly means 'distracted', 'half mad', as used by the *fin-de-siècle* literary men of Paris it was a compliment:

People wanted to be *détraqué*, mad in a brilliant and sensitive way. Behind this fashion lay the idea that the higher, more refined intellectual life was closely allied to madness, or that in any case it must appear so to the uninitiated masses. Psychiatric discoveries concerning the connection between genius and mental illness, as well as the examples of Poe, Baudelaire, and Verlaine, helped to foster this idea. Related to this new respect for madness was a notion that the use of alcohol and narcotics could contribute to the creation of a higher human type.[16]

It is clear that in his essay 'Deranged Sense Impressions' Strindberg thought of himself as just such a 'higher human type'. He was eager to believe himself capable of abnormal experiences, in whose objectivity – at the time he wrote the essay – he only half believed, but which he saw provided him with material for a dramatic presentation of himself as a 'modern human being'. His use of the word 'modern' indicates that he knew Verlaine's essay on Baudelaire, in which he talks of 'modern man, his senses sharpened and vibrant, his mind painfully acute, his brain saturated with tobacco, his blood burned by alcohol'.[17] Strindberg is expressing the same idea when, having caught himself regretting his insomnia, he pulls himself up and exclaims: 'But

15. S.S. 27, pp. 539–40.   16. Brandell–Jacobs, p. 189.
17. Brandell–Jacobs, p. 189.

why should I complain? Is it not insomnia and dissipation that have sharpened my senses and my nerves?'[18]

A letter to Richard Bergh of 26 November 1894 shows that by this time he was deliberately cultivating his hypersensitivity:

Sent you an article out of *Le Figaro* some time ago : *Deranged Sense Impressions*, in which I have tried, in a good frame of mind that I'd worked up, to anticipate the accomplishments of a more highly developed psychic life, a thing we still lack, and which I can only momentarily achieve before I sink back, tired by the exertion, into my old state.

What impression did it make on you who have delicate nerves? In Paris – at the café Napolitain, where I have my ear of Dionysus every evening from 6 to 7 – silence reigned! It was new, extraordinary, but mad. As my talent was not questioned, nor the novelty, my madness only served as seasoning, and they now call me Cher Maître!

'Deranged Sense Impressions' was written for a *fin-de-siècle* French audience which would not be surprised by the idea that a genius might be mad, nor think that any reason for shutting him up. It may be asked whether *Inferno* was not written for the same audience, and whether this may not be the reason for the bizarre character of the experiences it recounts. It is true that he had other reasons for making his story as lurid as he could, but it seems reasonable to suppose that he dared to do so because he was writing for a public who would not think him dangerous even if they thought him mad.

That the book was published in Sweden in a Swedish translation before it appeared in France was probably an accident; it certainly came as a surprise to its author. 'It is not worth while thinking of a publisher in Sweden for my *Inferno*,' he wrote to Hedlund in September 1896. 'I shall have to write in French if I want to be read.' But, in

18. S.S. 26, p. 543.

the event, the chance of publishing in Sweden did arise early in 1897, and no doubt his desperate need of money was his reason for taking it.

But although Strindberg did not write *Inferno* until after he knew that it would first be published in Sweden, the fact that he did not write it in Swedish confirms the idea that he wrote for French readers who would, he believed, understand him. His fears of being misunderstood in Sweden were acute, and reached a climax after the book appeared in November 1897: 'It is quite horrible, and made me afraid, surprised that I was able to laugh at those things!' he wrote to his publisher on 12 November.

'What will happen now?

'And is it possible that they will advance temporary conditions, delirium, madness, as explanations, or suggestion, hypnotism, and other circumlocutions?'

He was also afraid of another prosecution that might involve his publisher. In fact his fears of what might happen were so great that he decided to stay on in Paris for a time after the book had appeared. He had no such fears when the French edition was printed in Paris nearly a year later, although he had included in it his essay 'In the Cemetery', and parts of *Jardins des Plantes*, material of an 'occult' nature, but which he believed that the French would understand.

What was it about *Inferno* that so much alarmed Strindberg, although he says that he had laughed at what it described? Was it that the story it told was so convincing, and was it convincing because his attitude to his experiences had changed since the light-hearted days of 'Deranged Sense Impressions'? The answer to both questions is yes. As time passed, and his physical and mental health deteriorated, he had come more and more to believe, at least at times, in the objectivity of his experiences, and when he wrote *Inferno* he succeeded in conveying this belief.

His changed attitude is apparent in his letters. By the summer of 1896 he had become deeply involved with the French occultists, and their ideas of the possibility of bewitchment had taken a firm hold on a mind all too prone to believe in powerful enemies. When he had reached this point the most trifling incident was enough to convince him that these enemies intended to harm him, even to kill him at a distance.

At the time of his most severe crisis in July 1896 he wrote a series of letters to a friend in Sweden, some of which well illustrate his changed attitude. This friend had obviously accused him, not for the first time, of megalomania and persecution mania. On 6 July he replied:

I beg you, strike out these fatal words and concepts, fantasies, megalomania, and persecution mania, and new horizons will open up for you as they did for me when I struck out superstition, chance, and strange coincidences.

Nothing comes from nothing, and fantasies, like dreams, possess full, higher reality. A person who has great powers eventually becomes aware of them and will always appear conceited. The man who has so-called persecution mania is persecuted, either in actual fact, or because he feels the hatred of his fellow men, which is real.

Five days later he carried his argument about public hatred a stage further:

Don't you think that bewitchments are very common, even when we are not told of them? Hatred, evil desires, curses, murder more or less, depending on the hater's justification, or the lack of it in the hated.

Do you know that during, and particularly after the prosecution of *Getting Married*, when the whole Swedish nation hated me, it felt like a magnetic storm, which sometimes pressed me to the earth, and sometimes gave me tremendous power through induction.

Seven days later he wrote again:

I'm going to continue, whether you want me to or not. I'm writing this to clear my mind and to give myself relief; most of all perhaps to keep alive my interest in living. Hallucinations, fantasies, dreams, seem to me to possess a high degree of reality. If I see my pillow assume human shapes those shapes are there, and if any one says they are only (!) created by my imagination, I answer – you say only? What my inner eye sees means more to me! And what I see in my pillow, which is made of birds' feathers, once bearers of life, and of flax, in whose fibres vitality has travelled, is soul, creative power, and reality, as I can draw these shapes, show them to others.

And I hear a sound in my pillow, sometimes like a cricket. The noise that grasshoppers make in the grass has always seemed magic to me. Like a ventriloquist, for I have always fancied that the sound came from an empty hall under the earth. Suppose that the grasshopper has sung in a field of flax, don't you think that Nature or the creator can make a phonograph from its fibres, so that his song resounds for my inner ear when, by suffering, self-denial, and prayer, this has been prepared to receive more distant sounds than it normally does? But this is where your 'natural explanations' fail us, and I abandon them forthwith.

What had been a game had now become an obsession.

Torsten Hedlund, to whom the letters just quoted were addressed, can be identified with the 'occult friend' – although he was not an occultist – to whom reference is made in *Inferno* (p. 167). A Gothenburg publisher and a theosophist, he had first written to Strindberg in July 1891, asking if he shared his interest. To this Strindberg had replied that he knew all about theosophy, but did not much care for what he knew.

In July 1894 Strindberg wrote to him again to ask if he knew whether Jollivet-Castelot was a theosophist. To this Hedlund replied by warning him against the French occultists and their practice of black magic. After this the correspondence lapsed for a time, but in October 1895 Strindberg renewed contact with him and for about a year this new friend became indispensable. As well as acting as a confidant and safety-valve he was a financial support, since, with the help of a wealthy benefactor in Gothenburg, he supplied Strindberg with money during the difficult period of the spring and summer of 1896, when he would otherwise have been destitute.

Strindberg sent over eighty letters to Hedlund between 1891 and 1896. Of these letters eight of the fifteen written in July 1896 – among them those quoted above – are addressed to no one, all are unsigned, and he paginated them 1–59. Written at a time when Strindberg thought his death was imminent, they are in a sense a draft of some parts of *Inferno*. On 6 July Strindberg wrote to Hedlund: 'Life is short, had thought of writing a book, but feel I may not have time, shall therefore send you in letters, helter skelter, memories and experiences from these last strange years.' In fact the letters deal mainly with the events of July itself, the time when his persecution mania was at its height.

As has been shown, the causes of his trouble were many and various, and any attempt to pin-point them must to some extent be misleading. Ill-health, poverty, drink, disappointment over his literary career, and his failure as a husband were no doubt important ingredients. Behind them all lay the nagging feeling of guilt at being unable to support the children of his first marriage. That he did his best to suppress this last feeling, and argued that he was poor because he was working in the cause of knowledge, only made matters worse. In Brandell's view Strindberg's need to exonerate himself created his need to believe himself persecuted. This view is confirmed by a letter he wrote to his sister Elizabeth on 24 April 1898, when she was in a state of deep depression and restlessness :

As regards your impressions of being persecuted, they are just the same as mine were when I was ill; they lack all foundation in fact, though perhaps not all, as it seems we persecute ourselves. If you have read my book *Inferno* you will have seen the reasons for my illusions of persecution, which consisted chiefly of self-reproach. You will also have seen the way in which I sought to find resignation.

Don't move from where you are in a hurry, for it won't help. You can't run away from yourself – or from him who visits you.

The Veracity of Inferno

There is a vast difference between this balanced attitude to his troubles and the wild terrors of *Inferno*. By 1898 Strindberg had travelled a long way on the road to comparative serenity. But how far had he got by the time he came to write the book in May 1897? Evidence is to be found in its sequel, *Legends*, written between 22 September and 17 October 1897. The section which tells the story of his life in Lund from the end of 1896 to the time when he finished *Inferno* in June 1897 suggests that he was still very disturbed. It is full of strange stories, not only of his own experiences but also of those of his friends, 'my brothers in misfortune', as he calls them. He did not know that these friends were fanning the flame of his imagination by fictitious stories of strange experiences which they had never had, and in which he more than half believed. That he had some doubts about his own is shown by a remark he made to one of these friends, Axel Herrlin, in the early months of 1897. After giving him an impassioned account of the experiences he later described in *Inferno* he concluded his story with these words : 'With three fourths of my being I believe in the reality of these constellations, but with the fourth part I ask myself whether all this is not merely the play of my imagination.'[19]

Nevertheless, he did not allow these doubts to creep into *Inferno*, but wrote as convincingly as he could, and succeeded so well that most people have taken him at his word. This was his intention. By the time he had finished the book in June 1897 he had made up his mind that he wanted it to be regarded as an authentic account: 'The reader who is inclined to think that this book is a work of imagination,' he says on p. 274 of *Inferno*, 'is invited to consult the diary I kept day by day from 1895, of which the above is merely a version composed of extracts expanded and re-arranged.' Either he had forgotten what he had said on p. 134 ('I began to make notes which mounted up by degrees to form a diary'), or he did not expect that people would inquire too closely into the facts.

These throw a different light on the matter. He did not begin his diary until 21 February 1896, and then it was not kept as a day to day account. Under the heading 'Providential Events' he entered what he regarded as particularly significant incidents from the past year. It was not until the end of April that the notes applied to the date on which they were written.

This diary, which he kept in the strict sense of the word from April 1896 to July 1908, is the one which he later called his 'Occult Diary'. It is now always referred to by that title, though the word 'Occult' was first added in 1907, when he pawned the manuscript to Bonnier in order to raise money to pay his rent. The diary covers a wide range of subjects: his state of mind, his dreams, his journeys, the people he saw, the books he read, and so on. Many entries are purely factual, and the picturesque inter-

19. Axel Herrlin, *Från sekelslutets Lund*, C. W. K. Gleerups förlag, Lund, 1936, p. 162.

pretations of them were later additions made in the diary itself, or invented to suit his purpose when he came to write *Inferno*. The diary makes it clear that many of the incidents upon which he later built the book did not appear nearly so significant or alarming at the time they happened.

Take for instance the description of his walk in the gorge at Klam (*Inferno*, pp. 212–13). In the book this walk becomes a nightmare full of terrors; in the diary, except for one comparison, it is entirely factual. 'Walked to the gorge which is guarded by two dogs. A horn containing grease was hanging on the shed door; beside it leaned a broom. Next came a pig-sty that looked like a Columbarium (read Dante).'[20] Under this he drew a picture of a pig-sty with eight doors. But later, when he revised the diary, he crossed out two of the doors and wrote, '6 – a bad number', i.e., an ominous number, which eight would not have been.

Other entries tell the same story, such as that for 19 September, which runs:

Letter from Hedlund about the cyclone in Paris. Letter from Orfila. (Dreamed about Hans Forsell.)

Had heard noises from the attic in the night. Went up.* Saw spinning-wheels and a sewing-machine. Opened a chest: saw four black sticks making a pentagram; re-arranged them better.

*With my Dalmatian knife. The point is bent for no reason.

The following night a storm broke at 12 o'clock and lasted until 2. (The day before I had described the cyclones in Paris in a letter to Hedlund, not without some uneasiness.)[21]

In contrast, *Inferno* reads:

September 19. Went up to investigate the attic, where I found a dozen spinning-wheels that made me think of electric machines. I opened an enormous chest, empty except for five sticks painted black. What they were intended for I did not know, but they were arranged on the bottom of the chest to

20. O.D. 9 September 1896.   21. O.D. 19 September 1896.

form a pentagram. Who has played this trick on me, and what does it mean? I do not dare to inquire, and the mystery remains unsolved.

In the night a fearful storm raged between twelve and two o'clock. Usually the fury of the storm abates in a short time and it moves away, but this one remained over my village for two solid hours, and I am sure it was an attack on me personally, and each flash was aimed at me but failed to hit the mark.[22]

It is clear that the incidents recorded in the diary have been deliberately altered and touched up. The four sticks, which he re-arranged to look as much like a pentagram as possible, have become five, already placed in the form of a pentagram, and consequently put there with the intention of harming and frightening Strindberg. The treatment of the storm throws light on his methods. In the diary he only hints at its significance by mentioning that he had told Hedlund about the cyclone in Paris. In *Inferno* the description is far more dramatic. The cyclone is not mentioned, but its sinister characteristic is. Both Strindberg and the occultists believed that cyclones represented waves of hatred projected at some particular person or persons.

Sometimes there is no mention at all, at the time they happened, of incidents of which he later made much, for instance the one in which his little daughter sees a sweep. It runs as follows:

On another day, when there had been further speculation about the enigma I presented, they decided that I must be Robert le Diable (Robert Duke of Normandy, d. 1035, in legend the son of the devil). About the same time one or two things occurred that made me dread that I might be stoned by the populace. I will give you the plain facts. My little Christine was excessively afraid of the chimney-sweep. One evening at supper she suddenly began to scream at the top of her voice

22. *Inferno*, pp. 219–20.

and to point at some invisible object behind my chair, crying as she did so : 'Look, there's the sweep!'

My mother, who believes that children and animals are clairvoyant, turned pale. I was frightened too, especially when I saw her making the sign of the cross over the child's head. A deathly silence then followed, and my heart felt heavy within me.[23]

This incident is not mentioned in the diary at the time it is supposed to have happened in November 1896 because at that time Strindberg knew too little of Swedenborg to assign any special significance to sweeps. But by March 1897 he had read more of Swedenborg's works, including the one in which he deals with the spirits who inhabit Jupiter. A quotation from it entered in the diary on 21 March reads as follows : 'It is possible to distinguish among the spirits some who are called sweeps, because they have blackened faces and appear clad in dark, soot-coloured clothing . . .' This quotation is repeated in *Inferno* on p. 257. The six lines that follow it there do not occur in the diary, though other less colourful lines do. Under them Strindberg has written : 'Cp. Christine's fear of the sweep whom she sometimes saw when he was not there.'[24]

This is no more than a passing reference to an imaginative child's ability to see things which are not there, particularly things of which it is afraid. There is no hint in the entry that his daughter saw the sweep standing behind his chair, or that sweeps had any special significance in relation to him. This came later when he wrote *Inferno*, and after he had absorbed more of Swedenborg's teaching.

The above is only one of many examples of how Strindberg described and interpreted earlier experiences in the light of his later reading of Swedenborg. The diary is conclusive evidence that, whatever importance he seems to attach to Swedenborg in Chapter 9 of *Inferno*, he knew

23. *Inferno*, p.227.   24. O.D., 21 March 1897.

little of him in the autumn of 1896. With one exception, the only thing that made a deep impression on him at this time was Swedenborg's description of Hell. The exception was that he found support for his love of resemblances in Swedenborg's Law of Correspondences. We know this not from the diary but from a letter to Hedlund of 12 October: 'I have grown a whole ell in these last six weeks as a result of studying Swedenborg, where I have found the word "Correspondences", which gave me the clue to my method: see resemblances everywhere.'

Strindberg himself does not say precisely what work of Swedenborg's it was that he read in the autumn of 1896, he simply says in *Inferno* (p. 210) that his mother-in-law and her sister gave him 'an old German book' with the words: 'Take it and read it but do not be afraid.' We know that this happened a few days after he arrived in Klam, for he mentioned it in a letter of 7 September to Hedlund: 'Here Swedenborg's writings have fallen into my hands for the first time. There are miraculous things in them.' The next day he wrote a long entry in his diary headed: 'Swedenborg's Description of Hell; like Klam to a hair.'

Thanks to Swedish scholarship we now know that the 'old German book' was not a work by Swedenborg, but a German translation of a French book of extracts from his theological works, primarily *Vera Christiana Religio*. It was divided into chapters and Chapter XII, Hell, was the one Strindberg summarized in his diary on 8 September.[25]

The landscape described in this chapter was so exactly like the landscape of Klam that it confirmed Strindberg's long-held conviction that he was in hell, being punished for sins committed in a previous existence, or for sins of which he was well aware. But though the belief was there already he only realized the dramatic opportunities it offered after reading a fuller version of Swedenborg in 1897. The diary

25. Stockenström, pp. 55–7.

shows plainly that *Inferno* would have been a very different book had Strindberg's knowledge of Swedenborg been
as limited when he wrote it as it was in 1896. Except for
the one long entry of 8 September, where he simply summarized what he had read and did not relate any of it
to his own life, Swedenborg is never mentioned again
in any of the entries for September, October or November
1896.

Further proof that *Inferno* is a dramatized interpretation
of events is to be found in the paginated letters to Hedlund,
such as the one he wrote on 19 July about his flight from
Orfila to Rue de la Clé. It was presumably written in the
heat of the moment, for the diary confirms that this was
the date of his flight. He was certainly highly agitated when
he wrote it, but equally certainly he touched up his experiences when he came to write *Inferno*.

After telling Hedlund at considerable length about the
experiments he was conducting, the presence of his neighbours in the adjoining room, his belief that he was being
gassed, and his walk in the Luxembourg Gardens, he continues:

When I came home I wanted to write but could not do so,
and the stranger sat beside me.

At ten o'clock I went to bed, and immediately afterwards
the man crossed the room and lay down beside me. But then
the other individual woke and made a noise.

I lay awake and heard the two of them signalling to one
another with coughs and tappings. Lit the lamp again as I had
the feeling that I was being drawn between the two poles of
a powerful electric machine, or that I was being smothered between cushions.

There was no sign of the waiter whose window is opposite
mine, and I realized that I had not noticed the noise he usually
makes when he goes to bed; also noticed that I heard nothing
of my third neighbour. Shut up between what I supposed to be
two murderers I came to a decision; put on my clothes, went

down to the landlord, told him that my chemicals had made me ill, and asked for another room.

He was kind, gave me a drink and another room directly under the unknown man, whom I had not so much as hinted at by a word.

I now heard the unknown man leap from his bed. He's thinking of running away, I thought, believing that the police have been sent for.

He did not run away but banged once on the floor with a chair, and dropped something heavy like a suitcase. I slept, woke, and could only remember that I had dreamed about Ola Hansson.

It was a grey miserable morning, yellowish-grey! like murder and the fear of discovery.

At 11 o'clock I packed my bag, and a quarter of an hour later I fled, giving Dieppe as my address.

The same story as told in *Inferno* runs as follows:

In the evening I no longer ventured to sit at my desk for fear of a new attempt on my life. I went to bed not daring to sleep. Night had come and the lamp was lit. I saw, cast on the wall opposite my window, the shadow of a human being, whether man or woman I could not say, but the impression I retain is that it was a woman.

When I got up to look the blind came clattering down with a bang. After that I heard the unknown person enter the room next to my recess. Then all was silent.

For three hours I lay awake, unable to sleep, a thing that does not usually take me long. An uneasy sensation began to creep over me. I was being subjected to an electric current, passing between the two rooms on either side of mine. The tension increased still more and, in spite of the resistance I put up, I was obliged to get out of bed. I had only one thought in my mind:

'Someone is killing me! I will not be killed.'

I went out to look for the waiter whose room was at the other end of the corridor, but alas he was not there. Sent out on purpose, keeping out of the way, a secret confederate, bribed!

I went down the stairs and along various corridors to wake the proprietor. With a presence of mind of which I had not believed myself capable, I alleged that the fumes from the chemicals in my room had made me feel unwell, and asked if he could let me have another room for the night.

By an unlucky chance, which must be ascribed to an enraged Providence, the only vacant room was the one immediately under that of my enemy.

Left to myself I opened the window and inhaled the fresh air of a starry night. Above the roof-tops of the Rue d'Assas and the Rue de Madame the Plough and the Pole Star were visible.

So, to the North! *Omen accipio!*

As I was drawing the curtains of the recess I heard the enemy above my head get out of bed and drop some heavy object into a portmanteau, the lid of which he locked.

So there must be something he wanted to hide, an electric machine perhaps.[26]

In another place in this letter, and again in the corresponding passage in *Inferno*, Strindberg uses a quotation from the Bible. In each place he says it was taken at random, but the quotations are not the same and have not at all the same import. He leads up to them by describing an experiment. First the letter:

Yesterday, Saturday, I had bought a furnace (50 centimes) and crucibles (at 31 centimes) and was going to attempt a synthesis of gold over a fire by means of oxide of lead, which is on the way to being gold. In spite of the heat I was in good heart, and though I was working with soda and potassium cyanide, I felt no discomfort. But every time I left the stove and the furnace and sat at my desk I felt uneasy, partly because, on the other side of the wall, the unknown man sat a yard away from me shifting his chair, and partly because I felt suffocated. A great feeling of indisposition came over me, anxiety about something silent, hostile. At 12 o'clock I ate

26. *Inferno*, pp. 175–6.

from a tray, standing by the chest of drawers. Read the papers. Lay down on the bed to rest, but could not. Heard a man's voice and a woman's in the adjoining room but purposely speaking in the markedly low tones that conspirators adopt.

Got up : received a good letter.

Calm descended on me. Read Isaiah, chapter 54, opened at random.

'For a small moment have I forsaken thee but with great mercies will I gather thee.

'In a little wrath I hid my face from thee for a moment; but with everlasting kindness will I have mercy on thee saith the Lord thy Redeemer . . .

'Behold, they shall surely gather together, but not by me; whosoever shall gather together against thee shall fall for thy sake.'

Wonderfully comforted I sat in a chair and meditated.

Compare the corresponding passage in *Inferno*.

Alone, absolutely alone, I now had my dinner on a tray in my room, and ate so little that the good-natured waiter was inconsolable. I did not hear the sound of my own voice for a whole week, and I began to lose it for lack of exercise. I had not a sou in my pocket, no stamps or tobacco either.

I willed myself to make a final effort. I *would* make gold by the dry method with the aid of fire. Money was procured, a furnace, crucibles, charcoal, bellows, and tongs. The heat was intense and, stripped to the waist like a smith, I sweated in front of the open fire. But the sparrows had built a nest in the flue and the fumes made their way out into the room. My first attempt left me infuriated, partly because I had a headache but also because of the futility of my operations, as everything went wrong. After I had re-melted the stuff three times I looked into the crucible. The borax had formed a skull with two glistening eyes whose supernatural irony pierced my soul.

Still not a grain of metal, so I gave up further experiment.

Sitting in my armchair I read the Bible, opened at random.

'And none calleth to mind, neither is there knowledge or understanding to say, I have burned part of it in the fire; yea, also I have baked bread upon the coals thereof; I have toasted flesh and eaten it: and shall I make the residue thereof an abomination? Shall I fall down to the stock of a tree? He feedeth on ashes: a deceived heart hath turned him aside, and he cannot deliver his soul, nor say, Is there not a lie in my right hand?...

'Thus saith the Lord thy Redeemer, and he that formed thee from the womb: I am the Lord that maketh all things; that stretcheth forth the heavens alone; that spreadeth abroad the earth by myself; that *frustrateth the tokens of the liars, and maketh diviners mad; that turneth wise men backward, and maketh their knowledge foolish.*'

For the first time I was assailed by doubts about my scientific investigations. Suppose they were pure folly? Alas! if so, I had sacrificed a life of happiness for myself and for my wife and child too, all for a chimera.[27]

The reason that the quotation in the letter could not be used again in *Inferno* is that by the time Strindberg wrote the book his conception of God had changed. Swedenborg had convinced him that God was invariably a stern and relentless judge, who punished in order to reform, and who certainly did not approve of chemical experiments.

But this is not the last of the discrepancies between the letter and *Inferno*. In the former he tells Hedlund: 'My lungs and heart seem to be affected, not by recent events, but by two years of handling poisons, Sulphur, Iodine, Bromine, Chloride, and Cyanide. I've lost weight, food and strong drink revolt me, and I'm probably becoming paralysed.' This is a reasonable explanation of his symptoms. even if not the right one. But in *Inferno*, after a particularly violent attack at the Rue de la Clé, we find him rejecting it 'An illness? Impossible. I had been in excellent health up to the time I shed my incognito.'[28]

This attack took place on the night between 23 and 24 July, that is, after his letter to Hedlund admitting he was

27. *Inferno*, pp. 173-4.   28. *Inferno*, p. 182.

ill, so his statement that he had been 'in excellent health' does not represent what he thought at the time, but what he considered suitable for his purpose in May 1897.

Another thing that shakes belief in *Inferno* as a reliable account is that, except for what he himself admits was a happy period, briefly described in Chapter 4, the book depicts him as living in a perpetual state of crisis. For instance, take the visit he paid to Ystad from 31 July to 28 August 1896.[29]

From this visit Strindberg selected only those incidents which would enhance the impression of crisis, and even these he altered to suit his purpose. From *Inferno* one would suppose that his only regular companion was Eliasson. But the latter was a practising doctor and a busy man, so he had thoughtfully arranged for a friend to keep Strindberg company during the daytime. This friend was Eugen Hemberg, the local Forestry Supervisor, an ardent naturalist and consequently a man with whom Strindberg had much in common. Hemberg has left an account of the almost daily walks and expeditions they made together, and of Strindberg's keen and imaginative response to everything they saw and did,[30] but there is no mention of this in *Inferno*.

It is also odd that the letters written to Eliasson immediately after this visit, but before he had read Swedenborg, are affectionate and grateful whereas in one written on 17 September 1897, that is, after *Inferno*, he calls him 'a good but hard friend who was put over me "because of my sins!"'

But we have another important piece of evidence regarding the veracity of Strindberg's account of his visit to Ystad. After reading *Inferno* in November 1897 Eliasson wrote, but never sent, a long letter in which he refuted many of the

29. *Inferno*, pp. 188–20.

30. Sven Hedenberg, *Strindberg i skärselden*, Akademiförlaget–Gumperts, Göteborg, 191, pp. 54–60.

accusations Strindberg had made against him in that book. One was the story of the two-month-old foetus that Eliasson is said to have brought home with him one afternoon, his hands covered with blood, looking like a butcher. Eliasson's story is very different: 'A woman had had a miscarriage caused by another disease. The caul came away intact without being ruptured. I told you this relatively unusual fact. *You came with me* to the hospital on the following day, and I demonstrated the foetus to you in the presence of a nurse. My hands were clean when I commenced the demonstration, that they became bloody was unavoidable.'[31]

There is an explanation why Strindberg's account in *Inferno* of this visit to Eliasson differs so far from the true facts. He had reached a point in the book at which he had to show that his destiny was under the control of higher powers, and that these powers sometimes designated other human beings to be their instruments. This is what he means when he says: 'I parted from my friend the Tormentor without bitterness. He had only been the instrument of Providence.'[32]

An extension of the same idea is to be found in a letter written on 7 November 1897, after *Inferno*, in which he comments upon his attitude to Eliasson, Torsten Hedlund and Ossian Ekborn, another friend whom he suspected of tormenting him. In it he claims that his relationship to all three was ordained by higher powers: 'It was their mission to torment me, but it is highly probable that it was also my mission to be a scourge to them! The odd thing is: this time I haven't a trace of guilty conscience, of "ingratitude". *Ich dien', och wir dienen högre Magter.'*[33]

It is understandable that Eliasson was not able to see this distortion of the truth in the same light, with the result

31. Stockenström, p. 171.   32. *Inferno*, p. 201.
33. I serve and we serve higher powers.

that *Inferno* lost Strindberg a good friend, who had often stood by him in time of need.

Yet another feature of *Inferno* that disproves its complete veracity is the number of significant omissions and evasions. The first of these occurs right at the beginning of the book. Strindberg would have us believe that after parting from Frida he returned to his 'miserable student's room' and immediately started upon his chemical experiments. In fact he went to Dieppe to stay with his friend the Norwegian painter Fritz Thaulow, with whom he was later to take refuge after fleeing from the Rue de la Clé at the end of July 1896. At the end of October 1894 he stayed for nine days, and his visit would have lasted longer if Thaulow had not been recalled to Norway on the death of his mother. 'My nerves are now beautifully at rest, and I'm going to make another attack on Paris,' Strindberg wrote to Frida on 30 October. This visit obviously did not provide him with material suitable for use in *Inferno*.

The same is true of much of his life in 1895 and the first month of 1896, of which he says little in *Inferno*. The picture he paints of a recluse who had retreated into a world where no one could follow him is entirely false. He was alone only in the sense that he had no wife living with him, but in his lodgings in the Rue de la Grande Chaumière he was close to a number of friends and opposite the crémerie where he had his evening meal. He saw his friends daily, not only when he dined but on walks and at the jolly evening parties with the Mollards, the kind friends of whom he speaks so patronizingly in *Inferno* (p. 104): 'Their home was a meeting place for the whole circle of artist-anarchists, and I felt that I was doomed to endure there all the things I should have preferred not to see and hear.' He obviously wants it to be thought that he was the disdainful observer, the man superior to and remote from those with whom he was forced to associate. In fact he was an active partici-

pant in their revels, and the people he met at the Mollards',
at Gauguin's weekly receptions and at the crémerie were
his intimate friends, who gave him companionship, understanding and support. Some, like Frederick Delius, were
almost as interested in occultism as he was himself and
firmly believed in his gold-making, about which they
thought he was far too modest.

He did not finally break with his friends at the crémerie
until July 1896. In a letter to Hedlund of 17 July he gives
two reasons : first, 'the company there was too disreputable
even for me,' and second, 'there too they wanted to tamper
with my destiny.' The second was the real reason for the
rupture. His persecution mania was at its height, and he
now suspected even his best friends of wanting to torment
him, even to kill him. When he came to write *Inferno* he
conveniently forgot all that these people had meant to him.
It would not have suited his purpose to remember.

He also failed to mention a visit he paid to Eliasson in
June–July 1895 'to repair my health and particularly my
hands', and he passes over in silence the fact that his portrait
was painted by the Polish artist Slewinski, and a bust
sculptured by another of his friends, Agnes de Frumerie.
Though he constantly talks of Edvard Munch, whom he
calls the 'Danish painter', he nowhere mentions the fact
that in June 1896 Munch made his famous lithograph portrait of him. He was not very pleased with Munch's lithograph because his name was misspelt 'Stindberg', and
because the naked figure of a woman had been inserted
among the zigzag lines that framed his face, but he was
very proud of the bust and told Hedlund on 28 June : 'that's
what I'd like to look like.' The bust is eloquently proof
that he did not spend all his time in hell. It shows us a
proud man who looks confidently on a world he has
conquered.

This was not the impression he wanted to create when

he wrote *Inferno*. To produce the desired effect he had to alter, distort or omit unsuitable material, and add matter suggested by his fertile imagination. To say that he did so is no criticism of the book, only of his statement that it was an authentic account, based on extracts from his diary. These alone, even expanded and rearranged, would have made a far less effective book than the one he produced. Moreover, Strindberg was above all a dramatist, and he often thought that all the horrible things he had experienced had been 'staged' for him to enable him to become one. Even when he was not composing drama he wrote as if he were. He himself believed that he had cultivated the art of writing fiction dramatically. In a letter to Schering of 6 May 1907 he says: 'The secret of all my narratives, short stories, and sagas is that they are dramas. When, as you know, the theatres were closed to me for long periods, I hit on the idea of writing all my dramas in epic form – for future use.' *Inferno* is a perfect example of what happened when he did so. In it he also prepared the ground for his play *To Damascus*, Part I.

It is interesting to note that at one time he conceived of *Inferno* as a poetic, that is, fictional, work in prose. In a letter to Hedlund of 23 August 1896 he says:

You said recently that people are looking for the Zola of occultism. That I feel is my calling. But in a grand, lofty strain. A poem in prose called

INFERNO

The same theme as in *By the Open Sea*. The destruction of the individual when he isolates himself. His salvation through: work without honour or gold, duty, family, consequently – woman – the mother and the child!

Resignation through the discovery of the task allotted to everyone of us by Providence.

On 21 September he asked Hedlund if he might borrow a book on German mythology 'as preparation for my novel or whatever it should be called'.

But by May 1897, when he actually began to write *Inferno*, he was interpreting his experiences in the light of what he had learned from Swedenborg. They were a punishment, inflicted on him for his good. Consequently, not only did he want other people to believe in them, he believed in them himself and thought that they had given him greater insight into the workings of his own mind and the minds of others. Commenting to his German translator, Emil Schering, on the observation of some German author that he was not only a poet but an educator, he says on 26 March 1900: 'Grateful, but I'm not an educator, only a poet who, on his pilgrimage, lives through all the stations of human experience in order to portray humanity.'

Strindberg's Faith in a God

For Strindberg the most important experience was the experience of God, whom he thought of as the power outside himself who guided his destiny. Of the nature of this power he was often in doubt, as we see from *Inferno*, but the belief that some such power existed was a necessity to him.

A widespread belief exists that Strindberg had been a confirmed atheist and that the result of his Inferno crisis was a conversion. This is far from being true, although, after the prosecution of *Getting Married*, he did for some years become a reluctant and uneasy atheist. A year after this change, on 11 January 1886, he wrote to a friend: 'I've been spiritually bankrupt since the spring of last year when I turned atheist, and afterwards had to revise the whole of my ideology bit by bit!', and on 18 February to another friend: 'I sometimes wish that I still had God and Heaven. It was in any case a retreat. Now I see none. Or that I'd become an atheist when I was younger. Then I should have organized my life accordingly. Now it's arranged with Heaven as its fixed point. Therefore everything has gone to the devil. I see no way out. And no meaning in anything.'

Strindberg's atheism, like his God, was a very personal matter. God had let him down after the prosecution of *Getting Married*, so, like a rebellious child, he rejected him, but as Brandell says: 'Except for a time during the climax of his struggle in 1887–8, his efforts to suppress the idea of God met with little success. Whenever his defensive attitude deserted him, a tentative idea of God rose to the surface of his mind.'[34]

Strindberg himself on 19 June 1898 described his atheistic period as 'a psychic experiment that immediately failed'.

It is easy to see why. In spite of the complexity of his nature Strindberg had an urgent need of simple faith, what he called the fixed point outside himself. In a letter to Hedlund of 20 July 1896 he writes: 'Black magic is practised by godless or arrogant beings who make themselves one with God. God in us, yes, in the sense that we are emanations of His being, that's one thing; but God the fixed point outside us, by which alone we can achieve anything. The Creator above us, and we his creations, with traces of his being, under him, that's how I understand the matter.' This is an echo of the words he put into the mouth of his hero Axel Borg in *By the Open Sea*: 'Give me a few more hypotheses, above all the fixed point outside myself, for I am quite adrift.'[35]

This need of hypotheses was no doubt one of the things that drew him to Catholicism. 'It's a religion for children,' he wrote to Herrlin on 31 January 1898, 'and if we do not become as children etc.' But he could never take the final step, and a visit to a real monastery seems to have dis-

34. Brandell–Jacobs, p. 55.   35. S.S. 24, p. 238.

couraged him. After one night at Maredsous in Belgium he wrote to his daughter from Lund on 19 August 1898 :

As a guest I was very kindly received, slept there, ate in the Refectory with the 100 monks. All was peace and quiet except for me. Into the bargain we had five courses at dinner with beer and wine on the table for the guests, and that was too much food for me, so I came back here ... The brothers were very friendly, but they drank wine and took snuff which I didn't life. They were a bit too worldly for me.

Even had he found their life ideal it is unlikely that he would ever have committed himself to their faith. The real reason for his retreat from Catholicism was that he could never accept any form of religion other than his own. On 4 August 1899 he wrote to his eldest daughter, Karin, who had also been tempted to turn Catholic : 'Your religious anxieties don't alarm me at all, but do as I did when I found that I could not comply with the demands of any formulated dogma; keep what is essential : your relationship with God through prayer, even if you have to drop all the rest.'

He called his God by many different names, and his conception of him constantly changed. He was a fixed point only in the sense that he was a father-figure; like a human father, he was unpredictable, something of an enigma. Of one thing, however, Strindberg was certain; his God belonged to him personally and was concerned with everything that happened to him, good or bad. 'Impossible for me to exist with a collective God in whom I was part owner, for then I should be able to make slight changes in my destiny, and that I cannot do ...' he wrote to Hedlund on 1 July 1896. 'No, I experience God as an entirely personal acquaintance who during the past year has "sought" me so openly and tangibly that I have awakened, but I am still not sure what he wants of me. I don't think it is to come forward and make a personal proclamation, for every time I have come forward to speak my tongue has become paralysed and my understanding dimmed.'

At times he had difficulty not only in understanding but even in finding his God, but on 1 April he discovered a comforting explanation of his dilemma, writing to a friend:

Brand sent me a book about the Jesuits in which I found something that gave me relief. The author, Jean Wallon, writes in his preface: 'In 1876 ... I predicted in an article called *Providential Atheism* that God was going to hide himself in order to force people to seek him more diligently.' This neglect of the Powers because they had hidden themselves began in 1867 with Renan, Taine, and Zola (Darwin was not an atheist). But now the powers are about to return, and now people are seeking God with lighted candles, whether by God we mean a moral world order, an avenger, or a reconciler. And those who, in arrogant curiosity, delve too deeply into forbidden mysteries like the occultists (and me), they were allowed to see more than they wanted and the Sphinx clawed them, the one after the other. But occultism led back to a conception of God, and the certainty that there are others who guide our destinies. That is where I stand, and I have got no further, but it seems to me that, with the return of the powers, the old demands for law and order and so on will return too. And, as one who stands under the complete supervision of the unseen, I believe that I must deny myself some of life's little pleasures that have been my misfortune, most of all wine.

At the time he finished writing *Inferno* in June 1897 he was far less certain of his position. God was there indeed, but he was seen as a jester who mocks man and delights in tormenting him, and Strindberg's *Inferno*, unlike Dante's, ends without a glimpse of heaven.

But *Inferno* had served its purpose. It was not so much an end in itself as a means to an end. In it he had done what he set out to do in the letters to Hedlund: he had cleared his mind and relieved himself of some of his burden. He believed, as he had done in 1882, that 'to write and to relieve one's heart is the greatest joy and comfort,' and he could still tell Schering twenty-five years later to 'write the pain' out of himself.

Strindberg continued this process in *Legends* and *Jacob Wrestles*, the last work of the trilogy, but the latter was never finished. Writing to his publisher, Gustaf af Geijerstam, on 2 March 1898 he says:

> When I read the proofs of Part II, *Legends*, I see that we have miscalculated the length of the manuscript, and that the book will have a paltry, brochure-like appearance. As the third part that I'd begun has misfired, and I've been forced to cut short my religious brooding, I'm sending you the fragment which can be bound with Part II. With that my religious struggles are over, and the whole Inferno saga is at an end.

What had 'forced' him to give up his 'religious brooding'? Was it the realization that the time had come for him to return to drama? In November 1897 his play *Master Olof* had been staged with great success in Stockholm, and it was performed fifty-two times between 26 November 1897 and 23 January 1898. At first he thought of following this up by attempting to get some of his earlier plays performed, but by January the idea of writing a new play had germinated. An entry in his diary dated 19 January 1898 runs: 'Got back my theatre mania and began *Robert le Diable*.' This was the first title he gave to *To Damascus*, Part I.

Not much more than a month later, on 10 March, he wrote to Herrlin: 'I seem to have recovered the grace of being able to write for the theatre again, and have recently finished a big play that I'm grateful to have been allowed to do.'

He was back at what he always considered was his true vocation, from which he had been and would so often be debarred.

From an Occult Diary tells the story of Strindberg's strange love for Harriet Bosse, his third and last wife. As the extracts from the diary and his letters to Harriet show, he tried to compensate for the deficiencies and irritations of their relationship by transferring his love for her to a world of the imagination. This is how he describes the situation in *A Blue Book*:

There is a woman I cannot bear to be near, but who is dear to me at a distance. We write letters, always appreciative and friendly, but after we have longed for one another for a time and feel we must meet, we instantly begin to quarrel, grow coarse and disharmonious, part in anger. We love one another on a higher plane, but are not able to be in the same room, and we dream of meeting again, disembodied, on a verdant island, where only we two, and at most our child may be.[36]

Strindberg married Harriet on 6 May 1901. The ingredients for disaster were there from the beginning, and perhaps two wiser people would not have embarked on such a perilous adventure. Strindberg was fifty-two, Harriet only twenty-three. His habits and tastes were set by many years of living alone, whereas Harriet was still experimenting with life. What he wanted most of all was a quiet, disciplined existence which would leave his mind free for his work. In this life there was room for visits to or from old friends, but there was no place for the active social life likely to appeal to a successful young actress.

Most difficult of all for Harriet to understand must have been his conviction that many aspects of his life were governed by mysterious beings whom in *Inferno* he had called 'the Powers'.

After 1898 these powers lost their plurality and were referred to as 'the Unseen', 'the Unknown', 'Someone', but

36. S.S. 46, p. 175.

their function was the same. Writing to Harriet on 16 September 1905 he says: 'Of the Someone I only know that he steers my destiny, and always towards a goal, though sometimes by a roundabout route. This was what you found so hard to understand in our early days, when you still believed that man is the master of his fate. The fact that I could not convince you often drove me to despair.'

But Strindberg's eccentricity was not the only cause of their difficulties. Harriet was a tempestuous creature who took her own way if she was not given it. She was the thirteenth of fourteen children and after her mother's death was brought up by her older sisters, who probably spoiled her. During her childhood the family oscillated between Stockholm and Kristiania, as Oslo was then called, so Harriet was educated in both Sweden and Norway. She began her career as an actress in Norway but, in spite of her success there, she left Kristiania precipitately in 1898, possibly because of an unhappy love affair. After spending some time in Denmark and Paris studying the theatre she came to live with a sister in Stockholm, and by the autumn of 1899 had become one of the actresses at the Royal Dramatic Theatre. Her first big success was in Gustaf Wied's comedy *The First Violin*, but it was her rendering of Puck in *A Midsummer Night's Dream* which impressed Strindberg so favourably that he acceded to the suggestion that she should play the part of the Lady in *To Damascus*, Part I.

Harriet herself did not think much of the style of acting she found in Stockholm. 'In my youthful superiority,' she writes, 'I thought the acting I saw was stilted, declamatory, and false.' According to an eye-witness her own style was very different. 'Her only technique was the one she had created for herself – an individual, subdued and allusive style, that concentrated on the spiritual, and reduced the use of gesture to a minimum. Her most eloquent features were her eyes which, with vibrant intensity, reflected the innermost emotions of her spirit.'[37] Nothing like her acting had been seen in Stockholm before and the critics were somewhat baffled. The person who understood her best was Strindberg who wrote to her: 'Now stay on with us as *the* actress of the new century. You have struck a new note for us to hear, no matter where you found it.'

But Harriet was not only a very gifted actress on the brink of a successful career, she was also an intelligent and independent person, not at all the sort of woman to submit patiently to Strindberg's whims and habits. Nor did she take kindly to opposition. A member of the governing body of the Dramatic Theatre during her years there has this to say of her: 'There were times when not even the diplomacy of a Talleyrand could have made her see reason ... The most difficult time was in 1925 when she was playing Nora in *A Doll's House* and insisted on wearing a knee-length dress, the fashion of the day, but not at all that of the 1880s, the period in which the play was set.'[38] This of course led to a clash and resulted in Harriet's leaving the theatre in the middle of the season – another precipitate move.

Harriet and Strindberg were divorced in 1904 but remained lovers until January 1907. Her subsequent marriages did not last any longer. She left Gunnar Wingård – a fellow-actor of her own age – after three years in 1911, and did not marry again until 1927. Her third husband was the actor Edwin Adolphson, twelve years her junior. This marriage too lasted for only three years. According to him they were happy at first, but when his career flourished and hers did not – largely because of her quarrel with the Dramatic Theatre – she became jealous and bad-tempered,

37. Oscar Wieselgren, 'Harriet Bosse', in *Meddelanden* No. 29, December 1961.
38. ibid.

and when he annoyed her by looking at some of Strindberg's letters to her behind her back, and then insisting that she should publish them, she flew into a rage, broke a mirror over his head and left, never to return.

This is the Harriet that could go off without saying good-bye or telling Strindberg where she was going; who could wake him in the night and scold him for his supposed infidelity, or leave the fire burning all night 'out of spite' – in a word, the tempestuous Harriet to whom the quiet life that Strindberg loved was anathema.

No wonder that two such ill-assorted people could not get on. The real wonder is that they got as much out of their life together as they did, and that their child was always a bond between them. According to Harriet the weeks they all spent at Furusund in 1904 were happy. Harriet had just returned from France and she says:

Strindberg had, as usual, arranged everything beautifully for me, given me the best room, and done many little things to make me feel happy and at home. My memory of this summer is of the calmest period of our marriage. My little girl was always loved by her father, and now she was two, able to talk rationally and go walks with him. He was delighted by her fear of a large ant, and her refusal to cross the road on which it was unless her father carried her ... it made him happy just to have an excuse to take her in his arms.[39]

Another bond between them was their art. Harriet the actress was a source of joy and pride to Strindberg. 'Strindberg always took a sympathetic interest in my work. He comforted me when the critics were severe, and shone like the sun when I was successful. He overestimated my gifts as an artist, but I am certain that his admiration never made me vain. It only spurred me on – I strove to be the artist he believed I already was.'[40]

39. *Strindberg till Harriet Bosse*, p. 112.
40. *Strindberg till Harriet Bosse*, p. 83.

Strindberg's letters to her show how highly he valued her opinion of his work, and Harriet herself reports: 'I read all that he wrote as it came from his pen. During my time with him all the plays he wrote were handed to me to be read, act by act.'[41] This suggests that he got from her the intellectual companionship which his previous marriages had lacked. What then drove them so relentlessly apart? Harriet was always very circumspect in what she said about Strindberg and asserted that the difference in their ages was the cause of their discord. No doubt this played an important part, but it cannot account for everything. The entries in the diary, and in particular the letter of 28 August 1901, make it plain that in their early days their physical relationship was far from satisfactory. On the other hand it is not easy to decide precisely what was wrong. Harriet's accusations that he was 'not a man', and that a week after her marriage her sisters could say that she was still 'unmarried', seem to suggest impotence.

This was a subject on which Strindberg was always particularly sensitive. According to a letter of 18 August 1887 his first wife had accused him of being impotent, a charge that he indignantly denied. His anxiety to contradict the accusation that he had had the same trouble with Harriet may account for the long entry in the diary of 2 June 1904, in which he puts a very different interpretation on his early difficulties with her. Much of this entry was blotted out by Strindberg, and part of what remains has not previously been printed. It runs as follows:

On our first night H–t had a prolapsed uterus. I had heard that she had had a uterine complaint, and felt sorry for her, but when I tried to comfort her she was angry. Meanwhile I possessed her twice that night, but with distaste. The next day she said she was having her period. After some days we were reunited, but now I felt that she was using a preventive

41. *Strindberg till Harriet Bosse*, p. 112.

and was angry . . . She still complained of me saying she had no pleasure. I could not understand it, but possessed her twice each day, though without the expected pleasure. Often at the climax her uterus fell down and pushed me out. It felt as if a hand inside her slowly drove me back. Finally everything was as it should be, and she was declared to be pregnant.

It is obvious that if not actually impotent Strindberg was an inadequate lover, and that Harriet had no hesitation in telling him so. Perhaps Gunnar Ollén is right when he says: 'he was impatient and hypersensitive (ejaculatio praecox), and lacked the ability to show the necessary consideration for his female partner.'[42] Strindberg was certainly aware of his shortcomings, but he had early evolved the comforting theory that women did not need sexual satisfaction from intercourse, they got all they needed from maternity.[43]

Strindberg is often said to have disliked and despised physical love, and in his later life he said many things that support this theory. But it is equally possible that his professed dislike was again a way of comforting himself for his lack of success as a lover. At the time he wrote *Getting Married* in 1884 he undoubtedly thought that sex was fun and also vitally necessary. (One remembers poor Theodore in *The Reward of Virtue* who pined away and became perverse for lack of it.) But in 1901, after his marriage to Harriet, he had changed his mind and he wrote in his diary that the brutalities of marriage disgusted him, and that he never understood what 'the not very elegant act of procreation had to do with love for a beautiful female soul'. The truth is that physical love was only abhorrent to him when it was unsatisfactory, as it was in 1901. It is obvious from the entries in the diary and from his letters that after they had ceased to reside under the same roof he and Harriet got on better, even physically. On 27 May

42. *Strindbergs dramatik*, Sveriges Radio, Stockholm, 1961, p. 156.
43. S.S. 17, p. 139.

1904 he wrote to her: 'We must live as man and wife for I love your body as I love your soul, and I know that our knowledge of each other has gained ground, though this has required time, as I told you it would on our first night together.'

This does not sound like a man who was still disgusted by the 'brutalities' of marriage, nor does the entry in the diary for 2 June 1904 where he says: 'Harriet's return from Paris to Furusund is one of my loveliest memories. When she left my bed that night she did not look like herself ... and she gave off a fragrance so strong and delicious, that I fell into a state of ecstasy and almost lost consciousness. This thing is supernatural and sometimes makes me think she must be a being from a higher sphere, not an ordinary mortal.' There is no sign here of a conflict between physical love and the spiritual ecstasy to which it gave rise.

It is clear that the news of Harriet's engagement to Gunnar Wingård threw Strindberg into a state of abnormal erotic excitement in which his awareness of her – always acute – was enormously increased. The thought that she belonged to another man was intolerable and he rejected it absolutely. But the only way to escape from it was to retreat into a fantasy world where she could be his alone, and more satisfactorily his than when they were lovers.

Strindberg's attitude to his imagined telepathic intercourse with Harriet is as ambivalent as his attitude to their physical relationship in ordinary life. It was both horrible and marvellous, wedlock and a crime. But as time went on and this intercourse became more and more associated with acute physical suffering, he most often saw it as evil, something that should be resisted. Finally common sense got the upper hand. He wrote to his publisher Karl Otto Bonnier that he was sure he had cancer of the stomach, and he called a doctor.

A sensitive study of Strindberg's relationship with Harriet
Bosse has been made by an American psychiatrist, Donald
L. Burnham, in his 'August Strindberg's Need Fear Dilemma'.[44] Dr Burnham believes that Strindberg's need to meet
Harriet in a disembodied state was due to a deep-seated
conviction that sex was unclean and sinful, but he does not
explain how it was that Strindberg came to think thus about
something that he had previously regarded as delightful,
even necessary, nor the fact that Strindberg was by no
means always revolted by sex even in his later days. To me
Strindberg's idea that sex was sinful seems a rationalization
of his own lack of success as a lover, on a par with his theory
that women did not require sexual satisfaction.

Dr Burnham also seems to have fallen into the trap set
for all of us by the diary, and especially by *From an Occult
Diary*, which is to believe that they give us a complete picture of Strindberg's life. By 1900 he was using the diary in
two ways: as a record of selected events and, more impor-
tantly, as the confidant of his emotions, particularly those
connected with Harriet. The letters of the period show that
there were other important matters that he never mentioned
at all. Many of those in the 1901 to March 1904 volume are
business letters, and a large number are to his German translator, Emil Schering, who was actively engaged in promoting
the publication of his works and the performance of his
plays in Germany. This was a matter of vital importance
to Strindberg. His position in Sweden was much as it had
been in 1892. His plays were again being neglected and he
was living largely on the money he got from Germany. Yet
there is no hint in *From an Occult Diary* of the important
part that Schering and Germany played in his life. These
letters to Schering give no indication that he was undergoing any sort of emotional crisis, which does not mean

44. So far only published in a Swedish translation: 'Strindbergs
kontaktdilemma', in *Meddelanden* No. 50, May 1972.

that there were no crises, but simply that he was able to think of other things.

The recently published letters from April 1904 to April 1907 tell the same story, and we have yet another reliable guide to Strindberg's activities. This is August Falck's book *Five Years with Strindberg* (*Fem år med Strindberg*), which covers the years 1906–10. Falck was the young actor with whom Strindberg started his own Intimate Theatre in November 1907. It is hardly possible to overestimate the importance of this event to Strindberg. It meant that he would at last see his many neglected plays performed, and it was for this theatre that he wrote his four Chamber Plays, *Storm*, *After the Fire*, *The Ghost Sonata* and *The Pelican*, all in 1907, and *The Great Highway* in 1909. He had written no plays since 1903, largely because he saw no prospect of getting them performed in Sweden.

There is no doubt that work for and in the theatre occupied much of his time, yet this side of his life is not even hinted at in *From an Occult Diary*. Falck is mentioned once or twice, but there is no indication that he and Strindberg were close friends who met daily and who often sat up late into the night drinking whisky and discussing their plans. Falck was allowed to sit with him as he worked and was eventually given a key to his flat.

Strindberg was also deeply interested in the young actors and actresses who formed Falck's troupe and often arranged little supper parties for their entertainment and to show his gratitude. He could never bring himself to attend a public performance, but he often went to dress rehearsals or visited the theatre on other business. For almost the first time in his life he was actively collaborating with people who believed in him and in a venture that fulfilled a life-long dream. Moreover, the theatre was a refuge from his trouble. A sentence in the diary for 16 May 1908, not included in *From an Occult Diary*, reads: 'I went down to the

Intimate Theatre where Harriet does not exist.' The words
sound like a sigh of relief, and an answer to his prayer that
he might be rid of his obsession.

No doubt the move from Karlavägen 40, the flat in which
he and Harriet had lived, was also salutary, for it was after
this that he felt able to give the theatre even more of his
attention. In the late summer of 1908 he offered to direct
The Father. He must have seemed to the young company a
most unusual director, for he could never bring himself to
address them as a body but sat silent during rehearsals and
made his wishes known by writing little notes of criticism
or encouragement to each one individually.

It was because of his inability to address any gathering
of people that he wrote the essays now known as *The
Letters to the Intimate Theatre* (*Öppna brev till Intima
Teater*, 1908–9). In these he gave his young friends the fruits
of years of thought on the study, interpretation and performance of dramatic works, using as examples some of
Shakespeare's plays. These letters are lucid, wise and full of
common sense, and show no trace of the turmoil through
which he had passed and which would have shattered an
ordinary human being. Just as in 1896 he had broken away
from his nightmare of persecution in Klam and returned to
Sweden to seek medical aid, so now in 1908 he broke away
from the nightmare of his obsession with Harriet. On 11 July
he moved from Karlavägen to his last home in Drottninggatan 85, taking with him nothing that could remind him
of her. There, as in his Intimate Theatre, she did not exist.

His recovery was astonishingly rapid. On 1 August he
wrote to his friend Nils Andersson: 'Karlavägen 40 has
ceased to exist. A seven-year period has passed away. "The
Lord gave and the Lord took." ... I have been ill but I am
now well again.'

Three weeks later he wrote again. This time he mentioned
a violent crisis in his life and added:

I grieved myself ill and begged God to let me die, but I came through. To do so I wrenched myself free of my old state with a mighty tug – the flat was let, furniture and books had to go too, nothing for it but the pawnbroker. But everything worked out to my advantage. Freed from memories and books, my creativity broke through! And now I am living the life that suits me best. I am just at the end of the third Act of a young Gustav Vasa,[45] and life is pure joy.

No wonder that when he wanted an illustration of the creative artist's invulnerability the Swedish author Hjalmar Söderberg chose Strindberg. In his book *The Serious Game* (*Den allvarsamma leken*, 1912) he writes:

Creative artists are a breed apart, and I warn you to beware of them. They are a strong breed, though they often have weaknesses which serve as a protective disguise. A creative artist can stand up to blows that would kill an ordinary man. Of course he feels the pain, but its effect on him is not worth mentioning, on the contrary he converts it into a work of art, he makes use of it. Look at Strindberg. It isn't what he has experienced that is the reason for all the morbid, horrible, and distracted things in his writings. He himself thinks it is, but this is not so. Quite the reverse: the morbid, horrible, and distracted side of his own nature is what has obliged him to experience and endure. But what a man! Who but a great creative artist could have gone through all that *he* has gone through comparatively unscathed. And not only unscathed but strengthened. All the evil he has suffered has served him – as material, as nourishment, as medicine. It has almost given him health. I saw him out walking one morning on my way to the paper. And I cannot remember ever having seen a man of sixty looking so well, so strong, and so happy as he does.

Strindberg himself was well aware of the therapeutic effects of writing. 'Write the misery out of yourself,' he told Littmansson on 4 October 1907, 'then it will seem that

45. *The Last Knight* (*Sista riddaren*).

it has never existed.' That was advice he himself always followed.

After 11 July 1908 Strindberg ceased to keep his diary. He no longer needed it.

ABBREVIATIONS

The following abbreviations are used in the notes to the Introduction:

Inferno	August Strindberg, *Inferno*, translated by Mary Sandbach, Penguin Books, 1979
S.S. 1–2, etc.	*Samlade skrifter* 1-2, etc. (Strindberg's Collected Works), edited by J. Landquist, Bonniers, Stockholm, 1912–21
Ahlström	Stellan Ahlström, *Strindbergs erövring av Paris*, Almqvist & Wiksell, Stockholm, 1956
Ogonvittnen	Stellan Ahlström and Torsten Eklund (eds.), *Ogonvittnen* II, Wahlström & Widstrand, Stockholm, 1961
Brandell–Jacobs	Gunnar Brandell, translated by Barry Jacobs, *Strindberg in Inferno*, Harvard University Press, Cambridge, Massachusetts, 1974
Falck	August Falck, *Fem år med Strindberg*, Wahlström & Widstrand, Stockholm, 1935
O.D.	*Ockulta dagboken*, facsimile edition, Gidlunds förlag, Stockholm, 1977
Meddelanden	*Strindbergssällskapets Meddelanden* (journal), Stockholm
Stockenström	Göran Stockenström, *Ismael i öknen*, Acta Universitatis Upsaliensis, Uppsala, 1972
Sprinchorn	August Strindberg, *Inferno, Alone, and Other Writings*, translated, edited and introduced by Evert Sprinchorn, Anchor Books (Doubleday), New York, 1968

Strindberg till Harriet Bosse	*Strindbergs brev till Harriet Bosse med kommentar*, Natur och Kultur, Stockholm, 1932 (Strindberg's letters to Harriet Bosse with her commentary)
Söderström	Göran Söderström, *Strindberg och bildkonsten*, Forum, Uddevalla, 1972

NOTE ON THE TEXT

Inferno was written in French, but was first published in 1897 in a Swedish translation made by Eugène Fahlstedt. A second edition of the same year contained improvements, some made with Strindberg's advice. This text was reprinted, with further corrections by John Landquist, in 1914 (S.S. 28).

Strindberg's original French was corrected by Marcel Réja and published in 1898. This text was reprinted in 1966 with some notes and nearly a hundred pages in which are recorded the differences between Réja's French and Strindberg's autograph. The editor of this edition was C. G. Bjurström. These French editions contain three chapters not included in the Swedish editions, and the main text is preceded by a miracle play, *Coram Populo*, a version of the sequel to Strindberg's play *Master Olof*.

The present translation was made from John Landquist's Swedish edition checked against the French edition of 1898. Some of the notes have been emended in accordance with the notes in C. G. Bjurström's 1966 edition.

From an Occult Diary was first published in Sweden in 1963, and the English translation by Mary Sandbach in 1965. In the present edition some corrections have been made in the translation. The text is made up from the following sources : *The Occult Diary*; letters from Strindberg to Harriet Bosse; Harriet Bosse's explanatory notes to these letters; letters from Harriet Bosse to Strindberg.

Square brackets indicate omissions from any of the above mentioned sources. Italics within round brackets indicate that Strindberg wrote the original words, expressions or sentences in Greek characters. The Swedish editor's notes are signalled by * or † and the translator's notes by numerals.

The translator has felt that inconsistencies or deviations from the normal in spelling and punctuation, notably the erratic use of capitals and exclamation marks, should be retained in order to keep some of the colour of the original.

INFERNO

Courbe la tête, fier Sicambre!
Adore ce que tu as brûlé,
Brûle ce que tu as adoré!

St Remy, Baptizing Clovis the
Frank at Rheims

And I will set my face against that man, and will make him a sign and a proverb, and I will cut him off from the midst of my people; and ye shall know that I am the Lord.

Ezekiel xiv: 8

Of whom is Hymenaeus and Alexander, whom I delivered unto Satan, that they might be taught not to blaspheme.

I Timothy i: 20

Translator's Note: These mottoes preface the Swedish editions of *Inferno*.

Il n'y a personne de bonne foi et dont la raison ne soit pas obscurcie ou prévenue, qui ne convienne que la vie corporelle de l'homme est une privation et une souffrance continuelles. Ainsi, d'aprè les idées que nous avons prises de la justice, ce ne sera pas sans raison que nous regarderons la durée de cette vie corporelle comme un temps de châtiment et d'expiation; mais nous ne pouvons le regarder comme telle sans penser aussitôt qu'il doit y avoir eu pour l'homme un état antérieur et préférable à celui où il se trouve à présent, et nous pouvons dire, qu'autant son état actuel est borné, pénible et semé de dégoûts, autant l'autre doit avoir été illimité et rempli de délices.

Louise Claude de Saint-Martin

Translator's Note: This motto prefaces the first French edition, published in 1898, and the second, published in 1947.

I

THE HAND OF THE UNSEEN

IT WAS with feelings of savage glee that I returned homewards from the Gare du Nord where I had parted from my little wife. She was going to our child, who had fallen ill in a distant land. So now I had accomplished the sacrifice of my heart. Her last words, 'When shall we meet again?' and my answer, 'Soon,' still echoed in my ears as an untruth, a deception that I was unwilling to admit, even to myself, though something in me whispered that we had now parted for ever. Those farewell words that we exchanged in November 1894 were in fact our last, for up to the present time, May 1897, I have never seen my dear wife again.

When I got as far as the Café de la Régence I sat down at a table at which I had often sat with my wife, my beautiful wardress, who had spied upon my soul day and night, had guessed my secret thoughts, kept watch over the development of my ideas, observed with jealous resentment the striving of my spirit towards the unknown.

Restored to the world of the free, I became aware of a sudden expansion of my self that elevated me above the petty cares of life in the great city, that scene of intellectual strife, where I had just won a victory – no great thing in itself, but to me of enormous significance, representing as it did the fulfilment of a youthful dream. A play of mine had been performed at a Paris theatre, the dream of all contemporary authors in my country, but one which I alone had realized. But now the theatre was repellent, as is everything that one has attained, and science attracted me. Compelled to choose between love and knowledge, I had made up my mind that I would try to reach the summits of intellectual achievement, but in my willingness to make a sacrifice of my love I forgot the innocent victim of my ambition – or my vocation.

Back once more in my miserable student's room in the Latin Quarter, I delved into my trunk and drew forth from their hiding place six crucibles of fine porcelain which I had robbed myself to buy. A pair of tongs and a packet of pure sulphur completed the apparatus of my laboratory. All that remained to be done was to make a fire of furnace heat in the stove, secure the door, and draw down the blinds, for since the execution of Caserio, only three months earlier, it had become dangerous to handle chemical apparatus in Paris.

Night fell, the flames of hell rose from the burning sulphur, but towards morning I had ascertained the presence of carbon in sulphur, previously regarded as an elementary substance. By doing this I believed I had solved the great problem, overthrown the prevailing chemical theories, and won the only immortality accorded to mortals.

But from my hands, roasted by the intense heat, the skin was peeling off in scales, and the pain caused by the mere effort of undressing reminded me of what my victory had cost. Yet, alone in my bed, where the odour of woman still lingered, I was blissful. A feeling of spiritual purity, of masculine virginity, made me regard my past married life as something unclean, and I regretted that there was no one to whom I could render thanks for my deliverance from those degrading fetters, now broken without much fuss. The fact is, that in the course of years, as I came to notice that the unseen Powers left the world to its fate and showed no interest in it, I had become an atheist.

Someone to thank? There was no one, and the ingratitude thus forced upon me weighed me down.

*

Being jealously anxious about my discovery, I took no steps to make it known. My shyness prevented me from approaching authorities on the subject or the academies. All the same, I continued my experiments, but meanwhile my chapped hands became poisoned, the cracks widened, were filled with coke dust, blood oozed from them, and the agony became intolerable. Everything I touched caused me pain and I was in mind to ascribe my torment to those unknown Powers which, for so many years, had persecuted me and frustrated all my endeavours. Almost mad with pain, I avoided and neglected my fellow men, refused invitations, drove my friends from me. Silence and solitude encompassed me, the stillness of a desert, solemn, terrifying, in which I defiantly challenged the unseen Power to a wrestling match, body against body, soul against soul.

I had proved the presence of carbon in sulphur; I now had to show that it contained hydrogen and oxygen, for they also must be there. My apparatus was inadequate; I had no money, my hands were black and bleeding, black as was my need, bleeding as was my heart. For during all this time I had been carrying on a correspondence with my wife. I had told her of the success of my chemical experiments and she had replied with bulletins about our daughter, interspersed with warning hints about the futility of my scientific work and the imbecility of throwing away money on such things.

In an attack of righteous indignation, and overwhelmed by a furious desire to do myself an injury, I committed suicide by despatching an infamous, unpardonable letter, casting off wife and child for ever, and giving her to understand that I was involved in a new love affair.

My bullet hit the mark and my wife replied by demanding a divorce.

Solitary, guilty of suicide and assassination, my sorrow

and anxiety made me forget my crime. No one came to see me, and I could seek out no one, as I had given offence to all. This gave me a feeling of exaltation, of drifting over the surface of a sea, with my anchor weighed but without a sail.

Meanwhile, necessity, in the form of my unpaid rent, made her appearance, interrupted my scientific work and metaphysical speculations, and brought me down to earth once more.

Such was my state as Christmas drew near. I had rather curtly refused an invitation to visit a Scandinavian family, as certain painful irregularities made the atmosphere of their house offensive to me. But in the evening, sitting alone, I regretted what I had done and went there all the same. No sooner were we seated at table than the midnight revels began, with a great deal of noise and unrestrained hilarity among the young artists, who were very much at home in that house. An intimacy that was repulsive to me, gestures and looks, in a word behaviour that was quite out of place in a family circle and caused me indescribable discomfort and depression. In the midst of these saturnalian revels my sadness conjured up before my inward eye my wife's peaceful dwelling. I had a sudden vision of the room, the Christmas tree, the mistletoe, my little daughter, her deserted mother. Pangs of remorse seized me, I stood up, alleged that I was feeling unwell, and departed.

I walked along the horrible Rue de la Gaieté, but the artificial merriment of the crowds there wounded me. Then I went along the silent, gloomy Rue Delambre, a street which, more than any other in that quarter, can make one feel desperate. I turned off into the Boulevard Montparnasse and sank on to a chair outside the Brasserie des Lilas.

For a few moments a glass of good absinth gave me comfort, but then I was attacked by a party of cocottes and students who flicked me in the face with switches. As if pursued by the furies, I left my absinth to its fate and hurried off to get myself another at the Café François Premier in the Boulevard Saint-Michel.

I had only jumped out of the frying-pan into the fire. Another lot of people came hallooing at me, 'Hi, hermit,' and I fled back to my house, whipped by Eumenides and escorted and unnerved by the triumphant strains of their mocking song. The idea of a punishment, the consequence of a crime, never occurred to me. The part I was playing to myself was that of the innocent victim of unjust persecution. The unknown Powers were hindering me from carrying on my great work and it was essential to break through this hindrance if the crown of victory were to be won.

I had done wrong, and yet I was right and should be acknowledged right.

I slept ill that Christmas Eve. A cold blast swept over my face repeatedly and from time to time I was awakened by the strains of a Jew's harp.

A growing weakness of body and mind was gradually getting the better of me. My black and bleeding hands made it impossible for me to dress myself neatly. My anxiety on account of the rent I owed never gave me a moment's peace, and I paced up and down the room like a wild animal in a cage. I had given up eating regular meals and my landlord advised me to go to hospital; but this was no solution, as such places are expensive and demand payment in advance.

Then the veins in my arms began to swell, a sure sign of blood-poisoning. This was the final blow, and news of it spread to my fellow countrymen. One evening the kind woman from whose Christmas party I had so rudely and abruptly withdrawn – the very person for whom I had felt such antipathy, whom I had almost despised – sought me out, questioned me, learned of the deep distress in which I found myself, and, with tears in her eyes, tried to make me see that to go to hospital was my only hope.

Judge how forlorn and contrite I felt when my eloquent silence made it plain to her that I was without means. She was filled with compassion at seeing me reduced to such a state of misery. She herself was poor and oppressed by domestic cares and anxieties, but she announced that she would collect money for me among the members of the Scandinavian community and that she would go to see their chaplain.

The woman who had sinned had been merciful to the man who had just abandoned his truly wedded wife.

Once more reduced to beggary and appealing for charity through the agency of a woman, I began to suspect the existence of an unseen hand which was responsible for the irresistible logic of events. I bent before the storm, but was determined to rise again at the first possible moment.

A cab took me to the Hôpital de Saint-Louis. On the way there I got out in the Rue de Rennes and bought two shirts, shrouds for my last hour!

The idea that my death was imminent obsessed me. I cannot explain why.

I was accepted as a patient and I was forbidden to go out unless I had obtained permission. My hands were swathed in bandages so that any sort of occupation was out of the question. I felt as if I were locked up in a prison.

My room was impersonal, bare, furnished only with absolute necessities, without a trace of beauty, and situated close to the patients' common-room, where people smoked and played cards from morning till night.

The bell sounded for lunch, and at the table I found myself among a company of spectres. Faces like death's-heads, faces of the dying. A nose missing here, an eye there, a third with a dangling lip, another with a crumbling cheek.

Two of the individuals at the table did not look ill at all, but their expression was sullen and despairing. They were master thieves of a good family who, thanks to their powerful relatives, had been let out of prison on the grounds of illness. A nauseating smell of iodine took away my appetite; my bandaged hands obliged me to seek the assistance of my neighbours when I wanted to cut bread or pour myself out a drink. In the midst of this delightful company of criminals and those doomed to die there moved our kind mother, the Matron, in her austere habit of black and white, dealing out to each of us his poisonous draught. I toasted a death's-head in a mug of arsenic; he toasted me in digitalis. It was lugubrious and yet one had to be grateful. Grateful, for anything so ordinary and at the same time so offensive!

People dressed and undressed me, tended me like a child. The nun took a special fancy to me, treated me like a baby and called me 'my child', while I, like all the others, called her 'Mother'.

How wonderful it was to use that word 'mother', a word that had not crossed my lips for thirty years. This elderly woman, who belonged to the Augustinian Order, wore the garb of the dead because she had never really lived her life. She was gentle as resignation itself, and she taught us to smile at our sufferings as if they had been so many joys, for she knew how salutary pain can be. She never uttered a word of reproach, she never admonished us, she never preached to us. She knew the rule she must obey, that applying in secularized hospitals, and she knew too how to grant small liberties to her patients, though never to herself. For this reason she used to allow me to smoke in my room, even offered to roll the cigarettes for me, an offer I declined. She got me permission to go out at other times than the usual hours and, when she discovered that I busied myself with chemistry, she arranged that I should be introduced to the learned pharmacist in charge of the hospital's dispensary. He lent me books and, after I had acquainted him with my theories on the nature of the elements, he invited me to work in his laboratory. That nun did indeed play a part in my life. I began to be reconciled to my fate and praised the fortunate misfortune that had brought me under that blessed roof.

The first book I borrowed from the pharmacist's library opened of itself and my eye lighted like a falcon on a line in the chapter on phosphorus. In a few words its author described how the chemist Lockyer had shown by spectral analysis that phosphorus was not an elementary substance, adding that an account of the experiment had been handed in to the Académie des Sciences in Paris, which had not rejected his findings.

Feeling encouraged by this unexpected support for my theories, I set off into the city, taking with me my crucibles and what remained of the incompletely burnt sulphur. I handed these over to a firm of analytical chemists, who promised to give me, on the morning of the following day, a certificate of their analysis.

It was my birthday. When I got back to the hospital I found awaiting me a letter from my wife in which she mourned my calamities and declared that she wanted to come to me in order to tend me and to love me.

The joy of knowing myself loved in spite of everything made me feel I wanted to express my gratitude, but to whom?

To the Unknown, who for so many years had hidden from me?

My heart melted; I confessed to the base lie about my infidelity, I begged for her forgiveness, and in a trice I was involved in an exchange of love-letters with my own wife, though I nevertheless postponed our reunion until a more suitable time.

*

The next morning I hurried off to my chemist in the Boulevard de Magenta. I carried back with me to the hospital the certificate in its sealed envelope. As I passed the statue of St Louis in the inner courtyard I recalled to mind the Saint's three achievements, the great Asylum for the Blind, L'Hospice des Quinze-Vingts, the Sorbonne, and the Sainte-Chapelle, which I interpreted thus: from suffering, through knowledge, to penitence.

In my room, behind the closed door, I opened the envelope that was to decide my future, and I read as follows:

This powder, which has been handed in to us for investigation, has the following characteristics:
Colour: greyish black. Leaves a trace on paper.
Density: considerable, greater than the medium density of graphite; the substance appears to be hard graphite.
Chemical analysis:
This powder burns easily and in burning gives off carbon monoxide and carbon dioxide. That is to say, it contains carbon.

So pure sulphur contains carbon!

I was saved. From this moment I should be able to prove to my friends and relations that I was not mad. This would confirm the theories I had advanced in my work *Antibarbarus*, published a year before, which had been treated by the newspapers as the work of a charlatan or a madman, with the result that I had been cast off by my family as a good-for-nothing, a sort of Cagliostro.

Ha ha, thought I, now you are crushed, my worthy opponents! My whole self swelled with righteous pride. I wanted to go into the city to cry aloud in the streets, roar in front of the Institut, tear down the Sorbonne, but my hands were still bandaged, and when I got out into the courtyard its tall railings counselled me to have patience.

The hospital's pharmacist, to whom I had communicated the results of the analysis, proposed that he should call together a committee before whom I might demonstrate my thesis by an experiment on the spot.

In the meantime, rather than do nothing, and aware too of my timidity when compelled to make a public appearance, I put together an article on the subject and sent it to *Le Temps*, where it was published within two days.

The password had been given. I had answers from various quarters, but no one denied the validity of my claims. I gained adherents. I was urged to send the article to a chemical periodical and became involved in a correspondence that stimulated me to press on with the investigations I was pursuing.

One Sunday, the last that I spent in Saint-Louis, that place of purgatory, I was sitting at the window watching what was going on in the courtyard below. The two thieves were walking about with their wives and children, kissing them from time to time, and looking so happy as they warmed themselves at the flame of love that their misfortunes had only served to fan.

My own loneliness weighed heavily upon me, I cursed my fate. I thought it unjust because I had forgotten that my crime far exceeded theirs in baseness.

The postman arrived with a letter from my wife. It was cold and frigid. My success had wounded her and she pretended to base her scepticism on the opinion of a professional chemist. She added her advice on the perils of illusions that might lead to a mental breakdown. For that matter, what did I expect to gain by all this? Could I support a family by my chemistry?

The same alternatives again – love or knowledge. I did not hesitate, I struck her down with a final letter of farewell, and felt as pleased with myself as a murderer who has dealt his blow successfully.

In the evening I took a walk in that gloomy part of the

city. I crossed the Canal St Martin, black as a grave, a most suitable place for drowning oneself in. I stopped at the corner of the Rue Alibert. Why Alibert? Who was he? Wasn't the graphite that the analytical chemist had found in my sample of sulphur called Alibert graphite? What did that imply? It was odd, but I could not rid my mind of the impression that there was something inexplicable about this. Next the Rue Dieu. Why God, when the Republic has abolished him and is devoting the Panthéon to a new purpose? Rue Beaurepaire. The delightful retreat of malefactors! Rue de Bondy. Was I being led by the Devil? I gave up reading the names of the streets, got lost, retraced my steps, but still could not find my way, and finally recoiled before an enormous shed that stank of raw meat and mouldy vegetables, especially sauerkraut. Suspicious-looking persons brushed past me, shouting out coarse words as they did so. Fear of the unknown gripped me. I turned first to the right, then to the left, and stumbled into a sordid blind alley that seemed to be the abode of human trash, vice, and crime. Prostitutes barred my way, street arabs jeered at me. The scene from the night of the Christmas party was repeated, *Vae soli!* Who was it who was setting these ambushes for me the instant I detached myself from the world and from people? There was someone who had caused me to fall into this trap. Where was he to be found, that I might wrestle with him?

As I started to run, rain and slushy snow fell. In the background, at the end of a short street, I saw outlined against the sky a dark archway, an enormous, cyclopean structure. There was no place behind, only a sea of light. I asked a policeman where I was.

'At the Porte Saint-Martin, monsieur.'

A few steps more and I was out in the great boulevards and walking along them. It was a quarter past six by the theatre clock. Absinth time, and my friends would be waiting as usual at the Café Napolitain. Quickening my pace, I pressed on, forgetting the hospital, my grief, and my poverty. But outside the Café du Cardinal I happened to bump against a table at which a gentleman was sitting. I knew him only by name, but he recognized me and in an instant his eyes had told me what he was thinking: 'You here? So you are not in hospital after all! Fine humbug, that appeal for help!'

I was sure that this man must be one of my unknown benefactors, one of those who had given me alms, and I realized that to him I was a beggar who had no right to go to cafés. A beggar! Just the right word. It kept ringing in my ears, and drove a burning flush to my cheeks, a flush of shame, mortification, and rage.

To think that only six weeks before I had sat at this same table with the director of the theatre where my play was being performed. I had been his host and he had addressed me as 'dear Master'. Reporters had tumbled over one another to interview me; photographers had begged for the honour of selling my portrait. And now, a beggar, a branded man, an outcast from society.

Whipped, played out, hunted to death, I slunk along the boulevards like a night-bird and crept back to my hole among the pest-ridden. There I shut myself into my room. This was now my home.

When I reflect upon my fate I can see the hand of the Unseen at work, disciplining me, driving me on towards a goal that I myself was still unable to discern. He had granted me glory and at the same time He had denied me worldly honours. He had humbled me and simultaneously He had raised me up. He had made me grovel in the dust in order to exalt me.

The idea again occurred to me that Providence must have some mission which it intended me to carry out in this world, and that this was the beginning of my education for it.

*

I left the hospital in February, not cured of my illness, but proof against the temptations of the world. At our parting I had wanted to kiss the hand of our kind mother who, without preaching at me, had taught me the way to the Cross, but I had been held back by a feeling of veneration for something that must not be defiled.

May her spirit receive this tribute of gratitude from a stranger who had gone astray and who now dwells concealed in a distant land!

2

SAINT LOUIS INTRODUCES ME TO THE CHEMIST ORFILA

I pursued my chemical investigations throughout the winter in a modestly furnished house I had rented. I stopped at home all day, but in the evening I went out to eat my dinner at a crémerie, where artists of various nationalities had formed a club. After my dinner I usually visited the family whose house I had once quitted in a fit of puritanism. Their home was a meeting place for the whole circle of artist-anarchists, and I felt that I was doomed to endure there all the things I should have preferred not to see or hear: free and easy manners, loose morals, deliberate godlessness. There was much talent among them and infinite wit. Only one of them was a genius, a wild fellow, who has since made a great name for himself.[1]

Nevertheless, it was a family circle. They loved me there and I was indebted to them, so I shut my eyes and closed my ears to their little private affairs, which were no concern of mine.

If it had really been unjustified pride that had made me shun these people my punishment would have been logical, but as my aloofness had arisen from my efforts to purify my individuality and refine my spirit by contemplation in solitude, I find it difficult to understand the workings of Providence in this matter. I am by nature flexible and very willing to adapt myself to my surroundings, out of pure affability and the fear of appearing ungrateful; so, as I was excluded from society by my pitiable and scandalous poverty, I was thankful to find some place of refuge in the

1. Gauguin.

long winter evenings, even though the very free tone of the conversation there cut me to the quick.

After it had been revealed to me that an unseen Hand was guiding my steps along this rough path I no longer felt alone. I kept strict watch over my actions and my words, though in this I sometimes failed. But as soon as I sinned I was instantly caught, and the punishment administered was so punctual and so exactly suited to the crime that it left no room for doubts about the intervention of a Power who chastised in order to reform.

I felt that I was personally acquainted with this unknown Power. I talked to him, I thanked him, I asked his advice. Sometimes I imagined him to be my servant, the counterpart of Socrates' daimon, and consciousness that I could count on his assistance restored to me an energy and a feeling of confidence that spurred me on to exertions of which I had not thought myself capable.

Looked upon by society as a bankrupt, I was born again in another world where no one could follow me. Things that would previously have lacked significance now attracted my attention. The dreams I had at night assumed the guise of prophecies. I thought of myself as one of the dead, passing my life in another sphere.

I had already demonstrated the presence of carbon in sulphur. Analogy would suggest that hydrogen and oxygen were there too, but this I had still to prove. I spent two months making calculations and studying problems, but I lacked the apparatus for carrying out experiments. A friend advised me to go to the research laboratory at the Sorbonne to which even foreigners have access. But I was too timid and too frightened of crowds to dare to take such a step, so my work came to a standstill and a brief period of rest ensued. One beautiful spring morning I got up in a good mood, walked down the Rue de la Grande Chaumière and reached the Rue de Fleurus, which leads to the Luxembourg Gardens. The lovely little street lay before me perfectly quiet, its wide avenue of chestnuts a brilliant green and straight as a racecourse, with David's column like a winning post at the far end. In the distance the dome of the Panthéon towered above everything else, while the golden cross that crowned it was almost lost in the clouds,

I stood still, entranced by this symbolic sight, but when I at last lowered my gaze I became aware of a dye-house sign on my right, in the Rue Fleurus. Ha! here I saw something undeniably real. Painted on the window of the shop were my own initials, A.S., poised on a silvery-white cloud and surmounted by a rainbow. *Omen accipio.* The words of Genesis came into my mind :

'I do set my bow in the cloud, and it shall be for a token of a covenant between me and the earth.'

I no longer trod upon the ground, I floated through the air, and it was with winged footsteps that I entered the gardens, where there was not a soul about. At this early hour of the morning the place was mine. The rose-garden was mine. I recognized all my friends in the borders, the daisies, the verbenas, and the begonias.

After making my way along the course I reached the winning post and passed out through the iron gateway into the Rue Soufflot, turned towards the Boulevard Saint-Michel, and stopped beside the stall of second-hand books outside Blanchard's shop. Without thinking what I was doing, I picked up an old chemistry book by Orfila, opened it at random and read: 'Sulphur has been included among the elements. Nevertheless, the ingenious experiments made by H. Davy and the younger Berthollet seem to prove that it contains hydrogen, oxygen and some special base which no one has so far succeeded in isolating.'

You may imagine the feeling of almost religious ecstasy

that gripped me when confronted by this seemingly miraculous revelation. Davy and Bertholet had demonstrated the presence of oxygen and hydrogen, I of carbon. It had fallen to me therefore to provide the formula for sulphur.

A few weeks later I was enrolled as a student in the Faculty of Natural Sciences at the Sorbonne (St Louis's Sorbonne!) with the right to work in the research laboratory there.

The morning on which I betook myself to the Sorbonne was for me a holy day. Although I had no illusions about the possibility of convincing the professors there, who had received me with the chilly politeness accorded to foreigners who push themselves in, I yet experienced a calm joy, from which I derived the sort of courage a martyr must possess when he takes up the struggle against a multitude of enemies – because, of course, for me at my age, the young were my natural enemies.

When I arrived at the open space in front of the little church that is part of the Sorbonne I found the door open and went in, without really knowing why I did so. The Holy Mother and Child greeted me with a gentle smile. The figure on the cross, incomprehensible as always, left me cold.

My new acquaintance, St Louis, friend of all those smitten by poverty and disease, caused some young theological students to introduce themselves to me. Was it possible that St Louis was my patron saint, my good angel, and that he had driven me to the hospital, there to pass through the fire of agony before I could attain the glory that leads to dishonour and scorn? Was it he who had sent me to Blanchard's bookstall, who had drawn me here?

It was remarkable that, from being an atheist, I had sunk into a state of almost complete credulity.

The sight of the votive offerings, presented by candidates

who had been successful in their examinations, made me swear a solemn oath that, supposing I should succeed, I would under no circumstances accept worldly recognition of my merits.

The hour had struck. I had to run the gauntlet between lines of merciless young people who, already informed of my chimerical task, were waiting to mock and insult me.

After about two weeks I had obtained incontrovertible evidence that sulphur is a ternary compound, composed of carbon, oxygen, and hydrogen.[2]

I proffered my thanks to the Director of the laboratory, who pretended to take no interest in what I had been doing, and I left this new purgatory feeling at heart the most inexpressible delight.

Whenever I did not visit the Luxembourg Gardens I took my morning walk in the Cemetery of Montparnasse. A few days after I had concluded my investigation at the Sorbonne I happened to catch sight of a monument of classical loveliness near the circular open space in the cemetery. On a medallion of white marble I beheld the noble features of a wise old man. The inscription on the socle revealed to me who he was: Orfila, Chemist and Toxicologist. None other than my friend and protector, who has many times since then been my guide through the labyrinth of chemical operations.

A week later, as I was walking down the Rue d'Assas, I came to a halt in front of a house that looked like a monastery. A large signboard told me what manner of building it was: Hôtel Orfila.

Again and yet again Orfila!

2. Fod further details see *Tryckt och otryckt* (*Printed and Unprinted*) Stockholm, 1897; *Sylva Sylvarum*, Paris, 1896; *L'Hyperchimie*, Paris, 1897. (Author's note.)

In the following chapters I shall relate all that occurred in this old house, to which the unseen Hand drove me that I might be chastised, instructed, and – why not? – enlightened.

3

THE DEVIL TEMPTS ME

The divorce suit made very slow progress. It was held up from time to time by a love-letter, a cry of regret, or promises of reconciliation, always followed by a curt, irrevocable farewell for ever.

I loved her and she me, yet we hated each other with the savage hatred of a passion that was intensified by separation.

In spite of this, and also in an effort to free myself from toils so fraught with evil, I sought for an opportunity to transfer my tender feelings to another object. My dishonourable wish was instantly granted.

An English lady, a sculptress, came to dine at the crémerie. She addressed me first and I was immediately attracted to her. She was charming, beautiful, distinguished looking, tastefully dressed, with the easy-going manners of the artist, which made her seductive into the bargain. In a word, she was a de-luxe edition of my wife, her very image, but nobler and on a larger scale.

Intending to do me a kindness, the well-known painter who was the doyen of our dining circle invited this English lady to the Thursday soirées that he held in his studio. I went there, but kept in the background, as I am always very reluctant to expose my feelings to gossip-mongers. At about eleven o'clock the lady rose and signalled to me with a look. I likewise got up, rather awkwardly, took my leave, and, having asked if I might accompany her, followed the young lady to the door, at which all the impudent young people burst out laughing.

We went away looking ridiculous in each other's eyes and quite unable to utter a word, despising ourselves as much as if we had been stripped naked in front of a jeering mob.

To make matters worse we had to go along the Rue de la Gaieté, where the prostitutes and their pimps assailed our ears with abuse and insults, taking us I suppose for a couple of abandoned creatures like themselves.

It is not easy to be charming when one is mad with rage; put in the pillory and goaded as I was, I found it quite impossible to regain my composure. However, when we had got as far as the Boulevard Raspail a fine rain began that made our faces tingle as if they had been whipped. We had no umbrella, so the sensible course seemed to be to take refuge in a warm, well-lit café. With the gesture of a grand seigneur I pointed to the most elegant of all the restaurants, and we crossed the street, treading on air, when ... oh, horror! The realization that I had not a sou on me struck my pate like a hammer-blow.

I have forgotten now how I got out of my predicament, but I shall never forget the sensations that preyed upon me that night after I had left the English lady at her door.

My punishment, administered by a skilful hand which I could not fail to recognize, had been instantaneous and severe, but it seemed to me inadequate. I was a beggar, I had unfulfilled obligations to my wife and child, and yet I had been quite ready to commence a relationship which would have been compromising for an honourable woman. It was nothing less than a crime, and I imposed upon myself the appropriate penance. I refrained from going to our evening gatherings at the crémerie, I fasted and avoided doing anything that might stimulate this baleful passion.

But the Tempter was on the watch. At a studio party I met my adored one again. She was wearing an Eastern costume that enhanced her beauty to such a degree that I became more infatuated than ever. But when we came face to face I was such a nincompoop that I could not get out a word, and, realizing that this woman deserved nothing more than the plain and straightforward declaration, 'I desire you,' I went my way, consumed by my guilty passion.

The next day I went to our eating place again. She was there. She was charming, she caressed me by her coaxing way of talking to me, her cat-like eyes titillated me. We began to talk, and everything was going splendidly when, just at the critical moment, young Minna burst in upon us. Minna was the daughter of an artist, a model, of easy virtue, interested in literature, good-natured, and received everywhere. I knew her too, and one evening we had become really good friends, without however overstepping the bounds of propriety. To cut the story short, in she came, threw herself into my arms – she was not quite sober – kissed me on the cheeks, and called me by my christian name.

Up got my English lady, paid her bill, and left, and with that all was over. She never came again, thanks to Minna – who, for that matter, had once warned me against this particular lady for reasons that do not belong here.

No more love. The Powers had given the word of command and I was resigned, well aware that a special Providence lay behind this, as behind everything else.

My success with sulphur had encouraged me, and I now set to work on iodine. One day, after I had flung an article on one method of making synthetic iodine into *Le Temps*, I was visited at my hotel by an unknown gentleman. He introduced himself as the representative of all the iodine manufacturers in Europe, said he had just read my article, and promised that, the moment the business side of the matter was concluded, we should be able to bring about a financial crisis on the stock market, which would result in a gain of millions for us, if we had first taken out a patent.

The answer I gave him was that my invention was not intended for industry. It was merely a scientific discovery which was still incomplete, and I was not sufficiently interested in the business side of the matter to feel impelled to turn my hand to developing its practical use.

He departed. The manageress of the hotel, however, who knew him already, learned the great news from his own lips, and for two whole days I was regarded as a prospective millionaire.

This business man came again, even keener about the matter than before. He had collected further information and, as he was now convinced that my discovery could be made profitable, he tried to persuade me to go with him to Berlin immediately so that the idea might be converted to practical uses.

I thanked him, but advised him to have the necessary analyses carried out before he went any further.

He then offered to give me 100,000 francs before the evening if I would go with him, but, suspecting some trickery, I dismissed him, whereupon he went down to the manageress and told her I was mad.

The following days were quiet and gave me time for deliberation. On the one side the threat of want, my unpaid debts, an uncertain future, and, on the other, independence, freedom in which to pursue my studies, and an easy life. Moreover, wasn't a good idea worth its price?

Regrets got the upper hand, but I had not the courage to re-establish contact with the man. Then a telegram arrived from him, saying that an assistant chemist in the Medical Faculty and a Deputy – a man who had already made a name for himself and has since become altogether too notorious – were interested in the iodine question.

I then began a series of methodical laboratory experiments which invariably produced the same results. All seemed to prove that iodine could be derived from benzine. They were still in progress when, after a conversation with the chemist, a day was agreed upon for an interview, to be followed by the decisive experiments.

On the morning upon which the fate of the whole matter was to be settled I set off in a cab with my retorts and reagents to the appointed place, the house of the business man in the Quartier du Marais. He was at home, but the chemist, who had remembered that it was Sunday, had excused himself and postponed the conference to the following day.

It was Whit Sunday and I had not known it. The sight of the shabby office, overlooking the dark and dirty street, made my heart ache. Memories of my childhood stirred within me: Whitsun, that most ecstatic of all festivals. The little church, decked with greenery, with tulips, with lilac and lilies of the valley, its doors opened wide to all the young communicants. The girls all in white, like angels. The organ, the bells.

I was bowed down by a feeling of shame and returned to my home much perturbed and firmly determined to break with anything that might tempt me to make money out of my science.

I began to clear away the apparatus and reagents that were cluttering up my room. I swept and tidied and dusted. I sent someone to buy flowers, above all narcissi. After I had had a bath and put on a clean shirt I felt cleansed of my stains and went out to walk in the Cemetery of Montparnasse, where peace settled on my soul, and gentle thoughts, and a feeling of unaccustomed remorse.

O crux, ave spes unica! These words on the tombs were a prophecy of my destiny. No more love! No more money-making! No more honours! The way of the Cross, the only one that leads to Wisdom.

4
PARADISE REGAINED

I reckon the summer and autumn of 1895 – in spite of everything – among the happy resting places in my turbulent life. All my undertakings prospered, unknown friends brought food to me as the ravens did to Elijah. Money came to me of itself. I was able to buy books, natural-history specimens, and, among other things, a microscope that unveiled for me the secrets of life.

Lost to the world by renouncing the empty pleasures of Paris, I lived entirely within my own quarter of the city. Each morning I visited the departed in the Cemetery of Montparnasse, and afterwards walked down to the Luxembourg Gardens to say good morning to my flowers. Now and then some countryman of mine, on a visit to Paris, would call and invite me out to luncheon or to the theatre on the other side of the river. I always refused, as the right bank was forbidden territory. To me it represented the 'world' in the true sense of the word, the world of the living and of earthly vanity.

The fact was that a kind of religion had developed in me, though I was quite unable to formulate it. It was a spiritual state rather than an opinion founded upon theories, a hotchpotch of impressions that were far from being condensed into thoughts.

I had bought a Roman missal, and this I read and meditated over. The Old Testament comforted but also chastised me in a somewhat confused way, while the New Testament left me cold. This did not prevent a Buddhist work from making a far greater impression on me than all other sacred books, as it put the value of actual suffering higher than that of mere abstention. Buddha had had the courage to give up his wife and children when he was in the prime of life and enjoying the happiness of married bliss, whereas Christ had avoided all contact with the legitimate pleasures of this world.

In other respects I did not brood upon the emotions that possessed me. I remained detached, let things take their course, and granted to myself the same freedom that I was bound to accord to others.

The great event in Paris that season was the call to arms raised by the critic Brunetière about the bankruptcy of science. I had been well acquainted with the natural sciences since my childhood and had tended towards Darwinism. But I had discovered how unsatisfying can be the scientific approach that recognizes the exquisite mechanism of the world but denies the existence of a mechanic. The weakness of the theory was revealed by the universal degeneration of science, which had marked out for itself a boundary line beyond which no one was allowed to go :

'We have solved all problems, the Universe has no secrets left.'

This presumptuous lie had annoyed me even in 1880, and for the past fifteen years I had been engaged upon revising the natural sciences. Thus, in 1884, I had cast doubts upon the accepted theory of the composition of the atmosphere, and upon the identification of the nitrogen found in the air with that obtained by breaking down a compound of nitrogen. In 1891 I had gone to the Laboratory of Physical Science in Lund to compare the spectra of these two kinds of nitrogen, which I knew differed. Need I describe the sort of reception I got from the mechanistic men of science there? But with the year 1895 came the discovery of argon, which proved the rightness of the suppositions I had already ad-

*

vanced and infused new life into the investigations that had been interrupted by my rash marriage.

No, science had not gone bankrupt, only science that was out of date and distorted. Brunetière was right, though he was wrong.

Meanwhile, whereas all were agreed in recognizing the unity of matter and called themselves monists without really being so, I went further, drew the ultimate conclusions of this doctrine, and eliminated the boundaries between matter and what was called the spirit. In my book *Antibarbarus* I had discussed the psychology of sulphur and interpreted it in the light of its ontogeny – that is to say, the embryonic development of sulphur.

For further information I refer those interested to my book *Sylva Sylvarum*, published in 1896, in which, proudly aware of my clairvoyant faculty, I penetrated to the very heart of the secrets of creation, especially those of the animal and vegetable kingdoms. I would also refer them to my essay 'In the Cemetery' (included in *Printed and Unprinted*) which shows how in solitude and in suffering I was brought back to a faltering apprehension of God and immortality.

5

THE FALL AND PARADISE LOST

After I had been led into the new world where no one could follow me I conceived an aversion for the company of my fellow men and felt an irresistible desire to cut myself off from my intimates. For this reason I gave my friends to understand that I intended to settle down at Meudon, as I wanted to write a book for which I required solitude and quiet. Just about this time disagreements on perfectly insignificant matters led to a breach with my circle at the crémerie, so that one fine day I found myself completely isolated. This first resulted in an astonishing increase in my awareness, a feeling of psychic power that demanded some outward manifestation. I felt that I possessed boundless vitality and, inspired by self-conceit, I hit upon the mad idea of trying to work miracles.

At an earlier period in my life, and at times of great crises, I had noticed that I was able, even at a distance, to exercise an influence on absent friends. A study of folklore makes it quite clear that in bygone days people were much occupied by such problems as telepathy and bewitchment. I do not want to be too hard on myself, still less do I want to make myself out innocent of nefarious practices, but I do really think that the crushing reversal of fortune I sustained was out of all proportion to the ill I had intended.

An unwholesome curiosity, an outburst of perverted affection, the result of my horrible loneliness, filled me with a passionate desire to try to re-establish contact with my wife and child, for I loved them both. How was I to do this now that legal proceedings for a divorce were in progress? Perhaps some extraordinary happening, a common misfortune, like being struck by lightning, involved in a fire or a flood

... in a word, some catastrophe that might serve to reunite two hearts, the sort of thing that happens in novels, where enemies join hands by a sick-bed. Of course, the very thing! An attack of illness. Small children are always falling ill for one reason or another. A mother's tender heart always exaggerates the danger : a telegram, and that would be that.

I was quite unversed even in the simplest forms of magic, but some fatal instinct whispered in my ear what I must do to the portrait of my beloved little daughter, the one person who was later to be my only consolation in a damnable existence.

I shall now describe the results of this manoeuvre and how my evil intentions seemed to have taken effect through the medium of this symbolic act.

These results, however, did not follow immediately. I went on with my work, but was oppressed by a dim feeling of uneasiness, accompanied by a premonition of new disasters.

One evening, sitting alone before my microscope, something occurred that made a deep impression on me, even though at the time I did not understand it.

For four days I had been allowing a walnut to germinate, and I had then detached the embryo. Shaped like a heart, and no bigger than a pear pip, it lies between the two seed-lobes which also closely resemble a human heart. Imagine my emotion when, on the slide, I saw two tiny hands, white as alabaster, raised and clasped as if in prayer. Was it a vision? A hallucination? Not at all! It was a startling reality that filled me with horror. The hands did not move, they were stretched out towards me, I could count on each five fingers, the thumbs shorter than the rest. They were exactly like the hands of a woman or a child.

A friend, who surprised me in the act of gazing at this overwhelming sight, was invited to look for himself to verify the truth of what I had seen, and he did not require clairvoyance to enable him to see the two hands clasped in an appeal to the beholder.

What was the meaning of this? Here were the two first rudimentary leaves of a walnut, *Juglans regia*, Jupiter's acorn.[3] That was all. And yet it was an undeniable fact that ten fingers like those of a human hand were clasped together in a gesture of supplication : *de profundis clamavi ad te*!

But I was still too incredulous, too stupefied by an empirical education, and I left things as they were.

Then came my fall! I became aware that the displeasure of the Powers was lying heavy upon me. The hand of the Unseen was raised against me and its blows rained thick and fast upon my head.

First of all, my anonymous friend, the man who up to then had provided me with the means of existence, took offence at a presumptuous letter and withdrew his support. So there I was, left without any resources.

Then, when I received the proofs of my book *Sylva Sylvarum*, I discovered that the pages were put together exactly like a pack of well-shuffled playing cards. Not only were they muddled and wrongly numbered, but even the different sections of the book were jumbled together higgledy-piggledy, so that, ironically enough, they symbolized the theory of 'the great disorder' that prevails in Nature. At last, after endless delay and protraction, the booklet was printed, but then I was presented by the printer with a bill for more than twice the sum agreed upon. Very reluctantly I took my microscope, my evening clothes, and the few other valuables I still possessed to a pawnbroker, but at least my book had appeared in print and for the first time in my life I felt that I had said something new, important and splendid. You may easily imagine how insolent and

3. *Juglans*, 'walnut', from *Jovis glans*, 'Jupiter's acorn'.

self-assured I felt as I carried the copies to the post. Raising my hand heavenwards in a gesture of contempt, I threw the packages into the box, and, to show my scorn of the Powers, I thought as I did so:

'Listen to me, you Sphinx up there! I have solved your riddle and I defy you!'

When I reached my private hotel I found my bill awaiting me with an accompanying letter.

This unexpected rebuff annoyed me, as I had been a guest there for over a year, and I began to take notice of a number of trifling matters that I had previously not bothered about. One of these was that three pianos in adjacent rooms were all being played at the same time. I told myself that this must be an intrigue on the part of the Scandinavian females with whom I had refused to mix.

Just imagine it, three pianos! And I quite unable to change my place of residence for lack of money.

I was furious with those females and with Fate, and fell asleep cursing Heaven.

I was awakened by a dreadful din. Someone was hammering a nail in the next room alongside my bed. After that somebody began to hammer on the other side too.

Quite clearly a conspiracy, just about as stupid as those female pianists themselves; but I let it pass as not worthy of notice.

But after lunch, when I was about to take my usual nap on my bed, such a din broke out in the room over the recess in which it stood that the plaster from the ceiling fell down on my head.

I went down to find the proprietress to complain to her about the behaviour of the other guests. She asserted, very politely for that matter, that she had heard nothing, but she promised to get rid of anyone at all who dared to disturb me, for she was exceedingly anxious to keep me at her hotel, which was not going particularly well.

Though I put no faith in the word of a woman, it was to her own advantage to treat me well and I trusted to that.

But the row continued. I became convinced that those females wanted to make me believe that it was caused by a poltergeist. The fine fools!

It was at this juncture that the behaviour of my friends at the crémerie changed towards me. Their muffled hostility was shown by the hints they dropped and the sidelong glances they gave me. Sick of the struggle, I left both the hotel and the crémerie, robbed of my belongings, forced to leave my books and other small treasures behind me, naked as a little John the Baptist. The 21 February 1896 saw my entry into the Hôtel Orfila.

6

PURGATORY

The Hôtel Orfila, which looked like a monastery, was in fact a boarding house for students of the Roman Catholic persuasion. It was supervised by an abbé, a gentle, kindly man. Silence, order, and good habits were the rule there and, a thing that was particularly comforting to me after so many vexations, women were not admitted.

It was an old house with low rooms, dim corridors, and a labyrinth of winding wooden staircases. The whole building, that had exercised such an attraction upon me for so long, had about it an atmosphere of mysticism. My room looked out on a blind alley in such a way that when I stood in the centre of the floor all I could see was a moss-covered wall, in which were two small circular windows. But when I sat at my table by the windw I could gaze out over a charming and quite unexpected view. An ivy-clad wall enclosed the courtyard of a convent, a boarding school for young women. In it grew plane trees, Paulownias, and Robinias. There was also an exquisite Gothic chapel. Further off were high walls with innumerable little barred windows that made me think of a monastery. Still further up the valley, a forest of chimneys topping ancient, half-hidden houses, and in the distance the tower of Notre-Dame-des-Champs with its cross and, on top of that, the cock.

In my room were two pictures, an etching of St Vincent de Paul and, above my bed in the recess, one of St Peter, keeper of the gates of Heaven. This seemed to me a piece of scathing irony, as some years earlier I had made fun of the apostle in a fanciful drama.

Delighted with my room, I slept well that first night.

The next day I discovered that the outdoor convenience

was situated in the narrow courtyard just below my window, so close to it that I could plainly hear all the mechanism and the clatter of the movable iron trap. Furthermore, I learned by inquiry that the two bull's-eyes right opposite belonged to similar closets. Before very long I found out that the hundreds of small windows in the background indicated the presence of hundreds of closets placed behind a whole row of dwelling houses. At first I was furious, but, as I had no means of extricating myself, I had to make the best of it – but how I cursed my fate.

At one o'clock the waiter brought my lunch and, as I refused to disturb the things on my desk, he put the tray on the bedside commode in which the chamber pot was kept. I commented on this and the lad excused himself by saying that there was no other table available. He looked a pleasant fellow and not at all ill-intentioned; so I forgave him, but I made him take away the pot.

If at that time I had known anything about Swedenborg I should have realized that the Powers had condemned me to the Hell of Excrement.

At first I was infuriated by the persistent bad luck that had dogged my footsteps for so many years, but by degrees I grew calmer and gloomily resigned myself to my fate. For edifying reading I turned to the Book of Job, convinced that the Eternal had delivered me into the hands of Satan in order to test me. This thought gave me comfort and I rejoiced in my sufferings, believing that they testified to the confidence the Almighty placed in me.

From this time on there occurred a series of manifestations which I cannot account for, except by assuming the intervention of unknown Powers, and I began to make notes which mounted up by degrees to form a diary. It is extracts from this that I am now making public.

People had become icily silent about my chemical investigations. In order to reinstate myself and to strike a decisive blow, I attacked the problem of how to make gold. I took as my point of departure the following question: Why does sulphate of iron in a solution of chloroaurate of sodium precipitate metallic gold? The answer came out as follows: Because iron and sulphur are included in the composition of gold. In fact, all the compounds of sulphur with iron that occur in Nature contain some gold, more or less. Consequently I began to work upon solutions of ferric sulphate.

One morning I woke up with a vague feeling that I should like to make an expedition into the country. This was entirely against my inclinations and usual habits, and it was almost by chance that I arrived at the Gare Montparnasse and took a train to Meudon. I got off at the little place itself, which I had never visited before, walked up the main street and took a turning to the right up an alley that ran between two walls. Twenty feet ahead, half buried in the ground, I beheld a Roman knight, wearing iron-grey armour. The figure was beautifully modelled on a small scale, but I was not misled into thinking that it was in fact anything more than an unworked stone. When I got closer I could see that the thing was an optical delusion, but I stopped in front of it, intentionally holding fast to the illusion because it pleased me. The knight was looking at the wall close by and, following the direction of his gaze, I saw an inscription written in charcoal on the whitewash. The intertwined letters F and S made me think of the initials of my wife's name. She loves me still! A second later a light dawned upon me when the inscription decomposed before my eyes into the chemical symbols for iron and sulphur (Fe and S) and revealed to me the secret of gold.

I then turned to examine the ground and found two lead seals fastened together by twine. One was stamped with the letters V.P., the other with a royal crown. I was in no mood to analyse in detail what had happened to me here, but I returned to Paris with the very vivid impression that something miraculous had taken place.

In my stove I burned a sort of coal that is called 'sparrows' heads'[4] because it is round and smooth. One day, when the fire had gone out before all the fuel was consumed, I poked out a bit of coal of a fantastic shape. A cock's head with a splendid comb, the trunk almost like a human body with distorted limbs, it looked just like one of the demons that used to perform in the witches' sabbaths of the Middle Ages.

The next day I got out a capital group of two gnomes in billowing garments embracing each other, a masterpiece of primitive sculpture.

On the third day there was a Madonna and Child in the Byzantine style, incomparably beautiful in form.

After I had made drawings of them I left all three lying on my table. One of my friends, a painter, came to see me, and, after examining the statuettes with increasing curiosity, he asked, 'Who has made them?'

Made them? In order to test him I mentioned the name of a Norwegian sculptor.

'Really,' he said. 'I should have been inclined to guess that it was Kittelsen, the famous illustrator of the Norwegian fairy-tales.'

I did not really believe in the existence of demons but I was curious to see what impression my bits of sculpture would make on the sparrows who were accustomed to having crumbs given to them outside my window, so I set the figures out on the roof.

The sparrows were alarmed and kept away. So there was a resemblance that even these little creatures could detect, and there was some reality behind this interplay of inert matter and of fire.

The sun warmed my little figures and the demon with the

4. *Têtes de moineaux.*

cock's comb split in two. That reminded me a bit of folk-
lore which tells how the dwarfs are struck dead if they stay
out until sunrise.

Disquieting things happened in the hotel. The day after
my arrival I found, on the board in the vestibule upon which
the keys of the rooms were hung, a letter addressed to a Mr
X, a student whose name was the same as my wife's. The
stamp bore the postmark Dornach, the name of the Austrian village where my wife and child were living. This was
mysterious, as I was quite certain that Dornach had no post
office.

This letter, displayed in a way that was obviously intended to attract attention, was followed by several more.
The next one was addressed to Dr Bitter and postmarked
Vienna. A third bore an assumed Polish name, Schmulach-
owsky.

Clearly the Devil now had a finger in the pie, for that
name was pure fabrication. I realized where my thoughts
were being directed, namely to one of my mortal enemies
who lived in Berlin.

Yet another that arrived had on it a Swedish name that
reminded me of an enemy in my native land. Finally came
a letter posted in Vienna, on which was printed the name of
Dr Eder's firm of analytical chemists. In fact, someone was
spying on my synthesis of gold.

I had no doubts left. This was a plot, but the Devil himself
must have shuffled the cards for the tricksters. No ordinary
mortal could have hit on the idea of sending my suspicions
roaming to the four quarters of the globe; it was altogether
too contrived.

When I asked the waiter to tell me about Mr X he artlessly
replied that he was an Alsatian. I could get nothing more
out of him. Once, when I returned from my morning walk,
there was a card in the rack just by my key. For one moment

I was tempted to solve the riddle by having a look at it, but my good angel immobilized my hand at the very instant that a young man appeared from his hiding place behind the door.

I looked at his face. He was like my wife. We bowed to each other without uttering a word, and walked off in opposite directions.

I have never been able to get to the bottom of this plot and still do not know who the conspirators were, as my wife has neither brothers nor male cousins.

This state of suspense and the perpetual threat of vengeance was torment and enough for half a year. I bore this, like everything else, as a punishment for sins known and unknown.

The New Year brought a stranger to our circle at the crémerie. A painter, an American, he arrived just at the right moment to infuse new life into our society, which was growing languid. A lively, cosmopolitan, daring fellow, with a winning manner, yet he filled me with a vague feeling of mistrust. In spite of his assured manner, I knew instinctively that his affairs were in a bad way.

The crash came sooner than I had expected. One evening the unhappy man came into my room and asked if he might stay there a while. He looked like a lost man, as indeed he was.

He had been driven out of his studio by his landlord and deserted by his mistress. He was up to the ears in debt and harassed by duns. He was being abused in the streets by the souteneurs of female models who had not been paid. But the thing that had crushed him completely was that his cruel landlord had confiscated the picture which he had been intending to exhibit in the Champ de Mars, and which he had been certain would be a success, as the subject seemed to him both original and vigorous. It represented an emancipated woman, pregnant, crucified, and mocked by the mob.

He owed money at the crémerie too and found himself thrown out on the streets on an empty stomach.

After pouring out this first confession he made a clean breast of everything and admitted that he had taken a double dose of morphia but that death did not want him yet.

After we had discussed the matter thoroughly we agreed that he must move to some other part of the city, that the two of us would eat our dinner at a small cook-shop unknown to the others, so that lack of companionship should not deprive him of the courage to prepare another picture for the Salon des Indépendants.

The sufferings of this man, who became my sole companion, enhanced my own as I submerged myself in his anguish. This was a piece of bravado on my part, but through it I acquired a very valuable experience. He revealed to me the whole of his past life. A German by birth, he had lived for seven years in America owing to some family misfortune, and also because he himself, in a fit of youthful indiscretion, had published a blasphemous pamphlet, for which sentence had been passed on him.

I discovered that he was unusually intelligent, of a melancholy disposition, and an unbridled sensualist. But behind these human characteristics, whose more peculiar features had been rounded off by a cosmopolitan upbringing, I detected something that I found disturbing, something that I expected to discover fully sooner or later.

I waited for two months, during which time I so merged my own existence in that of the stranger that I had to suffer once again all the hardships of an artist who has not arrived. I forgot that my own career was already made, that I was a somebody, that my name was well known in dramatic circles in Paris and appeared in *Tout Paris*,[5] though this

5. A directory of important persons.

was a matter of no consequence to Strindberg the chemist. Moreover, so long as I managed to hold my tongue about my successes, my companion loved me, but whenever I was obliged to touch upon them he was hurt, and looked so unhappy and browbeaten that, out of pure compassion, I never spoke of myself except as an old wreck. Thus by imperceptible degrees I was humbled, while he, who had the future before him, recovered at my expense. I was like a corpse that lies buried beneath the roots of a tree which flourishes by sucking nourishment from the decomposing remains.

The study of Buddhist writings, that I was making at this time, provided me with a reason for admiring my act of self-denial in sacrificing myself for another. A good deed brings its reward, and mine was as follows.

One day in the *Revue des Revues* I found a portrait of the American seer and faith-healer Francis Schlatter, who in 1895 cured 5,000 sick and then disappeared, never to be seen again. I noticed that this person's features bore a striking resemblance to those of my companion. I wanted to get this confirmed, so I took the periodical with me to the Café de Versailles, where a Swedish sculptor was awaiting me. He too was struck by the likeness and pointed out how extraordinarily similar were some of their circumstances. Both were of German extraction and had been active in America. Schlatter's disappearance coincided with our friend's appearance on the scene in Paris. As I had by then become slightly familiar with the terminology of occultism, I hinted at the possibility that this Francis Schlatter might be our man's 'Doppelgänger', who existed independently of him and without his knowledge.

When I uttered the word 'Doppelgänger' my sculptor opened his eyes very wide and drew my attention to the fact that our man always had two abodes, one on the right bank of the Seine, the other on the left. I learned, furthermore, that my mysterious friend lived a double life. After having

spent the evening with me absorbed in a discussion of philosophical and religious matters, he was always to be seen late
at night at Bullier's dance saloon.

We had one trustworthy means of proving the identity
between these Doppelgänger, as a facsimile of Francis
Schlatter's last letter was reproduced in the periodical.

'Come and dine with me this evening,' I suggested. 'Then
I will get him to write down Schlatter's letter from dictation.
If the handwriting is the same in both cases, in particular the
signatures, that ought to be sufficient proof.'

At dinner that evening everything was confirmed. The
handwriting was the same, the signature, the flourish that
was appended, it was all there.

Our partner submitted to our examination with some surprise. When it was over he asked:

'What is it you are aiming at?'

'Do you know Francis Schlatter?'

'I never heard of him.'

'Don't you remember the faith-healer in America last
year?'

'Why, yes, I do remember now. The man was a charlatan!'

He remembered. I showed him the portrait and the facsimile. He just laughed and his face remained sceptical, un-
moved, and completely indifferent.

Some days later, just as my mysterious friend and I were
sitting calmly drinking our absinth outside the Café de Versailles, a man dressed like a workman, and with a malignant
expression of countenance, stopped in front of our table and,
without any sort of warning, began to create a disturbance
right in the middle of the other customers. Confronting my
companion, he shouted at the top of his voice:

'I've caught you at last, have I, you damned rogue! What
do you mean by ordering a cross from me for thirty francs

and letting me deliver it and then slinking off? You black-guard, do you think a cross makes itself?'

He went on like this for an eternity and when the waiters tried to remove him he threatened to call the police. All this time his wretched debtor sat motionless, dumb, annihilated, like a condemned man, disgraced in front of that gathering of artists, with all of whom he was more or less acquainted.

When this exhibition was over I was left in a state of be-wilderment, much as if I had witnessed a witches' sabbath, and I asked:

'A cross? A cross for thirty francs? I don't understand what it is all about.'

'Yes, it was for Joan of Arc's cross, the contraption I was painting from, you know, the things in my picture of the crucified woman.'

'But he was the Devil himself, that workman.' And, after a minute or two's silence, I continued:

'It is odd to be sure, but the Cross is not a thing to trifle with, nor is Joan of Arc.'

'Do you believe that?'

'I don't know, I really don't know what I believe now. But the thirty pieces of silver?'

'That's enough, that's enough,' he cried out, much upset.

When I arrived at our cook-shop on Good Friday I found my companion in misfortune fast asleep at the table. Over-come by merriment, I woke him up and asked in a voice of surprise:

'You here?'

'What if I am?'

'Oh, as it is Good Friday I thought you would be hanging on the cross, at least until six o'clock.'

'Until six o'clock! True enough, I have slept all day, right up to six o'clock, and I can't say why.'

'But I could, you know.'

'Of course, my astral body has been out and about in America, isn't that what you mean?' And so on . . .

From this time forth a certain chilliness crept between us, almost imperceptibly. We had been meeting constantly for four horrible months, during which time my companion had undergone a re-education, had had time to change his style of painting, and had come so far that he was quite contemptuous of his Crucified Woman, which he now regarded as worthless rubbish. He had learned to take suffering in his stride, as a bitter drink, but the only health-bringing one in this life; and upon this had followed resignation. His powers of endurance were heroic. I thought he was wonderful when in one single day he walked the distance between Montrouge and the Halles twice, there and back on down-at-heel shoes and without having tasted a morsel of food. By the evening, after making seventeen calls on editors of various illustrated papers, he had managed to place three drawings, but still without ready money, and after having had only a couple of sous' worth of bread to eat he had gone off to dance at the Bal Bullier.

In the end we arrived at an unspoken understanding that we should dissolve this association for mutual aid. We both had an odd feeling that we had had enough of each other, and that each must go his own way towards the accomplishment of his destiny, and I knew on the last occasion of our saying good-bye that we were parting for ever.

I have never seen this man again, nor have I heard what became of him.

In the spring, just at the time when I was so much oppressed by my own reverses as well as those of my companion, I had a letter from the children of my first marriage, telling me that they had been seriously ill and had had to go to hospital. When I compared the date they mentioned with the date of my experiment in bewitchment I was seized with horror. By playing with those mysterious powers out of pure folly I had given the reins to my evil desires, but they, guided by the hand of the Unseen, had struck at my own heart.

I am not trying to excuse myself. I am only asking the reader to bear these facts in mind, should he ever be tempted to practise magic, particularly the kind known as bewitchment, or witchcraft in the true sense of the word. De Rochas[6] has shown this to be a reality.

One Sunday morning close upon Easter I woke up, went to the Luxembourg Gardens, walked through them, crossed the road, and entered the arcades of the Théâtre de l'Odéon. Here I came to a stop in front of a row of Balzac's novels bound in blue, picked up his *Séraphita*, quite by chance. But why? Maybe it was because of some half-submerged memory left on my mind by a review of my book *Sylva Sylvarum* in *L'Initiation*, in which I had been referred to as a compatriot of Swedenborg.

When I got home I opened the book, which was practically unknown to me, as so many years had passed since I first read it. Now, with a mind prepared to receive it, I devoured the contents of this remarkable work as if it were something entirely new. In my homeland and his Swedenborg was regarded as a charlatan, a madman with a distorted and lewd imagination. I had never read a word he had written, and I was now carried away by admiration for this angelic giant of the last century, interpreted as he was here by the most profound of French geniuses.

I read on with devout attention until I reached page sixteen, on which the date of Swedenborg's death was given. It was 29 March. I paused, reflected, looked at the calendar. Sure enough, the day was 29 March and it was Palm Sunday too.

6. *L'Extériorisation de la sensibilité.*

So it was that Swedenborg came into my life, in which he has played an immense part. He came on the actual anniversary of his death, bringing me the palms of victory or of martyrdom, who could say which?

Séraphita became my gospel. It caused me to renew my ties with the beyond to such an extent that life filled me with repugnance and Heaven drew me to it, so that I yearned for it with the irresistible yearning one has for home. I doubted not that I was already prepared for a higher existence. I despised the earth, this unclean world, man and all his works. I saw in myself the righteous man upon whom the Eternal has visited temptations, but whom the purgatory of this earthly life would make worthy of imminent deliverance.

This arrogance, called into existence by the intimacy I had established with the Powers, went on growing, all the more so because my labours in the field of learning were going well.

According to my own calculations, which agreed with the observations made by the metallurgists, I had succeeded in making gold, and I was confident I could prove it. I sent a sample to a chemist in Rouen, with whom I was on a friendly footing. He replied refuting my contentions. For a week I had no answer to give him. But, turning over the pages of the book on chemistry by my protector and patron Orfila, I found there the secret of my method of procedure.

This old chemical treatise of 1830, forgotten and despised, helped me at a critical moment and became my oracle. My friends Orfila and Swedenborg protected, encouraged, and chastised me. I could not see them, but I was aware of their presence. They never appeared to me either as spirits or in visions, but I was made conscious of their intervention in the vicissitudes of my life by small, daily happenings.

Spirits have become positivists, in harmony with the

times, and are therefore no longer content to manifest themselves only in visions.

What follows ought to be sufficient proof of this, as it cannot possibly be explained by the word 'coincidence'.

After I had succeeded in producing specks of gold on paper I tried to obtain the same result on a larger scale by the dry process and by heat. Two hundred experiments were made without result and in despair I laid aside my blowpipe. A morning walk led me to the Avenue de l'Observatoire, where I often go to admire the group representing The Four Continents for a private reason, namely that the most pleasing of Carpeaux's female figures resembles my wife. She stands under Pisces beneath the celestial globe and sparrows have built their nests behind her back.

At the foot of the monument I caught sight of two oval pieces of cardboard. On one was stamped the number 207 and on the other 28. The meaning: Lead (atomic weight 207) and Silicon (atomic weight 28). I picked up my find and put it among my chemical notes.

When I got home I started a series of experiments with lead, but let the silicon wait for further instructions.

Metallurgy had taught me that lead, refined in a melting pot lined with bone-ash, always yields a little silver and that this silver invariably contains a minute quantity of gold. From this I concluded that, as calcium phosphate constitutes the most important part of bone-ash, it should be the essential factor in the production of gold from lead.

This proved to be true. Lead, melted on a bed of calcium phosphate, always turned golden yellow on the underside. But the Powers showed their disfavour by interrupting the experiment before it was complete.

A year later, when I was living in Lund in Sweden, a sculptor, who was working on the production of fine pottery, gave me a glaze composed of lead and silicon, from which I was able, by treating it over heat, to extract for the first time beautiful and absolutely perfect metallic gold.

When thanking him, I showed him the two bits of cardboard stamped with the numbers 207 and 28. Can one in such a case as this talk of chance or coincidence when it so clearly bears the mark of an unshakeable logic?

I repeat again, I was never haunted by visions, but that does not mean that actual objects did not assume human shape, often with magnificent effect.

For instance, I once found my pillow, which I had crumpled when taking my midday rest, so moulded that it looked like a marble head in the style of Michelangelo. And one evening, when I returned home accompanied by the American faith-healer's Doppelgänger, I observed in the shadow of the recess a gigantic Zeus[7] reposing on my bed. Confronted by this unexpected sight, my companion stood still, overcome by awe and terror, but, as he was an artist, the beauty of the lines appealed to him immediately.

'Why, this is the lost art reborn! There's a school of drawing, if you like!'

The more we looked at it the more lifelike and frighteningly real the manifestation became.

'Clearly the spirits have taken to realism just as we human artists have.'

These occurrences could not be regarded as accidental, for on some days the pillow presented the appearance of horrible monsters, of gothic gargoyles, of dragons, and one night, when I had been out merrymaking, I was greeted by the Evil One himself, the Devil Incarnate in medieval style, goat's head and all. These things never frightened me, they all seemed so natural, but there was implanted in my mind

7. G. E. Klemming (d. 1893), Librarian of the Royal Library in Stockholm when Strindberg worked there as a young man. Strindberg believed himself to be in contact with his old master when he saw the head of Zeus.

an impression that something unusual, quasi-supernatural, was going on.

My friend the sculptor, whom I called in to witness these phenomena, showed no surprise but asked me to accompany him to his studio. There, hanging on the wall, was a pencil drawing which greatly impressed me by the beauty of its lines.

'What was your model?' I asked. 'A Madonna?'

'Yes, the Madonna of Versailles. It is a drawing of the floating water-weeds in the Pièce des Suisses.'

A new art discovered. Nature's own! A natural clairvoyance. Why scoff at naturalism now that it has shown itself capable of inaugurating a new kind of art, full of youth and hope? The Gods have returned to us. Writers and artists have sounded the call to arms, 'Back to Pan!' and its reverberations have been so multifarious that Nature has awakened from her slumber of centuries. Nothing happens in this world that has not the approval of the Powers. Naturalism has come into existence. Therefore let there be naturalism, let there be a rebirth of the harmony of matter and spirit.

My sculptor was a seer. He told me that he had seen in Brittany the figures of both Orpheus and Christ shaped in the same rock, and that he intended to go there again, as he meant to make use of the figures in a group he was going to send to the Salon.

One evening, as I was walking down the Rue de Rennes with my clairvoyant friend, he suddenly came to a halt in front of the window of a book-shop in which were exhibited some coloured lithographs. These represented a sequence of scenes in which human figures all had pansies in place of heads. Though a practised observer of plant life, I had never noticed the likeness between a pansy and a human face. My companion, however, was quite unable to recover from his surprise, for two reasons.

'Would you believe it?' he said. 'Yesterday evening when

I got home the pansies in my window looked at me mockingly, and then suddenly I saw them replaced by human faces. I was convinced that it was an illusion, produced by my nervous condition, but here today I see the same thing on cards printed and published long ago. So it cannot have been an illusion but reality, since an unknown artist observed the same thing before I did.'

We made progress as seers. I, in my turn, saw Napoleon and his marshals under the cupola of the Hôtel des Invalides. If you walk down the Boulevard des Invalides from Montparnasse, when you have passed the Rue Oudinot, you see the cupola in all its splendour at sunset. In that light the consoles and the other projecting parts of the drum at the base of the dome take on the shape of human figures, which change according to the distance from which they are viewed. Napoleon is there, Bernadotte and Berthier too, and my friend has drawn them all 'from Nature'.

'How are you going to explain these phenomena?' he asked.

'Explain it? Has anyone ever explained anything except by paraphrasing one set of words by another set?'

'You don't think the architect worked on those particular portions with an idea in his mind of which he was only half aware?'

'Listen, my friend, Jules Mansart, who built that dome in 1706, could not possibly have foreseen what Bonaparte would look like. Bonaparte was born in 1769 ... need I say more?'

Occasionally at night I had dreams that foretold the future, forewarned me against dangers, or disclosed secrets. For instance, in one dream a friend, long since dead, appeared to me bearing an unusually large silver coin. When I asked him where it came from he answered, 'From America,' and disappeared with his treasure.

The next day I received a letter with an American stamp. It came from a friend over there whom I had not seen for twenty years, and informed me that a request that I should write something in connection with the Chicago Exhibition had been travelling round Europe in search of me. The fee offered had been 12,000 francs, an enormous sum of money in the desperate straits in which I found myself at that time, and this was now lost to me. Those 12,000 francs would have meant an assured future. Only I could know that the loss of this money was a punishment inflicted upon me for a wicked action, something I had done in a moment of anger caused by the duplicity of a literary rival.

In another dream of even greater significance Jonas Lie[8] appeared to me bearing a clock of gilded bronze ornamented in an unusual way. Some days later, when I was walking along the Boulevard Saint-Michel, the window of a watchmaker's shop attracted my attention.

'Why,' I cried, 'there is Jonas Lie's clock!'

It was indeed the self-same clock. It was crowned by a celestial globe, against which leaned two women, and the works rested on four pillars. Inserted in the globe was a dial giving the date, 13 August.

I will postpone until a later chapter the story of how calamitous this date 13 August was to be for me. Trifling incidents of this kind, and many other things of a similar nature, happened during the period of my stay at the Hôtel Orfila, which lasted from 6 February until 19 July 1896.

Concurrent with these incidents, and interspersed at intervals between them, was a series of happenings which resulted in my being driven out of the hotel and which inaugurated a new phase of my life.

Spring had come. The vale of tears that stretched beneath

8. A famous Norwegian author and one of Strindberg's friends and benefactors.

my window was turning green and blossoming anew. Verdure covered the ground and hid the filth, so that this Gehenna became a veritable Vale of Sharon, where not only lilies bloomed but also lilac, Robinias, and Paulownias.

I was grieved to death, but the happy laughter of the young girls at play, hidden by the trees, floated up to me touching my heart and revivifying me. My life was ebbing away, old age was creeping on. Wife, child, and hearth of my own, all was wrecked. Autumn within, spring without!

The Book of Job and the Lamentations of Jeremiah brought me comfort, for between my fate and Job's there was assuredly some analogy, at least. Was not I, too, afflicted by incurable ulcers? Had not poverty fallen heavily upon me, and my friends deserted me?

> I go mourning without the sun.
> I am a brother to jackals
> And a companion to ostriches.
> My skin is black and falleth from me,
> And my bones are burned with heat.
> Therefore is my harp turned to mourning
> And my pipe into the voice of them that weep.

So said Jacob. And Jeremiah expressed in three words the depths of misery into which I had sunk:

'I forgot prosperity.'

It was in this frame of mind, one sultry evening as I sat bent over my work, that I heard the sound of a piano coming from behind the foliage in the valley beneath my window. I pricked up my ears like a charger at the blast of a trumpet. I straightened my back, drew a deep breath, my whole self metamorphosized. It was Schumann's *Aufschwung*. And what was more, I was sure that it was *he* who was playing it. My friend the Russian, my pupil who had called me 'Father' because I had taught him all he knew, my *famulus* who had called me 'Master' and had kissed my hands because his life had begun where mine had ended. He had come from Berlin to Paris to kill me, just as he had killed me in Berlin, and for what reason? Because Fate had decreed that the woman who was now his wife had been my mistress before he had known her? Was it my fault that things had happened that way? Of course not, but nevertheless he had conceived a deadly hatred for me, slandered me, prevented me from having my plays accepted at the theatres, woven intrigues that had bereft me of the remuneration I needed in order to exist. In a fit of rage I had struck him a brutal, a cowardly, blow, so cowardly that I regretted it as much as if I had assassinated him.

Now the fact that he had come here to kill me was a relief, for death alone could deliver me from remorse.

It must have been he who had annoyed me by sending all those letters with faked addresses, that I had found in the porters' lodge. 'Good,' thought I, 'let the blow fall. I shall not defend myself, for he is in the right and life means nothing to me.'

He was for ever playing *Aufschwung* as only he could play it. Invisible behind that wall of greenery, he sent the enchanted strains soaring over the blossoming creepers, so that I fancied I could see them fluttering like butterflies in the sunshine.

Why was he playing? Was it to let me know of his arrival with the object of terrifying me and pursuing me as I fled?

Perhaps they would know at the crémerie, where the other Russians had long been predicting the arrival of their fellow countryman. I went to dine there that very evening, but was met at the door by hostile looks. The whole assembly, already informed of my quarrel with the Russian, were now in league against me. I decided to disarm them by firing the first shot.

'Popoffsky[9] is in Paris, isn't he?' I asked challengingly.

'No, not yet,' replied one of them.

9. Stanislav Przybyszewski, Polish author, 1868–1927.

'But he is,' asserted another. 'He has been seen at the office of the editor of the *Mercure de France*.'

This was denied by some of the others, and the discussion ended leaving me knowing as little as before, but pretending to believe all that I had been told. Their all too obvious hostility made me swear to shun the place in future. I did so with regret, as there were people there with whom I got on very well. Isolated once more, driven out by this accursed enemy of mine, I became resentful, hatred stung me and poisoned my mind. I renounced the idea of dying. I was not going to be beaten by someone who was inferior to me. It would be far too great a humiliation for me, and far too great an honour for him. I would accept the challenge. I would defend myself. In order to ascertain the true facts, I went to the Rue de la Santé, behind the Val-de-Grâce, to seek out a Danish painter[10] who was an intimate friend of Popoffsky. This man, who had once been my friend too, had come to Paris six weeks previously, and when I had met him in the street had greeted me like a stranger, almost like an enemy. He had called on me the next day and, possibly with the idea of varnishing over the bad impression he had made, invited me to his studio and said all kinds of polite things to me. They were, however, so exaggerated that they left me with the feeling that he was a false friend. When I asked him if he had heard from Popoffsky he became very reserved and evasive, but did confirm the report that Popoffsky was expected shortly in Paris.

'To murder me,' I put in.

'Of course. Be on your guard!'

On the morning on which I returned his visit I opened the door only to find a gigantic Danish mastiff, a monstrous object lying on the paving stones of the courtyard, blocking my way – just by chance, of course. Instinctively, and with-

10. Edvard Munch, the Norwegian painter whom Strindberg had known in Berlin.

out a moment's doubt or hesitation, I turned back into the street and retraced my steps, perfectly certain that I had escaped some unknown danger and thanking the Powers for having warned me of it. Some days later, when I was trying to repeat the visit, a child was sitting on the threshold of the open doorway, holding a playing card in its hand. A flash of superstitious insight prompted me to glance at the card. It was a ten of spades!

'They are up to no good here,' thought I, and retreated without putting a foot inside.

That evening I was absolutely determined, after what had happened at the crémerie, to defy both Cerberus and the ten of spades. But Fate had ordained otherwise, as I came upon the man I was looking for at the Brasserie des Lilas. He was delighted to see me and we sat down together at a table outside.

As we refreshed our memories of the times we had had together in Berlin, he warmed up and resumed his old rôle of intimate friend; minor matters of discord between us were forgotten, and he even admitted that a number of the things he had denied in public were in fact true. Then suddenly he seemed to recollect some duty he had to perform or some promise he had given, and fell silent. His manner became cold and hostile, as if he were annoyed that he had been enticed into betraying secrets.

When I asked him point blank if Popoffsky was in Paris he replied with such an abrupt 'No' that I was sure it was a lie, and we parted.

It is worth while pointing out that this Dane had been Mme Popoffsky's lover before I was, and bore me a grudge because his mistress had deserted him for me. Now he was playing the part of friend of the family, thanks to Popoffsky's lack of taste; for the latter knew very well what his wife's relationship to 'handsome Henrik' had been.

The strains of Schumann's *Aufschwung* resounded over

the bosky tree-tops, but the player remained invisible and I could not discover his whereabouts. He played every afternoon between four and five for a whole month.

One morning, after I had walked down the Rue de Fleurus to comfort myself by having a look at my rainbow in the paint-shop window, I entered the Luxembourg Gardens, now in full bloom and lovely as a fairy-tale. There on the ground I found two dry twigs, broken off by the wind. They were shaped like the Greek letters for P and y. I picked them up and it struck me that these two letters P—y must be an abbreviation of the name Popoffsky. Now I was sure it was he who was persecuting me, and that the Powers wanted to open my eyes to my danger. I became very agitated, notwithstanding this indication that the Unseen was benignly disposed towards me. I called upon Providence to protect me. I recited the Psalms of David in the face of my enemies. I hated my enemy, and my hatred was a religious, Old Testament hatred; at the same time I did not dare to make use of the black art, of which I had recently been making a study.

> Make haste, O God, to deliver me.
> Make haste to help me, O Lord.
> Let them be ashamed and confounded
> That seek after my soul:
> Let them be turned backward and brought
> to dishonour that delight in my hurt.
> Let them be turned back by reason of their shame
> That say, Aha, Aha.

At that time this prayer seemed to me righteous and the mercifulness of the New Testament cowardly.

I know not to what Unknown my invocation found its way, but the sequel to this story will at least show that my prayer was heard.

May 13th. Had a letter from my wife. She has learned from the papers that a Herr Strindberg is going to the North Pole in a balloon. It is a cry of anguish. She assures me that she still loves me and begs me on her knees to abstain from an undertaking which is the equivalent of suicide.

I have informed her that she is mistaken, and that it is my cousin's son who is going to risk his life in the cause of an important scientific discovery.

May 14th. I had a dream last night. An amputated head had been stuck on to a man's trunk, making him look like a drunken actor. The head began to talk. I was terrified and knocked over my folding screen in trying to push a Russian in front of me to protect me against the furious creature's onslaught.

This same night I was bitten by a mosquito and killed it. In the morning the palm of my right hand was covered with blood.

During a walk along the Boulevard Port-Royal, I saw a pool of blood on the footpath. Sparrows have built a nest in the flue of my stove. The homely sound of their twittering makes me feel as if they were actually living in my room.

May 17th (and subsequent days). Absinth at six o'clock outside the Brasserie des Lilas, just behind the statue of Marshal Ney, is now my only vice and my last remaining pleasure. When the day's work is done, and body and soul are worn out, I restore myself with a glass of the green liquor, a cigarette, and *Le Temps* or *Le Journal des Débats*. How sweet life can still be when the misery of one's existence is blurred by slight intoxication. Probably the Powers grudge me this one moment of blissful make-believe between the hours of six and seven, since from this very

11. Very little of what follows is in the diary itself.

evening my felicity has been disturbed by a series of unpleasant incidents which I am not disposed to ascribe purely to chance.

For instance, on this 17th day of May I found the spot that I have occupied for two years already taken. No other seat was vacant and I was forced to go to another café, which depressed me more than I can say.

May 18th. Found my nice corner at the Brasserie des Lilas empty. Sitting there under my chestnut tree behind Marshal Ney I was content, yes, positively happy. My absinth was before me, mixed to perfection; my cigarette was lit, *Le Temps* opened, when, looking up, I saw a drunken man passing by, a disgusting, a horrible, sight. He fastened his eyes on me with a sly, mocking expression that embarrassed me. His face was the colour of wine dregs, his nose Prussian blue, his eyes evil. I sipped my absinth, thankful that I did not look like that sot, but suddenly, and I still do not know how, I found my glass upside-down and empty. I had no money with which to buy another, so I paid, got up, and left the café convinced that the Evil One had cast a spell on me.

May 19th. Dare not go to the café today.

May 20th. Strolled about outside the Brasserie des Lilas for a while and at last found my corner vacated. One must fight with the Evil One, so I took up the struggle. My absinth was ready, I was puffing away at my cigarette, *Le Temps* was full of interesting news, when – you must believe me, reader, I am not lying! – just above my head, in the same building as the café, a chimney caught fire. General panic. I kept my seat as I had only just got it. But a will stronger than mine brought down a cloud of soot so well aimed that two large smuts fell in my glass. Thoroughly discouraged, I went on my way, still incredulous or, at most, sceptical.

June 1st. After prolonged abstinence I was again overcome by a desire to seek comfort under my chestnut tree. My table was occupied, so I sat down at another where I could be on my own and in peace. One must fight the Evil One but – would you believe it? – a lower-middle-class family came and sat down quite close to me. They were too numerous to count, their glasses were replenished again and again, the females bumped against my chair, small children calmly did their little business in front of me, young men took matches from my table without so much as asking my leave. Though surrounded by these boisterous and insolent persons, I was determined not to budge. Then followed a scene which must, without any doubt, have been arranged by the skilful hands of the Unseen, for it was far too cleverly contrived for it to be possible for me to suppose a plot on the part of the persons concerned, to whom I was completely unknown.

One of the young men laid a sou on my table with a gesture that I could not understand. As a foreigner, and alone among a crowd of strangers, I did not dare to make a fuss. So I just sat there, blinded by rage, trying to fathom what had really happened.

He had given me a sou as if I had been a beggar.

A beggar! The very dagger with which I so often stab myself.

A beggar, yes, for you earn nothing, and you . . .

The waiter came and offered me a more comfortable seat, and I left the coin lying on the table. The waiter brought it to me. What an insult! But he informed me, very politely, that the young man had seen it lying under the table and thought it belonged to me.

I felt ashamed and, to calm myself, ordered another absinth.

It came, and everything was fine, when the foul stink of sulphate of ammonia began to suffocate me.

What do you suppose it was? Something quite natural, not a miracle, not a trace of malice about it, merely the gaping vent of a sewer at the edge of the pavement close to my chair. Then, for the first time, I realized that the good spirits intended to help me to free myself from a vice that must inevitably lead to the mad-house. Blessed be Providence for having saved me.

May 25th. Notwithstanding that according to the rules of the hotel women are not allowed to enter it, a family has been given a room next to mine. A babe in arms cries day and night, but this gives me real pleasure. It reminds me of the good old days when I was in my thirties and life was full of promise.

May 26th. The family next door are squabbling, the child is yelling its head off. It is just like old times and how sweet it is – now.

This evening I saw the English lady again. She was charming, and gave me such a kind, motherly smile. She has painted a picture of a snake-dancer that resembles a walnut or a brain. Her painting hangs almost hidden behind Mme Charlotte's bar at the crémerie.

May 29th. A letter from the children of my first marriage informs me that they have received a communication summoning them to Stockholm, to be present at the farewell feast to be held before my departure for the North Pole. They cannot understand it; no more can I. What a fatal error!

June 2nd. In L'Avenue de l'Observatoire I found two pebbles shaped exactly like hearts. In the evening I found a third heart of the same size and exactly like the other two in the garden of a Russian painter. I never hear Schumann's *Aufschwung* now, so my mind is at rest again.

June 4th. I went to see the Danish painter who lives in the Rue de la Santé. The huge dog had gone, the way in was clear of obstacles. We set off to get some dinner at a pavement café in the Boulevard Port-Royal. My friend was cold and felt indisposed. As he had forgotten his overcoat I put mine over his shoulders. That soothed him immediately. He became most amenable, I could do what I liked with him. He did not dare to oppose me and we were in complete agreement on all points. He admitted that Popoffsky was a scoundrel, and that it was he I had to thank for all my reverses. Then, suddenly, he had a nervous seizure, he began to shake like a medium under the influence of a hypnotist, he fidgeted, shook off my overcoat, stopped eating, threw down his fork, got up, gave me back my coat, and said good-bye.

What could be the meaning of this? A tunic of Nessus? Was my garment impregnated with my nervous fluid, and had its opposite polarity subjugated him?

This must be what Ezekiel means in chapter xiii, verse 18 :

Thus saith the Lord God : Woe to the women that sew pillows upon all elbows and make kerchiefs for the head of persons of every stature to *hunt souls* ... Behold, I am against your pillows ... and I will tear them from your arms and I will let the souls go, even the souls that ye hunt to make them fly.

Had I become a magician without being aware of it?

June 7th. I visited my friend the Dane to look at his pictures. When I arrived he was hale and hearty, but after I had been there for half an hour he had such a severe attack of nerves that he had to undress and go to bed.

What can be the matter with him? Bad conscience?

June 14th. Sunday. I found another heart-shaped pebble, exactly like the others, this time in the Luxembourg Gardens. A golden-yellow spangle was glued to the stone. I cannot solve the riddle, but I have a presentiment that it must be an omen. I was comparing these four stones in front of the open window when the bells of Saint-Sulpice began to ring; the great bass bell of Notre-Dame joined in, but through these accustomed chimes there penetrated to me the sound of a deep, solemn beat that seemed to proceed from the bowels of the earth.

The waiter came in with my post and I asked him what it was.

'It is the great bell of Sacré-Cœur in Montmartre,' he replied.

'So it is the Feast of the Sacred Heart today,' thought I, and looked at my four stone hearts, rather impressed by this striking coincidence.

I have just heard the cuckoo from the direction of Notre-Dame-des-Champs. But that is impossible. Or have my ears become so hypersensitive that I can detect sounds uttered as far away as the Forest of Meudon?

June 15th. I went down to the city to change a cheque into notes and gold. The Quai Voltaire rocked under my feet, which caused me some surprise. I know, of course, that the weight of passing vehicles makes the Pont du Carrousel tremble, but on this particular morning the motion continued through the courtyard of the Tuileries and on through L'Avenue de l'Opéra. Naturally, a city always vibrates to some extent, but only supersensitive nerves can detect it.

The far side of the river is foreign territory to us denizens of Montparnasse. It is almost a year since I was last there, and I never got farther than the Crédit Lyonnais and the Café de la Régence. In the Boulevard des Italiens I was seized by homesickness and hurried back to the other bank, where the sight of the Rue des Saint-Pères put new heart into me. But near the Church of Saint-Germain-des-Prés I met, first of all, a hearse, and after that a cart carrying two colossal images of the Virgin. One of these, a kneeling figure with clasped hands and eyes raised to Heaven, made a deep impression on me.

June 16th. In the Boulevard Saint-Michel I bought a paperweight. It had a marble base and a glass dome enclosing a figure of Our Lady of Lourdes, framed in the famous grotto, with a veiled woman kneeling before her. Placed in the sunlight the image casts strange shadows on to the wall. By an accident, unforeseen by the artist, the plaster behind the grotto is shaped like the head of Christ.

June 18th. My Danish friend entered my room in a state of collapse, trembling from head to foot. Popoffsky has been arrested in Berlin, charged with the murder of a woman and two children, his mistress and their two children before his marriage. My first feeling was amazement, mixed with genuine sympathy for a friend who had once shown me such importunate affection; then peace descended upon my spirit which for many months had been in a state of turmoil thanks to the imminent danger in which I had lived.

I was unable to conceal my justifiable selfishness and expressed my feelings quite openly.

'Of course it is terrible; all the same I cannot help feeling relieved when I think of the danger that I have escaped. His motive? Shall we say his present legitimate wife's jealousy of his illegitimate family, and the expense it involved? Maybe also . . .'

'What?'

'Maybe his bloodthirsty impulses, frustrated here in Paris, have had to seek another outlet, no matter where.'

Is it possible, I thought to myself, that my fervent prayers have succeeded in turning aside his dagger? And had they parried the blow so well that it had struck the murderer himself, right in the heart? I did not go into the matter any further but, as the victor, made a generous proposal.

'Let us at least save our friend's literary reputation; I will write an article on his merits as a writer, you shall illustrate it with an attractive portrait, and we will offer it to the *Revue Blanche*.'

In the Dane's studio (the dog no longer guards it) we stood looking at a portrait of Popoffsky painted two years before. It was just the head, cut off by a cloud, and underneath it a pair of crossbones such as one sees on gravestones. The amputated head made us shudder and the dream I had had on May 14th rose up before me like a ghost.

'What gave you the idea of beheading him?'

'Hard to say; there was a sort of fatality about him in spite of his great gifts. Even these were in some ways those of a factitious genius who aspires to the highest honours without being prepared to pay the price. Life offers us a choice of only two things, laurels or sensuality.'

'Indeed! So you have found that out at last, have you?'

June 23rd. I have picked up a pin of mock gold set with an artificial pearl. Fished up a heart-shaped piece of gold out of my bath for gold synthesis.

This evening I walked along the Rue du Luxembourg and, looking up the first avenue to the right, I saw in the background, above the trees, a hind outlined against the sky. It was exquisite both in shape and colour, and as I looked it made a sign with its head towards the south-east (the Danube)!

These last few days, ever since I heard about the catastrophe to the Russian, a new uneasiness has come upon me. I feel as if someone were working upon me somewhere or other. I have confided to the Danish painter that, since his arrest, the Russian's hatred is causing me pain such as one might feel from the current of an electric machine.

There are moments when I have a presentiment that my stay in Paris will soon come to an end and that I may expect my fate to take a new turn.

The cock on the top of Notre-Dame-des-Champs seems to me to be flapping his wings as if he intends to fly off to the north. As I feel that I shall very soon be departing, I am pressing on to complete my studies at the Jardin des Plantes.

The zinc bath in which I make my synthesis of gold by the wet method has on its inner surface a landscape formed by the evaporation of salts of iron. I interpret it as a warning, but I have tried in vain to guess in what part of the world this remarkable landscape may be. There are small hills covered with conifers, particularly firs, and between these eminences plains, with orchards and cornfields, and everything suggests that there is a river in the neighbourhood. One of these hills, which has a precipice formed by stratified rocks, is crowned by the ruins of a castle.

(I did not yet recognize the place but I should do so before long.)

June 25th. Invited to the house of the leader of scientific occultism, the editor of *L'Initiation*. When the Doctor and I arrived at Marolles-en-Brie we were greeted by three items of bad news. A weasel had killed the ducks. A maid had fallen ill. I have forgotten the third.

When I got back to Paris in the evening I read in a paper a description of the haunted house at Valence-en-Brie, later to become so notorious.

Brie! My suspicious nature makes me fear that the other people living in my hotel will draw their own conclusions about my expedition to Brie, and will think that it was I who contrived these practical jokes or, perhaps I should say, this black magic.

I have bought myself a rosary. Why? It is beautiful and the Evil One dreads the Cross. As a matter of fact I no longer try to find a motive for my actions. I act extempore, which makes life much more amusing.

Things have taken a new turn in the case against Popoff-sky. His friend the Dane has begun to dispute the likelihood that he committed the crime, alleging that the accusation was refuted at the inquiry. As a result, our article has been postponed and the relationship between us is again chilly. Also, that horrible monster of a dog has reappeared, a re-minder to me to be on my guard.

A storm broke in the afternoon while I was writing at my table by the window. The first drops of rain fell on my manuscript and smudged it so that the letters of the word

'Alp'[12] ran together forming a blot that looked like a giant's face. I have preserved it, as it looks exactly like the Japanese Thunder God as he is portrayed in Camille Flammarion's work *L'Atmosphère*.

June 28th. Saw my wife in a dream. She had lost her front teeth, and she gave me a guitar that looked like a Danube boat. The same dream threatened me with imprisonment.

This morning I found a bit of paper of all colours of the rainbow in the Rue d'Assas.

This evening I ground together a little quicksilver, tin, sulphur, and ammonium chloride on a piece of paste-board. When I removed them the imprint of a face was left on the board. It was exactly like my wife's as I had seen her in my dream last night.

July 1st. I am expecting an eruption, an earthquake, or a thunderbolt, but I don't know where it will strike. I am as nervous as a horse when wolves are near. I scent danger and pack my bags in readiness for flight, but I cannot budge.

The Russian has been released from prison for lack of evidence. His friend the Dane is now my enemy. My friends at the crémerie are persecuting me. When I last ate dinner there it was served in the yard because of the heat. The table was placed between the rubbish-bin and the conveniences. Over the rubbish-bin was the picture of the crucified woman by my former friend the American, hung there as a revenge because he had gone off without paying what he owed. Near the table the Russians had set up a statuette of a warrior armed with a sickle, their national emblem. To scare me, of course. A young guttersnipe, who lives in the house, went to the closet at my rear with the evident intention of annoying me. That yard is as narrow as a well and the sun cannot reach it because of the high walls. The cocottes, who have taken up residence here and there on every storey above

12. German 'demon' or 'nightmare'.

the yard, had opened their windows and were raining indecent remarks upon our heads. Servants came out with buckets and emptied garbage into the rubbish-bin. It was Hell let loose. As for my two table companions, they were known perverts and carried on a disgusting conversation for the purpose of trying to engage me in a quarrel.

What was I doing there? The fact is that loneliness had compelled me to seek the company of other human beings, to listen to the sound of the human voice.

Then, just as my state of spiritual torment reached its peak, I caught sight of some pansies that were blooming in the narrow flower-bed. They shook their heads at me as if they wanted to make me aware that some danger was threatening me, and one of them, whose face was like a child's, signalled to me with her large, deep, shining eyes:

'Leave this place!'

I got up and paid my bill. As I was leaving, the gutter-snipe bade me a surly farewell, using some opprobrious epithet that nauseated me but did not make me lose my temper.

I commiserated with myself and blushed for the others.

I absolved them on the ground that they were merely demons performing their duty.

Nevertheless, it was only too obvious that I had displeased Providence and when I got back to my room I began to scrutinize my debit and credit accounts. Up to now, and in this had lain my strength, I had found it impossible to admit that others could be in the right. Now, broken as I was by the hand of the Unseen, I tried to confess that I myself was in the wrong. When I examined my conduct of the last few weeks I was seized with dread. My conscience had no mercy but stripped me naked.

I had sinned out of arrogance, *hubris*, the one vice that the Gods do not forgive. The friendship that Dr Papus had shown me and the praise he had bestowed on my investigations had so much encouraged me that I had persuaded myself that I had solved the riddle of the Sphinx. I had set myself up as a second Orpheus; Nature had died at the hands of the learned, and it was my task to bring her back to life.

I had been so conscious of the protection of the Powers and had flattered myself that my enemies could not get the better of me; this had gone so far that I had scorned the notion of showing even the most elementary humility.

I think this is a suitable place in which to insert the story of the occult friend[13] who played such a decisive part in my life as my mentor. He gave me advice, comfort, and chastisement; and, in the periods of acute poverty that recurred from time to time, he it was who stood by me and provided me with the means of subsistence.

As early as 1890 he had written to me about a book I had published. He had found that on some points my ideas agreed with those of the theosophists, and he asked me to give him my views on occultism and on that priestess of Isis, Mme Blavatsky. The rather presumptuous tone of his letter displeased me, and I told him so point-blank in my reply. Four years later I published *Antibarbarus*, and at this critical moment of my life I received another letter from this unknown man, a letter that struck an elevated, almost prophetic, note. In it he foretold for me a future that would be rich in suffering and in honour. Into the bargain he gave me his motive for renewing our correspondence. This arose from a presentiment he had that I was at that moment passing through a spiritual crisis and that a word of comfort was perhaps necessary. Finally he offered me material assistance; but this I refused, as I was jealous of my independence, however wretched it might be.

In the autumn of 1895 it was I who wrote to him, to ask him to assist me by publishing my articles on natural his-

13. Torsten Hedlund, Swedish theosophist and publisher.

tory. From that day we have kept up by letter very friendly and even intimate relations, except for one brief rupture occasioned by some hurtful expressions of which he made use when he took it upon himself to instruct me upon things I already knew or lectured me in a highfalutin' way for my lack of modesty.

Meanwhile, after our reconciliation, I communicated to him all my observations and was more free with my confidences than was wise. To this man, whom I had never seen, I confessed everything. From him I put up with the most severe reproofs, because in him I saw an idea rather than a person. He was a messenger from Providence, a Paraclete.

There were two fundamental differences of opinion between us, which led to very animated arguments, though these never degenerated into bitterness or quarrelling. As a theosophist he preached the doctrine of Karma — that is to say, the sum total of human destinies which counterbalance one another, so as to result in a kind of Nemesis. He was in fact a mechanist and an epigone of the so-called materialistic school. I, on the other hand, saw the Powers as one or a number of concrete, living, individualized personalities, who directed the course of events and the lives of human beings, consciously and hypostatically, as the theologians would put it. Our second difference of opinion concerned the denial and mortification of the Ego, which to me seemed and still seems an insane idea.

All that I know, little as that may be, springs from one central point, my Ego. It is not the cult but the cultivation of this which seems to me to be the supreme and final goal of existence. My answer to his objections was always given in the same decisive form: to kill the Ego is to commit suicide.

For that matter, to whom shall I submit? To the theosophists? Never. Before the Eternal, the Powers, and Providence I do try to curb my bad impulses always and every day, as far as is possible. To strive for the preservation of my Ego in the teeth of all the influences that a domineering sect or party may try to impose upon me, that is my duty, dictated by the conscience I have acquired through the grace of my divine protectors.

Because of the qualities that I loved and admired in this man whom I had never seen, I put up with the censorious tone he adopted when he was treating me as an inferior being. I always answered his communications and never concealed my aversion for theosophy.

At last, just in the middle of the Popoffsky affair, he addressed me in such haughty language that his tyranny became intolerable. I feared he regarded me as insane. He called me 'Simon Magus', a practitioner of black magic, and he advised me to read Mme Blavatsky. I retorted by giving him to understand that I had no need of Mme B, and that *no one could teach me anything*. Thereupon he threatened me with what do you think? He said that he would see to it that I was set upon the right path once more, and this with the assistance of Powers that were stronger than those I acknowledged. I then begged him not to interfere with my destiny, so well guarded by the hand of that Providence which had always guided me. In order to make my faith plainer to him by an example, I told him the following story, a detail from my life-history, which had been so rich in providential happenings. At the same time I warned him that I dreaded giving away my secret, as I had a misgiving that I might, by so doing, bring upon myself the vengeance of Nemesis.

It happened ten years ago, at the most tumultuous period of my career as an author. I was attacking the feminist movement, which was supported by everyone in Scandinavia except myself. I had allowed myself to be carried away by the heat of the moment and so far overstepped the limits of decency that my fellow countrymen regarded me as insane.

I was living in Bavaria with my first wife and our children when I received a letter from a friend[14] I had known since my youth, inviting me to spend a year with him, me and the children. My wife was not mentioned.

My suspicions were aroused by this letter, partly because of its affected style and partly because of the erasures and corrections, which revealed the hesitation the writer had felt in the choice of arguments to advance. I scented a trap, and rejected his proposal in vague but grateful terms.

Two years passed; the divorce from my first wife was an accomplished fact, and I wrote to my friend inviting just myself to stay with him on the island, in the outer skerries of the Baltic, where he functioned as an Inspector of Customs.

He received me warmly, but there was an atmosphere of falsehood and equivocation, and he spoke to me with the air of a police inspector. After a night's reflection the whole position became clear to me. I had wounded this man's self-conceit by something I had said in one of my novels and, in spite of the sympathy he otherwise felt for me, he bore me a grudge. He was exceedingly despotic by nature, and now he wanted to tamper with my destiny, to tame my spirit, to subdue me in order to demonstrate his superiority.

He was anything but careful of his choice of the means he employed. He tortured me for a week, poisoned my mind with slanders and lies that he invented for the purpose, but he did it so clumsily that I remained convinced that the trap he had set for me on the previous occasion had been laid with the object of getting me shut up as insane.

I let him have his own way without opposition, trusting that my lucky star would deliver me when the time was ripe.

14. Ossian Ekbohrn, of Sandhamn.

My apparent submissiveness caused my tormentor to grow fond of me. Isolated from the world on his island out in the ocean, he was disliked by his neighbours and subordinates and at last yielded to his desire for a confidant. With a naïvety quite incomprehensible in a man of fifty, he told me that the previous winter his sister had lost her reason and, in a fit of frenzy, had burnt up all the money she had saved.

The next day he took me into his confidence again. This time I learned that his brother was shut up somewhere in the country because he was insane.

I asked myself whether it was for this reason, and because he wanted to be revenged on Fate, that he was aiming at getting me shut up too.

Meanwhile I heartily commiserated with him about his family misfortunes and won him over completely, so that I was able to leave the island and rent a house on another in the vicinity, where I had my own people with me. After I had been there a month I was recalled to my 'friend' by a letter, and found him shattered by the news that his brother had battered in his own head in a manic fit. I comforted him, my tormentor, and then, to crown it all, his wife confided in me, weeping as she did so, that she had long been expecting her husband sooner or later to fall victim to the same fate that had overtaken his brother and sister.

A year later I read in the papers that my friend's elder brother had taken his life in circumstances that indicated mental derangement. So three thunderbolts had fallen on the head of this man who had tried to play with lightning.

You may well say what an extraordinary coincidence! And, more than that, what a fatality there is in this coincidence, so that every time I have told this story I have been punished for it.

The intense heat of July had descended upon Paris and life

became unendurable. Everything stank, most of all the hundred conveniences.

I was expecting a catastrophe, though I could not say what.

In one street I found a piece of paper on which was written the word *Marten*, in another street a similar piece on which the word *Vulture* was written by the same hand. Popoffsky is exactly like a marten, his wife like a vulture. Had they arrived in Paris to kill me? He, as a shameless murderer, is capable of anything if he could poison his wife and children.

I had been reading the lovely little pamphlet *The Delight of Dying* and it had made me long to leave this world. To reconnoitre the borderland between life and death I would lie down on my bed, uncork a bottle of cyanide of potassium and allow its deadly fumes to escape into the room. He would draw near, that old Reaper, so mild and so seductive, but at the last moment someone always appeared or something always happened to cut me short. The waiter would enter on some errand, a wasp would fly in at the window.

The Powers refused me this one and only happiness, and I bowed to their will.

At the beginning of July all the students left for their holidays and the hotel was unoccupied. My curiosity was therefore aroused by the arrival of a stranger, who was put into the room adjacent to my writing desk. This unknown man never uttered a word; he seemed to be occupied in writing something behind the wooden partition that separated us. All the same, it was odd that he should push back his chair every time I moved mine. He repeated my every movement in a way that suggested that he wanted to annoy me by imitating me.

This went on for three days. On the fourth I made the following observation. When I went to bed the man in the room next to my desk went to bed too, but in the room on the other side, next to my bed. As I lay in my bed I could hear him getting into his on the other side of the wall; I could hear him lying there, stretched out parallel to me. I could hear him turning the pages of a book, putting out the lamp, breathing deeply, turning over and falling asleep.

Complete silence then reigned in the room adjacent to my writing desk. This would only mean that he was occupying both rooms. How unpleasant to be besieged on both sides at once!

Alone, absolutely alone, I now had my dinner on a tray in my room and ate so little that the good-natured waiter was inconsolable. I did not hear the sound of my own voice for a whole week and I began to lose it for lack of exercise. I had not a sou in my pocket, no stamps or tobacco either.

I willed myself to make a final effort. I *would* make gold by the dry method with the aid of fire. Money was procured, a furnace, crucibles, charcoal, bellows, and tongs. The heat was intense and, stripped to the waist like a smith, I sweated in front of the open fire. But the sparrows had built a nest in the flue and the fumes made their way out into the room. My first attempt left me infuriated, partly because I had a headache but also because of the futility of my operations, as everything went wrong. After I had re-melted the stuff three times I looked into the crucible. The borax had formed a skull with two glistening eyes whose supernatural irony pierced my soul.

Still not a grain of metal, so I gave up further experiment. Sitting in my armchair I read the Bible, opened at random.

And none calleth to mind, neither is there knowledge or understanding to say, I have burned part of it in the fire; yea, also I have baked bread upon the coals thereof; I have roasted flesh and eaten it : and shall I make the residue thereof an abomination? Shall I fall down to the stock of a tree? He feedeth on ashes: a deceived heart hath turned him aside, and he cannot deliver his soul, nor say, Is there not a lie in my right hand? ...

Thus saith the Lord, thy redeemer, and he that formed thee from the womb: I am the Lord, that maketh all things; that stretcheth forth the heavens alone; that spreadeth abroad the earth by myself; *that frustrateth the tokens of the liars, and maketh diviners mad; that turneth wise men backward, and maketh their knowledge foolish.*

For the first time I was assailed by doubts about my scientific investigations. Suppose they were pure folly? Alas! if so, I had sacrificed a life of happiness for myself and for my wife and child too, all for a chimera.

Woe is me, madman that I am! And a gaping abyss opened between that hour of parting from my family and this fleeting moment. A year and a half, all those days, all those nights, all that suffering – for nothing.

No! it could not be so! It was not so!

Was I lost in the dark forest? No, the Angel of Light was guiding me along the true path towards the Islands of the Blessed, and this was the Devil tempting me or I was being punished.

I sank down into my armchair. A torpor, such as I have seldom experienced, weighed upon my spirit. It seemed to me that a magnetic fluid was proceeding from the partition wall, my limbs were overcome by drowsiness. With a great effort I got up and made haste to get into the open air. As I was walking down the corridor I heard two voices whispering in the room adjacent to my desk.

Why were they whispering? To maintain secrecy, of course.

I walked down the Rue d'Assas and entered the Luxembourg Gardens. I could hardly drag myself along. I felt as if I were paralysed from my hips to the balls of my feet, and fell on to a bench behind Adam and his family.

I was poisoned, that was my first thought. Popoffsky had killed his wife and children with poison gas. He must have arrived. He must have sent a stream of gas through the wall as Pettenkofer had done in his famous experiment. What was I to do? Go to the police? No, for if there was no proof I shoud be locked up as insane.

Vae soli! Woe to the solitary, a sparrow on a roof! Never had my existence seemed more wretched, and I wept like an abandoned child who is scared of the dark.

In the evening I no longer ventured to sit at my desk for fear of a new attempt on my life. I went to bed not daring to sleep. Night had come and the lamp was lit. I saw, cast on the wall opposite my window, the shadow of a human being, whether man or woman I could not say, but the impression I retain is that it was a woman's.

When I got up to look, the blind came clattering down with a bang. After that I heard the unknown person enter the room next to my recess. Then all was silent.

For three hours I lay awake, unable to get to sleep, a thing that does not usually take me long. An uneasy sensation began to creep over me. I was being subjected to an electric current, passing between the two rooms on either side of mine. The tension increased still more and, in spite of the resistance I put up, I was obliged to get out of bed. I had only one thought in my mind:

'Someone is killing me! I will not be killed.'

I went out to look for the waiter, whose room was at the other end of the corridor, but alas he was not there. Sent out on purpose, keeping out of the way, a secret confederate, bribed!

I went down the stairs and through various corridors to wake the proprietor. With a presence of mind of which I had not believed myself capable, I alleged that the fumes from the chemicals in my room had made me feel unwell, and I asked if he could let me have another room for the night.

By an unlucky chance, which must be ascribed to an enraged Providence, the only vacant room was the one immediately under that of my enemy.

Left to myself, I opened the window and inhaled the fresh air of a starry night. Above the roof-tops of the Rue d'Assas and the Rue de Madame the Plough and the Pole Star were visible.

So, to the North! *Omen accipio!*

As I was drawing together the curtains of the recess I heard the enemy above my head get out of bed and drop some heavy object into a portmanteau, the lid of which he locked.

So there must be something he wanted to hide; an electric machine perhaps?

On the following day, which was a Sunday, I packed my bag and pretended that I was going to the seaside.

At the door I called out 'Gare Saint-Lazare' to the cabby, but when he had got to the Odéon I redirected him to drive me to the Rue de la Clef, near the Jardin des Plantes, where I intended to stay incognito and finish the studies on which I was engaged before leaving for Sweden.

7

INFERNO

At length there was a pause in my torments. Installed in an armchair on the top of the flight of steps leading up to the Pavilion, I used to sit for hours looking at the flowers in the garden and meditating on past events. The calm that succeeded my flight was a proof that it was no illness that had struck me, rather that I had been persecuted by enemies. I worked during the day and slept peacefully at night. Delivered from the sluttishness of my former surroundings, I became sensible that I was being rejuvenated by the hollyhocks, those flowers of my youth.

The Jardin des Plantes, that wonder of Paris unknown to the Parisians, had become my private park. The whole of Creation was encompassed by its walls, a Noah's ark, a Paradise Regained, in which I could saunter without danger, though in the very midst of the wild beasts; my happiness was too great. Taking the minerals as my starting point, I made my way through the vegetable and animal kingdom and came at last to Man, behind whom I found the Creator. The Creator, that great artist who Himself develops as He creates, who makes rough drafts only to cast them aside, who takes up abortive ideas afresh, who perfects and multiplies His primitive conceptions. Most certainly, everything is the work of His hand. Often He makes prodigious advances in His invention of new species, and then Science comes along and establishes the existence of gaps, of missing links, and persuades itself that there have been intermediate forms that have now disappeared.

Meanwhile, certain that I was now secure from my enemies, I sent my new address to the Hôtel Orfila, so that I might resume contact with the outside world through my post, which had not been reaching me since my flight.

Hardly had I shed my incognito than my peace was broken. Things began to happen that made me uneasy and I was oppressed by the same disagreeable sensations as before. It all began when objects whose purpose I could not possibly explain were heaped up in the room next to mine on the ground floor. An old gentleman, with evil grey eyes like a bear's, carried in empty packing cases, sheets of iron, and other objects that I could not identify. At the same time the noises from which I had suffered in the Rue de la Grande-Chaumière began again above my head. Cables were dragged about, and people banged and hammered exactly as if they were assembling an infernal machine like those of the nihilists.

Then, too, my landlady, who had been extremely obliging when I first took up residence there, became more formal. She spied upon me, and her manner of addressing me was annoying.

Furthermore, new lodgers moved into the room on the floor above me. The taciturn old gentleman, whose heavy footfall I knew so well, was no longer there. He was a retired man of independent means, who had lived in that house for many years. He had not left it now, no, he had simply moved to another room. Why?

The servant girl, who cleaned my room and served my meals, wore a serious expression and cast surreptitious glances at me, full of pity.

In the room above mine they had set up a wheel that went round and round all day. Condemned to death! I was convinced of it. But by whom? By the Russians? By the devout, by the Catholics, the Jesuits, the theosophists? For what reason? As a sorcerer or a practitioner of the black arts? Perhaps it was by the police, as an anarchist? That is a charge very commonly employed for getting rid of personal enemies.

Even to the moment at which I write this down I have no idea what was going on that July night when death hurled itself upon me, but I well know and shall never forget the lesson I learned from it, which will last me the rest of my life.

If those who were let into the secret should ever own up and confess that what happened was the result of a conspiracy, woven by the hands of men, I shall not bear them a grudge, for I am now convinced that it was another and mightier hand that set theirs in motion, without their knowing or willing it.

If, on the other hand, there was no plot, then it must have been I who, by the power of my own imagination, had created these disciplinary spirits in order to punish myself.

We shall see from the sequel how improbable this supposition is.

On the morning of my last day I got up with a resignation that I would describe as religious. Nothing bound me to life any more. I put my papers in order, wrote the essential letters, and burnt all that had to be destroyed.

After so doing I went out for a walk in the Jardin des Plantes, to bid farewell to Creation.

The blocks of lodestone from Sweden that stand in front of the Museum of Mineralogy gave me a greeting from my native land. To the Robinia, the Cedar of Lebanon, memorials to the great days of a still living science, I offered salutations. I bought some bread, and some cherries with which to regale my old friend Martin the bear, who knew me personally, because I was the only human being who ever offered him cherries when he woke up or before he went to sleep. I held out some bread to the baby elephant, who spat in my face when he had finished up every scrap, the ungrateful, perfidious young thing.

Farewell vultures, inhabitants of the heavens, shut up in a muddy cage. Farewell bison, thou behemoth, thou fettered demon. Fare you well sea-lions, well-matched couple, consoled by conjugal affection for the loss of the ocean and its wide horizons. Fare you well stones and plants, flowers and trees, butterflies, birds and snakes, all of you created by the hand of a good God. And you, great men, Bernadin de Saint-Pierre, Linnaeus, Geoffroy Saint-Hilaire, Haüy, you whose names are inscribed in letters of gold on the pediment of the temple – farewell! But no : I shall soon be among you.

I left that earthly paradise and, as I did so, those sublime words from *Séraphita* came into my mind : 'Farewell thou wretched earth! Farewell!'

When I entered the garden of the hotel I sensed that someone had arrived while I was out. I could not see him, but I felt that he was there.

My uneasiness was increased by the visible alterations that had been made in the room next to mine. To begin with, a length of cloth had been stretched across a rope, evidently with the intention of concealing something. On the mantelpiece of the stove were piles of metal plates separated by wooden slats. A photograph album, or some other book, had been placed on top of each pile, clearly in order to lend an appearance of innocence to these diabolical machines, which I would describe as being like batteries. To crown it all, I caught sight of two workmen perched on the roof of a house in the Rue Censier, exactly opposite the wing in which I lived. What they were doing up there I could not see, but they kept pointing at my French window as they handled objects the nature of which I could not make out.

Why did I not flee? Because I was too proud, and because what is inevitable must be endured.

I made my preparations for the night. I had a bath and

made sure that my feet were spotlessly clean, a thing to which I attach great importance, as my mother had taught me when I was a child that dirty feet are a disgrace. I shaved and sprinkled perfume on the shirt I had bought in Vienna three years earlier for my wedding ... A condemned man's last toilet.

From the Bible I read those psalms in which David calls down the vengeance of the Eternal upon his enemies.

But what of the penitential psalms? No, it would not be right for me to repent, for it was not I who had guided my destiny. I had never done evil for its own sake but only in defence of my person. To repent is to criticize Providence, who imposes sin upon us as a form of suffering in order to purify us through the disgust engendered in us by a bad deed.

I settled my account with life. We were quits. If I had sinned then, upon my word, I had suffered punishment enough. Should I fear Hell? But indeed, I had passed through a thousand hells in this life without faltering and endured more than enough to awaken in me a passionate desire to leave all the vanities and false pleasures of this world that I had always abhorred. Born as I was with a longing for Heaven, I had wept, even as a child, over the filthiness of existence and had felt myself a stranger to my parents and in the community. Ever since my childhood I had sought God but found the Devil. In my boyhood I had borne the Cross of Jesus Christ but I had repudiated a God who was content to rule over slaves cringing before their tormentors.

As I was drawing down the blind of my French window I noticed a party of ladies and gentlemen who were drinking champagne in the private reception room. Clearly some travellers who had arrived that evening. But they were not assembled just for pleasure since they were all looking serious. They were discussing something, making suggestions, speaking in hushed voices as if they were conspirators. The torture was intensified by the fact that they turned round as they sat and pointed in the direction of my room.

At ten o'clock I put out the lamp and fell asleep, as calm and resigned as one who was breathing his last.

I awoke. A clock in the house struck two, a door was shut, and I was drawn from my bed as if by a vacuum pump that was sucking at my heart.

Hardly had my feet touched the floor than a stream of electricity was discharged upon the nape of my neck, pressing me to the ground. I struggled up, grabbed my clothes, and tore out into the garden, a prey to the most horrible palpitations.

When I had got into my clothes my first lucid thought was that I must go to the police and ask to have the place searched. But the main gate was closed, the porter's lodge too, so I groped my way forward, opened a door on the right, and entered the kitchen, where a night-lamp was burning. I upset it and was left standing there in inky darkness.

Terror brought me to my senses again and, actuated by the thought that if I made a mistake I was lost, I went back to my room.

I dragged an armchair into the garden and, sitting there under the starlit sky, I went over in my mind all that had taken place.

An illness? Impossible. I had been in excellent health up to the time that I shed my incognito. An attempt upon my life? Yes, for I myself had watched it being prepared. Moreover, I felt completely restored here in the garden, out of reach of my enemies, and my heart was functioning perfectly normally. While in the midst of these reflections I heard someone cough in the room next to mine. Instantly from the room above came a slight, answering cough. Probably signals, and exactly like those I had heard the last night I spent in the Hôtel Orfila. I stepped forward and tried to burst open the French window of the ground-floor room, but the lock held.

Worn out by a useless struggle against these invisible enemies, I sank into the armchair. Sleep took mercy upon me and there, under the stars of a lovely summer night, lulled by the whisper of the hollyhocks as they swayed in the gentle July breeze, I knew no more.

I was woken by the sun and returned thanks to Providence for rescuing me from death. I packed my few belongings and prepared to leave for Dieppe, there to seek refuge with friends, people I had neglected as I had everyone else, but who were lenient and generous to all hapless and shipwrecked beings.[15]

When I asked for the proprietress I was told she could not see me, the excuse being that she was indisposed. It was just what I should have expected, certain as I was that she was one of the accomplices.

As I took my departure I called down a curse upon the heads of the evil-doers and implored Heaven to rain fire upon that nest of robbers. Who can tell whether I was right or wrong?

When I arrived at Dieppe my kind friends were appalled as they saw me come creeping up the slight incline to the Villa des Orchidées, my bag heavy with manuscripts.

'Where have you come from, you poor fellow?'

'I have come from death.'

'I thought as much, you look like a corpse.'

And so saying, the sweet and charming lady of the house took me by the hand and led me to a mirror so that I might

15. Fritz Thaulow, Norwegian painter. One of the other outcasts to whom he showed kindness and hospitality was Oscar Wilde.

see myself. My face was blackened by smoke from the engine, my cheeks sunken, my greying hair damp with sweat, my eyes haggard, my shirt filthy. I was a miserable sight.

But when my amiable hostess, who treated me like a sick and abandoned child, had left me alone in front of a dressing-table, I examined my face at close quarters. There was something about its expression that made me shudder. It was not that it bore the imprint of death or of vice, it was something else. If at that time I had read Swedenborg, the marks that the evil spirit had stamped there would have revealed to me the truth about my mental state and the events of the past weeks.

Then I felt ashamed and disgusted at myself. My conscience pricked me for the ingratitude I had shown to a family who had thrown open this harbour of refuge to me before, as they had done to so many other shipwrecked mariners.

The furies had driven me here to be punished. It was the beautiful home of an artist, a home of happiness, of married bliss, enchanting children, luxury and spotless cleanliness, of boundless hospitality, liberal and humane views, pervaded by an atmosphere of beauty and kind-heartedness that seared my soul. In the midst of all this I felt as dissatisfied with myself as a damned man would in Paradise, and it was here that I began to discover that I was damned.

Every blessing that life can offer was spread out before my eyes, every blessing that I had lost.

I was given an attic room with a view towards the top of the hill, where there was an asylum for the elderly. In the evening I observed two men leaning against the garden wall, spying on our villa and indicating my window by gestures. The idea that I was being persecuted by enemies who employed electricity began to obsess me again.

It was the night between the 25th and the 26th of July, 1896. My friends had done everything they could to re-assure me. Together we had inspected all the attics near mine, even the loft, to convince me that no one was hiding there with criminal intent. But, as it happened, when we opened the door of a lumber room, an object, quite harm-less in itself, made me lose heart. It was the skin of a polar bear used as a rug, but its gaping jaws, threatening fangs, and sparkling eyes upset me. Why was it we had found that brute there just at this moment?

I lay down on my bed fully dressed, determined to remain awake until the fateful stroke of two.

Until midnight I occupied myself by reading. Another hour passed, and the whole household was now fast asleep. At last the clock struck two. Nothing happened. I became arrogant and, to provoke my invisible enemies, also perhaps with the idea of making a physical experiment, I rose, opened both windows, and lit two candles. Then I sat down at the table with the candlesticks in front of me, and thus, offering myself as a target, my breast bared, I challenged the unknown with these words:

'Here I am, you fools!'

An emanation, that might have been electrical, made it-self felt. It was very slight at first. I looked at the compass that I had by me to provide evidence, but it showed not the least variation; therefore there could be no electricity about. All the same, the tension increased and my heart began to beat rapidly. I put up a resistance, but in a flash my body was charged with a fluid that suffocated me and drained my heart.

I rushed down the stairs and made for the drawing-room, where a temporary bed had been arranged in case I should have need of it. I lay down on it for five minutes, trying to collect my thoughts. Could it have been radiant electricity? No, the compass had refuted that possibility. An illness, brought on again by fear of the stroke of two? No, since my courage had not failed me when I dared my enemies to attack me. But why had it been necessary to light the candles to attract the unknown fluid?

Unable to find an answer, and lost in a labyrinth from which there was no escape, I tried to force myself to sleep. But now a discharge like a cyclone fell upon me and tore me from my bed. The hunt was on once more. I hid behind walls, I lay down close to doorways, in front of fireplaces. Wherever I went, the furies sought me out. Mental agony got the better of me, an unreasoning terror of everything and of nothing had me in its grip. I fled from room to room, finally taking refuge on the balcony, where I crouched in a heap.

Dawn broke with a yellowish-grey light, sepia-coloured clouds assumed strange and monstrous shapes which increased my despair. I found my way to my friend the painter's studio, lay down on the carpet, and closed my eyes. After five minutes I was awakened by an irritating noise. A mouse was looking at me and evidently wanted to come nearer. I shooed it away, but back it came with a second mouse. Good heavens, was I suffering from delirium tremens, I who had not abused wine for the last three years? (The next day I satisfied myself that there really were mice in the studio, so of course it was just a coincidence. But by whom had it been prepared and for what purpose?)

I moved again, and this time lay down on the carpet in the lobby. There merciful sleep descended upon my tortured soul and I was unconscious of my sufferings for perhaps half an hour.

A clearly articulated 'Alp!' woke me with a start. Alp! The German word for nightmare. Alp! The word that the raindrops had smudged on my manuscript in the Hôtel Orfila.

Who was it who was calling? No one; everyone in the

house was asleep. Demons at play. This was only a poetic image, but all the same it may have embraced the whole truth.

I climbed the stairs right up to my attic room. The candles had burnt down, all was quiet.

Then the angelus rang out. It was the Lord's day.

I took up my Roman missal and read: *De profundis clamavi ad te, domine.* This comforted me and I sank down on my bed more dead than alive.

On Saturday the 26th of July the Jardin des Plantes was devastated by a cyclone. Details of the disaster appeared in the newspapers and I found them exceptionally interesting, I cannot explain why. It was the day on which Andrée's balloon was going to ascend for the attempt upon the North Pole, and the omens were unfavourable. The cyclone had brought down a number of balloons in various places, causing the death of several aeronauts. Elisée Reclus had had a leg broken. Also, someone of the name of Pieska had committed suicide in Berlin in a most unusual way, by disembowelling himself in the Japanese fashion; a very bloody drama.

The next day I left Dieppe, this time bestowing a blessing on the house whose well-deserved happiness had been overclouded by my anguish.

I still spurned the idea that the spirits had played any part in what had occurred, and persuaded myself that I was suffering from a nervous disease. For this reason I was determined to go to Sweden, there to seek the help of a friend who was a doctor.[16]

As a memento of Dieppe I took with me a bit of rock, a kind of iron ore shaped like the trefoil of a Gothic window and marked with a Maltese cross. It was given to me by a child, who had found it on the beach. He told me that these

16. Anders Eliasson.

stones fall from the sky and are washed ashore by the waves.

I was very willing to believe what he told me, and I have kept his gift as a talisman though its significance is still a mystery to me.

(After a storm the inhabitants of the coast of Brittany collect stones called staurolites, that are shaped like crosses and have the appearance of gold.)

The little coast town to which I went is in the extreme south of Sweden.[17] It was once a nest of pirates and smugglers and has preserved traces of exotic features from all parts of the world, introduced by mariners who had circumnavigated the globe.

For instance, my doctor's dwelling presented the appearance of a Buddhist monastery. The four wings of the building, one storey high, enclosed a quadrangular courtyard, in the middle of which stood a dome-shaped building, an imitation of Tamburlain's grave in Samarkand. The pitch of the roof, and the Chinese tiles that covered it, reminded one of the Far East. An apathetic tortoise crawled about on the paving stones, or buried itself in the weeds in a state of Nirvana which seemed likely to endure for ever.

A thicket of Bengal roses adorned the outer wall of the east wing, in which I lived alone. To reach the two gardens belonging to the house you crossed a yard, a narrow, dark, damp place, which had in it a chestnut tree and some angry black hens.

In the flower garden was a pagoda-like summer-house, completely overgrown by clematis.

This monastery, with its innumerable rooms, was inhabited by a single human being, the superintendent of the district hospital. A widower, a solitary, he had gone his own independent way through the hard school of life, and looked

17. Ystad.

down on his fellow human beings with the sturdy, noble scorn that springs from a profound knowledge of the relative worthlessness of everything, including one's own self.

This man's entrance upon the stage of my life was of such an unexpected character that I am tempted to reckon it as a theatrical *Deus ex machina*.

At our first meeting after I arrived from Dieppe he looked searchingly at me and exclaimed:

'What is the matter with you? Your nerves! Good, but there is something else as well. You have the evil eye, a thing I do not remember your having of old. What have you been up to? Debauchery or vice? Or have you lost your illusions, or taken to religion? Tell me all about it, old boy.'

But I could not tell him anything at all, because the first idea that took hold of my suspicious mind was that he had been prejudiced against me in advance. Someone had informed him of my condition and I was going to be put away.

I pleaded insomnia, nervousness, nightmares, after which we talked of a number of other matters.

The doctor installed me in a small flat in his house. My attention was immediately attracted to an American bedstead of iron, whose four uprights were surmounted by brass knobs that resembled the conductors of an electric machine. In addition there was a flexible mattress, the springs of which were made of copper wire, twisted into spirals like those of a Ruhmkorff induction coil. You may judge of my fury when I found myself faced by this piece of devilish bad luck.

It was quite impossible to ask for another bed, as that would have aroused suspicions about my sanity. To convince myself that nothing was hidden above me, I went up into the attic. There, just to make matters worse, I found precisely one object, an enormous coat of chain mail, placed exactly over my bed. 'That is an accumulator,' thought I. 'If a storm breaks, a thing that very often happens in these parts, the network of iron will attract the lightning and I shall be lying on the conductor.' But I did not dare to say a word about it. I was also much disturbed by what sounded like the steady roar of a machine. As it happened, I had been plagued by a buzzing in my ears ever since I left the Hôtel Orfila, a noise that resembled the pounding of a water-wheel. I was therefore doubtful whether the roaring noise I heard was real or not, and inquired about it.

'The press in the printing house next door.'

There was a simple and natural explanation for every-thing, but it was just this simplicity in the means employed that so much alarmed me and drove me mad.

Then came night with its terrors. The sky was overcast, the air heavy; there was thunder about. I did not dare to go to bed and spent two hours writing letters. Annihilated by weariness, I undressed and crept between the sheets. An awful silence reigned over the house as I put out the lamp. In the gloom I could feel someone watching me, someone who touched me lightly, groped for my heart and sucked.

I promptly threw myself out of bed, opened the window, and precipitated myself into the courtyard, but the rose bushes were waiting and my shirt was no protection against the lash of their thorns. Slashed to bits and bleeding, my naked feet flayed by stones, scratched by thistles, stung by nettles and slipping all the time on unknown objects, I crossed the courtyard and reached the kitchen door that led to the doctor's flat. I banged on it. No answer. Only then did I notice that it was raining. Oh, depth of misery! What had I done to deserve such torture? Clearly this was Hell itself. *Miserere! Miserere!*

I banged again and again.

How extraordinary that no one was ever there when I was attacked!

People always had alibis, so there must be a conspiracy in which everyone was involved!

At last I heard the doctor's voice.

'Who is there?'

'It is me, I am ill. Open or I shall die!'

He opened the door.

'What is the matter with you?'

I started to tell him my story, beginning with the attempt on my life in the Rue de la Clef, which I said I attributed to enemies who employed electricity.

'Be quiet, unhappy man. You are suffering from a mental disorder.'

'Hang it all! test my intelligence, read what I write every day and get published.'

'Hush! Don't say a word to anyone. The textbooks on insanity know all about these stories of electricians.'

'The Devil take them! I don't care a bit about your textbooks and, to get the whole matter cleared up, I shall go to the lunatic asylum in Lund tomorrow and have myself examined.'

'If you do you will be lost. Not another word; go and lie down in the next room.'

I persisted in demanding that he should listen to me, but he refused to let me speak.

Left alone I asked myself the following question: Is it possible that this friend, a man of honour who has always kept clear of any kind of dirty business, is now, at the close of an honourable career, giving way to temptation? But who was tempting him? The answer eluded me, but many possibilities sprang to my mind.

Every man has his price. But if the payment had been proportionate to his virtue this man's price must have been a high one, and what was the object of it? Straightforward revenge sets limits to what it will pay. Some interest of tremendous importance must be involved. But wait, I have it! I had made gold. The doctor had half admitted it, but today he had denied that he had copied the experiments which I had communicated to him by letter. He had denied it, yet that evening I had found samples of what he had made scattered over the paving stones of the courtyard. So he had lied.

Moreover, that very evening he had expatiated upon the unfortunate effects that mankind would suffer should it prove possible to manufacture gold. Universal bankruptcy, general confusion, anarchy, the end of the world.

There would be nothing for it but to kill the gold-makers. Those had been his final words.

There is another point worth mentioning. My friend's economic position was a pretty humble one. I had therefore been astonished to hear him say that he was intending, in the immediate future, to buy the property where he was living. He was in debt, in a very tight corner, yet he was dreaming of becoming a property owner.

Every circumstance combined to make me suspicious of my good friend.

Was I suffering from persecution mania? Granted that this was the case, who was the artificer who forged the links in these infernal syllogisms? Where was he?

'There would be nothing for it but to kill the gold-maker.' That was the last thought which my tortured mind could retain before I fell asleep about sunrise.

We started the cold-water treatment and I was given another room in which to sleep. My nights were now tolerably quiet in spite of a few relapses.

One evening the doctor noticed the prayer book on my bedside table and fell into a fury.

'Still meddling with religion! Can't you understand it's a symptom?'

'Or one necessity among others.'

'Be quiet! I am no atheist, but I am sure the Almighty

has no use today for that sort of old-fashioned familiarity. That fawning upon the Eternal is finished and I hold to the fundamental principle of the Mohammedans that one should pray for nothing except to be able to bear the burdens of existence with resignation.'

High-sounding words from which I washed a few grains of gold.

He took the missal and the Bible away from me.

'Read things that do not excite you, things of secondary interest, world history or mythology, and take leave of these chimerical dreamers. Above all, beware of occultism, that abuse of science. We are forbidden to pry into the Creator's secrets, and woe betide those who come upon them.'

When I objected that a school of occultism had been formed in Paris he roared, 'Woe betide them!'

That evening he gave me Victor Rydberg's *Germanic Mythology*, but I am absolutely sure that he had no ulterior motive.

'Look, here is something that will send you to sleep as you stand. This is much stronger than sulphonal.'

Had my excellent friend had any idea what a fuse he was lighting, he would have chosen almost anything else.

This mythology, in two volumes, comprising about a thousand pages in all, had hardly been put into my hand before it fell open, of itself as it were, and my eyes instantly became glued to the following lines, which engraved themselves on my memory in letters of fire.

According to the legend, Bhrigu, who had learned everything from his divine father, became so proud of his knowledge that he believed it to surpass that of his master. For this the latter sent him to the underworld where, to humble his pride, he was made to witness many terrible things of which he had previously known nothing.

My own case precisely: arrogance, conceit, hubris, punished by my father and master. And I was in Hell too, hunted here by the Powers.

Who then was my master? Swedenborg?

I went on turning over the pages of that marvellous book.

This may be compared with the Germanic myth of the Field of Thorns that lash the feet of the unrighteous and . . .

But enough, enough! Even the thorns too! This was too much.

No doubt about it. I was in Hell. And in truth the facts gave such reasonable support to this apparently fanciful idea that at last I really believed it.

The doctor seemed to me to be torn between the most conflicting emotions. At times he was preoccupied, watched me furtively, and treated me with humiliating brutality. At others, himself unhappy, he would tend and comfort me as he might have done a sick child. Then again, he would rejoice in the power of trampling underfoot a man of importance, for whom he had previously felt respect, and he would play the tormentor and lecture me thus:

'It is your duty to work. You must curb your overwhelming ambition. You have a duty to fulfil to your country and your family. Leave chemistry alone. It is a chimera, and in any case there are plenty of specialists, people who are authorities on the subject, professionally trained people who know what they are doing.'

One day he suggested that I should write for the worst among the inferior Stockholm newspapers, saying that it paid well.

I replied that I did not need to write articles for the worst of the Stockholm papers when the leading paper in Paris, and in the world, had offered me space in its columns. He put on a show of scepticism and treated me like a braggart, though he had read my articles in *Figaro* and had himself arranged for one of my leaders in *Gil Blas* to be translated.

I was not angry with him, as I knew that he was only playing the part assigned to him by Providence.

I forced myself to suppress my rising hatred for this impromptu demon of torment, and I cursed Fate for seeking to pervert my feelings for a generous friend from gratitude to ingratitude.

Insignificant things happened which constantly fanned the flame of my suspicions regarding the doctor's evil intentions.

One day he placed some axes, saws, and hammers under the veranda facing the garden. They were quite new and served no apparent purpose. He also put two rifles and a revolver in his bedroom, and another collection of axes, too large for any domestic use, out in the corridor. What a devilish piece of bad luck that these appurtenances of the hangman and the torturer should have been put where I could not fail to see them. They made me uneasy because they seemed so strange and so useless.

My nights had become fairly quiet, but the doctor, on the other hand, had begun to wander about alarmingly. In the middle of one very dark night I was awakened by hearing a gun go off. I discreetly pretended not to have heard anything, but in the morning he explained the incident by laying the blame on a flock of magpies which had flown into the garden and disturbed his sleep.

On another occasion it was the housekeeper who uttered some hoarse shrieks in the small hours. On yet another, the doctor moaned and sighed deeply and called upon the 'Lord of Hosts'.

Was this a haunted house? And who was it that had sent me here?

I could not help smiling when I saw how the nightmare that was riding me had also settled on my gaoler. My unholy joy was followed by instant punishment. A frightful

attack seized me, and I was awakened by hearing an unknown voice cry out these words: 'Luthardt, druggist.'

Druggist! Was I being slowly poisoned by alkaloids that
produce delirium, like hyoscyamin, hashish, digitalis, or
atropine?

I did not know, but from that moment my suspicions
were doubled. They did not dare to kill me outright, only
to drive me mad by underhand methods, so that they could
cause me to vanish behind the gates of the madhouse.

Appearances now argued even more strongly against the
doctor. I discovered that he had developed my gold synthesis, so that he knew more about it than I did myself.
Into the bargain what he said one minute he contradicted
the next and, faced by his lies, my imagination took the bit
between its teeth and bolted off beyond the bounds of
reason.

On the 8th of August I took a morning walk outside the
town. A telegraph post beside the road was making a humming noise. I put my ear to it and listened as if bewitched.
A cast horseshoe lay by chance at the foot of the post. A
good omen! I picked it up and carried it home.

On the evening of August the 10th I said good night to
the doctor, whose behaviour during the past few days had
made me more uneasy than ever. He had been looking most
secretive, as if he were having a struggle with himself. His
face was ashen, his eyes lustreless. He sang or whistled all
day long. A letter had arrived that had made a deep impression on him.

That afternoon he had come home with his hands covered with blood from an operation, bringing with him a
two-months-old foetus. He looked like a butcher, and expressed himself on the subject of the mother's delivery
in a manner that I found most unpleasant.

'We must kill the weak and shield the strong. Away with
tender-heartedness, it only causes the race to degenerate.

He filled me with horror and, after we had bidden each other good night on the threshold that separated our rooms, I continued to note his every movement. First he went out into the garden, but I could not hear what he was doing there. Then he returned to the veranda outside my bedroom. He stopped there, handling some very heavy object and winding up a spring that was certainly not part of the works of a clock. Everything was done quietly, in a way that suggested that he wanted to make a mystery of it or that he was executing some dubious manœuvre.

Partially undressed, I stood motionless, holding my breath as I awaited the effects of these mysterious preparations.

Then, through the dividing wall beside my bed, I felt the usual current of electricity streaming towards me, felt it groping over my breast as it sought its way to my heart. The tension increased. I seized my clothes, slipped out through the window, and did not dress until I was far beyond the gate.

Turned out at night once more, out on to the hard paving stones of the street, but this time with my last refuge, my only friend, behind me. I walked on and on, aimlessly. Then I began to think more clearly, and made straight for the house of the Medical Officer of Health for the town. I rang the bell and waited, meanwhile trying to decide what I could say without incriminating my friend.

At last the doctor appeared. I asked him to excuse this late visit, but I was a sick man, suffering from insomnia and fainting fits, who had lost confidence in his doctor and so forth – I said that the excellent friend whose hospitality I had accepted had treated me as a hypochondriac and had refused to listen to me.

Almost as if he had expected that I should come, the doctor invited me to be seated, offered me a cigar and a glass of wine.

It was a relief to be received like a well-bred man after having been hounded about like a complete idiot. We sat chatting for two hours, and I found out that the doctor was a theosophist to whom I could tell everything without fear of compromising myself.

Finally, a little after midnight, I rose, saying I would try to find a room at an hotel, but the doctor advised me to go back to my friend.

'Never, he would be likely enough to murder me.'

'But if I come back with you?'

'Well, then, we will go together and face the enemy's fire. But I am sure he will never forgive me.'

'We'll go all the same.'

So we returned the way I had come and, finding the door locked, I banged on it.

After a minute my friend opened the door, and it was my turn to feel compassion. This man, a surgeon, accustomed to inflicting pain on others without showing a trace of pity, this prophet of premeditated murder, he looked such a pitiful sight. He was wan as a corpse, he trembled and stammered, and when he saw the doctor standing behind me he sank to the ground in the grip of a terror which appalled me more than all the horrors that had gone before.

Was it possible that this man had been intending to commit murder and was afraid of exposure? Certainly not! and I thrust the impious thought out of my mind.

After we had exchanged a few meaningless words, half jesting on my side, we parted for the night.

There are times in our lives when things happen so pregnant with horror that our minds refuse to accept them at the moment of impact. But the impression they have made is there all the time and very soon returns with irresistible force.

When I got home after my nocturnal visit a sight, that for a fleeting moment had attracted my attention in the doctor's drawing-room, suddenly came back to my mind.

The doctor had gone to fetch some wine. Left alone I started to look at a cupboard with panels inlaid with walnut or alder, I forget which. As usual, the grain of the wood produced various shapes. As I looked, I beheld a goat's head, executed by a master hand, upon which I instantly turned my back. Pan himself! just as the tradition of antiquity had portrayed him. Pan! whom the Middle Ages had transformed into Satan. It was he all right!

I confine myself here to a bare narration of fact. The doctor to whom the cupboard belongs would be doing a service to the science of occultism if he would have the panel photographed. Dr Marc Haven in *L'Initiation* (November 1896) discussed these phenomena, which are very common in all the realms of nature. I recommend the reader to examine carefully the face that is drawn on the shell of the crab.

After this adventure my friend and I openly declared our hostility to each other. He made it plain to me that my presence was superfluous. I let him know that I was prepared to move to an hotel while I waited for important letters. He then pretended to be offended.

As a matter of fact, I was unable to budge for lack of money, and for the rest I had a premonition that a change in my destiny was about to take place.

My health was now restored. I slept well at night and worked during the day. Providence adjourned any further expressions of its displeasure and my endeavours were all crowned with success. If I picked up a book at random in the doctor's library it was sure to give me just the information I needed. For instance, in an old chemistry book I found the secret of the process by which I had been making gold, so that I was able, by means of metallurgy, to prove by calculations and analogies that I had made gold and that in fact people had always made gold when they thought they had merely extracted it from ore.

An article on the subject was sent off to a French periodical and immediately accepted. I hastened to show it to the doctor who, when he could not deny the facts, plainly showed how much he disliked me.

After this I had to admit to myself that he was no longer my friend, since my success gave him pain.

August 12th. Bought a sort of notebook from a bookstall. Splendidly bound in tooled and gilded leather. My attention was attracted by the design of the tooling, which, strangely enough, contained a prophecy. Its interpretation will be given in the sequel. The composition, very artistically executed, showed on the left-hand side the first quarter of the new moon, encircled by a branch in blossom; three horses' heads (trijugum) springing out of the moon; above this a laurel branch and beneath it three chevrons (3 times 3). On the right-hand side a bell from which a spray of flowers was cascading, also a wheel like a sun.

August 13th. The day foretold by the clock in the Rue Saint Michel has arrived. I have been expecting something to happen, but in vain. Nevertheless, I am convinced that something has happened somewhere and that the result will shortly be communicated to me.

August 14th. Found a leaf torn from an office calendar in the road. On it was printed in large type August 13th (the clock's date again). Under the date, in small type, the words 'Never do in secret what you would not do in public.' (Black magic!)

August 15th. A letter from my wife. She laments my fate, says she still loves me, that our child is with her and she hopes for its sake that matters will improve between us.

Her relations, who used to hate me, are not insensible to my sufferings and have invited me to visit my daughter – that little angel – who lives in the country with her grandmother.

For me this was like being recalled to life. My child, my daughter, had supplanted her mother. I longed to embrace the innocent little mite, whom I had actually been prepared to injure. I wanted to beg her to forgive me, to make life happier for her by small, fatherly attentions. I was eager to lavish on her all the tenderness I had been hoarding for years. I began to feel like one reborn, as if I were awakening from a long and evil dream. I saw in all this the goodwill of that severe Master who had punished me with such a heavy but understanding hand. Now I grasped the meaning of those sublime but obscure words from the Book of Job : 'Behold, happy is the man whom God correcteth.'

Happy indeed, for about the 'others' he troubles himself not at all.

Whether or not I should find my wife down there by the Danube I did not know and it mattered very little to me because of the indefinable lack of harmony between us. I prepared for my pilgrimage, well knowing that it would be a penitential journey, and that new Calvaries were being held in reserve for me.

Thirty days of torment. I had not long to wait before the gates of the torture-chamber were opened.

I parted from my friend the Tormentor without bitterness. He had only been the instrument of Providence.

'Behold, happy is the man whom God correcteth.'

8

BEATRICE

In Berlin a cab took me from the Stettiner to the Anhalter Bahnhof. For me this half-hour journey was like being dragged through a hedge of thorns, stabbed to the heart as I was by the memories it revived. First I passed through the street where my friend Popoffsky had lived with his first wife, unknown or rather ignored, struggling with passion and poverty. Now his wife was dead, his child too – both had died in that house on the left – and our friendship had degenerated into ugly hatred.

There on the right was the ale-house,[18] the meeting place of artists and writers and the scene of so many intellectual and amorous orgies.

Over there was Cantina Italiana, the spot where, three years ago, I used to meet my fiancée and where we had converted my first Italian royalties into chianti.

There was the Schiffbauerdamm and Pension Fulda, where we had lived together as newlyweds. And here was my theatre, my book-shop, my tailor, and my chemist.

What fatal instinct was it that had led my driver to bring me through this *via dolorosa*, paved with buried memories which at this nocturnal hour rose up like ghosts? I could not imagine why he had to drive down this particular alley, past the Black Boar, once our place of refreshment and famous as the favourite haunt of Heine and E. T. A. Hoffmann. Its host was there too, standing outside on the steps under the monster's head hung out as a signboard. He looked at me, but without seeing me. For a single instant the chandelier inside sent out a beam of light coloured by the hundreds of bottles displayed in the window,

18. Zum schwarzen Ferkel.

causing me to relive a year of my life, richer than others in sorrow and joy, friendship and love. At the same time I was acutely aware that all this was over and ought to remain buried, leaving room for what was to come.

That night I slept in Berlin and when I awoke in the morning I saw over the roof-tops a roseate flush, carnation pink, greeting me in the eastern sky. Then I remembered that I had seen the self-same colour in Malmö on the evening before my departure. This Berlin that I was leaving had been my second fatherland. In it I had lived through my *seconda primavera*, which was also to be my last. At the Anhalter Bahnhof I left behind me not only my memories but all hope of renewing a springtime and a love that were never, never to return again.

After spending a night in Tabor, where the roseate flush followed me, I travelled through the Bohemian Forest down to the Danube. Here the railway came to an end, and it was by carriage that I made my way into the depths of the country that borders the Danube as far as Grein. My route lay between apple and pear trees, cornfields and green meadows. At last I saw in the distance, on a hill on the other side of the river, the little church that I had never entered, but which had been the most prominent landmark in the view we had had from the cottage where my daughter had been born on that unforgettable May morning two years before. I drove through villages, past castles and monasteries, along a road lined by innumerable penitential chapels, Calvaries, votive offerings, monuments raised to commemorate accidents, thunderbolts or sudden deaths. Most certainly, at the yet distant end of my pilgrimage, I should find awaiting me Golgotha's twelve stations of the Cross.

Every hundred yards or so the crucified figure with the crown of thorns saluted me, reinforced my courage, and bade me welcome to the Cross and its torments.

To mortify my flesh I kept telling myself that my wife would not be there, which indeed I already knew. But now that she would not be there to prevent those tempestuous family rows, I should have to endure reprisals from her elderly relatives. When I had last left their house the circumstances had been so painful that I had refused to bid them goodbye. Now I was coming back resigned to the idea of receiving punishment in order that I might regain peace, and by the time I had passed the last village and the last crucifix I was already feeling in anticipation the torments of a condemned man.

My daughter had been a baby of six weeks when I left her; now she was a little girl of two and a half. At our first encounter she studied me with an expression on her face that was serious without being severe, probing my soul to its depths, apparently with the idea of trying to discover whether I had come for her sake or for her mother's. When she felt reassured she allowed me to kiss her and put her tiny arms round my neck.

It was like Dr Faustus's reawakening to an earthly existence, but sweeter and purer. I was never tired of holding the little one in my arms, of feeling her tiny heart beating against mine. When a man loves a child he becomes a woman; he casts off his masculinity and experiences what Swedenborg calls the sexless love of those who dwell in Heaven. This was how I could begin to prepare myself for Heaven. But first of all I must expiate my sins.

Briefly the situation was this. My wife was living elsewhere with a married sister, as her grandmother, who was in possession of all the family property, had sworn that our marriage should be dissolved. The old lady hated me for my ingratitude, and for other reasons too. I was welcome to see the child, who would never cease to be mine, and could remain a guest in my mother-in-law's home for an indefinite period. I accepted the situation as I found it, and

did so gladly. My mother-in-law had forgiven me everything, in the gentle and submissive spirit of a deeply
religious woman.

September 1st, 1896. I have been given the room which
my wife has used during the two years of our separation.
It is here that she suffered while I was undergoing my torments in Paris. My poor, poor wife. Is this our punishment
for the crime we committed in trifling with love?

A strange thing happened yesterday evening at supper.
My little daughter cannot help herself to her food; so, wanting to assist her, I touched her hand, quite gently and with
the kindest intentions. The child gave a shriek, snatched
away her hand, and darted at me a look that was full of
horror. When her grandmother asked her what was the
matter she replied:

'He hurt me.'

I sat there quite taken aback and unable to utter a word.
I had done much harm intentionally; could I now have
come to do it without wishing it?

That night I dreamt that an eagle was pecking my hand
to punish me for some crime. I knew not what.

This morning my daughter came in and greeted me ten-
derly and with loving caresses. She had coffee with me and
I let her spend some time at my writing desk, while I showed
her picture books. We have become really good friends
already, and my mother-in-law is delighted to think she has
someone to help her with the little one's upbringing. In the
evening my little angel insisted that I should watch her
being put to bed and hear her say her prayers. She is a
Catholic, and when she urged me to pray too and to cross
myself, I did not know what to say to her, as I am, of
course, a Protestant.

On September 2nd there was a great commotion. My
mother-in-law's mother who lives down by the river, a few

kilometres from here, had issued orders that I was to be sent away. She wanted me to leave immediately, and threatened to disinherit her daughter if she was not obeyed. My mother-in-law's sister, a most kind-hearted woman, who was herself divorced, invited me to spend some time with her in a neighbouring village until the storm had blown over. With this in mind she came to fetch me. We drove up a two-kilometre-long hill, and when we got to the top we had a view over a circular valley that lay below us, sunk between the surrounding mountains. In the valley itself, numberless hills, spiky with pine trees, rose up like the craters of volcanoes. In the very centre of this funnel-shaped valley lay the village and its church and, high up on a steep rock, the castle, like a medieval fortress in appearance. Interspersed here and there were cornfields and meadows, watered by a stream that cut its way through the gorge beneath the castle.

The sight of this singular landscape, unique of its kind, filled me with sudden amazement. It struck me that I had seen it before, but where, where?

Why, of course, in that zinc bath in the Hôtel Orfila, the picture made by the iron oxide. It was the same landscape, there was no doubt about it.

With this lady, whom I call my aunt, I drove down the hill to the village, where she had three rooms in a large building, which also housed a bakery, a butcher's shop, and a tavern. The house was equipped with a lightning conductor, as lightning had set fire to the loft the previous year. When my kind aunt, who is just as pious as her sister, led me into the room she had set aside for me, I halted on the threshold, as much moved as if I had seen a vision. The walls were painted pink, the very same pink as the flush of dawn that had haunted me on my journey. The curtains too were pink, and the windows were full of flowers that coloured the light as it entered. Everything was exquisitely clean, and the old four-poster bed with its canopy was a couch fit for a virgin. The whole room and the manner in which it was furnished was a poem, the inspiration of a mind that lived only in part on this earth. There was no crucifix, only a figure of the Blessed Virgin and a stoup of holy water to keep off evil spirits.

Shame seized me. I was afraid of defiling this creation of a pure soul who had raised this temple to the Holy Mother over the tomb of her only love, whom she had buried more than ten years before. In halting phrases I tried to refuse her noble offer, but the kind old lady was obstinate.

'It will do you good to sacrifice your earthly love to the love of God and the tenderness you feel for your child. Believe me, this love without thorns will give you peace of heart and a quiet mind and, under the protection of the Virgin, your nights will be tranquil.'

I kissed her hand as a token that I was grateful for the sacrifices she was making, and with feelings of compunction, of which I had not known myself to be capable, I finally accepted her offer, certain that I should be granted a reprieve by the Powers, who seemed to have postponed for the time being the punishments they intended to inflict upon me for my good.

For some reason or other I reserved myself the right to remain one more night in Saxen and put off moving till the morrow. So with my aunt I set off to return to my child, but when we got outside into the street I observed that the rod and wire of the lightning conductor were fixed exactly over the spot where my bed stood.

What devilish bad luck! It made me feel sure I was the chosen object of persecution.

Moreover, I also noticed that the only view I had from my window was of the poor-house, inhabited by released criminals and sick people, some of them at the point of death. What a sorry company and what a gloomy prospect to have before one's eyes!

When I got back to Saxen I packed my things and prepared for my departure. It pained me to have to part from my daughter, of whom I had grown so fond. My resentment was aroused by the cruelty of the old woman in dividing me from my wife and child, and in a fit of rage I shook my clenched fist at an oil painting of her that hung above my bed. A muttered curse accompanied the gesture.

Two hours later a frightful thunderstorm broke over the village, flashes of lightning intersected one another, and rain poured down from the murky heavens.

When I arrived at Klam the next day my roseate room was all ready for me, but on looking up I saw a cloud, shaped like a dragon, hovering over my aunt's house. Furthermore, I learned that a thunderbolt had set fire to a neighbouring village and that the cloudburst had ravaged our parish, destroying haycocks and washing away bridges.

(On September the 10th a very remarkable cyclone had ravaged Paris. It had started, in the middle of a dead calm, in the Luxembourg Gardens behind Saint-Sulpice, had swept across to the Théâtre du Châtelet and the Préfecture de Police, and finally dispersed by the Hôpital de Saint-Louis, after having torn up fifty metres of iron railings. On the subject of this cyclone, and the one that had preceded it in the Jardin des Plantes, my theosophist friend posed me the following questions.

'What are cyclones? Are they waves of hatred, surges of passion, or emissions of psychic power?' to which he later added: 'Are the followers of Papus aware of the manifestations they produce?'

By what appeared to be chance, but was in fact not chance at all, I had written to him and our letters had crossed. As one initiated into the mysteries of the Hindus, I had asked him the following blunt question:

'Can the Hindu sages produce cyclones?'

The fact was that I had begun to suspect that the adepts in magic were persecuting me, either because of my goldmaking or because I had so obstinately refused to be dominated by them. I had also learned, through my reading of Rydberg's *Germanic Mythology* and Hiltén-Cavallius's *Wärend och Wirdarne*,[19] that witches sometimes amused themselves by appearing as a tempest or a short, violent blast of wind.

I mention these things in order to shed some light on my state of mind in the period that preceded my study of the teachings of Swedenborg.

The sanctuary in pink and white was ready, and the Saint would take up residence there with his disciple, who had been summoned from their common fatherland that he might revive the memory of the man who, more than any other born of woman in recent times, was possessed of the gift of grace.

France had despatched Ansgar to baptize the Swedes, and a thousand years later Sweden had despatched Swedenborg to rebaptize the French through the mediation of his disciple Saint-Martin.[20] The order of Saint-Martin well knows the role it plays in founding a new France. It will not undervalue the purport of these words and even less the significance of the thousand years of this millennium.

19. A book on the antiquities and folk-lore of Wärend, a district in southern Sweden, and the Wirdar, its inhabitants.
20. Louis Claude de Saint-Martin, 1743–1803, French theosophist.

9

SWEDENBORG

My mother-in-law and my aunt are identical twins, exactly alike in character, with the same likes and dislikes, so that each appears to be the other's double. If I talked to one of them when the other was not present, the absent one always knew what I had said, so that I was able to confide in either without having to repeat myself. I don't therefore distinguish between them in this account, which is not a novel with pretensions to style and literary form.

On the first evening we spent together I confessed to them my inexplicable experiences, told them of my doubts and my terrors. With an air of satisfaction they both exclaimed:

'Just think of it, you have now reached the stage that we have passed.'

They had started out with the same indifference to religion as myself and they too had studied occultism. From this had come sleepless nights, mysterious happenings followed by mortal anguish, and finally nocturnal attacks, so that they had sometimes been driven to the verge of insanity. Unseen furies had hounded them on ceaselessly, until at last they found a safe harbour: religion. But before they reached it a guardian angel had made his appearance, none other than Swedenborg. They assumed, wrongly, that I was thoroughly familiar with my countryman's teachings and were astonished at my ignorance. These two good woman gave me an old German book, though with a reservation that implied that they were holding something back.

'Take it and read it, but do not be afraid.'

'Afraid of what?'

Alone in my roseate chamber, I opened the book at random and started to read.

I leave it to the reader to imagine what I felt when my eyes fell on a description of Hell, and I recognized in it the landscape around Klam, the landscape of my zinc bath, drawn as if from Nature. The enclosed valley, the pine-clad hills, the dark woods, the stream cutting through the gorge, the village, the church, the poor-house, the manure heaps, the puddles of muck, the pig-sties, they were all there.

Hell? But I had been brought up to regard Hell with the deepest contempt as an imaginary conception, thrown on the scrap-heap along with other out-of-date prejudices. All the same, I could not deny a matter of fact, the only thing I could do was to explain eternal damnation in this new way: we are already in Hell. It is the earth itself that is Hell, the prison constructed for us by an intelligence superior to our own, in which I could not take a step without injuring the happiness of others, and in which my fellow creatures could not enjoy their own happiness without causing me pain.

It is thus that Swedenborg, perhaps without knowing it, depicts our earthly life when meaning to describe Hell.

Hell-fire is our desire to make a name for ourselves in the world. The Powers awaken this desire in us and permit the damned to achieve their objectives. But when the goal is reached and our wish fulfilled, everything is found to be worthless and our victory meaningless. Vanity of vanities, all is vanity. Then, after our first disillusionment, the Powers fan the flame of desire and ambition. Yet it is not unappeased hunger that plagues us most but gratified greed, which leaves us with a loathing for everything. Thus the Devil is made to suffer endless punishment by having every wish granted, and granted instantly, so that he is no longer able to take pleasure in anything.

When I compared Swedenborg's description of Hell with the torments mentioned in the *Germanic Mythology*, I saw that there was an unmistakable similarity between them, but to me personally the essential point was the fact that these two books had overwhelmed me at the same moment. I was in Hell and damnation lay heavy upon me. When I subjected my past life to close scrutiny and thought of my childhood, I could see that even that had been like a prison sentence, an inquisitorial court. The tortures to which an innocent child had been subjected could be explained in no other way than by assuming that we have had a previous existence, from which we have been removed and sent here to suffer the consequences of misdemeanours of which we ourselves have no recollection. Because of a faint-heartedness from which I often suffer, I pushed away into the furthest recesses of my soul the impression that my reading of Swedenborg had made upon me. But the Powers would no longer give me any peace.

When I took a walk in the outskirts of the village, the little stream led me towards the gorge between the two hills. The truly magnificent entrance to it, between masses of fallen rocks, lured me on with a strange and irresistible fascination. The perpendicular side of the rock, upon which the ruined castle stood, came down right to the bottom and formed a gateway to the ravine itself at the spot where the stream became the mill-race. By a freak of nature the top of the rock looked like the head of a Turk, so like, that everyone in the district had noticed it.

Under it, nestling against the wall of rock, was the miller's wagon shed. On the door handle hung a goat's horn, containing the grease for lubricating the waggons, and close by, leaning against the wall, was a besom.

In spite of the fact that all this was perfectly natural and just as it should be, I could not help asking myself what demon it was who had put those two insignia of witches, the goat's horn and the besom, just there and right in my way on this particular morning.

I walked on along the dark, damp path, feeling decidedly uneasy, and pulled up sharply before a wooden building of unusual appearance. It was a low, oblong shed with six oven doors. Ovens!

Good heavens, where had I got to?

The image of Dante's Hell rose up before me, the coffers, the sinners being baked red hot ... and the six oven doors. Was it a nightmare? No, it was a commonplace reality, that was made perfectly plain by a horrible stink, a stream of mire, and a chorus of grunts coming from the pig-sty.

Exactly under the Turk's head the path contracted to a narrow passage between the miller's house and the rock wall. I went on, but in the background I espied an enormous Danish mastiff, the colour of a wolf, the very image of the monster who had guarded the studio in the Rue de la Santé in Paris.

I shrank back a couple of paces, then I remembered Jacques Cœur's motto: 'To a brave heart nothing is impossible', and pushed on into the abyss. Cerberus pretended not to notice me, and I marched on between two rows of low, gloomy houses. A black hen with the comb of a cock. A woman who at a distance seemed beautiful and bore on her forehead a mark like a blood-red half-moon, but who turned out, when I got closer, to be toothless and hideous.

The waterfall and the mill-wheel made a noise that was just like the humming in my ears that had been with me ever since those first nights of agitation in Paris. The mill-hands, white as false angels, handled the machinery like executioners, and the great paddle-wheel performed its Sisyphean task of sending the water running down ceaselessly over and over again.

Further on was the smithy, with the begrimed, naked smiths armed with firetongs, pincers, sledge-hammers, standing in the midst of fire and sparks and glowing iron and melted lead and a din that made my head whirl and my heart thump against my ribs.

Next came the saw-mill and the huge saw, gnashing its teeth as it tortured the giant logs lying on the rack, while from them colourless blood trickled down on to the slimy ground.

The ravine, devastated by pelting rain and whirlwinds, followed the course of the stream. Floods had left a layer of greyish-green slime that covered the sharp pebbles on which I slipped and hurt my feet. I wanted to cross the water-course, but the plank had been carried away and I was brought to a halt under an overhanging precipice where the rock had been undermined. It was threatening to fall on an image of the Virgin, whose divine but slender shoulders alone seemed to be holding it up.

I returned the way I had come, lost in contemplation of a sequence of accidental circumstances which, taken together, formed one great whole, awe-inspiring but by no means supernatural.

I passed eight days and nights of calm in my roseate chamber. My daughter's daily visits brought peace to my soul. She loved me and I her, for she was always kind to me and my relatives indulged me as if I were a poor, spoiled child.

I spent my days reading Swedenborg and was overwhelmed by the realism of his descriptions. I found everything there, all my observations, all my impressions and ideas, so that his visions seemed things actually experienced, truly human documents. There was no question of blind faith. All one had to do was to read and compare what was there with one's own experiences.

It was unfortunate that the volume I now had only contained extracts. It was not until later on, when the complete edition of *Arcana Coelestia* fell into my hands, that I was able to discover the answer to the principal riddles of our spiritual life.

Meanwhile, the conviction that there was a God and that He punished sinners awakened doubts within me, but in the midst of these some lines of Swedenborg's gave me comfort, and immediately my arrogance and my ability to exculpate myself reappeared. One evening therefore, when I was making my usual confession to my mother-in-law, I said to her:

'Do you really believe I am damned?'

'No, but all the same I have never before met with a human destiny quite like yours. I am sure that you have not yet found the true path which will lead you to God.'

'But,' I replied, 'do you remember Swedenborg's maxims for reaching Heaven? He places first the desire to dominate with some high aim in view. This is the predominant feature of my character, though I have never striven for public honours or absolute power. Next, he puts a love of prosperity and riches, directed to the furtherance of the general good. You know that I have never been interested in profit and despise money. If I make gold, now or at any time, I have given the Powers my solemn promise that anything I may gain thereby shall be devoted to humanitarian, scientific, and religious purposes. Last of all comes conjugal love. Need I tell you that, ever since my youth, any warm sentiments that I have entertained for a woman have all been concentrated round the idea of marriage and family life. If life reserved for me the lot of being married to the widow of a man who was still alive, that is simply an irony of Fate which I cannot comprehend. As for the irregularities of my bachelor life, they do not count.'

The old lady sat for some moments lost in thought, then she said:

'I cannot deny the truth of what you say. When reading your books I have found in them a soul that aimed at the heights but always failed to reach them in spite of itself. There is no doubt that you are being punished for sins you committed in another world. You must have been a great slayer of men in a previous existence, and therefore you will have to suffer the pangs of death a thousand times without actually dying before your penance is completed. Now that you have become devout, on with the good work.'

'Are you trying to tell me that I ought to become a prac-tising Catholic?'

'Of course.'

'But Swedenborg has said that it is wrong to abandon the religion of one's forefathers, as every individual belongs to the spiritual territory in which his people were born.'

'The Catholic religion is a sublime grace which is granted to all who seek it.'

'I am content with something lower. If the worst comes to the worst, I am prepared to stand before the throne behind the Jews and the Mohammedans, who will certainly be there too. I believe in being modest.'

'You are being offered forgiveness. It is your birthright, but you prefer a mess of pottage.'

'The right of primogeniture for the Son of a Servant?[21] That is far, far too great an honour!'

From that moment, rehabilitated by Swedenborg, I began again to imagine that I was Job, the righteous and blameless man, put to the test by the Eternal, in order to demonstrate to the wicked how well an upright man can endure suffering unjustly inflicted.

This conception took a firm hold on my mind and I became puffed out with pious vanity. I boasted of my re-verses as if they had been favours, and I never tired of ex-claiming, 'Look how much I have suffered!' I lamented the

21. The title of Strindberg's autobiography.

good treatment I was receiving at the hands of my relatives. My roseate room was a bitter mockery, people were scoffing at my genuine remorse by loading me with kindnesses and small attentions. Briefly, I was one of the chosen; Swedenborg had said so, and thus, feeling assured of the protection of the Eternal, I challenged the demons.

On the eighth day of my stay in the roseate room we received news that the old great-grandmother down by the banks of the Danube had fallen ill. She was suffering from some ailment of the liver accompanied by vomiting, insomnia, and nightly heart attacks. The aunt with whom I was staying was called to her bedside, so I was invited to return to my mother-in-law's home in Saxen.

When I objected to this, on the grounds that the old lady had forbidden it, I was told that she had revoked her expulsion order and that I was free to stay where I pleased.

I was greatly surprised that such a spiteful woman should suddenly change her mind, but did not dare to ascribe this favourable turn of events to the calamity that had befallen her.

The next day I was told that the sick woman was worse. My mother-in-law gave me a bunch of flowers from her mother as a token of reconciliation, and told me that the old lady imagined that there was a snake in her abdomen and had other fanciful ideas of a like nature.

We learned later that the sick woman had been robbed of 2,000 marks and that she suspected her confidential maid. The latter was so deeply indignant at being wrongfully suspected that she was threatening to bring an action against her mistress for slander. So now this helpless invalid, who had withdrawn from the world in order that she might die in peace, had not even a tranquil home.

Every messenger who came from her house brought us flowers, fruit, game, pheasants, chickens, or pike.

Was it divine justice that had smitten her, and did the sick woman realize it? Did she remember that she had once driven me out on to the highway that had finally led to the hospital? Or was she perhaps superstitious? Did she think I had the power to bewitch her and were all these gifts merely burnt-offerings laid at the feet of the sorcerer to appease his thirst for revenge?

Unfortunately, just at that time I received a book on magic from Paris. From it I learned more of the practice called bewitchment. Its author warned his readers not to imagine that they were free from blame if they merely avoided using the magic arts that aim at causing injury. They must keep guard over their evil desires, which are quite sufficient to produce an effect on somebody, even if such a person is not actually present.

This information had a twofold consequence. In the first place, it pricked my conscience about the present situation, since in a fit of rage I had muttered curses and raised my fist at the old lady's portrait, and next it revived my former suspicion that I myself was secretly being made the object of nefarious practices.

On one hand remorse, on the other fear; these two mill-stones began to grind me to powder.

This is the picture Swedenborg paints of Hell. The damned being is lodged in an enchantingly beautiful palace, finds life there sweet, and believes that he is among the chosen. One by one all the delights begin to vanish like smoke, and the wretched creature finds that he is shut up in a miserable hovel, ringed round with excrement (note the sequel).

Farewell, roseate chamber! When I entered the large room adjoining that of my mother-in-law I felt in my bones that my stay there would not be a long one. In actual fact, all the trifles that can poison one's existence now conspired to destroy the peace that my work demanded. The floor-boards rocked beneath my feet, the chair was tottery, the table wobbled, the commode swayed, the bed creaked and the rest of the furniture shook when I walked about the room. The lamp smoked; the ink-pot neck was too narrow, so that the penholder got inky. This was a country mansion that reeked of dung, filth, sulphuretted hydrogen, sulphate of ammonia, and carbon disulphate. The hubbub from the cows, the pigs, the calves, the hens, the turkeys, and the doves went on all day long. Flies and wasps annoyed me by day and mosquitoes by night.

There was hardly anything to be bought at the grocer's shop in the village. For lack of anything better, I had to make do with what ink they had; it was carnation pink. Another strange thing, a packet of cigarette papers included, among a hundred white, one that was pink. Pink! It was like being roasted over a slow fire, and, used though I was to enduring great afflictions, I still suffered immoderately from these paltry pin-pricks, all the more because my mother-in-law thought I was dissatisfied in spite of her attempts to meet my every wish.

September 17th. Woke up in the night and heard the village clock strike thirteen times. Instantly I became aware of the usual electric sensations, also of a noise in the attic above me.

September 19th. Went up to investigate the attic, where I found a dozen spinning-wheels that made me think of electric machines. I opened an enormous chest, empty except for five sticks, painted black. What they were intended for I did not know, but they were arranged on the bottom of the chest to form a pentagram. Who has played this trick on me and what does it mean? I do not dare to inquire and the mystery remains unsolved.

In the night a fearful storm raged between twelve and

two o'clock. Usually the fury of the storm abates in a short time and it moves away, but this one remained over my village for two solid hours, and I am sure that it was an attack on me personally, that each flash was aimed at me but failed to hit the mark.

Every evening my mother-in-law used to give me an account of current events in the neighbourhood. What a vast collection of domestic and other tragedies! Acts of adultery, divorces, lawsuits between kinsfolk, murders, thefts, rapes, incestuous relationships, slanders. The castles and the villas, as well as the cottages, housed wretches of every description, and I never took a walk along the roads without thinking of Swedenborg's Hell. Beggars, lunatics of both sexes, the sick and the crippled, filled the ditches beside the highway, kneeling at the foot of a crucifix, or before an image of the Virgin or a martyr.

At night those unfortunates who suffered from insomnia or nightmare used to wander about in the fields or the woods, trying to reach a pitch of exhaustion that would give them back the power of sleep. Among these afflicted creatures were people from the upper classes, well-educated women – why, there was even a parish priest!

Quite close to our house was a convent that served as a place of detention for fallen women. It was in fact a real gaol, governed by the strictest rules. In the winter, in a temperature of twenty degrees of frost, the prisoners had to sleep in their cells on the icy flagstones and, as fires were forbidden, their hands and feet were covered with broken chilblains.

Among these women was one who had sinned with a priest, a mortal sin. Ground down by remorse and reduced to despair, she had run to her father-confessor, but he had refused to confess her or to give her the sacrament, as the penalty for mortal sin is damnation. Then the wretched woman had lost her reason and imagined she was already dead. She wandered about from village to village, calling upon the priesthood to be merciful and let her be buried in consecrated ground. Excommunicated and hunted, she went hither and thither baying like a stag, and when they met her people would cross themselves and say, 'There goes the damned one!'

No one had any doubt that her soul was already in everlasting fire, while her wraith roamed about the earth, a wandering corpse, to serve as a terrifying example.

I was also told of a man possessed by a devil who had changed the unfortunate creature's character and forced him to go about uttering blasphemies against his will. After looking for an exorcist for a long time, at last they found a young Franciscan monk, a virgin and well known for his purity of heart. He prepared himself for his task by fasts and penances and, when the great day arrived, the possessed man was led to the church, where he confessed before the whole congregation. *Coram populo.* Then the young monk went to work with prayers and invocations from morning till late at night, when he at last succeeded in ousting the Devil. The latter fled in a manner so horrifying that the spectators never dared to tell of it. A year later the Franciscan died.

Such stories, and others that were even worse, strengthened my conviction that this district was predestined to be a place of penance, and that there was some mystic correspondence between this country and the places in which Swedenborg locates the hells he describes. Had he visited this part of lower Austria, and had he drawn his hells from the life in the manner of Dante, who described the district south of Naples?

After fourteen days, during which I worked and studied, I was again wrenched from my lair. With the approach of autumn, my aunt and my mother-in-law both wanted to move to Klam, so we broke up camp. In order to preserve my independence I rented a little cottage consisting of two rooms and a kitchen, quite close to where my daughter was living.

On the evening of the day on which I took possession of my new dwelling I experienced fearful physical distress, as if the very atmosphere were poisoned. I went down to see my mother and said: 'If I sleep up there tonight you will find me dead in my bed tomorrow. Shelter a homeless man for one night, dear Mother.'

The roseate room was immediately put at my disposal, but good heavens! what a transformation had been effected there since my aunt moved out! Black furniture, a library of empty shelves like so many gaping mouths, the flowers gone from the windows, a cast-iron stove, tall, narrow, black as a spectre, and decorated with gruesome and fantastic shapes, salamanders, and dragons. It struck such a discordant note that I felt quite sick. In fact everything was getting on my nerves, because I am a man of very regular habits and like to live by the clock. Though I made every effort to conceal how upset I was, my mother knew how to read my hidden thoughts.

'Always dissatisfied, my child.'

She did her best, and more than that, to please me, but a spirit of discord always put a spoke in the wheel, and nothing seemed to mend matters. She tried to remember what were my tastes and habits, but things always went wrong. For instance, there are few things I detest more than calf's brains and browned butter.

'I've got something especially good today, just to please you,' she would say.

And then she would place before me calf's brains and brown butter. I would realize that she had made a mistake

and eat it, but with a reluctance that an affectation of en-
joyment could ill conceal.

'You are not eating anything!'

And she would replenish my plate.

This was too much. Formerly I used to ascribe all my
misfortunes to female malice; but I recognized that this
woman was innocent and told myself it was the Devil.

Ever since my youth my morning walk has been dedi-
cated to meditation as a preparation for the day's work.
I have never allowed anyone to accompany me, not even
my wife.

The fact is that in the morning my mind rejoices in a
state of equilibrium and a feeling of expansion that
approaches ecstasy. I do not walk, I fly. My body becomes
weightless, all my melancholy evaporates and I am pure
spirit. It is for me the hour of inward concentration, the
hour of prayer, of worship.

But now that I must sacrifice everything, renounce myself and my most legitimate preferences, the Powers found
a way to force me to abstain from this last and most sublime pleasure – my little daughter came asking to accompany me.

I tried to put her off with a very affectionate embrace but
she could not understand my excuse that I needed to be
alone with my own thoughts. She started to weep, and as
that made her irresistible I took her with me, but I made
up my mind that I would not allow this abuse of my rights
to continue. Of course a child is enchanting, captivating in
its spontaneity, its light-heartedness, its gratitude for the
least little thing; that is to say if one has nothing else to do.
But when one is preoccupied by one's own thoughts, abs-
tacted or absend-minded, how terribly soul-destroying
a little tot can be, with its endless questions, its fancies and

whims! My little girl, jealous as a lover of my thoughts, just waited for the moment when her chatter would be most likely to ruin a cleverly spun network of ideas. No, of course she did not intend it; I was suffering from my usual delusion of being the victim of a deliberate plot on the part of an innocent little thing.

I climbed slowly, I no longer flew. My soul was captive, my brain empty as a result of the efforts I was making to come down to the level of a child's understanding. What made me suffer, almost to the point of torture, was the searching and reproachful look she gave me when she thought she was being a nuisance and imagined that I did not like her. Her little face darkened, that frank, radiant face of hers; she looked away and withdrew into herself, and I felt deprived of the light that this child had shed on my gloomy soul. I kissed her, carried her in my arms, collected flowers and pebbles for her, cut a switch and pretended to be a cow that she was driving out to graze.

Then she was happy and pleased, and life smiled upon me once more.

I had sacrificed the hour in which I usually rallied my ideas. It was a penance for the evil that, in a moment of delirium, I had been prepared to bring upon this angelic little head.

Fancy being allowed to expiate a crime by making oneself loved! In truth, the Powers are not as cruel as we.

10

EXTRACTS FROM THE DIARY OF A CONDEMNED MAN

October, November 1896.

The Brahmin fulfils his duty to life by putting a child into the world. That done, he goes out into the desert and dedicates himself to solitude and self-abnegation.

My mother.[22] 'Unhappy man, what did you do in your last incarnation to cause Fate to ill-treat you in this way?'

I. 'Guess! Think of a man who first marries another man's wife, as I did. Who then parts from her to marry an Austrian girl, as I did. And then people tear his little Austrian from him, as they have torn mine from me, and their only child is hidden away on the slopes of the Böhmer Wald, as my child has been. Do you remember the hero of my novel *By the Open Sea*, the man who died in such a pitiful way on an island out in the ocean?'[23]

My mother. 'Enough! enough!'

I. 'You do not know that the name of my father's mother was Neipperg . . .'

My mother. 'Hush, unhappy man!'

I. 'And that my little Christine is very like the greatest manslayer of the century, forelock included. Just look at her, the little despot, subjugating men even at the age of two and a half.'

My mother. 'You are mad!'

I. 'Yes. But what about you women? What sinners you must have been since your lot is more cruel than ours! You

22. By 'my mother' Strindberg means his mother-in-law, whom he called 'Mutter'.
23. Strindberg here suggests that he is a reincarnation of Napoleon.

see how right I am to say that women are our devils. Everyone gets what he deserves.'

My mother. 'True, it is hell twice over to be a woman.'

I. 'And woman, is she not a devil twice over? As for reincarnation, that is a feature of Christian teaching that the priesthood has discarded. Jesus Christ claimed that John the Baptist was a reincarnation of Elijah. Is he to be regarded as an authority or not?'

My mother. 'Of course, but the Roman Catholic Church forbids us to inquire into what is hidden from us.'

I. 'And occultism allows it. Every realm of science is open to us.'

The spirits of discord did their utmost and, in spite of the fact that we were fully aware of the game they were playing and knew that we were both of us blameless, we frequently had misunderstandings that left behind them dregs of bitterness.

On top of this, both sisters began to suspect that my ill-will might have had something to do with their mother's mysterious illness. In view of the interest I had in seeing the obstacle that separated me from my wife removed, they could not dismiss from their minds the quite natural idea that the old lady's death would necessarily give me pleasure. The mere existence of this wish on my part made me odious and I no longer dared to inquire after their mother for fear of being treated as a hypocrite.

The situation was tense, and my old friends wore themselves out by endless discussions about my appearance, my character, my opinions, and the genuineness of my affection for the child. One day they would think of me as a saint, and the cracks in my hands as the stigmata. In actual fact the marks on my palms did look like holes left by large nails, but, in order to remove the idea that I had any claim to saintliness, I said that I was the good thief come down from the cross and making a pilgrimage to win my way to Paradise.

On another day, when there had been further speculation about the enigma I presented, they decided that I must be Robert le Diable. About the same time, one or two things occurred that made me dread that I might be stoned by the populace. I will give you the plain facts. My little Christine was excessively afraid of the chimney-sweep. One evening at supper she suddenly began to scream at the top of her voice and to point at some invisible object behind my chair, crying as she did so :

'Look, there's the sweep!'

My mother, who believes that children and animals are clairvoyant, turned pale. I was frightened too, especially when I saw her making the sign of the cross over the child's head. A deathly silence then followed, and my heart felt heavy within me.

Autumn had come, bringing with it storms, rain, and gloom. In the village and in the poor-house the number of the poverty-stricken, the sick, the dying or the dead increased. At night I used to hear the little bell rung by the choir-boy who headed the procession of the last sacrament. In the daytime the passing-bell would sound from the church tower, and one funeral procession after another would follow in quick succession. Life was deadly dull and dreary. My attacks during the night started again. Intercession was made for me, paternosters were said, the holy-water stoup in my chamber was filled by the priest himself.

'The hand of the Lord rests heavy upon you,' my mother would say, crushing me to earth with these harsh words. And I would bow my head but soon raise it again.

Having a naturally resilient mind and being armed with a deep-rooted scepticism, I managed to shake my spirit free of these dark imaginings and, after reading certain occult works, I persuaded myself that I was being persecuted by elemental and elementary spirits, incubi, lamias, who were trying with all their might to prevent me from finishing my great work on alchemy. In accordance with the instructions of the initiated, I obtained a Dalmatian dagger and felt myself well armed against evil spirits.

A shoemaker in the village, an atheist and a blasphemer, had recently died. He had owned a jackdaw which after his master's death had taken up residence on a neighbour's roof. During the wake the jackdaw had appeared in the room, though none of the people present could explain how it had got in. On the day of the funeral the bird had led the burial procession and at the church-yard had flown down on to the lid of the coffin in the middle of the service. This creature used to follow me along the roads on my morning walks, which made me very uneasy because of the superstitious tendencies of the villagers. On the last day that this happened it flew before me down the village streets uttering horrible cries, interspersed with coarse words that it had learnt from the blasphemer. Then two small birds, a robin and a wagtail, came on the scene and pursued the jackdaw from roof to roof. The jackdaw flew out of the village and settled on the chimney-stack of a cottage. At the very same moment a black rabbit scuttled away in front of the house and disappeared into the grass. A few days later we heard that the jackdaw was dead. It had been killed by some boys who hated it for its thieving ways.

Meanwhile, I spent my days working in my cottage, but it was easy to see that I had for some time been in disgrace with the Powers. When I entered the house I often found the air as heavy as if it had been poisoned, and I had to work with the door and windows open. Clad in a thick cloak and a fur cap, I used to sit at my desk, struggling against the so-called electric attacks that cramped my chest and stabbed me in the back. I often felt as if someone were standing behind my chair. Then I would strike out backwards with my dagger, imagining that I was fighting an enemy. This would go on until five o'clock in the evening. if I tried to work on after this hour, the struggle became truly formidable and, utterly worn out, I would light my lantern and go down to be with my mother and the child. On only one occasion did I manage to prolong the struggle until six o'clock in order to finish an article on chemistry. Then I had to sit in a double, even a treble, cross draught, as in spite of the open window the air in my room was thick and oppressive. A ladybird was crawling about on a bunch of flowers. Her colours, yellow spotted with black, were those of Austria, and she was feeling her way and trying to get down. Finally, she dropped on to my writing-paper and flapped her wings, just as the cock on the top of Notre-Dame-des-Champs in Paris had done. After that she crawled along the edge of the manuscript, reached my right hand and climbed on to it. She looked at me and then flew towards the window. The compass on my desk showed that she had set off northwards.

'Good,' thought I, 'to the North, then, but at my leisure and when it suits me. Until I get further orders I shall stay where I am.'

After the clock had struck six it was impossible to remain in that haunted place a moment longer. Unknown forces lifted me from my chair and I had to shut up shop.

On All Soul's Day, at about three o'clock in the afternoon, the sun was shining and the weather was calm. The procession of the villagers, led by the priests with banners and music, marched to the churchyard to salute the departed. The church bells began to toll. Suddenly, without any preliminaries, without a warning cloud in the pale-blue sky, a storm broke loose. The banners flapped and beat against the poles, the clothes of the men and women in the procession tossed about in the wind, whirling clouds of dust rose up, the trees bowed and bent. It was a truly miraculous occurrence.

I dreaded the coming night, and my mother was fore-warned of its dangers. She gave me an amulet to wear round my neck. It was a Madonna and a cross of sanctified wood, which had once formed part of the beam of a church more than a thousand years old. I accepted it as a precious gift kindly offered, but some remnant of the religion of my ancestors forbade me to hang it round my neck.

At about eight o'clock we had our supper. An ominous silence reigned over our little circle round the lamp. It was pitch dark outside, the trees were hushed, all was silent. Then came a sudden gust of wind, just one. It forced its way through the chinks in the window uttering a wail like the sound of a Jew's harp. Then it was over.

My mother looked at me with horror and clasped the child in her arms. I instantly realized what her glance implied:

'Leave this place, doomed man, and bring not the wrath of demons upon innocent heads!'

My world collapsed in ruins. My last remaining happiness, that of being with my daughter, had been snatched from me, and, as we sat there speechless and mournful, I bade a silent farewell to life.

When the meal was over I retired to my room, once roseate, now black, and prepared for a nocturnal struggle; for I felt I was being menaced. By whom? I did not know, but I challenged the Unseen whoever he might be, the Devil or the Eternal, and prepared to wrestle with him as Jacob did with God.

There came a knock at the door. It was my mother, who had had a premonition that this was going to be a bad night for me and had come to invite me to sleep on the sofa in her sitting-room.

'The nearness of the child will save you,' she said.

I thanked her, but assured her that there was no danger and that I had nothing to fear so long as my conscience was clear.

She bade me good night with a smile.

I donned my cloak, my cap, and my boots, in which to do battle, firmly determined to sleep fully dressed, and ready to die like a bold warrior who, having faced life bravely, defies death. But towards eleven o'clock the air in the room began to thicken and a deadly anxiety got the better of my courage. I opened the window. The draught threatened to put out the lamp and I shut it again. The lamp began to sing, to moan, to whine. Then all was silent.

Nearby a dog set up a miserable howl, a sound that popular tradition interprets as a funeral chant.

I looked out of the window. Only the Great Bear was visible. Down below in the poor-house a single candle was still alight; an old woman was stooping over her work, awaiting release or perhaps dreading sleep and dreams.

Tired out, I lay down on my bed and tried to sleep. Immediately the same old game began again. An electric current sought out my heart, my lungs ceased to function, I had either to get up or die. I sat down on a chair, too utterly exhausted to read, and remained sitting there in a stupor for half an hour.

Then, having made up my mind that I would wander about until day broke, I went out. The night was dark, the village was asleep, but the dogs were not, and, at a summons from one, the whole pack swarmed round me, their gaping jaws and gleaming eyes forcing me to beat a retreat.

When I got back and opened the door of my room it seemed to me that the whole place was filled by animate and hostile beings. There was not a bit of room anywhere, and I felt as if I were pushing my way through a crowd of people as I tried to reach my bed. Resigned, and resolved to die, I sank upon it. But at the last moment, just as I was suffocating in the grip of the invisible vulture, someone pulled me from my bed and the hunt of the furies was on again. Defeated, all my courage gone, driven frantic, I yielded to the Unseen and abandoned the battlefield of this unequal struggle.

I tapped on the door of the sitting-room on the other side of the passage. My mother, who was still up and rapt in prayer, opened it.

The expression that came on to her face as soon as she saw me gave me a feeling of deep aversion for myself.

'What is it you want, my child?'

'I want to die and then to be burned, or rather to be burned alive.'

Not another word did I need to utter. She had understood me, but, even as she struggled against her feeling of dread, compassion and pious mercy got the upper hand and she herself made the sofa ready for me, before retiring to the inner room where she slept with the child.

By chance, always the same satanic chance, the sofa was exactly opposite the window and, as the same chance would have it, the window had no blind. The black window, giving on to the dark of night, stared me in the face, and, what was more, it was through this very window that the gust of wind had whistled that evening as we sat at table.

At the end of my tether, I sank on to my couch, cursing this omnipresent, inescapable chance that pursued me with the obvious intention of making me the victim of persecution mania.

For five minutes I was allowed to rest, my eyes fixed on the square of black. Then the unseen spectre came creeping upon my body and I got up. I remained standing in the middle of the room like a statue for I do not know how long, transformed into a stylite, sleeping or waking by turns.

Who was it who had given me the strength with which to suffer? Who was it who denied me death, which would deliver me from my tortures?

Was it He, the Lord over life and death, to whom I had given offence when, after reading the work *On the Delight of Dying*, I had experimented with suicide, believing myself ripe for eternal life?

Was I Phlegyas, doomed for his arrogance to suffer the agonies of Tartarus, or Prometheus, punished by the devouring vulture because he had revealed the secrets of the Powers to mortal man?

(As I write these things I am reminded of the scene from the story of the Passion where the soldiers spat in Jesus' face and some buffeted him and others smote him with the palms of their hands, saying as they did so, 'Prophesy unto us, thou Christ, who is he that struck thee?'

The friends of my youth should be able to remember an orgiastic evening in Stockholm on which the author of this book played the soldier's part.)

'Who is he that struck thee?' That was the unanswered question, the doubt, the uncertainty, the mystery; in a word, my Hell.

My constant thought was, 'If he would but reveal himself I would wrestle with him and bid him defiance.'

But this was just what he avoided, in order to drive me mad, to scourge me with the bad conscience, which sufficed in itself to make me look for enemies on all sides. Enemies, yes, those who had been injured by my ill will;

and each time I tracked down a new enemy it was because my conscience had been pricked.

The next day I was awakened, after a few hours' sleep, by the sound of my little Christine's chirruping, and all was forgotten. I applied myself to my usual occupations, which were going well. Everything I wrote was accepted immediately, proof enough that my sound sense and my intellect were unimpaired.

At the same time the newspapers circulated a rumour that an American scientist had discovered a way of turning silver into gold. This cleared me of the suspicion that I was a practitioner of the black art, a madman, or a charlatan. It was at this moment that my friend the theosophist, who had been sending me pecuniary assistance, made efforts to win me over to his sect.

When he sent me Madame Blavatsky's *The Secret Doctrine* he did not succeed in concealing his anxiety to know my opinion of it. This put me in something of a dilemma, as I suspected that our friendly relations depended on how I answered him. *The Secret Doctrine*, that hotchpotch of all the so-called occult theories, that rehash of every scientific heresy, ancient and modern, utterly worthless when the lady is expressing her own foolish and conceited ideas, and only interesting for the quotations it contains from little-known authors, helpful because of the conscious or unconscious deceptions it perpetrates, and because of the stories it tells about the existence of Mahatmas. The work of a virago, who wants to beat men at their own game and who plumes herself that she has dethroned natural science, religion, and philosophy, and set up a priestess of Isis on the altar of the Crucified.

With the reserve and consideration due to a friend, I gave him my views, telling him candidly that the idea of the collective deity, Karma, did not appeal to me, and that for this reason I could not join a sect that denied the existence of a personal God, the only belief that satisfied my religious needs. This was the confession of faith that was demanded of me and, though I was convinced that my words would bring about a rupture, and the consequent withdrawal of my allowance, I had to speak my mind.

This changed my upright and noble-minded friend into a vengeful demon. He flung a sentence of excommunication at me, threatened me with the occult powers, intimidated me by hints of some form of coercion, and uttered prophecies like some heathen, sacrificial priest. He concluded by summoning me to appear before an occult tribunal, and swore that I should never forget the 13th of November.

I was in a painful predicament. I had lost a friend and was threatened by want. By a devilish piece of bad luck, just as we were in the middle of our postal battle, a most unfortunate thing happened.

L'Initiation published an article of mine in which I criticized the prevailing astronomical systems. A few days later Tisserand, the director of the Paris Observatory, died. In an excess of jocularity I hinted at a connection between these two events, recalling the fact that Pasteur had died the day after the distribution of my book *Sylva Sylvarum*. My friend the theosophist had no sense of humour. Being the most credulous man in the world and perhaps better initiated than I into the black art, he was led to say that he believed that I was practising bewitchment.

Imagine my terror when, after the letter that closed our correspondence, the most distinguished of Sweden's astronomers died from apoplexy. My anxiety increased, not without reason. To be accused of practising sorcery puts one in danger of one's life, and 'he who slays such a man need fear no punishment.'

To add to my alarm, within the space of one month no fewer than five more or less well-known astronomers died, one after another.

The man I stood in fear of was a fanatic, whom I credited with the cruelty of a druid, combined with the Hindu sorcerer's alleged power of killing at a distance.

A new Hell of agonizing fear! From that day I forgot the demons and turned my mind entirely towards the fatal intrigues of the theosophists and the Indian magicians, gifted with unbelievable powers, whom they were reputed to have among them. Now I really felt that I was doomed to die, and I put into a sealed envelope a paper denouncing my assassins in the event of my being overtaken by sudden death. Then I waited.

Ten kilometres further east along the Danube lay the little town of Grein, the most important place in the district. Towards the end of November, when full winter had already set in, word was brought to me that a stranger from Zanzibar had taken up his abode there, calling himself a tourist. This was quite enough to awaken all the apprehensions and dark imaginings to which a sick mind is prone. I tried to find out more about this stranger, whether he really was an African, what he was doing there, where he came from.

No information was to be had. A veil of secrecy enveloped this unknown man, who haunted me night and day. In my great need, and always in the spirit of the Old Testament, I called upon the Eternal for His protection and for vengeance upon my enemies.

The Psalms of David were those that best expressed my thoughts and old Jacob was my God. The eighty-sixth psalm was the one I had most in mind and I repeated it time after time.

EXTRACTS FROM THE DIARY OF A CONDEMNED MAN

O God, the proud are risen up against me
And the congregation of violent men have sought after my soul,
And have not set thee before them.

Shew me a token for good;
That they which hate me may see it, and be ashamed,
Because thou, Lord, hast holpen me, and comforted me.

It was a token I was invoking, and mark, reader, how soon my prayer was heard.

II

THE VOICE OF THE ETERNAL

Winter came, bringing skies of yellowish grey, unrelieved for several weeks by so much as a glint of sunshine. The muddy lanes made walking impossible, the fallen leaves were rotting, the whole of Nature stank of disintegration and decay.

The autumn slaughtering had begun. All day long the grey heavens rang with the piteous cries of the victims. One walked through blood between the carcasses.

It was all dreadfully depressing, and I inflicted my low spirits on the two sisters of charity, who cherished me as if I had been their ailing child. My poverty, which I had to conceal, and my fruitless attempts to avert approaching disaster, made me even more downcast.

Besides, my friends wanted me to leave them for my own sake. They considered my isolated existence was an unnatural life for a man. Moreover, they both agreed that I ought to see a doctor.

I waited in vain for the necessary money from my homeland; so, to prepare myself for an escape on foot, if it came to that, I tramped the main roads.

> I am like a pelican of the wilderness.
> I am become as an owl of the waste places.

My presence was a torment to my relatives, and had it not been for the child's affection for me they would have turned me out. Now that the mud and snow made it impossible for her to walk, I used to carry the little one in my arms along the lanes. I climbed hills and scrambled over rocks, until the old ladies begged me to be more cautious.

'You are undermining your health, you will end up

with consumption and bring about your death if you go on like this.'

'What a sweet death that would be!'

We were sitting at dinner on the 20th of November, a grey, gloomy, abominable day. I was completely burnt out after a sleepless night and repeated struggles with my invisible foes, and I cursed my life and bewailed the absence of the sun.

My mother predicted that I should not regain my health until after Candlemas, when the sun would return to us.

'My only ray of sunshine is here,' I said, pointing to my little Christine, who was sitting opposite me.

At that very moment the clouds, that had been growing ever heavier for the past weeks, suddenly parted and a beam of sunshine penetrated the room, lighting up my face, the tablecloth, and the china.

'Look, the sun, Papa! It's the sun!' cried the child, clasping her hands together.

I rose from the table, confused, a prey to the most conflicting emotions. Was it chance? No, I said to myself. The miracle, the token? No, that would be too much to expect for one so out of favour as myself. Besides, the Eternal does not concern Himself with the insignificant affairs of a worm.

Yet this beam of sunshine remained with me like a broad smile in the face of my discontent.

During the two minutes that elapsed while I walked to my cottage, the clouds banked up into the strangest shapes, and in the east, where they had drifted away, the sky was green – emerald green, like a meadow in midsummer.

I remained standing in my room, waiting for an indefinable something, lost in a feeling of contrition that was tranquil and unmixed with fear.

Then, unheralded by lightning, came a clap of thunder, a single clap, just above my head. My first feeling, as I waited for the usual rain and storm, was fear. Nothing happened. Complete calm reigned. It was all over.

Why, I asked myself, did I not prostrate and humble myself before the voice of the Eternal?

Because when the Almighty deigns to speak to an insect, and that in a majestic setting, the insect grows in stature, he is inflated by the honour conferred on him and his pride whispers to him that he must be a particularly worthy individual. The truth is that I believed myself to be the Eternal's equal, believed that I formed an integral part of His personality, emanated from His being, was an organ of His organism. He needed me in order to manifest Himself, otherwise He would have made the lightning destroy me on the spot.

What had caused such boundless conceit in a mortal? Did I originate from the beginning of time, when the rebel angels united in revolting against a ruler who was content to reign over a realm of slaves? Was that why my pilgrimage on earth had been like a running of the gauntlet, in which the meanest of the mean had rejoiced in whipping me with rods, spitting on me, and defiling me?

There was not one among all imaginable humiliations that I had not endured, yet, all the same, my pride had grown continuously, in exact proportion to my abasement. What was the meaning of this? Jacob, wrestling with the Eternal and emerging from the struggle, somewhat disabled, but with the honours of war. Job, put to the test and persevering in justifying himself in the face of punishment unjustly inflicted?

Shaken by all these incoherent ideas, I was forced by weariness to give in. My inflated ego collapsed and dwindled, so that the incident that had brought about all these speculations was reduced to a mere nothing, a clap of thunder in November!

But the echo of that clap of thunder began to resound

again and, once more overcome by ecstasy, I opened the Bible at random, praying to the Lord as I did so that He would speak yet louder so that I might understand.

My eyes instantly fell upon the following verses from the Book of Job.

> Wilt thou even disannul my judgement?
> Wilt thou condemn me, that thou mayest be justified?
> Or hast thou an arm like God?
> *And canst thou thunder with a voice like Him?*

I doubted no longer. The Eternal had spoken.

'Eternal! What do you demand of me? Speak, and your servant will harken unto your words.'

No answer!

It is well. I will humble myself before the Eternal who has deigned to humble Himself before His servant. But bend my knee to the masses or to the mighty, that I will never do.

That evening my kind mother greeted me in a manner that is still a mystery to me. She watched me surreptitiously, but with a searching glance, as if she wanted to discover what sort of an impression that majestic and spectacular performance had made.

'Did you hear it?' she asked.

'Yes, indeed. It was very strange, thunder in winter!'

At least she no longer believed that I was one of the damned.

12

HELL LET LOOSE

At this same time, in order to confuse me yet further as to the true nature of the mysterious illness from which I was suffering, a number of *L'Evénement* circulated the following report:

The unfortunate Strindberg brought his misogyny with him to Paris, but it was not long before he was obliged to run away. Since he left, all those like him have held their tongues when confronted by the flag of feminism. They do not want to share the fate of Orpheus, whose head was torn from his body by the Thracian Bacchants.

So, it was true that someone had laid a trap for me when I was living in the Rue de la Clef; true too that an attempt had been made on my life and that it was the direct cause of the malady of which I still had symptoms. Oh, those women! Their spite was evidently due to the article I had written about the feminist pictures painted by my woman-worshipping friend the Dane. At last I had something factual, a tangible reality, something that would set me free from all those terrifying fears of a mental disorder.

I hastened to my mother with the good news, saying:

'Just look here, this should show you that I am not mad.'

'No, of course you are not, you are only ill. The doctor says you should take up some bodily activity, like chopping wood for example.'

'Is that going to dispose me to like women or the reverse?'

My retort had been too hasty and it made a breach between us. I had forgotten that a female saint is after all a woman – that is to say, man's enemy.

I pushed them all out of my mind, the Russians, the Rothschilds, the magicians, the theosophists, even the Eternal. I was the victim Job. I was blameless. The women had wanted to kill the Orpheus, who had written *Sylva Sylvarum*, the man who had revived the dead natural sciences. I was lost in a forest of indecision. I pushed aside the idea, so recently conceived, that there had been a supernatural intervention by the Powers with some high aim in view. I made no efforts to fill out the details of the bare fact that an attempt had been made on my life. I did not try to discover who the actual originators of the crime had been.

Thirsting for revenge, I began to prepare a letter of denunciation, addressed to the Préfecture of Police in Paris, and another to the Paris Press. Fortunately a well-timed change occurred in the course of events, putting an end to this boring drama, which was threatening to turn into a farce.

One yellowish-grey day, after dinner at one o'clock, my little Christine insisted on accompanying me to my cottage, to which I was about to betake myself for my usual afternoon nap. She was irresistible and I gave way to her pleading.

Once up there, my Christine demanded pen and paper, then she issued orders for picture books, wanted me to look at them too, to explain them and draw things for her.

'Don't go to sleep, Papa.'

Tired, completely exhausted, I could not imagine why I obeyed the child, but there was something in the tone of her voice that I could not resist.

Then an organ-grinder began to play a waltz, just outside the door. I suggested to the child that she should dance with her nurse, who had come with her. Attracted by the sound of the music, the neighbour's children came in too, and soon, after the organ-grinder had been invited into the kitchen, there was an improvised ball going on in my hall.

This went on for an hour and my dejection disappeared. But, in order to take my mind off what was going on, also to ward off my desire to sleep, I took up my Bible, always my oracle, and opening it at random I read:

Now the spirit of the Lord had departed from Saul, and an evil spirit from the Lord troubled him. And Saul's servants said unto him, Behold now, an evil spirit from God troubleth thee. Let our Lord now command thy servants, which are come before thee, to seek out a man who is a cunning player on the harp; and it shall come to pass, when the evil spirit from God is upon thee, that he shall play with his hand and thou shalt be well.

An evil spirit! That was just what I had suspected.

Then in the middle of all this merriment, my mother came to look for the child and, seeing the dance that was going on, she stood amazed. She told me that quite suddenly, within the last hour, a woman of good family had gone mad.

'What form does her madness take?'

'She dances, that old lady dances, dances indefatigably, dressed like a bride. She imagines herself to be Burger's Leonora.'

'She dances, do you say? Anything else?'

'Yes, she weeps, too, and fears that Death is coming to fetch her.'

The thing that made this horrible situation worse was that the woman in question had once lived in this cottage and that her husband had died in the very room in which the dance was in progress.

Explain this if you can, you doctors, psychiatrists, and psychologists, or confess that science is bankrupt.

My little daughter had exorcized the Devil, and the evil

spirit, driven away by her innocence, had rushed into the old woman, who had boasted that she was a free-thinker.

The dance of death went on all night, the lady's friends watching over her and shielding her from the attacks of her assailant. As she denied the existence of evil spirits, she called him Death. Yet at times she asserted that she was being persecuted by her dead husband.

My departure was postponed and, in order to regain my strength after so many nights without sleep, I moved into a bedroom in my aunt's flat on the other side of the street. So I left the roseate chamber. (What an extraordinary co-incidence that the torture-chamber in Stockholm in the good old days was called the Rose Chamber!)

I passed my first night in a tranquil room. The white-washed walls were covered with pictures of male and female saints and over my bed hung a crucifix.

But on the second night the spirits started their old games again. I lit candles, meaning to spend some time reading. An ominous silence reigned, and I could hear the beating of my heart. Then I was disturbed by a little sound like a crackle of electricity.

What could it be?

A very large drip that had formed on the candle had fallen to the ground. Nothing else, but this was always regarded as a harbinger of death in my country. 'Here goes for death, then,' thought I. After I had read for a quarter of an hour I wanted to use my handkerchief, which I had put under the bolster. It was not there, but when I looked I found it on the floor. I bent down to pick it up. Something fell on my head and, when I ran my fingers through my hair, what should I find but another piece of candlewax.

Instead of being alarmed, I could not refrain from smil-ing, so absurd did the incident appear. Smile at death! That would not be possible if it were not that life itself is so ridiculous. Such a lot of fuss for so little result. It may even be that in the recesses of our souls there lurks a vague notion that everything here on earth is but a masquerade, a semblance, an illusion and that the Gods make merry over our suffering.

High up, above the rock on which the castle stands, there rises one crag that dominates all the others and provides a view-point overlooking the inferno-like gorge. The approach to it is through a grove of oak trees that are perhaps a thousand years old. Legend has it that it was a druids' grove, as mistletoe is found there in abundance, growing everywhere on lime and apple trees. The path rises steeply above this parkland and passes through a dark wood of pines.

I had tried to reach this summit many times, but something unforeseen had always happened to drive me back. Now it would be a roe-buck who broke the silence by an unexpected leap, now a hare, that was quite unlike any ordinary hare, or a butcher-bird, uttering its alarming cry. On my last morning, the eve of my departure, I defied all hindrances, and, after making my way through the dark and gloomy pine wood, I climbed right up to the very top. From there I had a splendid view over the valley of the Danube and the Styrian Alps. When I had left that dark funnel of a valley below me I breathed freely for the first time for ages. The sun shone upon the surrounding country with its endless horizons, and on the white crest of the Alps that merged into the clouds. It was as beautiful as Heaven. Could it be that the earth contained both Heaven and Hell and that there was in fact no other place for punishment or reward? Perhaps. One thing is certain. When I think of the loveliest moments of my life I remember them as heavenly, the worst as hellish.

Had the future still in store for me any hours or minutes of this happiness, which cannot be purchased except by anxious care and a tolerably clear conscience?

I lingered on up there, little inclined to descend again into the vale of suffering, and as I walked over the plateau behind the crag to admire the earth's beauty I noticed that the isolated crag that forms the actual summit had been hewn by Nature into the shape of an Egyptian sphinx. On the gigantic head was a cairn, topped by a little stick with a bit of white linen fastened to it as a flag.

I was seized by an uncontrollable desire to take the flag away with me, and, ignoring the danger and without pausing to consider why it had been put there, I stormed the precipice and captured the flag. At the same moment, from the slopes beside the Danube, I heard the unexpected strains of a wedding march, accompanied by joyous singing. It was a bridal procession, invisible to me, but recognizable by the customary rifle-shots.

Childish enough, and sufficiently unhappy to be able to extract the poetry from the most everyday and the most natural events, I accepted this as a good omen.

Very unwillingly, and with lagging footsteps, I descended into that valley of pain and death, of sleepless nights and demons. My little Beatrice[24] was waiting for me and for the mistletoe I had promised her. The mistletoe, that green twig that grows in snowy places and should really be cut with a golden sickle.

For a long time the old great-grandmother had been expressing a wish to see me, whether to bring about a reconciliation or, since she was a visionary and a clairvoyant, for reasons which may have had roots in the occult, I did not know. I had made various excuses whereby to postpone seeing her, but when the date for my departure was fixed

24. Strindberg is thinking of himself as Dante, his daughter as Beatrice.

my mother insisted that I must visit the old lady to bid her farewell, probably for the last time on this side of the grave.

On the 26th of November, a cold clear day, my mother, the child and I set off on our pilgrimage to the family mansion beside the Danube.

We established ourselves at the inn and my mother-in-law went on to her mother's house to announce my visit. While I waited for her to return I wandered about in the fields and groves which I had not seen for two years. Memories crowded upon me, the image of my wife was intermingled with everything. Frost and autumn rain had left a trail of devastation; there was not a flower, not a blade of grass, where we two had once plucked all the flowers of spring, and summer, and autumn. In the afternoon I was taken to see the old lady, who was living in the summer cottage belonging to the villa, the place in which my child had been born. We met with decorum, but without warmth. It appeared that a scene reminiscent of the return of the prodigal had been expected. I feel nothing but repugnance for demonstrations of that kind so I confined myself to recalling memories of a vanished paradise. My wife and I had painted the door and the window-frames in honour of little Christine's arrival in the world. I had planted with my own hands the roses and clematis that adorned the outside walls. The path that crossed the garden had been cleared by me. But the walnut tree that I had planted the day after Christine's birth, that had vanished. The 'Tree of Life', as we had called it, was dead.

Two years, two eternities, had passed since we said our farewells, she on the bank, I in the boat that was to carry me as far as Linz on my way to Paris.

Which of us was responsible for the rupture? I was, I who had murdered my own love and hers. Farewell, white house of Dornach, field of thorns and of roses. Farewell, Danube. I comfort myself with the thought that you were never more than a dream, brief as summer, sweeter than reality, and that I do not mourn you.

We spent the night at the inn. At my urgent request my mother and the child stayed there with me to preserve me from a further tussle with death, of which, thanks to the sixth sense that had developed in me during six consecutive months of martyrdom, I had a premonition.

At ten o'clock that evening a gust of wind started to rattle the door that opened on to the passage. I put in wooden wedges. It was no use, it went on rattling. After that the wind whistled through the window, the stove howled like a dog, the whole house rocked like a ship.

I could not sleep. At times it was my mother who moaned, at others the child who cried.

In the morning my mother was absolutely worn out by lack of sleep and other troubles that she concealed from me.

'Go, my child,' she said. 'I have had enough of the fumes of Hell.'

So I went, on a pilgrimage to the North, there to face the fire of the enemy at yet another station on the road to atonement.

13

PILGRIMAGE AND ATONEMENT

There are ninety towns in Sweden, but it was to the one I most abhor that the Powers had condemned me.[25]

I began by visiting the doctors.

The first labelled my trouble neurasthenia, the second angina pectoris, the third paranoia (mental illness), the fourth emphysema. This was enough to make me feel secure against being shut up in a madhouse.

Meanwhile, to earn my bread I had to write articles for a newspaper, but every time I sat down at my desk and took up my pen, Hell was let loose. They had hit upon a new device for driving me mad. As soon as I had settled in a hotel an uproar would break out, very like that in the Rue de la Grande Chaumière in Paris. People walked about, dragging their feet and moving furniture. I changed my room, changed my hotel; the noise was always there, just above my head. I visited restaurants, but hardly had I chosen a seat in the dining-room before the row would begin. And, please note, I always asked the other people present if they could hear the same noise that I did, and they always answered 'Yes', and their impression of it always tallied with mine.

'So,' said I to myself, 'this is not an aural delusion but a carefully planned and widespread intrigue.' But one day, when I entered a shoe-shop quite by chance, the noise instantly began there too. So it was not a well-planned intrigue, it was the Devil himself. Hunted from hotel to hotel, beset where ever I went by electric wires that passed along the very edge of my bed, attacked by those currents

25. Malmö.

of electricity that lifted me off chairs and out of bed, I prepared to commit suicide in due form.

The weather outside was horrible, and I dispelled my misery by carousing with my friends. One day, after such a bacchanal, I had just finished breakfasting in my room. The tray of china and cutlery was still on the table and I had my back turned to it. A dull thud attracted my attention and I saw that a knife had fallen to the floor. I picked it up and put it back carefully, so that the same thing should not happen again. It was lifted up of itself and fell.

So, it was electricity.

That same morning I was writing to my mother-in-law, complaining to her about the bad weather and life in general. Imagine my surprise when, just as I had finished writing the words 'the earth is dirty, the sea is dirty, and the heavens rain slush', I saw a drop of crystal-clear water fall on to the paper.

Not electricity this time. A miracle!

That evening I was still at my desk when I was alarmed by a noise from the direction of the washstand. I looked round and saw that the piece of oil-cloth, upon which I stood when performing my morning ablutions, had fallen down. In order to get to the bottom of the mystery, I hung it up again in such a way that it could not possibly fall. It fell all the same.

What did this mean? My thoughts reverted to the occultists and their hidden powers. I left that town, taking with me my letter of denunciation, and went to Lund, where I had friends, doctors, psychiatrists, even theosophists, on whose support I counted for my temporal salvation.

How or why was I led to settle in that little university town? Was it not always regarded as a place of exile or penance for Uppsala students when they had caroused more than was good for their purses or their health? Was it a Canossa, where I should have to renounce my exaggerated opinions before the same young people who, between 1880 and 1890, had called me their standard-bearer? I well knew the situation there, and I was not ignorant of the fact that I had been excommunicated by the majority of the professors as a seducer of the young, and that fathers and mothers feared me as if I had been the Devil himself.

In addition, I had made personal enemies there, and I had incurred debts in circumstances that shed an ugly light on my character. Popoffsky's sister-in-law and her husband lived there and, as they both occupied a prominent position in society, they were well placed for causing me grave annoyance. I even had relatives there who had disowned me, friends who had renounced our acquaintanceship and become my enemies. In a word, it was the worst possible place to have chosen for a period of peace and quiet. It was a Hell, devised with masterly logicality and divine ingenuity. It was there that I had to drain my cup to the dregs and reconcile the youth of Lund with the outraged Powers.

By an accident, which had its picturesque side, I had recently bought myself a fashionable cloak with a cape and hood, of a flea-brown colour and very like the habit of a Capuchin friar. Thus it was in the garb of a penitent that I re-entered Sweden after six years of exile.

About the year 1885 a student society had been formed in Lund which went by the name of 'The Young Gaffers', and whose literary, scientific, and social interests could all be characterized as radical. Their programme, always in harmony with the ideas of the moment, was first of all socialist, then nihilist, and ended by making an ideal of general disintegration and fin-de-siècle, with a suggestion of satanism and decadence about it.

The leader of this society and the bravest of the paladins,

a friend of mine for years, though it was three since I had last seen him, came to visit me.[26]

He was dressed as I was in a cloak, but his was that of a Franciscan friar. He had aged greatly and grown very thin. He was a pitiable sight and his face alone told me his story.

'What, you too?'

'Yes, but it is all over now.'

When I offered him a glass of wine he refused it, saying that he was a teetotaller and no longer touched strong liquor.

'And what about "The Young Gaffers"?'

'They are dead. They went downhill, turned philistine, and enrolled in the accursed ranks of society.'

'Canossa?'

'Canossa all along the line.'

'It looks as if there is something providential about my arrival here.'

'Providential! That is just the right word for it.'

'The existence of the Powers is recognized in Lund, is it?'

'The Powers are preparing to return here.'

'Can one sleep at night here in Skåne?'

'Not really. Everyone is complaining that they suffer from nightmares, difficulty in breathing, affections of the heart,'

'This is where I belong, then. I too suffer from the self-same things.'

We talked for a couple of hours about the signs and wonders that were taking place, and my friend told me of the singular experiences in which first one and then another had been involved. In conclusion he told me that the youth of the present day was expecting something new.

'People are longing for a religion, a reconciliation with

26. Bengt Lidforss.

the Powers (their exact words), a re-establishment of harmony with the unseen world. The naturalistic phase was potent and fruitful, but it has served its turn. There is nothing adverse to be said about the movement, nothing to regret, since the Powers ordained that we should pass through it. It was an experimental phase, in which experiments that produced negative results have proved to us the emptiness of certain of the theories tested. A God, unknown for the present but who has within himself the capacity for growth and development, reveals himself from time to time, though in the intervals he seems to leave the world to its fate, like the husbandman who lets the tares and the wheat both flourish until the harvest. Each time he has revealed himself his views have changed and he has begun his new reign by introducing improvements, the fruits of his experience.

'So we know that religion will appear, but it will take other forms, for a compromise with former religions seems out of the question. It is not a reactionary phase that awaits us, nor is it a return to what has already run its course; it is an advance towards something new. We must wait and see what that will be.'

Towards the end of our conversation I flung out a question, much as one shoots an arrow at the clouds.

'Do you know anything about Swedenborg?'

'No, but my mother has his works and, what is more, miraculous things have happened to her.'

It was no more than a step, then, from atheism to Swedenborg.

I asked if I might borrow Swedenborg's writings, and my friend, that Saul among the young prophets brought me *Arcana Coelestia*. He also brought with him a young man who had been pardoned by the Powers, an infant prodigy who told me of an incident in his life history which was quite like my own experiences, and as we compared our tribulations light dawned upon us and we won deliverance with the help of Swedenborg.

I thanked Providence, which had sent me to that despised little town, there to atone for my sins and find salvation.

14

THE REDEEMER

When Balzac, in his book *Séraphita*, introduced my sublime countryman Emanuel Swedenborg to me as the 'Buddha of the North', he showed me the evangelistic aspect of the prophet. Now it was the Law that impressed me, overwhelmed me, and set me free.

By a single word, just one, he brought light to my soul, dispelled my doubts, my vain speculations about my imaginary enemies the electrical experts and the practitioners of black magic, and this little word was *Devastation*. Everything that had befallen me I found again in Swedenborg. The sensations of acute anxiety (angina pectoris), pressure on the chest, palpitations, what I called the electric girdle, they were all there, and the sum total of these phenomena constituted the spiritual purification known even to the apostle Paul, and mentioned by him in the Epistles to the Corinthians and to Timothy.

I have judged that he that hath so done this deed, he shall be delivered unto Satan for the destruction of the flesh, that the spirit may be saved in the day of the Lord Jesus.

Of whom is Hymenaeus and Alexander, whom I delivered unto Satan, that they might be taught not to blaspheme.

When I read Swedenborg's dreams of 1744, the year before he established relations with the unseen world, I discovered that the prophet had endured the same nocturnal tortures as myself. In fact, so striking was the similarity between our symptoms that I was no longer in any doubt about the nature of the malady that had struck me down. *Arcana Coelestia* solved for me all the riddles of the past two years with such accuracy and force that I, a child of the latter half of this renowned nineteenth century, became unshakably convinced that Hell exists, but that it is here, on earth, and that I had just passed through it.

Swedenborg explained to me the reason for my stay in the Hôpital de Saint-Louis thus: Alchemists are attacked by leprosy, which produces itching scabs like fish-scales — my incurable skin disease in fact.

Swedenborg interpreted the meaning of the hundred conveniences at the Hôtel Orfila: They were the Hell of Excrement. The sweep that my little girl had seen in Austria, he was there too.

It is possible to distinguish among the spirits some who are called sweeps, because they actually have blackened faces and appear clad in dark, soot-coloured clothing ... One of these spirit sweeps came to me and pressed me urgently to intercede for him so that he might be admitted to Heaven. 'I do not believe,' he said, 'that I have done anything for which I deserve to be excluded. I have reproved the earth-dwellers, but I have always seen to it that instruction followed reprimand and chastisement ...'

The spirits who are our censors, who discipline or instruct, place themselves on a man's left side when they bend over his back to scrutinize the book of his memory and read his deeds, yea, even his thoughts; for when a spirit insinuates itself into a man it takes possession of his memory. When they see people doing wrong, or contemplating a wrong, they punish them by giving them a pain in their foot or the hand (!) or in the region of the stomach, and they do this with incomparable skill. A shudder foreshadows their arrival.

Besides pains in the limbs, they make use of a painful contraction round the navel, like that produced by a stinging girdle, and from time to time of sensations of suffocation, driven to the length of anguish, and of a distaste for all food other than bread.

Other spirits seek to convince me of the opposite of what the educative spirits have told me. These contradictory spirits have been men on earth, banished from the community because of their villainy. Their approach is foreshadowed by a flickering flame that seems to come down in front of one's face. They take up a position at the base of the back, from which they manifest their presence through the limbs.

(Flickering flames or sparks have appeared to me twice and on both occasions in moments of revolt, when I had repudiated everything as empty dreams.)

They preach that one shall put no faith in the teaching of the educative spirits, which agrees with that of the angels. They say that one shall not adapt one's conduct to this teaching, but that one shall live in self-indulgence and liberty, just as one pleases. They usually make their appearance immediately after the others have gone. People know them for what they really are and do not take much notice of them, but learn through them what good and evil are. For one acquires a knowledge of the nature of goodness through its opposite, and every perception or idea that one has is formed by reflecting upon the difference between opposites, considered in different ways and from different points of view.

The reader may remember the human faces, resembling the marble sculptures of antiquity, into which my white pillow-slips used to shape themselves at the Hôtel Orfila.
This is what Swedenborg has to say about them :

There are two characteristic signs which show that they (the spirits) are with a person. One is an old man with a white face. This is a sign that they should always speak the truth, and do only what is right ... I have myself seen this old man's face ... Shining white, the countenance very beautiful and radiating both integrity and modesty.

(In order not to alarm the reader I have purposely concealed the fact that all that I have quoted above refers to the inhabitants of the Planet Jupiter. Judge of my surprise when, one day this spring, I came across a periodical which reproduced a picture of Swedenborg's house on Jupiter, drawn by Victorien Sardou. First of all, why Jupiter?

What an extraordinary coincidence! And had this laureate of French drama noticed that the left façade, seen from a sufficient distance, looks like an antique face? It was the face that my pillow-slip had made, but the outlines of Sardou's drawing showed a number of human silhouettes of the same kind. Had the Master's hand been guided here by another hand so that he has, in fact, given us more than he was consciously aware of?)

Where did Swedenborg see these Hells and these Heavens? Were they visions, intuitions, inspirations? I hardly know, but the correspondence between his Hell and Dante's and those of the Graeco-Roman and Germanic mythologies disposes me to believe that the Powers, to realize their plans, have always made use of means that were very similar. And what are these plans? The perfection of the human type, the procreation of the Superman (Übermensch), that rod of chastisement, established in a place of honour by Nietzsche but too soon worn out and cast upon the fire.

So the problem of evil has reappeared and Taine's moral indifference crashes to bits when faced by this new demand.

The demons follow as a necessary consequence. What then are demons? As soon as we have admitted immortality the dead become nothing more than survivors who continue their association with the living. The evil geniuses are therefore not wicked, since their aim is good, and it would be better to use Swedenborg's expression, 'disciplinary spirits', and thus dispel fear and despair.

The Devil, as an autonomous personality and God's equal, does not exist, and the undeniable manifestations of the Evil One, in his traditional form, are simply scarecrows, conjured up by a Providence, unique and good, who governs by means of an immense staff of servants made up of the departed.

Be therefore comforted and be proud of the grace that has been granted you, all ye who are sorrowful, who suffer from sleeplessness, nightmares, visions, anguish, and palpitations. *Numen adest.* God wants you.

15

TRIBULATIONS

Shut up in that little city of the Muses, without any hope of getting away, I fought out a terrible battle with the enemy, my own self.

Each morning, when I took my walk along the ramparts shaded by plane trees, the sight of the huge, red lunatic asylum reminded me of the danger I had escaped and of the future, should I suffer a relapse. By revealing to me the true nature of the terrors that had beset me during the past year, Swedenborg had set me free from the electrical experts, the practitioners of the black arts, the wizards, the envious gold-makers, and the fear of insanity. He had shown me the only way to salvation: to seek out the demons in their lair, within myself, and to destroy them by — repentance. Balzac, as the prophet's adjutant, had taught me in his *Séraphita* that 'remorse is the impotent emotion felt by the man who will sin again; repentance alone is effective, and brings everything to an end.'

To repent, then! But was not that to repudiate Providence, that had chosen me to be its scourge? Was it not to say to the Powers: 'You have misdirected my fate, you have allowed me to be born with a mission to punish, to overthrow idols, to raise the standard of revolt, and then you have withdrawn your protection and left me alone to recant and thus to earn ridicule. Do you now ask me to submit, to apologize, to make amends?'

Fantastic, but exactly the vicious circle that I foresaw in my twentieth year when I wrote my play *Master Olof*, which I now see as the tragedy of my own life. What is the good of having dragged out a laborious existence for thirty years only to learn by experience what I had already anticipated? In my youth I was a true believer and you made of me a free-thinker. Of the free-thinker you made an atheist, of the atheist a monk. Inspired by the humanitarians, I extolled socialism. Five years later you showed me the absurdity of socialism. You have cut the ground from under all my enthusiasms, and suppose that I now dedicate myself to religion, I know for a certainty that before ten years have passed you will prove to me that religion is false.

Are not the Gods jesting with us mortals, and is that why we too, sharing the jest, are able to laugh in the most tormented moments of our lives?

How can you require that we take seriously something that appears to be no more than a colossal jest?

Jesus Christ our Saviour, what is it that he saved? Look at our Swedish pietists, the most Christian of all Christians, those pale, wicked, terror-stricken creatures, who cannot smile and who look like maniacs. They seem to carry a demon in their hearts and, mark you, most of their leaders end up in prison as malefactors. Why should their Lord have delivered them over to the enemy? Is religion a punishment, and is Christ the spirit of vengeance?

All the ancient Gods reappeared as demons at a later date. The dwellers in Olympus became evil spirits, Odin and Thor the Devil himself, Prometheus – Lucifer, the Bringer of Light, degenerated into Satan. Is it possible – God forgive me – that even Christ has been transformed into a demon? He has brought death to reason, to the flesh, to beauty, to joy, to the purest feelings of affection of which mankind is capable. He has brought death to the virtues of fearlessness, valour, glory, love, and mercy.

The sun shines, daily life goes on in its accustomed way, the sound of men at their everyday tasks raises our spirits.

It is at such moments that the courage to revolt rears up and we fling our challenge and our doubts at Heaven.

But at night, when silence and solitude fall about us, our arrogance is dissipated, we hear our heart-beats and feel a weight on our chests. Then go down on your knees in the bush of thorns outside your window, go find a doctor or seek out some comrade who will sleep with you in the same room.

Enter your room alone at night-time and you will find that someone has got there before you. You will not see him, but you will sense his presence. Go to the lunatic asylum and consult the psychiatrist. He will talk to you of neurasthenia, paranoia, angina pectoris, and the like, but he will never cure you.

Where will you go, then, all you who suffer from sleep-lessness, and you who walk the streets waiting for the sun to rise?

The Mills of the Universe, the Mills of God, these are two expressions that are often used.

Have you had in your ears the humming that resembles the noise of a water-mill? Have you noticed, in the still-ness of the night, or even in broad daylight, how memories of your past life stir and are resurrected, one by one or two by two? All the mistakes you have made, all your crimes, all your follies, that make you blush to your very ear-tips, bring a cold sweat to your brow and send shivers down your spine. You relive the life you have lived, from your birth to the very day that is. You suffer again all the suffer-ings you have endured, you drink again all the cups of bitterness you have so often drained. You crucify your skeleton, as there is no longer any flesh to mortify. You send your spirit to the stake, as your heart is already burned to ashes.

Do you recognize the truth of all this?

These are the Mills of God, that grind slow but grind exceeding small – and black. You are ground to powder and you think it is all over. But no, it will begin again and you will be put through the mill once more.

Be happy. That is the Hell here on earth, recognized by Luther, who esteemed it a high honour that he should be ground to powder on this side of the empyrean.

Be happy and grateful.

What is to be done? Must you humble yourself?

But if you humble yourself before mankind you will arouse their arrogance, since they will then believe themselves to be better than you are, however great their villainy.

Must you then humble yourself before God? But it is an insult to the All-Highest to drag Him down to the level of a planter who rules over slaves.

Pray! What? Will you arrogate to yourself the right to bend the will of the Eternal and His decrees, by flattery and by servility?

Seek God and find the Devil. That is what has happened to me.

I have done penance, I have mended my ways, but no sooner do I begin the work of re-soling my soul than I have to add yet another patch. If I put on new heels the uppers split. There is no end to it.

If I give up drinking and come home sober at nine o'clock of an evening to a glass of milk, my room is full to overflowing with all manner of demons, who pluck me from my bed and smother me under the bedclothes. If, on the other hand, I come home drunk, towards midnight, I fall asleep like a little angel and wake up in the morning as fresh as a young god, ready to work like a galley-slave.

If I shun women unwholesome dreams come upon me at night. If I train myself to think well of my friends, if I confide my secrets to them or give them money, I am betrayed, and if I lose my temper over a breach of faith it is always I who am punished.

I try to love mankind in the mass, I close my eyes to their faults, and, with limitless forbearance, forgive them their meanness and their back-biting, and then, one fine day, I find that I am an accomplice. If I withdraw from the company of people I consider bad I am immediately attacked by the demon of solitude. If I then seek for better friends I fall in with worse.

Furthermore, when I vanquish my evil passions, and reach at least some measure of tranquillity by my abstinence, I experience a feeling of self-satisfaction that makes me think I am superior to my fellow men, and this is the mortal sin of egotism, which brings down instant punishment.

How are we to explain the fact that each apprenticeship in virtue is followed by a new vice?

Swedenborg solves this riddle when he says that vices are the punishments man incurs for more serious sins. For instance, those who are greedy of power are doomed to the Hell of Sodomy. If we admit that the theory holds good we must endure our vices and profit by the remorse that accompanies them as things that will help us to settle our final account.

Consequently, to seek to be virtuous is like attempting to escape from our prison and our torments. This is what Luther was trying to say in article XXXIX of his reply to the Papal Bull of excommunication, where he proclaims that 'The Souls in Purgatory sin incessantly, since they are trying to gain peace and to avoid their torments.'

Similarly in article XXXIV: 'To struggle against the Turks is nothing more than rising in rebellion against God, who is chastising us for our sins through the medium of the Turks.'

Thus it is clear that 'all our good deeds are mortal sins,'

and that 'the world must be sinful in the eyes of God, and must understand that no one can become good except by the grace of God.'

Therefore, O my brethren, you must suffer without hope of a single lasting happiness in this life, since we are already in Hell. We must not reproach the Lord if we see innocent little children suffer. None of us can know why, but divine justice makes us suppose that it is because of sins committed before ever they arrived in this world. Let us rejoice in our torments which are so many debts repaid, and let us believe that it is out of pure compassion that we are kept in ignorance of the primordial reasons for our punishment.

16

WHAT IS OUR GOAL?

Six months have ebbed away and I still take my walk on the ramparts. As I let my eyes stray over the lunatic asylum and try to catch sight of the blue streak in the distance that is the sea, I fancy that I am on the look-out for the new era that is coming, the new religion of which the world is dreaming.

Dark winter is buried, the fields are growing green, the trees are in blossom, the nightingale is singing in the Observatory Gardens, but the melancholy of winter still weighs upon our spirits because of the many ominous things that are happening, the many inexplicable things that make even the sceptical uneasy. Cases of sleeplessness are increasing, serious nervous disorders are multiplying, invisible presences are of common occurrence, real miracles are taking place. People are waiting for something to happen.

A young man came to visit me. He asked:

'What ought I to do to sleep peacefully at night?'

'What has happened?'

'Upon my word, I cannot tell you, but I have a horror of my bedroom, and I am moving elsewhere tomorrow.'

'Young man, you are an atheist and a believer in naturalism. What has happened?'

'Devil take it! When I got home last night and opened my door someone took hold of my arm and shook me.'

'So there was someone in your room.'

'Why, no! I lit the candles and I could not see anyone.'

'Young man, there is one whom we cannot see by the light of a candle.'

'What manner of thing is he?'

'He is the Unseen, young man. Have you taken sulpho-nal, potassium bromide, morphia, or chloral?'

'I have tried them all.'

'And the Unseen won't decamp? Well, then, you want to sleep peacefully at night, and you have come to ask me how to do so. Listen to me, young man. I am no doctor, nor am I a prophet; I am an old sinner, doing penance. Do not expect any sermons or prophecies from a ruffian who needs all the time he can spare to preach sermons to him-self. I too have suffered from sleepless nights and deep de-jection. I too have fought face to face with the Unseen, and I have at last regained the power of sleep and got back my health. Do you know how? Guess!'

The young man guessed what I meant and lowered his eyes.

'So you have guessed. Depart in peace and sleep well.'

You see, I had to hold my tongue and let people guess what I meant, for the instant I presumed to play the friar people turned their backs upon me.

A friend asked me, 'What is our goal?'

To him I said, 'I cannot tell you, but for me personally it seems that the way of the Cross is leading me back to *the faith of my forefathers.*'

'Catholicism?'

'It seems so. Occultism has played its part by giving me a scientific explanation of miracles and demonology. Theo-sophy, having opened the road to religion, is outworn now that it has re-established a cosmic system that pun-ishes and rewards. Karma will become God, and the Mahat-mas will be revealed as regenerated Powers, as disciplin-ary spirits (demons) and spirits that instruct (spirits of in-spiration). Buddhism, much extolled by the youth of France, has introduced resignation and a worship of suffering that leads directly to Calvary.'

With regard to my homesickness for the Mother Church, that is a long story, but I should like to give a summary of it.

Swedenborg, by teaching me that one is forbidden to abandon the religion of one's fathers, had clearly pronounced a judgement upon Protestantism, which he says constitutes an act of treachery against the mother religion. To put it better, Protestantism is a chastisement, inflicted upon the barbarians of the North. Protestantism is the Exile, the Babylonian Captivity, but a return to the promised land seems imminent. The tremendous strides that Catholicism has made in America, in England, and in Scandinavia are a prophecy of the great reconciliation that is to come. The Greek Orthodox Church, too, has recently been stretching out a hand to the West.

Here you have the socialists' dream of a United States of the West, interpreted in a spiritual sense. But I beg you not to believe that political theories are what is leading me back to the Roman Church. It is not I who have sought out Catholicism; it is Catholicism that laid hold on me, after pursuing me for years. My child, who has been brought up a Catholic, and that against my will, has taught me what beauty there can be in a cult that has been preserved intact since its inception. I have always preferred the original to the copy. My prolonged stay in my daughter's homeland taught me to admire the sincerity of the religious life there. My stay in the Hôpital de Saint-Louis had the same effect, and finally came my experiences of the past months.

After making this survey of my life, which showed me that I had been delivered over to the whirlwind like certain of the damned in Dante's Hell, and after recognizing that, all in all, the only purpose of my existence had been to humble and besmirch me, I decided to meet the hangman halfway and conduct the torture myself. I felt I wanted to live my life in the midst of suffering, filth, and the agony of death. To this end I resolved to apply for a situation as a male nurse at the hospital of the Frères Saint-Jean-de Dieu in Paris. This idea came to me on the morning of the 29th of April after an encounter I had with an old woman with a face like a death's-head. When I got home I found *Séraphita* lying open on my table and, on the right-hand page, a sliver of wood pointing to the following sentence:

Do for God what you have done for the furtherance of your own ambition, what you do when you devote yourself to an art, what you did when you loved one of his creatures more than you loved Him, or when you sought to explore some secret of human knowledge. Is not God Himself knowledge . . .?

That afternoon the newspaper *L'Eclair* arrived and – what a coincidence! – the hospital of the Frères Saint-Jean-de-Dieu was twice mentioned in its columns.

On May the 1st I read for the first time Sar Peladan's book, *Comment on devient mage.*

Sar Peladan, about whom I had until then known nothing now burst upon me like a tempest, a manifestation of Nietzsche's Superman, and with him Catholicism made its solemn and triumphant entry into my life.

He who shall come, had he indeed come in the person of Peladan? Poet, prophet, philosopher – is it really he, or must we wait upon the coming of another?

I do not know, but after having passed through this gateway to a new life I began to write this book on the 3rd of May.

On the 5th of May I received a visit from a Catholic priest, a proselyte.

On the 14th of May I saw Gustavus Adolphus[27] in the ashes of the stove.

On the 14th of May I read the following in Sar Peladan.

27. King of Sweden, 1611–32, and champion of Protestantism.

Around the year one thousand one could believe in spell-casting; now, as we approach the year two thousand, it has been established beyond doubt that there are certain individuals who possess the fatal power of bringing misfortune upon those who injure them. If you refuse such a person his demands your mistress will be unfaithful; lash out at him and you will have to take to your bed. Any evil that you inflict upon him will rebound twofold upon your own head. Never mind; chance will explain this inexplicable combination of circumstances; chance meets all the requirements of modern determinism.

On May 17th I read what the Dane Jörgensen, a convert to Catholicism, has written about the Monastery of Beuron.

On May 18th a friend, whom I had not seen for six years, arrived in Lund and took a flat in the same house as myself. Imagine my emotion when I discovered that he had recently been converted to Catholicism. He lent me a copy of the Roman missal that I had lost the preceding year, and when I read the Latin hymns and songs of praise again I felt as if I had returned home.

On the 27th of May, after a series of conversations on the subject of the Mother Church, my friend despatched a letter to the Belgian monastery where he had received baptism, requesting them to allow the author of this book to seek refuge there.[28]

On May 28th I heard a rumour that Annie Besant had become a Catholic, but it has not been confirmed.

I am still awaiting an answer from the Belgian monastery. By the time this book has been printed I shall have received one. What then? And thereafter? A new jest on the part of the Gods? For when we weep scalding tears they roar with laughter.

28. Solesmes. But on 3 September 1897 Strindberg read in a French newspaper that the Prior had been dismissed for immorality and he never went there.

EPILOGUE

I first concluded this book with the words: 'What a jest, what a miserable jest, this life is after all!'

After a little reflection it seemed to me that they were unworthy and I crossed them out. But I could not rid myself of my perplexity, and I therefore turned to the Bible, to find in it the illumination I so ardently desired.

The holy book, endowed more than any other with the marvellous gift of prophecy, answered me in the following words:

And I will set my face against that man, and will make him a sign and a proverb,[29] and I will cut him off from the midst of my people, and ye shall know that I am the Lord.

And if the prophet be deceived when he has spoken a thing, I the Lord have deceived that prophet, and I will stretch out my hand upon him, and will destroy him from the midst of my people Israel.

This is what my life amounts to then, to be a sign and an example for the betterment of others, to be a laughing-stock to show the futility of glory and fame, a laughing-stock to enlighten youth about the way in which they should not live. A laughing-stock who thought he was a prophet, but stands revealed as an impostor. But it is the Lord who has led this false prophet astray and caused him to speak, so the false prophet can feel that he is blameless, as he has only been playing the part assigned to him.

Behold, my brothers, one human destiny among many, and confess that the life of a man may well look like a jest.

29. The word used in the 1820 French Bible from which Strindberg quoted was *jouet*, laughing-stock.

Why has the author of this book been punished in such an extraordinary way? Read the miracle-play that concludes his drama *Master Olof* (verse edition). He wrote this miracle-play thirty years ago, before he knew anything about the sect of heretics who called themselves Stedinger. Pope Gregory IX excommunicated them in the year 1232 because of their satanic teaching, which was that 'Lucifer the good God, expelled and dethroned by "The Other", will come again when the usurper, who is called God, has earned the contempt of mankind through his wretched rule, his cruelty, and his injustice, and has himself become convinced of his incompetence'.

This Prince of the World, who condemns mortals to sin and punishes virtue by the Cross and the stake, by sleeplessness and nightmares, who is he? The tormentor, to whom we have been consigned because of some unknown or forgotten crime, committed in a previous existence? And what of Swedenborg's disciplinary spirits, those guardian angels who shield us from spiritual evils?

What a Babylonian confusion!

St Augustine considered it imprudent to foster doubts about the existence of demons. Thomas Aquinas declared that demons could summon up storms and call down thunderbolts, and also that these spirits were able to confer their power upon mortals. Pope John XXII bewailed the illicit practices of his enemies when they tormented him by sticking nails into his portrait (bewitchment). Luther believed that all accidents, broken limbs, falls, outbreaks of fire, and most illnesses, arose from the machinations of devils. What is more, Luther held that certain individuals have already found their Hell in this life.

Is it not with good reason, then, that I have christened my book *Inferno*?

If the reader doubts that what I say is true and thinks it

is too pessimistic, let him read first my autobiography *The Son of a Servant*, and then *A Madman's Defence*.

The reader who is inclined to consider that this book is a work of imagination is invited to consult the diary I wrote up day by day from 1895, of which the above is merely a version, composed of extracts expanded and rearranged.

FROM AN OCCULT DIARY

1900

From Harriet Bosse's explanatory notes to the 1932 volume of Strindberg's letters to her.

The spring of 1900 brought me a lot of work and much success. I played Puck in *A Midsummer Night's Dream* and Anna in *The First Violin*. [. . .] Just at that time a production of Strindberg's *To Damascus* was being planned for the coming autumn season, but those concerned had not made up their minds who should play the part of the Lady. August Palme, who was seeing a great deal of Strindberg just then, suggested that they should try me. [. . .]

Strangely enough I was chosen. [. . .]

I had still not met Strindberg in person, but one day Palme arrived with a message from him to say that he wanted me to visit him at a certain time on the following day.

[. . .]

From Strindberg's Diary, May 31st.

Fröken Bosse visited me, 1st time.

July 5th.

Fröken Bosse visited me, 2nd time. She accepted the part in *Damascus*. Her sister waited outside in a cab.

November 15th.

First dress-rehearsal of *Damascus*. The inexplicable scene with (Bosse).

It happened like this! After the 1st act I went on to the stage and thanked (Bosse). Made some comment about the final scene where the kiss has to be given with the veil down. As we stood there on the stage, surrounded by a lot of people, and I was talking seriously to her about the kissing scene (*Bosse's*) little face changed, grew larger and became supernaturally beautiful, seemed to come closer to mine while her eyes enveloped me with their luminous blackness. Whereupon, without excusing herself, she ran away and I stood amazed, feeling that a miracle had happened and that I had been given an intoxicating kiss.

After this (B) haunted me for three days so that I could feel her presence in my room.

Then I dreamt about her, thus. (*I was lying in a bed, B came to me in her Puck's costume from the play. She was married to me. She said of me: 'Behold, the man who brewed me,' gave me her foot to kiss. She had no breasts, absolutely none!*)

Gustaf Strindberg,* who had been to see *Damascus*, said that B was exactly like Aunt Philp (my sister Anna). Now my second wife (the Lady in *Damascus*) was like my sister Anna. Consequently, (B) like both. Some years ago (B) played the girl in my play *In the Face of Death*.† (*B's*) sister and brother-in-law lived in the same pension as I did in Paris.

(B) lives at 12 Gref Magnigatan, right opposite the house I was living in when I wrote *Master Olof*.‡

November 19th.

After a long absence the sun is shining. It is dry and cold. *To Damascus* is being performed tonight.

[. . .]

---

* Strindberg's elder brother Oscar's son.

† Harriet Bosse played this part in the Central Theatre in Kristiania. The theatre was run by her sister and brother-in-law, Alma and Johan Fahlström, whom Strindberg had met in Paris in 1895.

‡ From 1872 to 1873 Strindberg lived at 7 Gref Magnigatan, opposite the house in which Harriet Bosse was living in 1900.

Strindberg to Harriet Bosse, November 19th.

As I shall not be putting in an appearance at the theatre tonight may I thank you now for what I saw at the dress-rehearsal? It was great and beautiful [. . .]

August Strindberg

Strindberg to Harriet Bosse, December 5th.

Fröken Harriet Bosse,

Having in mind that our Journey to Damascus ended today, I ordered some roses – with thorns, of course – they say there are no others! I send them with a simple 'thank you'. Now stay on among us, *the* actress of the new century. You have struck a new note for us to hear, no matter where you found it!

And allow me to hope I may hear you again, in the spring, in *Easter*, as I think you have promised me!

August Strindberg

December 12th.

Sent (*Easter*) to (B) this evening. Sat down in the evening to write an analysis of the part for (B). Fancied I was having telepathic relations with (B). At night I dreamed . . . [. . .]

1901

January 3rd.

Have been plagued for a couple of months by a smell of Celery. Everything tastes and smells of Celery. When I take off my shirt at night it smells of Celery. What can it be? My (*chastity*), my celibacy?

January 5th.

Finished *The Bridal Crown* and in doing so had a feeling that there would be a pause in my work as a dramatist.

Longing for Paris; planning a visit.

January 8th.

Met (*Bonnier*) who dissuaded me from the Paris project. Read *Echo de Paris* sent by *Courier de la Presse*, and was frightened off. Had a message from (*Bosse*) saying that I must not go. Saw in the paper that 9 people had frozen to death in Paris. Decided not to go, for on the previous day I had (*begged God*) to signify (*his will*).

January 9th.

Reading Balzac. 'Lucien, in short, was loved absolutely, and in a way in which women very rarely love a man.' (Woman does not love; it is man who loves and woman who is loved.)

January 13th, Sunday.

(*B*), who read *Creditors* and *Simoon* on the 12th, haunted me on the 12th. This haunting grew more intense on the 13th, and at night she persecuted me. (First telepathic 'intercourse' with B.) When she appeared telepathically during the night I 'possessed' her. Incubus.

The whole thing seemed to me quite ghastly and I (*begged God to deliver me*) from (*this passion*).

January 14th, Monday.

Passed two ladies in the street; it was 6 degrees below zero and a fresh wind. A smell of Celery (*lasciviousness*).

Passed two ladies again in the evening, and there was a smell of Celery.

January 15th, Tuesday.

What is all this leading to? I want to flee to Berlin, but I cannot.

Last year (*Fru Geijerstam*) felt she was in telepathic communication with (*Arvid Ödman*) or that he was hypnotizing her from a distance. She had, in fact, been in love with him in her youth.

January 25th.

I saw a flag flying this morning from a house in Strandvägen. It made me happy. Coming closer I saw it was the 'clean' Norwegian flag,[1] at half-mast, with a wreath of laurel round a coat of arms, and something in the centre. What could it mean? But, of course! They were flying the English flag in honour of Queen Victoria who died recently!

(*Aversion to B*)

It is evening now, I am sitting alone at home while they perform *The Saga of the Folkungs*. The excitement of it all is with me, though from time to time it relaxes, probably when the curtain falls.

Going over in my mind what my life has been I wonder whether all the horrible things I have experienced have been staged for me to enable me to become a dramatist, and depict all mental states and all possible situations. I

---

1. The Norwegian flag without the union device, a combination of the flags of Norway and Sweden which was carried in the upper square next to the flagstaff in the flags of both countries.

was a dramatist at twenty, but if the course of my life had run smoothly, I should have had nothing to write about.

[...]

January 28th.

Played *The Midsummer Night's Dream* (Mendelssohn). Had a feeling that (*B*) would come. Then in came the maid and announced Fröken (*Vallberg*). I refused to see her!

Soon afterwards, as I was turning over the pages of Euripides, I came upon this: 'But do not take a fancy to an evil woman' and immediately after that: 'The visits of wicked women were my ruin.'

Let this suffice!

Cf: my peculiar performance in the street last year. I was busy wondering whether it was my duty to marry again, when I fell and hurt my ring-finger.

February 4th.

[...]

Read Maeterlinck's *Princess Maleine*. Was sensible all the time of the scent and taste of incense. (Incense=The prayers of the pious.) N.B.! *Easter* was being rehearsed and collated at Dramaten for the first time. Incense, Olibanum =(*B*), see below, the 16th.

[...]

February 8th, Friday.

[...]

Went on writing *Damascus III* in the morning. Shaved myself towards dinner-time. (*Kissed kind B's picture. Prayed God to bless her.*) Then B arrived. (*I was ashamed ... She was serious, lovely*), she said: (*God bless you*) for the beautiful things you have said in *Easter*! In the presence of (*this perfect specimen of a female child*) I felt like old Faust, mourning his lost youth.

Her mouth when she smiled was like that of an eight-year-old child.

She had an eagle's quill-feather* in her hat and a strange ornament, a golden heart, on her breast.

Strindberg to Harriet Bosse, February 8th.

Kind Fröken Bosse,

Happy to have had a talk with you at last about *Easter*. I feel now that I forgot so much of what I meant to say to you, and I am afraid too of appearing to want to interfere with your development. But since you so kindly and so charmingly thanked me today, when it was really I who wanted to thank you, I will first say a few words about Eleanora, and then about something else!

As a result of family troubles Eleanora had developed a certain mental condition, some would call it an ailment, by reason of which she has entered into rapport (telepathic) both with those related to her and with mankind as a whole, and finally with the lower forms of creation, so that she suffers with all living things, or realizes the idea of 'Christ in Man'. She is therefore kin to Balzac's Seraphita, Swedenborg's niece, whose acquaintanceship I had meant to recommend to you as an introduction to *Easter*, had I not feared – yes – to make a nuisance of myself. Had even intended to ask you to read Hannah Ioël's *Beyond*, Fru Skram's *Hieronymus*, and, above all Maeterlinck's *Le Trésor des Humbles*.[2] But as I have just said, I was afraid you would not want to be instructed. [. . .]

Some other time, soon, I shall hope to hear your impressions of *La Princesse Maleine*, and after you have read *The*

---

* This was clearly the occasion on which Strindberg was given the well-known eagle-pen.

2. The first two works deal with mental derangement and life in the lunatic asylums of the time; the third, by Maeterlinck (English translation. *The Treasures of the Humble*), is a book of essays of a mystical and philosophical nature.

Bridal Crown, I shall introduce you to the enchanting girl Judith in *The Dance of Death*.

August Strindberg

February 10th, Sunday.

Woke up and went out in a wonderful mood. The sun was shining and I saw a rosy glow in the north-east (Furusund).

(*Experienced the feeling*) that life might again begin to smile. On a new house in Karlavägen saw a notice: 'Flats, 3 to 5 rooms, available April 1st.' (This was the house into which we moved when we were newly married.)

... Went out in the evening and noticed that the city was illuminated; but now, on the 11th, still do not know why. That, and the sound of a festive march being played out on the ice, affected me oddly.

February 11th, Monday.

Cut the ring-finger of my left hand just where the ring had been. A large drop of blood oozed out.

Alone the whole day, in quiet mood, reading Peladan[3] and (*thinking of B and begging her to forgive my evil thoughts*). This evening a beam of green light from the lamp fell on my breast and followed me wherever I went. Is the light really coming back at last?

Since (*B's visit*) I have entered on a new phase of my life. I long for purity, beauty, and harmony. The 2nd act of *Damascus III* is influenced by (*B*) who has now entered my life [...] Harriet and I have, periodically, lived together telepathically and have 'enjoyed' each other from a distance – after she had initiated me into the secret of it.

February 12th.

Night before: uneasy. Woke at 2 o'clock. (*Possessed her when she sought me.*) My telepathic relationship with (*B*)

3. J. Péladan (Sar), the French occultist.

has intensified alarmingly. In my thoughts I live solely with her. (*Pray God to resolve this matter.*) It threatens to bring about a catastrophe.

[...]

I woke this morning with a fever and a pain in my chest. Went out all the same. Saw the golden cross on Jakob's church, that you see above the Synagogue, lit up by the sun, provocatively.

When I got home a parcel arrived from Maredsous Monastery, which I visited a couple of years ago.

What I am now going through is horrible and marvellous – I feel as if I were expecting a death-sentence. Sometimes I think that (*she loves me*), sometimes not. God's will be done! If I only knew what it was. Up to now there have been as many premonitory signs for as against. On her last visit I felt as if an angel were in the room and I decided in favour of the good; hoping to achieve reconciliation with woman through woman. For three days now I have had her in my room and experienced an elevating, *ennobling* influence, which surely no demon could possess.

If the Supreme Powers are jesting with me, I am prepared to bear that too!

[...]

My fate will probably be decided today.

Will even love, great, sublime love come again? And have we seen the last of the economic-bargain marriages of the previous century?

February 13th, Wednesday.

[...]

This has been a brighter day than yesterday. The fever has left me.

I sent (*B*) a letter this evening, and an Easter birch[4] and a daffodil. It is odd: yesterday, my feverish day, everything

4. A bunch of birch twigs tipped with brightly coloured feathers.

was black; nothing seemed to make the rooms lighter. They were dark ... today they are strikingly bright, yet the illumination is the same as it was yesterday.

[...]

Strindberg to Harriet Bosse, February 13th.

Kind Fröken Bosse,

[...]

In the meantime, as the answer may come soon, I beg you to tell me quickly if I may count on you to play Kersti?* Then I can immediately secure the role for you. [...]

It is not impatience on my part that dictates this letter. It is the fear of not getting you for the role, which they might give to someone else.

August Strindberg

February 14th.

Disharmonious, though the sun is shining. All my thoughts are centred on (B), but as if she were coming; good, loving, to give me back my faith in the good in woman, and in mankind. (B) is like (1) my second wife (whom she played in Damascus), (2) my sister Anna, (3) my mother, (4) M'lle Lecain, the beautiful English woman who wanted to capture me in Paris, and who was like all of them. She frequently gave me the impression of being warm and motherly, so that when I was at Mme Charlotte's† I would often wish myself under her beautiful, warm, woollen cloak, as in a mother's womb. But Gauguin said she was a demon, and that she tempted men – and women. (5) She smiles like my son Hans did when he was four years old, angelically.

Every evening I pray to (B's) guardian angel to make her good and me good through her. Is it all a delusion?

* The leading part in *The Bridal Crown*.

† Mme Charlotte was the proprietress of the eating-place in Paris at which Strindberg was a regular customer in the middle of the nineties.

Demons can dress up like angels.

... I waited the whole of this morning in deadly anxiety. The clock struck the half hour. I collapsed as if the thought 'she is not coming' had brought my life to an end ... Soon after, she arrived. Unaffected, gentle, kind, not so glowing ... as last time. Talked warmly and with dignity, kept the conversation above trifles ...

I rallied, but was so much affected by the joy of seeing her that I wept ... Finally I kissed her little hand and thanked her for wanting to visit me. When I showed her my alchemist's cupboard my hand bled. – She said: 'You have your secrets, I see!' (à propos the pieces of paper in the cupboard).[5]

At 4 o'clock I was overcome by an attack of weeping – wept in general over my own misery and that of mankind, wept without reason, with a dim feeling of happiness, of pain because I had no happiness, with a premonition of coming disaster.

February 16th.

Letter from (B) that made me calm and happy.

I answered it. She was so glad to have my photograph.*

The strange smell of incense manifested itself again today, more intensely than usual. The idea struck me that it was (B). I sniffed her letter, it smelt of incense! So it is her!

---

5. Pieces of paper on which Strindberg believed that he had laid a film of gold of his own making.

* Strindberg had given Harriet Bosse a photograph of himself with the following dedication: 'To the "Lady" from the "Unknown One". This is what he looked like during his journey to Damascus of 1896, in Ystad.' During his courtship of Harriet Bosse Strindberg often referred to himself as the Unknown One and to Harriet Bosse as the Lady, the hero and heroine of his play *To Damascus*. In 1896, at the height of his Inferno crisis, Strindberg spent some weeks in Ystad, a small town in the south of Sweden.

But the smell has become nauseous. At first it was good, uplifting; then it smelt of madness and witchcraft. Finally it has become nauseous and terrifying.

[...]

Harriet Bosse to Strindberg, c. February 16th.

Herr August Strindberg,

Thank you for the photograph. You made me so happy by sending it. I have only read part of *The Dance of Death*. I cannot bear to read much at a time; it affects me so deeply. May I please keep it for a few days longer?

Harriet Bosse

Strindberg to Harriet Bosse, February 16th.

Kind Fröken Bosse,

I go on calling you kind because last Friday you were kind and begged God to bless me. – Nobody has blessed me for years! – I hardly know whether you believe in a good God, but He took you at your word and listened to you! Can you imagine it? I was ill and in darkness; then light came to me, good intentions and peace! That was why I kissed the little hand that had blessed me. Pray understand! That was why I wept. It is many yesterdays since I last wept! Understand that too!

Of course you may keep *The Dance of Death*. I await your verdict with patience, and I beg you to tell me exactly what you think of the play.

[...]   Your,

August Strindberg

February 17th, Sunday.

Night before: tranquil, wonderful. Woke clear-eyed and happy. Loathed coffee and drank milk. A walk in Djurgården. A flag was hoisted on Skansen. Two dogs made much of me! Read in Stockholms Dagblad the words 'Love is best'. The text for the day treated of love = Caritas, not Eros – Amour –

Discovered the plan of a tour to Italy in Maeterlinck. Now contemplating a journey to an Italian monastery that Richard Bergh found. The smell of incense, which succeeded that of Celery and had become nauseating, is less strong today. Oh that I might have a new one!

This evening I saw the cross that is formed by the gas-lamps on Slottsbacken. I see it occasionally, not always.

February 18th.

Fairly quiet. The smell of incense less strong. Went on writing *Damascus III* but slept for the most part. x x x* She sought me and I responded!

February 19th.

[. . .]

As I was about to go to bed this evening I became sensible of (B) out in the dining-room, of her smell of incense too. Later on in my room, but with such intensity and so weirdly that I grew afraid.

[. . .]

February 20th.

Went on writing *Damascus III*. (B) arrived, kind, friendly, diffident. I revived! She had her veil down the whole time. She likes babies. She had read *The Dance of Death* – I asked her if she had not herself experienced Judith's first love . . . Poor child; she did not answer! When she had gone it grew dark again. She had a fur round her neck with two little claws, sharp, black. There was a moment when the smell of incense came from her. The strange thing is, however, that every evening when I change my cotton shirt, I am aware of a smell of incense from myself. It used to be celery. What does this mean?

* The x sign by which Strindberg indicates here and subsequently the number of 'telepathic embraces'.

A tranquil night until 4 o'clock. Said my morning prayers.
x x x Possessed her.

Who will deliver me from this sinful flesh?

February 23rd.

Woke firmly determined to release myself from (B). Sent
both photographs of her to Germany and felt freer!* Went
on writing *Damascus III*.

Beethoven evening with Axel, Richard B and Gyllen-
sköld.⁶ Pleasant atmosphere. I thanked God for letting me
have such an agreeable time after so many years of misery.

February 24th.

Night before: Dreamt about storks. N.B.! There are two
pictures of storks in my present rooms, or rather three, now
that I have bought a Japanese screen.

[...]

(B) haunting me.

About midday I wrote and sent off a letter to Personne
at the theatre. There was a matinée and (B) was acting. I
asked him to delete *Casper†* and put *Simoon* in its place
with (B) in the female part. For two whole hours afterwards
I felt I was in friendly rapport with (B). So strong was the
feeling that it gave me palpitations. I felt happy, as if she
(*loved me*) and as if my fate were now decided. Smell of
incense intense but not disagreeable.

My whole existence is now intertwined with hers. May
God help me out of this!

---

* Strindberg sent photographs of Harriet Bosse in her roles as the
Lady in *To Damascus* and Eleonora in *Easter* to his German translator
Emil Schering, who was going to negotiate guest-artist appe   ances
for her in Germany. Cf. the entry of March 4th 1901 in the diary.

6. Axel Strindberg, Strindberg's eldest brother; Richard Bergh the
painter; Vilhelm Carlheim-Gyllensköld the physicist.

† The play *Casper's Shrove Tuesday* which Strindberg had just
written.

February 25th.

x x x She offered herself and I possessed her.

Wrote more of *Damascus III*.

At midday, books lent to (B) returned along with a letter, stiff, cold, friendly.

[. . .]

Harriet Bosse to Strindberg, February 25th.

Herr August Strindberg,

I have grown to like Mäterlinck more and more. There is a peculiar elegance about his art that impresses one as being strange at first, because of its originality, but later enchants by its sublime power of giving colour to a mood.

I am thinking here particularly of *Les Sept Princesses, Intérieur* and *Les Aveugles.*

I am grateful to you for having introduced me to him.

Harriet Bosse

[. . .]

Strindberg to Harriet Bosse, February 25th.

Fröken Harriet Bosse,

Please have patience with me and my letter-writing for a little longer. Our great mutual interest, Eleonora, is its ultimate objective. Even the books I send you are concerned with her. You say that the part is so sensitive that it hardly bears touching. True, that is why I do not want to analyse it, or pick it to bits, or philosophize about it. [. . .]

February 26th, Tuesday.

[. . .]

Woke in the morning determined to free myself from (B). Thought of her stiff, arrogant letter of yesterday. Thought of the consequences of surrendering my power and my property, my freedom and my honour to a hard, calculating woman of an enemy nation![7]

[. . .]

7. Harriet Bosse was Norwegian by birth.

(B) haunted me continuously from noon to evening. Then I went to Gyllensköld to be quit of her. Before going I wrote a cold, stiff letter to (B) and put it in the pillar-box.

The conception of *Swanwhite* has kept me in a state of intoxication all day.

February 27th.

Night before fairly quiet x x x (=Possessed her). Woke obsessed by *Swanwhite* and worked on it the whole day. Heard nothing from (B). The smell of incense seems to be coming to an end. Have my three weeks of asceticism made me impervious to her Aura? Or has her Aura merged into mine and become refined through it?

Free of any contact with (B) all day, but longed for her at times. And, although I longed intensely, I got no response. Is the thread severed?

The day was really grey and rather dismal.

Strindberg to Harriet Bosse, February 27th.

Fröken Harriet Bosse,

I have much to tell you and many things to ask, but I have got it into my head that my friendly advances give you pain and that my concern for your welfare embarrasses you. [...]

It would, of course, be improper if I asked you to come here, and I do not dare to do so either. But if I tell you that the importunate table will certainly be laid at 2 o'clock, but cleared at 2.30, then you can please yourself whether you honour me by a visit as hitherto. If I am too bold in offering even this piece of information, please forgive me. I cannot at the moment see any other alternative.

[...]

February 28th.

Sent off a friendly letter to (B) this morning.

She came at 3 p.m., dressed in black, delightful, charming,

good. We talked intimately, intimately! She told me she had had a feeling that I had been angry with her the last few days! Etc. I gave her *Damascus III* which is a confession.

[. . .]

Strindberg to Harriet Bosse, March 1st.

Kind Fröken Bosse,

Come and give me your impressions of *Damascus III* before they are washed away by other things.

I attach so much value to your opinion because you have played the part of the Lady, you see!

Your

August Strindberg

March 1st.

Woke with a feeling that my fate had now been decided. Wrote a letter to (*B*) asking her to tell me what she thought of *Damascus*.

Spent the rest of the day in a state of great tension, waiting for her to come. (The clock has just struck 6.) This afternoon, immediately after dinner, I was certain she would come. Could not smell the scent but my heart beat violently.

(N.B.! The pendulum clock in the dining-room stopped this morning. My pocket watch stopped three days ago.)

(Telephone call from Branting this evening, which I refused to take.)

Very strange; I feel as if I were engaged. I have today chosen furniture for 'my wife's' room from Bodafors' catalogue. I have bought new clothes, as if I were expecting visits of congratulation. Suppose the whole thing is and remains make-believe? What then? Why, I shall write a poem, a beautiful poem, and the anguish of loss will be transformed into song! Dante never got his Beatrice, and therefore he remained faithful to her, in spite of the fact that she was married to another man!

On the other hand, I had a feeling this evening that my contact with her was broken off and as if all were over.

[. . .]

March 2nd.

Received a letter from Germany about (*B's*) visit as a guest artist. Engaged a messenger and sent it to (*B*). Thought to myself, now I have her in a trap. She came: lovely, child-like, gentle, wise. But immediately a rapping started on all the walls. She had with her *Damascus III* and to what was (as I thought) the question that would decide matters: 'Ought I to let "the Unknown One" end up in a monastery?' She answered: 'No, he has more to accomplish in life.' ... I had now intended to strike my great blow and ask ... but the question was not forthcoming and she slipped through my fingers. (In fact, she had written a letter accepting me. I did not receive it until April 25th, where it is now to be found.)*

In order to reveal my feelings I had put out (as if by accident) one of her green seals with four cords laid in a cross. She noticed it and smiled – smiled like a little girl when she has succeeded in catching her adorer off his guard. One thing is certain: she knows where she has me!

She offered to play the piano for me. Oh!

[. . .]

March 3rd.

Woke resolved to disclose my feelings to (*B*). Wrote a long letter and sent it off ... It should be being delivered at this moment.

It was delivered, to (*B*), who was at home. (Instantly the sky cleared and turned bright blue over the Baltic.) I was, however, not sensible of any smell, none at all, but I was

* This letter from Harriet Bosse is the one dated March 4th 1901, on page 295 of this book.

overcome by sleep, . . . and I was so cold that I had to light a fire and put on my brown cloak.

It is now 4.30. I know nothing. I have no presentiment of anything.

Read the text for the day, Passion Sunday, but could not feel devout!

What will happen now?

Evening, 9 o'clock. Nothing has happened. Have been uneasy and tense, but have experienced no contact with (B).

[. . .]

March 4th.

[. . .]

It is 10.30 a.m. Nothing has happened! G.H.M.[8]

At 11 o'clock a letter arrived from Schering giving his impression of (B's) portrait: 'ethereal'. Sent it on immediately to (B). Not so much as a whisper in reply, nor did I experience any sensation of her having received it.

It is now 6 o'clock. Nothing has happened.

Horrible shivering fit at dinner-time.

Another attack of drowsiness.

Wrote a letter to (B) and gave up hope. Suddenly the smell of incense returned! What can it mean?

Harriet Bosse to Strindberg, March 4th.

Herr Strindberg,

Thank you for your letter, it was so kind and gentle.

I should like with all my soul to give you the advice you ask for, but oh, what a very, very heavy responsibility!

If you believe that the woman you want to create for the Unknown One has the power to bind him fast to life by taking his hand and showing him all the brightness and goodness that is also to be found in the world, then he is not doing right by entering a monastery.

8. God Help Me.

But suppose she is not capable of it?

How disappointed he will be if he discovers by degrees that she is far from being as gifted, as intelligent and as wise as he had imagined her to be!

Suppose he comes to feel that her spirit is too small to keep pace with his great and mighty one? Do you not think that he will lose heart, and that all his hopes will collapse, so that darkness will enfold him even more closely than before?

And she! She will suffer, suffer because she cannot attain her great goal, which was to lead him forward to a reconciliation with mankind – the thing he so much wanted and hoped for.

I can so well imagine to myself that little woman's exultation and joy if the Unknown One, in spite of all her forebodings, quite calmly and quietly took her hand in his and walked onwards with her, towards the goal.

And forgot the monastery!

Your Harriet Bosse

March 5th.

Sent off my letter to (B) from the corner of Strandvägen. Then walked round the block, expecting that when going along Gref Magnigatan I should somehow become aware of her answer. I got to the corner of Storgatan . . . a window in her flat was open and out of it popped a little female head . . . What does that mean?

This morning, after I had drunk my coffee, I heard my name whispered in the room, though no one was with me in the flat.

At noon I played *The Midsummer Night's Dream.* Was overcome by evil thoughts, and threw (B's) picture into a cupboard.

Immediately afterwards she arrived!

It was then 4 o'clock!

At 5 o'clock I was engaged!

Think of it! I have kissed her beautiful little mouth and her tiny milk-teeth! And this morning I gave up hope! How strange life is!

[. . .]

Harriet Bosse's explanatory notes, 1932.

[. . .] He told me how severely and harshly life had treated him, how much he longed for a ray of light, a woman who could reconcile him with mankind and with woman. Then he laid his hands on my shoulders and looked deeply and ardently at me and asked: 'Will you have a little child by me, Fröken Bosse?' I curtsied and answered quite hypnotized: 'Yes, thank you,' and then we were engaged.

March 6th.

Had intended to go into town to buy rings when a letter arrived from (B) in which she warned me of her wickedness.

I have now written to her and am waiting.

When I returned home from my morning walk I found that my landlady had put the key of the dining-room on the inside and made up my sofa as a bed. Why, I wonder? Shall we fall so quickly? That is the way things go! The way they should go! The way they always go, must go!

Why wait? Perhaps she cannot be a mother? Why all these prosaic preliminaries?

Waited for 3.30, when she had promised to come! She did not come! Evil thoughts and passions raged!

The clock struck 6. She came, bright, calm, radiant, her mind made up; whereupon the matter was settled. She gave me violets! We went out to put an announcement in a newspaper. Went with Harriet and the Möllers* to Rydberg's in the evening.

* Harriet Bosse's sister Dagmar Möller, the singer, and her husband Carl Möller, the architect.

March 7th.

Dinner at Lidingöbro, a drive in Djurgården. Met the

March 8th.

Dinner at Lidingöbro, a drive in Djurgården. Met the King ... Beethoven evening at home, with Harriet, the Möllers, Axel, Carl Larsson, Richard Bergh and Gyllensköld. [...]

Strindberg to Harriet Bosse, March 31st.

Beloved,

[...]

To me you are 'Swanwhite', and when last night I laid my great, terrestrial-globe of a forehead beneath your little celestial one, then I knew that the universe had fallen into a state of harmony, and I noticed how I, an earth-spirit, was winning heavenwards through you, a spirit of the air!

This had to be written, for I could not say it. Hide it, for it is true, truer even than reality, knowledge, or experience!

Your Gusten

Harriet Bosse's explanatory notes.

As a fiancé Strindberg was a very attentive cavalier – sent flowers, presents, thought of everything that might give me pleasure. He even forced himself to take me out to dine at Rydberg's – he hated appearing in public. [...]

He liked taking a drive in a victoria, sometimes all went well, but alas, many were the occasions when a victoria was engaged, and I just about to get into it in eager anticipation, when 'No, I *cannot*, we must go in again,' would come from tightly compressed lips.

My memories of our engagement – apart from my own anxiety about how it would all turn out – are purely bright and beautiful. During it Strindberg himself was certainly in a very happy frame of mind, which inspired him to write the fairy play, *Swanwhite*.

Strindberg to Harriet Bosse, April 17th.

Beloved little Bosse,

[...]

Forgive me, friend, for spoiling your pleasure yesterday, but there are certain Powers that I cannot control.

When I stay quietly in my home, I am at peace. But if I go out among people, then Inferno is let loose.

That is why I long to have a home!

Your

Strix

April 18th

[...]

After many wonderful hours with Harriet – who really loves me – we managed today to get permission for the banns to be published. Our joy this morning was great, especially as we have been confronted by difficulties.[9]

Alone and at peace the whole day. At 6 o'clock this evening grew uneasy. Harriet was by then at the Möllers. At 7.30 I went to see her. She was (*poisoned*), and taking arsenic pills into the bargain, so that the place reeked of arsenic.

April 19th.

Olavus Petri. We shall publish the banns today. I got up at 5 o'clock and saw the sun rise in a marvellous sky. A bright heart of light with a green rim fell on my bed three times.

In the evening walked with Harriet towards the setting sun, which lit up our faces.

May 6th.

Married for the third time, after an engagement full of marvellous moments and brave struggles against the ugly.

9. Strindberg is here referring to the fact that he had not had all the necessary documents to prove that he was divorced from his second wife, Frida Uhl.

Our home-coming, to a room full of flowers and the whole flat illuminated, was like a fairy story.

[...]

May 7th.
Harmony.

May 8th.
She says I am the very husband for her – in all respects! – and I am certain she was made for me. I call her my first 'wife'.

We walk about the flat and wonder if it is true, if we shall be allowed to stay here or not. We do not feel it belongs to us.

This home has been paid for by my *Collected Dramatic Works*, the labour of 30 years.

Have been seized by an inexplicable longing to run away and rent an attic. I have told my wife about it. She says she understands!

[...]

The week of the Press Congress* and (*Dagmar's*) innocent activities as a procuress[10] saw the beginning of our dissensions. Harriet wanted to go to a masked ball. I bought trunks and threatened to go away.

May 30th.
Explanations. (*Sleeping apart.*)

May 31st.
[...]
(*Reconciliation.*)

---

* A Press Congress was held in Stockholm in the week of 23–31 May 1901. Strindberg here, as in other parts of the diary, has added a comment referring to an event of a later date. N.B. There are no entries between May 8th and May 29th 1901.

10. Dagmar Möller was in the habit of introducing Harriet to other men, a thing to which Strindberg strongly objected.

June 22nd.

Harriet went into the country: Two white pigeons, two small children beside the cab.

June 23rd.

Finished *Charles XIIth* this evening. At that same moment the music struck up on Gärdet[11] and the flags round the Maypole unfurled in the wind. Letter from Harriet, loving, tender.

June 25th.

Harriet home. Radiant with joy. She is reading *Charles XIIth* for me. We are now convinced that our union will be a lasting one, for we are living in complete harmony. I am telegraphing to Kymendö, trying to rent a cottage for the summer. If nothing is vacant we shall go abroad. Harriet is overjoyed at being back in her 'yellow room'* which is so beautiful, and peaceful, and according to her (*chaste*). It (*smells*) of incense.

June 26th.

Radiant morning, full of joy and hope.

Telegram from Kymendö to say it is let ... I now feel that I am not 'allowed' to leave Sweden, but must stay in my own country. H. is angry.

In the evening she set off, without saying goodbye, without saying where she was going!

What a night of anguish!

June 27th.

Horrible morning. Loss, sorrow, despair.

11. Ladugårdsgärdet. A large open space to the north-east of Stockholm, of which Strindberg had an uninterrupted view when he lived in Karlavägen. In his day it was used primarily by the military as an exercise ground, but also by the general public as a place of assembly on festive or political occasions.

* The Strindbergs' bedroom in their flat at 40 Karlavägen was decorated and furnished in yellow.

June 29th.

Letter from Harriet. She is on the Danish coast.

Harriet Bosse's explanatory notes, 1932.

One day Strindberg told me – to my great joy – that we were going to travel in Germany and Switzerland. We made our plans, booked tickets for the round trip and packed our bags. I was indescribably excited at the prospect, but on the very morning of our departure – we were actually on the point of setting off with our luggage – he groaned out: 'We are not going, the Powers will not allow it.' [. . .]

I grew impatient and nervy when, as a substitute for my summer trip, he gave me books to read in German, French and English. On top of everything else it appeared that he meant me to grind away at foreign languages! So I sobbed out that if he would not come too, I should go away on my own, to Hornbaek in Denmark. And that is what I did!

Strindberg to Harriet Bosse, June 29th.

[. . .]

After weeping for three days in my monastery – from which I have not stirred – I have your letter! [. . .]

Beloved! Do you not feel, even at a distance – for distance does not exist for us – that I only live for you, that I love you?

You are with me all day long and your incense travels through space to me, here in my room! [. . .]

What is this? Well, something to test us, I hope, just to test us! I am lacerated by self-reproach, but in my extremity I cry out: 'I could do nothing else'. I *could* not go, but I had no right, when it came to the point, to try to prevent you!

[. . .]

July 1st.
I went to meet Harriet at Hotel Monopole in Copenhagen. Slept at Hotel Kramer in Malmö. (Horrible.)

July 2nd.
Met Harriet. We went to Hornbaek. Stayed at The Kro.

July 10th.
Moved into 'The Red House' in Hornbaek, the one with the ivy.

August 1st.
Left for Berlin. Put up in the evening at Aachener Hof.

August 3rd.
Out to Charlottenburg (*terrible day*) after a scene with Harriet. She wanted me to take her to a whores' café, but I would not.

August 6th.
Returned, by the continental route.

August 7th.
Home again at 40 Karlavägen.

August 9th.
Visited a doctor. Pregnancy confirmed.

August 20th.
(*She said that the child's name was to be Bosse. Tit for tat! Crash!*)
This evening a meteor fell into the constellation of the Waggoner.

August 21st.
Fairly quiet, but horrible. Did not see Harriet until dinner time. This evening, at the same time, a meteor again fell in the neighbourhood of Capella; later on a shooting-star, *Easter* was being performed.
[. . .]

August 22nd.

Woke up with a disinclination for *Engelbrecht*, on which I have been working. Took out *The Corridor Play* and *Setting up House*.*

Overcome several times by drowsiness. Read about Beethoven.

Dinner time arrived and with it a letter from Harriet in which she announced that she had 'gone forever' ... What is to happen now? What am I to make of this affair that I took in holy earnest?

[...]

It is the anniversary of my father's birthday, and Harriet's name-day.

Received a letter from Gyllensköld. It contained some most remarkable news. It might have been written especially with me in mind, to comfort me. The fact is that his wife, with their unborn child, has left him.

[...]

August 23rd.

Alone. Dismal. Wept a great deal. Life seemed to me a cruel jest, especially with our finest feelings. Life is all humbug!

August 24th.

Alone. An attack of weeping in the morning. Took a walk on Gärdet later. On my way home I found first a hairpin, then an undamaged *horseshoe*.

[...]

August 25th, Sunday.

Alone. Wept a great deal. Given comfort by a book of devotions.

'You have passed through the like before and you survived it.'

* The names Strindberg gave to *A Dream Play* while he was working on it. They refer to the scenes between the Officer and the Lawyer.

Read my diary and all my letters to Harriet. Everything that had been great and lovely rose before me. I blessed her memory and thanked her for bringing light and joy into my life. (?)

August 26th, Monday.

Wept the whole day. From morning till evening my study was filled with the scent of incense (See Feb: Mar: of this year), sometimes refreshing, sometimes suffocating and exciting. I had the feeling that she was thinking kindly of me, perhaps longing for me!

[. . .]

Strindberg to Harriet Bosse, August 27th.

Say one single word! Tell me what you intend to do as soon as you yourself are sure.

I cannot hit upon any means of persuading you to return, as I do not know why you went. But if you, on your side, are waiting for a word from me, then I need hardly tell you, that your home here awaits you, just as pure as when you left it.

[. . .]   August Strindberg

Harriet Bosse to Strindberg, August 27th.

Can you not understand why I went? I did so to save at any rate the last remnants of feminine modesty and self-respect, that is why.

The language you used to me on that memorable day in Berlin has been for ever ringing in my ears. The things you then imputed have so sullied me that the most loving words you could utter would never wash them away or cover them up!

It was this feeling of outraged modesty that came over me the other day, and with such overwhelming force, that I felt I should be the most worthless of women if I went on enduring it by remaining with you.

I blame myself for being a coward, a *coward* in that I did not leave you on the spot, in Berlin. My excuse is that I was ill.

And suppose I were to return to you? Then, of course, you would despise me even more, and the next time you got annoyed over something or other, you would again – only worse – deluge me with the sort of words that I do not understand how a man can utter, even to the filthiest prostitute, let alone to his wife.

No Gusten, I cannot be trampled in the dirt, least of all now, when I am going to have a darling little baby. It shall come into the world *pure*.

You may imagine that things have not been easy for me lately for, after all, you are the father of my little baby. But rather than face a horrible future, full of unjust insults and pain for us both, I am going now, while I still have fresh in my memory all you have given me that is beautiful. –

[. . .]

Strindberg to Harriet Bosse, August 28th.

I stretched out my hand to you yesterday – that usually means let all the evil be forgotten; it usually means : forgive and forget. But you would not accept it. May you never regret it! [. . .]

There are things one is forced to say, even though one deprecates them. The thing that you recently took so badly was one of them. But it was a detonator, laid on the railway line at the last moment to give warning of danger.

Call to mind how it was set off. You wanted to deprive my child of my name. My comment was that, if my child was called B, it might harm it later in life and that its comrades might sometimes get it into their heads that it was illegitimate! [. . .]

Call to mind the first days of our marriage. The day after

our wedding you declared that I was not a man. A week later you wanted to let the whole world know that you were not yet Fru Strindberg, and that your sisters regarded you as 'unmarried'!

Was this kind? And was it wise?

If this child was not mine, then it must be another's. But that was not what you meant. You merely wanted to poison me, and that you did, but without being aware of what you were doing. That was why I had to bring you to your senses with a bang. [. . .]

August 29th.

Dreadful! Particularly having to see what is beautiful being dragged through the mud as now. Fie for shame!

August 31st.

Just as dreadful! Oh, how many tears!

September 1st.

Horrible to be living, alone!

Strindberg to Harriet Bosse, c. September 2nd.

[. . .]

Every hour is agony and I must leave this place if you do not come!

What do you demand of me? What are your conditions?

Tomorrow I intend to break up this home, our home, eradicate our memories, all of them, and – as I cannot go abroad – put myself among other people's things again, in a furnished room!

That done, I shall pray God to grant me the grace of forgetting you, of forgetting your name, that you have ever existed, you, whom I called my 'first wife'.

One thing gave me hope: Your letter from Denmark when you went off last time without saying goodbye. In it I read: 'Darling, what has happened? Our hearts that have been kissed together by God ...' And it ended with this cry of love in distress: 'Oh, my beloved friend!'

I have wept outwardly so that my eyes have paled, and inwardly so that my soul is washed clean! [. . .]

Harriet Bosse to Strindberg, September 3rd.

I have been putting myself to the test for a long time, so that I might finally be able to give you a decisive answer. It is best for both of us that I should not return. To live with you again with suspicion lurking under every word, every deed, would kill me. And you, on your side, would be tortured and hurt by things you were imagining, so that words – which you would certainly come to regret – would again slip from your lips. [. . .]

Our little child shall be kind and good. I shall always speak well of you to it. Of course it shall be called Strindberg if you wish. *If you can* I think you should go on living at Karlavägen. You have a home there, *which you ought not to break up.*

[. . .]   Harriet

September 3rd.

Letter from Harriet.

[. . .]

Rooms being torn to pieces!

A big rainbow. A hawk and a crow.

September 4th.

A ray of light. Wrote a letter 'To my child'. Had a friendly answer.

[. . .]

Strindberg to 'My unborn Child', September 4th.

To my child! (The little unborn one.)

My child! Our child! Our Midsummer child!

Your parents went about their home waiting for something; and, as all time spent in waiting is long and perhaps dreary, they thought *they* were dreary.

They were expecting something to come, and they did not know that it had come already, come beneath a white canopy in a silent, fragrant room with yellow walls, yellow as the sun and as gold!

Then your mother was seized by a longing to see her mother's country,* a wonderful longing that, though her heart bled, reft her from hearth and home.

And you, child of the South and the North, you were carried in the green fresh beech-woods, beside the blue sea.

And your beautiful mother rocked you on the blue waves of the sea that washes the shores of three kingdoms, and in the evenings, when the sun was going down, she sat in the garden and turned her face to the sun that you might drink light.

Child of the sea and the sun, you slept your first sleep in a little red, ivy-clad house, in a white room, where no word of hate was so much as whispered, and where nothing impure was so much as thought.

Then you made a black journey, a pilgrimage to the City of Sin,† where your father was to weep and your mother learn from his tears where that road was leading . . .

Then you came home to the golden room where the sun shines night and day, and where tenderness awaited you, and then you were carried away! . . .

Harriet Bosse to Strindberg, September 4th.

My child thanks you for your kind and beautiful message!

Harriet

* Harriet Bosse's mother was born in Denmark.
† Berlin.

September 5th.
Frightful!

September 6th.
I painted today!

For the first time in recent years the thought of suicide has risen in my mind. My motive: I am so keenly aware that this woman is going about with my gift to her of all that is finest in my soul, and inviting gatherings of people to partake of me. I feel defiled through her. Unknown men defile me by the glances with which they defile her. Through this woman I am sinking into the mire because, even if we are parted, I am sensible of her from a distance. Schopenhauer explains the meaning of 'la jalousie légitime' thus: 'My thoughts are led through my woman to the sexual acts of an unknown man. In certain respects she makes a pervert of me, indirectly and against my will.'

Suicide is a deadly sin, but Dante considered Cato* was reprieved from Inferno because he left the world of sin and bondage when he no longer saw any possibility of keeping his soul out of the dirt.

I feel that my spirit is bound down to the lower spheres of activity where my wife now operates. This love story, that to me was so extraordinarily great and beautiful, but which has dissolved into a mockery, has fully convinced me that life is an illusion. All our most beautiful encounters are made to dissolve like bubbles in dirty water in order to imbue us with a loathing for life. We do not belong here and we are too good for this miserable existence.

It was my soul that loved this woman, and the brutalities of marriage disgusted me. For that matter, I have never really been able to understand what the not very elegant act of procreation has to do with love for a beautiful

* Cato the Younger committed suicide after Julius Caesar had overthrown the Roman Republic.

female soul. The organ of love is the same as one of the ex-
cretory organs. How characteristic that is! (I discovered
four years ago that Hegel had said the same thing!) But I
cannot have a spiritual marriage with a woman who is not
my faithful wife, for if she is free and has an affair with
another man, she delivers over my soul and transmits my
love to that man, and thus forces me to live in a forbidden
relationship with a man's soul or body or both.

E. V. Hartman says that love is a farce invented by
nature to fool men and women into propagating their
species.

Life disgusts me and has always done so. Everything
is worthless! I have fulfilled my obligations and I have
been tortured enough. I think I have the right to go my
way!

This time I took life in a spirit of holy seriousness, and
look how cynically it has treated me.

It has always been the same! When I was a believing
young idealist, I was mocked for it! When I turned material-
ist, I was persecuted for that!

Life, for me, was as unmanageable as a woman; whatever I did was wrong and I was rebuked!

When I was immoral, abuse was heaped upon me, and
when I became moral I got even more of it!

People are not born wicked, but life makes them wicked.
So life cannot be an education, nor can it be a punishment
(that improves); it is simply an evil! In order to live at all
one must do evil to others just by getting in their way.

I was born for family life and a mate – and look what I
have got!

(My latest reflections on women and love – firmly based
on my own experiences – are to be found in *Damascus*,
Part Three.)

'Resignation!' Yes indeed, that was what I tried last.
But if you put up with everything, you have in the end to

endure filth and humiliation, and that is what you have no right to do!

September 7th.
    A terrible day. Painted! . . .
    Saw a one-legged pigeon hopping along the road this morning. (Compare a dream of 1906 in which I saw Harriet with only one leg.)
    [. . .]
    Impossible to know where you are with women. Whatever you do is wrong. One day they call you a (*satyr*), the next day a (*Joseph*). You can never tell what they want, if they are (*sensual*) or (*chaste*). One fine day they find they are with child. Then they 'wonder' how it happened. 'It is impossible!' In a word, the poisoning has begun. They begrudge a man paternal happiness and will deprive him of it even at the risk of drawing upon themselves the suspicion that they are (*whores*). Give but a hint of that suspicion and all h—l is let loose!
    Most women complain of disappointment in the matter of physical satisfaction. But a man would rather die before he complained. It never occurs to a woman to think that her husband may also have miscalculated about her. Oh this eternal torment of mutual recriminations, as if the bedroom held the keys to paradise!
    Sent a letter to Harriet. She was very ill yesterday and had to call two doctors. She was still in bed today. What has happened?

Strindberg to Harriet Bosse, c. September 8th.
Harriet,
    Before I put an end to my misery by entering a monastery or by some other means please write me that long letter and tell me why you cannot see me again. [. . .]

Harriet Bosse to Strindberg, September 8th.
Dear Gusten!

I ought to write you a long letter, but I have been and still am ill, so I shall not be able to collect my thoughts for a long, explanatory letter until a later date.

One thing I must tell you now. I cannot come home again, cannot, cannot! Forgive me if I cause you pain!!!

Harriet

September 8th.

A letter from Harriet. She says she *cannot* return!

Cato = the symbol of a voluntary decision to cast off the bondage of sin.

This evening she summoned me to visit her at the Möllers'. I saw her again. She behaved like an actress, insincere, scheming, as if she wanted to get something out of me. She was so changed that after ten minutes I got up saying: 'I do not know you. You are a stranger.' Then I left, without saying goodbye.

(She was like Nenny Geijerstam.)

September 9th.

Cleared the yellow room of her things! God was gracious and gave me strength to bear it, though I bled inwardly.

[. . .]

September 11th.

Sent away the grand piano! At it Harriet had her greatest and most beautiful moments. She was ethereally lovely. Only I have seen her like that!

September 13th.

Harriet came to see me. Started to reproach me, but when I reminded her of some of the many wicked things she had done she left, of course. For four months she pecked away at my liver, and I considerately held my tongue. Now, when I utter one single *justifiable* word of reproach, she departs, as if it were I who had ill-treated her! Just like a woman!

After she had gone I calmed down and did not feel the loss of her.

[. . .]

September 16th.

The determination to cut short my life is not new, it began when I was 8. Now it has reawakened in me as if it were an imperative duty.

The woman who has left me has taken with her all that is best and finest in my soul. I can feel from afar that she is going about befouling my soul which during my Inferno period I washed fairly clean. It is as if, through her, I was entering into forbidden relationships with men and with other women. This torments me, for I have always had a horror of intimacy with my own sex; so much so that I have broken off friendly relations when the friendship offered became of a sickly nature, resembling love. (I have never been able to explain these breaches to other people.)

Cato = the symbol of a voluntary decision to cast off the bondage of sin.

Yes, that is how I now feel. 'The decision' is coming to a head. I regard this act as a sacrifice of myself to God. He demands this proof of my faith that He is good and that I have nothing to fear as, through my sufferings, I have atoned for most things. He demands of me this deed of manly courage.

Terrible days! So many tears! Oh woe!

Harriet Bosse to Strindberg, September 20th.

Dear!

[. . .]

I woke at exactly 2 o'clock with a feeling that something

near me was striving to wake me up. Then by the light of the lamp I saw some roses that were on my table bending over me, half dead with suspense and weariness, and looking at me with large, dry, tired eyes . . .

Then followed violent palpitations and meaningless dread.

[. . .]

Your
Harriet

Strindberg to Harriet Bosse. September 21st.
My friend,

Only want to thank you for your letter. Am sending some roses which will certainly not look upon you with *dry* eyes. [. . .]

To see why you were woken on the stroke of 2 with palpitations and dread – read *Inferno*. You will find the explanation there.

Your friend,
August Strindberg

Harriet Bosse to Strindberg. September 21st.
Dear!

Thank you for the lovely flowers. They are filling the room with the most heavenly perfume!

Who do you think can miss our times together at table more than I? Or the happiness of being beside you as you work?

Your
Harriet

Strindberg to Harriet Bosse. September 22nd.
Dearest,

You complain most of all that you *may* not sit with me. Who is forbidding you?

Can you give me an answer to that?

Only recently you promised God that you would sit at table with me for the rest of your life!

[...]

Harriet Bosse to Strindberg, September 21st.

I may not sit with you any more for this reason: if we come together again you will see things as unlovely. Oh, *that* is what I am so afraid of!

[...]

The next time we exchange views or either of us expresses a wish, the bomb will explode again.

I with my unshakeable opinions and you with yours, though of course we can adapt ourselves to each other – to some extent.

But just think what it would be like for me to have to hear, yet again, that I drag you down! I, who want nothing so much as to see you raised on high!

[...]

There are times too, when I am overcome by a mad desire to *laugh*, to rejoice, to embrace everything and everyone out of sheer delight. You would never understand that. If I suppress this impulse I shall wither and die, and into the bargain it would only make you unhappy to hear me talk like that. What then is it best for us to do, dear? If you dare to take me back after what I have told you, prepared as you now are for my way of looking at things, and if you *promise* me the sort of understanding that I will try to show you, then I will come.

[...]   Harriet

September 22nd, Sunday.

Terrible day. Suicide an obsession. Harriet came in the evening, meaning to stay, but left again. (She told me later that she thought she was on the brink of insanity. Went from here down to Munkbron, but did not know why. Afterwards sat on her sofa all night – until the morning.)

September 23rd, Monday.

Moved to 7 Brahegatan. Drove with Harriet to Liding-öbro and had lunch.

Most extraordinary day! C'est la vie! Complete harmony, everything hopeful!

Christina is finished!

Harriet Bosse to Strindberg, September 23rd.

Dear!

My thoughts follow you, as always. Oh that I could slip into your new home with them, and let you feel all the good I wish you : that you may find peace and rest from all sick and dismal thoughts.

[...]

Went to Karlavägen this evening to talk to Lovise; but there was no one at home. Shut up and dark. So dark that it can surely never be lit up again. –

It is so strange, all this that is happening ... Good night – I should like to lay my hand on your forehead this even-ing –

[...] Your Harriet

September 24th.

Moved out of Brahegatan in terrific haste.

(This is what happened there. When I moved in the lock flew out of the door, so that it could not be closed; the wardrobe smelt of carbolic acid, everything was dirty, and the landlady said her belongings must be left in the drawers with mine. Mat-beating in the courtyard and piano lessons going on somewhere.

The next morning the earthenware stove in my bedroom was demolished.)

Back again at Karlavägen. A visit from Harriet.

September 25, 26, 27, 28th.

Terrible days. The impulse to die by my own hand grows stronger. It will soon be irresistible.

Why do I want to die? ... To escape from the bondage of sin. To free myself from an evil to which I can put no name! To offer myself up as a sacrifice for all my sins! God demands of me this act of faith! My blood shall atone for my past, and with my blood my longing for evil will be obliterated.

It is not Harriet's fault! The part she played in my life was, as she said herself, a 'task'. She was my last ray of sunshine, and for that I thank her. I loved her so deeply that I had to be punished!

My past? Can one ever fathom the depths of a creative artist's life? Has a man any right to repent of his past, from which he has learnt and which he did not stage himself? I have lived as I could and not as I should have wished! Being dragged through the mire, as I have been, was in itself a punishment! Like other people I acted evilly from lack of judgement or in the heat of the moment. And have I not suffered punishment enough? (See *Damascus, Part Three.*)

When I looked upon Harriet's beauty, which was sometimes 'ethereal', I trembled in awe and my former belief in woman as the connecting link between man and child was shaken. Then I told myself that though woman is, in origin, a higher being than man, she has fallen lower. For the wickedness and falsehood of woman is boundless – 'she cannot speak a word of truth.' ...

When Harriet was in our flat there was light, literally. When she left, it grew dark, literally, not figuratively. But this was not always so, often quite the contrary!

(But how can what is dark spread light? For she comes from the dark underworld. She is 'the wickedest woman ever born' as she said herself in a letter of 1901.)

All the same, her bright (?) little spirit could not prevail over my darkness, and when I saw that this was so, I begged her to save me, but too late!

'Poor friend,' I said, 'it is for me to go and by doing so to give you back your freedom and your light.'

Negotiations, doubts, this way and that.

October 4th.

Went out to Djurgårdsbrunn and had dinner with Harriet. Home afterwards. x x x. Then she left promising to return home tomorrow.

October 5th.

Harriet returned in . . . light! T.B.t.G.*

October 6th, Sunday.

. . . Peace reigns! Went to the Opera! Heard Aida!

October 10th.

Peace and light; but mixed with some fears that it may not last.

October 11th.

Darkness!

November 18th.

Am reading about Indian religions.

The whole world is but a semblance (=Humbug or relative emptiness). The primary Divine Power (Maham-Atma, Tad, Aum, Brama), allowed itself to be seduced by Maya, or the Impulse of Procreation.

Thus the Divine Primary Element sinned against itself. (Love is sin, therefore the pangs of love are the greatest of all hells.)

The world has come into existence only through Sin, – if in fact it exists at all – for it is really only a dream picture. (Consequently my *Dream Play* is a picture of life), a phantom and the ascetics allotted task is to destroy it. But this

* Thanks be to God.

task conflicts with the love impulse, and the sum total of it all is a ceaseless wavering between sensual orgies and the anguish of repentance.

This would seem to be the key to the riddle of the world.

I turned up the above in the History of Literature,* just as I was about to finish my Dream Play, *The Growing Castle*,[12] on the morning of the 18th. On this same morning I saw the Castle (= Horseguards' Barracks) illuminated, as it were, by the rising sun.

Indian religion, therefore, showed me the meaning of my *Dream Play*, and the significance of Indra's Daughter, and the Secret of the Door = Nothingness.

Read Buddhism all day.

* For his account of Indian religion Strindberg used Arvid Ahnfelt's *History of World Literature* (1875).

12. This was the title Strindberg often gave to *A Dream Play*, but by it he also meant an actual building, the Horseguards' Barracks, built in 1897, which he could see from his windows in Karlavägen. Resting on the pillars of the small balcony on top of the dome is a curious bud-shaped baldachin.

1902

Harriet Bosse's explanatory notes, 1932.

While I was expecting little Anne-Marie, Strindberg was always kind and considerate. Sometimes he could not resist raking up the touchy subject of women's rights. His whiskers would bristle and I would weep; then off he would go to a wash-stand he had in his room, wash his hands several times in nervous haste – as he always did when he was upset – and the storm would blow over. [. . .]

Strindberg promised, as he had done in 1901, that we should spend the summer in the country. Suitable places were discussed this way and that, but we could not agree. I was afraid that, when it came to the point, Strindberg would decide to stay on in Stockholm. I was longing to get into the country, which I have always loved, and I also wanted to escape from my sedentary life in Karlavägen.

If, now and then, I complained of feeling lonely, I was told: 'How can you say that you are lonely? When you are on the stage you are among your friends and you have the whole of the audience as well.' As time was dragging on and we remained firmly stuck in Stockholm, I made up my mind to take my little girl to Rävsnäs, an estate on the shores of Mälaren, where I had spent a year as a girl.

January 1st.

When Harriet returned to me on October 6th she was carrying Lillan[13] and she did so until March 25th.

13. Lillan, meaning the little girl, and Lillen, the little boy, are used as pet names in Sweden, often for as long as the girl or boy remains the youngest in the family.

Atmosphere calm but heavy. We play chess, we play the piano, Harriet works at her modelling, reads, goes for walks. Few visitors. Axel comes occasionally to play Beethoven.

January 9th.
[. . .]
Harriet crocheted a black collar; went to bed at 8 o'clock. She rejoices at the thought of the child.

March 8th.
Harriet ill this evening and during the night. She thought the child was about to arrive. A (*strange*) day. (My clothes caught fire in the night.) Harriet gave the alarm and I jumped out of bed to telephone for the midwife. When I lit the lamp my fluffy dressing-gown caught fire and burst into flames.
It was a false alarm.

March 25th, Lady Day.
Our daughter was born at 7.15 p.m.

April 5th, Saturday.
Explanations! Dark!

May 6th.
Anniversary of our wedding!! (*No flowers.*) Only (*Axel*) came.

June 4th.
All well after (*a long period of coldness*).

June 15th.
(*Crash, while at table. Dinner.*) [. . .]

July 3rd.
Absolutely awful. But ended well! Harriet left for the country, perfectly friendly. (*Räfsnäs*).

Strindberg to Harriet Bosse, July 4th.

My darling Wife,

Naturally there was a calm at first – as there always is after an earthquake, accompanied by thunder ... but then it became rather too calm. I missed the patter of your restless little spirit on the floors; I missed the doors not being left open, and most of all perhaps (?), I missed the little cries from the nursery. But when I think how irreconcilably horrible my feeling of loss would have been if we had parted in anger yesterday, why then I am happy, and the calm is as refreshing as a rest!

[...]

Moreover, when I am alone you are present with me, but when I have company you disappear, and contact with you is broken.

[...]   Your little husband,

                                              Gusten

Harriet Bosse's explanatory notes, 1932.

Of course Strindberg longed for me and for Anne-Marie. Left on his own in town, solitude became burdensome, and he wanted to join us. Nothing ever came of this. Our dissensions had already begun. I felt myself imprisoned and shut up in a cage, and he thought it was quite normal that I should stop at home.   [...]

With him, resignation was only a momentary thing. He was not sufficiently balanced to be resigned. He always flared up again. To the very last he struggled against his Karma.

It was probably the great difference in our ages that separated us most of all. Strindberg had lived his life and he had finished with a whole lot of things on which I had not even begun.

July 3rd.

Stiff letter from H—t. I answered it sharply and frankly, for the first time.

July 26th.

Harriet came. Had dinner ... and left again uncertain whether we should have any more children.

August 1st.

Harriet came and left again. All was quite pleasant and affectionate!

August 22nd.

Harriet telephoned this morning to say that she was returning. By noon she had changed her mind.

September 1st.

Gyllensköld, Geijerstam and I at Rydberg's.

The night that followed at home was terrible.

September 2nd.

The first half of today was very nearly the most frightful time I have had. At 5 p.m. things took a turn for the better.

October 14th.

Today, in the early morning, she was aware of the smell of incense from herself, and I noticed it too. After that I was persecuted by it all day. It was exactly like the smell that occurred in the early days of our acquaintanceship. It began at noon on February 4th, 1901, when Harriet was collating in *Easter* and I was reading Maeterlinck's *Princess Maleine*.

This smell throws me into a state of ecstasy and makes me happy when I first notice it, though my sensations are mixed with terror. (Witchcraft and madness.)

[...]

October 24th, Friday.

Fair Haven and Foul Strand published. Fetched Harriet from *Simoon.** Restaurant in Masonic Lodge ... pleasant walk home. Crash when we got home, on the subject of my book.[14]

[. . .]

November 18th.

Harriet intending to go to a concert with (*Dagmar*). The idea of their meeting frightened me. A couple of hours later came a telephone message to say (*D*) was ill and could not go.

November 19th.

Incense again, very strongly.

November 20th.

Fröken Key called. Driven out by me, with good reason.[15]

November 22nd.

At the dinner table, while Harriet was out, the following inexplicable thing happened. My wedding ring, which I wear on the inside of my engagement ring (with the sapphire) fell from my finger on to the floor, but N.B.! my engagement ring remained on. This is quite inexplicable.

[. . .]

* Harriet Bosse was at this time playing Biskra, the leading part in Strindberg's one-act play, *Simoon.*

14. *Fair Haven and Foul Strand* contained the story of his second marriage.

15. Ellen Key, the author and ardent apostle of female emancipation, with whom Strindberg had at one time been on the best of terms. She had called to ask Harriet Bosse to take part in an evening of readings and recitations to be held in honour of Bjørnson's 70th birthday. Strindberg, who suspected her of wanting to disrupt his third marriage, would have none of it.

1903

March 4th.

[...]

When (*Harriet*) got back from Lindberg's *Peer Gynt* this evening I gave her a piece of my mind and there was a terrible scene. Went to bed in a state of the most frightful disharmony. Thought I should die of contrition. But then in my Book of Devotions I read: 'This was he whom we had sometimes in derision ... We fools accounted his life madness and his end to be without honour. How is he numbered among the children of God and his lot is among the Saints?' Wisdom of Solomon 5: 3, 4, 5. This book, usually so severe, was gentle and gave me comfort, so that I fell asleep under the impression that I had been right to speak out even as brutally as I had. It is true that I was woken up a few times during the night, but my dreams were more beautiful than any I had had before.

[...]

March 5th.

Woke in the morning with a delightful sense of peace, as if all evil had departed from my house. It seemed to me purified and serene (just as it was last summer when Harriet was away).

Set out for my morning walk without having seen either my wife or my child. It had rained in the night; spring-like air, sunshine and gentle breezes. People struck me as being kindly disposed towards me.

[...]

When I got home after my walk there was dead silence in the house. I thought everyone had gone, but only Madam had departed. Indescribable peace reigns as I write this. She came back again!

March 6th.
    Dark in the flat, oppressive, poisonous.
    Sultry days. Calm but threatening, Lillan ill.

March 15th, Sunday.
    Had been thinking of going away but saw a newspaper on a chair with an advertisement in huge print: *Do not travel!* underlined. Pointed it out to Harriet! An hour later she had laid out a card on which was written: 'Thou shalt not kill!' What can she mean? Does she think I intend to kill her?

March 18th.
    Crash! Harriet is telephoning to a lawyer about a divorce.
    N.B.! The whole nursery and Madam's room are infested by vermin.

March 19th.
    Alone! Horrible.

March 20th.
    This morning I gave Harriet back my wedding ring. Then I went to the telephone. When I returned to my room the ring was lying on my desk. I took this to imply that she did not want to break with me. Curiously enough, though I should like to be free, the thought that she was still fond of me gave me a certain sense of satisfaction, almost pleasure. I sat down to write in good spirits – until one o'clock. Then for the first time it occurred to me to look at the ring, which I had put in a drawer. It was *her* ring! What my feelings were then is not clear to me . . .

April 4th, Palm Sunday.
    Alone at home this evening a feeling of anxiety came over me. I got it into my head first that Harriet was in mortal

danger, then that she had been brought home dead and that I was alone with Lillan. My sorrow was great.

[. . .]

May 27th.

Electric fire left on all night ! ! ! (Out of spite on Harriet's part.)

May 28th.

On the night of the 27th Harriet came home at about 11 p.m. friendly and bringing various pieces of good news for me. She kissed me good-night and went to bed.

At 1.30 she woke me up and let fly at me the most appalling scolding because she believed I was having an improper affair with our maid, Ellen. It is simply not true, I swear it! Poor Harriet, who tried to poison me by making me jealous. Now the demon has taken hold of her!

[. . .]

June 9th.

Harriet and Lillan have gone to Blidö.

June 22nd.

Went to Blidö.

[. . .]

July 6th.

Left Blidö after a terrible scene.

[. . .]

July 31st.

Harriet came to town. Telephoned to Axel asking him to meet her, but he would not. Harriet did not come. I was not sorry.

August 1st.

Cleared the flat of all the odds and ends that belonged to Harriet.

[. . .]

August 15th.

Harriet came to town this morning, but I did not see or hear anything of her.

I bought flowers this morning; needed some light but got darkness that grew blacker towards the evening. Axel here. He played Brahms, which made me nervous and disharmonious. The lamps were not burning properly, the sideboard creaked, the tray clinked, the clock behaved uncannily.

Then came a telephone call from Harriet. She was mournful, gentle; ('Do you love me?'). She is in difficulties at her new home at 30 Biblioteksgatan.

Harriet Bosse's explanatory notes, 1932.

In the autumn of 1903 I moved with Lillan into a furnished flat. This did not mean that Strindberg and I had broken with each other. He often came to see us, and Anne-Marie and I fell into the habit of dining with him every Sunday. This way of life brought our daily disputes to an end and we met only in a happy and festive mood. Of course Strindberg sometimes became bitterly aware of his loneliness, and then I would receive a letter like the one below.

Strindberg to Harriet Bosse, August 25th.

How are things with me? Think what you would feel if you were forcibly torn from your child, and then you will know!

[. . .]

What do you want of me? You are free now and have the peace and happiness that you lacked at my side. Did you not discover that I was the reason for your lack of peace?

Grasp happiness, which I denied you, but let me keep my sorrow pure. Follow your own destiny, which you feel you can control, but do not interfere with my destiny, which is controlled by another! the one of whom you know nothing!

August 21st.
  [...]
  During the night I was woken by a feeling that Harriet was attacking me, out of spite. Then I dreamt that I was lying on the sofa in my study; somebody came in with Lillan and held her out to me to fondle. I took her little face between my hands, wanting to look at her, but I could not open my eyes; it was dark, I was blind. Thereupon I woke up and wept a great deal. Felt sure that Lillan was ill. Dreamt about her time after time.

August 22nd.
  Worked on the play about Luther.[16] Was aware of a friendly Harriet all day (Incense).
  [...]

September 5th.
  Re-established relations with Harriet and Lillan. They are living at 30 Biblioteksgatan. Harriet has bought a grand piano.[17] The first time she played it her engagement ring broke. Later she hurt her mouth on the music rack so that her lip swelled up.
  [...]

October.
  It is two years since Harriet left me!
  We are now enjoying the best time we have had together. Harmony in *all* respects! We live apart but meet at dinner with Lillan and in the evening.

16. *The Nightingale of Wittenberg.*
17. Strindberg hated grand pianos and was angry because Harriet Bosse had insisted on having one at Karlavägen. No doubt he thought these accidents were a punishment.

November 1st.

Harriet, I and Lillan were going for a drive in Djurgår-den. However, when Harriet and Lillan were waiting out-side their door for the cab, Harriet saw the heads of two horses appearing round the corner; 'There comes our cab,' she said. The horses moved forward, – they were pulling a hearse –

Was this a warning?

November 2nd.

A rupture with Harriet, for no reason!

November 3rd.

Alone!

November 5th.

Saw the 'Castle' illuminated by sunshine. In a bright mood. Saw a picture of 'Victoria with a triumphal wreath'[18] in a window in Banérgatan. Met all my Djurgård friends in a body. Flags are being flown! Finished *The Lamb and the Beast*.

Harriet with me in the evening.

December 2nd.

Harriet to dinner. Subsequently in the yellow room! In dread of a child. Went to see Harriet in the evening. Harriet extremely nervous and I was frightened. When I got home I 'saw' a child's face on a card decorated with roses that had been placed on the calendar showing the date. Thought: now we are going to have another child.

18. The name Victoria had a special significance for Strindberg. When returning to Sweden from Switzerland to face a charge of blasphemy, after the publication of his book *Getting Married*, he was very depressed until he saw that the name of the boat that was to take him from Kiel to Denmark was *Augusta Victoria*. He interpreted this to mean Victory for August. He was in fact acquitted.

December 4th.

Gustav Adolf being performed in Berlin.

Sunshine reflected on all the window-panes this morning.

A cart with palms and laurels dogged my footsteps. Rose-red and yellow.

Harriet with me in the evening; very pleasant atmosphere.

[...]

1904

January 22nd.

My birthday. Harriet brought roses.

January 23rd.

Rupture again, for the thousandth time.

January 24th.

At the dinner-table today the petals from Harriet's roses came showering down on the plates like so many red hearts.

February 1st.

A reunion with Harriet. In dread of a child.

Believe we are going to have a child.

February 9th.

Harriet here this evening. We talked about getting a divorce. Crash! – *She went away; probably for the last time* – Horrible!

[. . .]

March 7th.

Harriet here again.

March 20th, Sunday.

Anniversary of Mother's death. Went for a drive in Djurgården with Harriet and Lillan. In mood and manner Harriet was just like she used to be when we were engaged, kind, . . . Slept in the yellow room. In dread of a child. (She behaved like a girl of fourteen.)

March 27th.

Harriet and Lillan to dinner. (Afterwards – in dread of a child.) That evening H. was taken ill at the theatre and the performance had to be broken off.

March 29th.

Harriet went to Saltsjöbaden.

April 9th.

Letter from Harriet in which she asks for a divorce.
[. . .]

Harriet Bosse's explanatory notes, 1932.

It was impossible to go on living as we were, to all appearances in different places; either we had to live together
or to get a divorce. We decided that we would apply for a
divorce.

Being wrenched first one way and then another in my
marriage, combined with over-exertion in my theatrical
work was too much for me, and I broke down completely.

Strindberg to Harriet Bosse, April 10th.

My friend,

So you really think that a simple-minded lawyer can
achieve what we ourselves have tried to do but failed. Or
is it that you feel your bonds are too irksome? If so, then
it must be as you wish, though it seems to me that you
have availed yourself of your freedom without much regard for your bonds. The marriage ceremony could not
bind us, but you think that divorce can part us; very well
then! I, who have felt myself bound by my vows, might
derive benefit from it. I could then associate with whom I
pleased, furnish my home as I pleased, keep what servants
I pleased, think and act as I pleased, without anyone having the right to object. [. . .]

April 12th.

Harriet back from Saltsjöbaden.

April 13th.

Harriet with a lawyer. Divorce proceedings started.
[. . .]

April 18th

Went to the lawyer's and signed the petition for a divorce. I experienced a sensation of great and solemn calm. Axel and Gyllensköld came of their own accord this evening. We had some Beethoven. I put away the Venus – which I bought with the Jason* on my wedding day – and took out the portraits of my children.

Had a very friendly telephone call from Harriet in the morning.

April 19th.

This is Master Olof's day (Olaus Petri). N.B. *The Gothic Room* comes out tomorrow.

In Djurgården met two riders (separated by a long interval) both unable to control restive horses, though in the end they did get the upper hand. – I went up to Hasselbacken and looked at the veranda window and the Bird-Cherry, where I had sat in the Sun at my wedding breakfast, when I married Harriet. I experienced next to no emotion, only a quiet satisfaction at being free. I did not regret what had happened; on the contrary it seemed to me bright, almost beautiful, though it has been so ugly.

N.B! Three years ago today I published the banns!

[...]

April 24th, Sunday.

Went for a walk in Djurgården. Saw the figure IX, 9 three times. 'Saw' Harriet, dressed in blue on my special path by the shore. Am still not certain whether it was her or not.

This evening, in the neighbourhood of the setting sun, I saw clouds which formed themselves into peaks, mountains,

---

* Two statues, the latter by Thorvaldsen. Strindberg had obviously bought them because they symbolized Woman and Man, i.e. Harriet Bosse and himself.

wooded eminences and castles (resembling Valhalla in *Rhinegold*). N.B! For three years now, in the spring, the summer and the autumn, I have seen these same cloud-formations in a west or north-westerly direction after sun-set. I am beginning to think that these 'cloud-formations' must have a foundation in fact, for they are invariably the same. They must be optical illusions (or mirages) of places on the earth of which we know nothing. Sweden-borg speaks of high places on the earth, unknown to us, where mighty beings dwell.

[...]

Harriet was acting in *A Venetian Comedy*, but in the middle of it she became convinced that her jaw was locked, and that she was unable to speak. A doctor had to be sent for!

May 5th.

Harriet is taking mud baths. (!)

Lillan came to see me; lost a button from her coat.

May 6th.

Axel, Rich. B. C., Gyllensköld and Nordström here this evening, for the last time until the autumn. Axel played Beethoven's Ninth Symphony, the Concerto in G major and the Overture to Egmont. I have never been so much moved. We were all happy and in good spirits. At about 12 o'clock the electric light failed and we had to sit in darkness. I took this to mean that all was over between me and Har-riet. We said goodbye to this flat as if we never expected to meet here again. I took a candelabra and retired to bed. A memory of the wonderful atmosphere of my wedding night came upon me; but strangely enough, I did not re-member that it was the anniversary of my wedding day; did not remember it until today, the 7th, in the evening. Three years have passed since then!

May 7th.

Have been re-reading *Inferno* and *Legends* in a reverent frame of mind, but I still do not understand the intentions of Providence. Are we to be made to suffer in order to learn, or are we to be punished and frightened off?

May 16th.

Received an impertinent letter from Harriet; conceited and wicked.

Axel here this evening. *The Growing Castle* (Horse-guards' Barracks) was lit up by the setting sun for the first time for ages.

[...]

May 17th.

Saw a white cross outside my front-door. Whitsun cold and dismal.

May 24th.

When I drew up my blind this morning two white pigeons were sitting on a chimney, caressing each other demonstratively. Had a loving, rapturous letter from Harriet.

[...]

May 27th.

A book on Buddhism arrived by post from Schering this morning. My eye was immediately caught by one chapter-heading 'The Permissibility of Suicide', and these words of Buddha's: 'In three months from today the man who has run his course will go to his eternal rest.'

A letter from Harriet and we took up the threads again. She will come to Furusund at midsummer, after she has been in Paris.

(I have just remembered that last autumn, when I ordered legs for Harriet's bed, the carpenter made them exactly like the legs of a coffin.)

Strindberg to Harriet Bosse, May 27th.

Beloved!

Is one not doing the right thing if one follows one's best feelings, especially when they direct one to do what is right?

Is there not clear enough indication that we are drawn to each other, in spite of all our differences?

[...]

[...] Just as your theatrical work is your affair, so my writing must be mine. We must have nothing in common but our home, our child and our friends. If we each have our own circle of friends, we shall drift apart and be unfaithful.

[...]

But we must live as man and wife, for I love your body as I love your soul, and I know that our knowledge of each other has gained ground, though this has required time, as I told you it would on our first night together.

[...]

May 28th.

Harriet broke with me by letter and took everything back.

May 30th.

The first thing I saw outside my front-door this morning was a cart labelled 'Victoria'.

Harriet here to dinner and we 'came together' again. (In dread of a child!)

May 31st.

Another crash! Rich. Bergh, Gyllensköld and Axel here.

June 1st.

Left for Furusund at 1 o'clock with Lillan. Harriet, who was leaving for Copenhagen that evening to facilitate her divorce, stood on the quay waving to us. I experienced no emotion, merely noted, with complete detachment, that I had had a beautiful young wife and felt grateful for that, and justifiably proud.

Met Svennberg on the boat. We celebrated.

Beautiful evening at Furusund.

Somewhat overwrought during the night.

June 2nd.

Glorious morning. Walked to Monte Bello alone. As I stood there again, after the lapse of four years, and saw my archipelago with its stretches of water and its islands, I rediscovered myself. Then, when I saw the northern point of Köpmansholm – the one I sailed past last year, when I was fleeing from Blidö and Harriet's violent behaviour – it seemed to me that I had again found purity, freedom and peace.

[...]

Am now recalling several minor aspects of my relationship with Harriet in our early days. A couple of months before we were engaged I woke at night in my bed and felt as if H—t were there. I 'possessed' her before we were engaged. I did not seek her; on the contrary she sought me. When I visited Harriet during our engagement, I used to be overcome by an inexplicable sensation of *weight*, so that I would collapse on her sofa saying: 'I feel so heavy, just as if I were sinking through all the floors and being drawn to the centre of the earth.' (Opposite of levitation.) In the early days of our marriage Harriet used to get cramp in the calf of her leg as she lay in my arms.

[...]

On our first night Harriet was so like my 2nd wife that it frightened me. We were also disturbed on those first nights by the 'nightmare'. We both used to wake up suffering from palpitations and dread, so much so that we had to get out of our beds.

June 3rd .

[...]

Even though Harriet is now in Denmark I sense her presence in my mouth, like violets. Very close in the early morning. x x x.

June 4th. Saturday.

Axel came. Beethoven night, Harriet is so close to me that I think she must be in Stockholm, or even here in Furusund.

June 6th.

Harriet so close to me this morning that she seemed to be in the room. A card from Harriet this evening, from Korsör and Cologne. At Cologne on the 4th, i.e. Saturday. That means she is in Paris today, yet I could feel her in this room! She was friendly and gave no hint of any kind of divorce.

June 16.

Harriet's perfume has been absent. Today it returned, strongly!

June 17th.

Card of Notre-Dame from Harriet. She lit a candle there for me on Sunday.

[...]

June 18th.

[...]

Letter from Harriet saying she went to a service in Sacré-Cœur on the 16th and lit a candle.

June 22nd.

Harriet came!

Harriet's return from Paris to Furusund is one of my loveliest memories. When she left my bed that night she did not look like herself. Her face was long and oval (as it is in the portrait of her as Miss Hopps (?)* and she gave off a fragrance so strong and delicious, that I fell into a state of ecstasy and almost lost consciousness. This thing is supernatural and sometimes makes me think she must be a being from a very high sphere, not an ordinary mortal.

[...]

July 18th.
Crash! I thought of going back to town.

[...]

August 9th.
Left Furusund without saying good-bye to Harriet. Axel and Gyllensköld came to my home in the evening.

August 12th.
Harriet came to town. A strangely uneasy evening at her home. The plants in her room had been removed. It was desolate, bare.

August 13th.
When I was on my way to Biblioteksgatan at 7 o'clock this evening, the sun was right in the middle of the background at the end of Kommendörsgatan, 1½ times as high as the trees in Humlegården, so that no part of the street was in shadow.

August 22nd.
Harriet's name-day. It is 3 years since she left me. She came to dinner; became unwell; in dread of a child.

[...]

August 23rd.
[...]
Harriet to dinner. Left the table in a temper.

* Jerome K. Jerome's play *Miss Hobbs* which was performed at Dramaten in 1902–3 with Harriet Bosse in the leading part.

August 26th.

Harriet here for dinner. Left. Axel and Anna with me in the evening.

Lillan ill in the night.

[...]

September 3rd.

Life is so horribly ugly, we human beings so abysmally evil, that if a writer were to describe *all* that he had seen and heard no one could bear to read it. I can think of people I have known, good, respectable, popular people, who have said or done things that I have crossed out, things I can never bring myself to mention and that I refuse to remember. Breeding and education seem to do no more than mask the beast in us, and virtue is a disguise. Our highest achievement is the concealment of our vileness.

Life is so cynical that only a swine can be happy in it, and anyone who can see this hideous life as beautiful is a swine!

Sure enough, life is a punishment! A hell. For some a purgatory, for none a paradise.

We are absolutely forced to do evil and to torment our fellow men. It is all sham and delusion, lies, faithlessness, falsehood and self-deception. 'My dear friend' is my worst enemy. Instead of 'My beloved' one should write 'My hated'.

September 6th.

Letter from Harriet, in which she humbles herself. Wants to leave the theatre and stay with me; but I have already written to Miller* telling him to start divorce proceedings.

[...]

October 29th.

Lillan left me today. Harriet returned from Finland.

* James Millar, the lawyer who was handling the Strindbergs' divorce.

October 30th, Sunday.

Very close contact with Harriet. x x x though divorced!

Harriet Bosse's explanatory notes, 1932.

I got my divorce from Strindberg during my season in Helsingfors in 1904. As in the preceding year Strindberg often came to see us, and Lillan and I went on being his guests at dinner on Sundays.

December 6th.

[...]

Very close contact with Harriet during the night of the 5th and for the whole of this day. The Growing Castle (Horseguards' Barracks) magically lit up while I was writing *Black Flags*.* Two white figures standing on the balcony of the tower.

December 10th.

Nobel's day.

Yesterday evening, the 9th, I sent off the letter I wrote to Harriet 14 days ago. We were divorced on October 27th.

[...]

December 20th.

Letter from Harriet in which she tells me, among other things, that on the previous night the oil-painting of Möller fell from the wall, knocking a large palm that was underneath it to the floor, while it remained upright, as if it had been lifted down. M. so much alarmed by this that he postponed his proposed trip to Paris until Christmas.

December 21st.

The Möllers went all the same, but only to Copenhagen. Letter from Harriet. 'The Distant One'.[19]

[...]

* *Black Banners.*
19. *'Die Ferne'.*

December 24th, Christmas Eve.

Strange day. I had made up my mind to being alone at home. At 6 o'clock Emil Sjögren arrived. He sat down to the piano and began to play. The telephone rang. It was Harriet asking me to go and spend Christmas Eve at her home. I went! Everything was peaceful and pleasant. At 10 o'clock Inez and Alf* arrived and we sat having supper until 11.30. Down in the street Inez fell and lost all her money in the snow. (The following year Inez went bankrupt.) Then I remembered that Harriet had just been telling us upstairs how her elder sister (Dagmar) had fallen on the self-same spot sometime ago and had sprained her ankle. She had had to lie there calling for help as she could not get up. A passing butcher's boy would not touch her. She got help in the end and was taken home in a cab. She had to stay in bed for a week. (She was the person who parted me from my wife and child!)

* Inez and Alf Ahlqvist, Harriet Bosse's sister and her son.

1905

Strindberg to Harriet Bosse, January 1st.

Beloved,

Want to thank you for Christmas Eve, which I shall treasure as one of my most beautiful memories. You let me see you in your rightful setting, alone, your own mistress, but with your loveliest jewel – the child!

And you let me see the mother undressing her child for the night! Your bedroom should always look as it did then!

You, who are so proud, wanted to have a husband at your side! That was a mistake which is now put right. But it was made because of the child. I feel honoured, to be sure.

[...]

Our visible bonds could be severed, but not our invisible ones. I think things are beautiful as they are and, at a distance, I can see you as a being from a higher sphere. I do not believe that we two are real mortals. We are creatures cast far down from a loftier home. That is why our bodily clothing is so irksome and why we are so ill at ease together.

Last night at 12 o'clock your perfume seemed to me like a sudden cry, to which I responded!

Wonder at times if there is not some little soul that drives us together because it wants to make parents of us again.

January 1st.

[...]

A cold day, but calm and sunny. My clouds appeared over 'The Castle' this morning. (Cf. 1904–24/4.) These clouds were like the steep coast of Rügen, with tree-clad heights, and glens running inland. But there are some formations that recur and that I recognize again. (See Plato's *Phaedo*.) It follows therefore that these are mirages, optical illusions of the 'high places' that Swedenborg speaks of. (The Monastery at Lhassa resembles these cloud fortresses. See Hellwald, *Countries and Peoples of the World*, new edition.)

Axel, Maggie,* Anna, Märtha, and Hugo Fröding† to dinner. Loving letter from Harriet.

January 3rd.

The hall door was open this morning; was closed, but opened again of itself, twice. Signifies a death!

Now associating with Harriet as before!

January 21st.

The bill for my Divorce arrived from Millar this morning. It came to 196 crowns. 196 is the atomic weight of gold. When I got out into the street there was a flag flying (just as there was on the parson's house – the house I was married in – the day divorce proceedings were made public).

[...]

January 22nd.

Harriet and Lillan to dinner. H—t taken ill in the evening.

[...]

January 30th.

[...]

Harriet ill. Dark.

January 31st.

Harriet ill. 'Nearly died' this morning.

Dark, bad weather too.

---

* Axel Strindberg's wife Margarethe.

† Anna von Philp, Strindberg's sister, his niece Märtha and her fiancé, Hugo Fröding.

February 1st.

Brighter. The sun illuminated 'The Growing Castle'. My sister Anna visited me. Among other things we talked about 'cello playing. I said a 'cello sounded like the bellowing of cattle. When I went to bed at 10 o'clock I heard a 'cello solo in the distance. Thought: Now I've got to put up with one of those blessed things in the house.

Went to see Harriet this evening. *Violent quarrel* over some *china*!

February 10th.

Harriet was here this evening until 1.30 a.m. Her face changed after 12 o'clock, grew old and ugly. This indicates that she is another person at night, exteriorized.[20] She was always ugly when she was asleep; ugly and repulsive.

I took her down to her cab. When I came up and shut the hall door, it opened again of itself.

[...]

May 6th.

Anniversary of my wedding with Harriet. Visited Hasselbacken in the morning. Broke off a twig of the birdcherry outside the window of the room where we celebrated it. Spent the evening with Harriet at her home. Nothing was said about the significance of the day.

May 13th.

Harriet had supper with me!

May 14th.

Went to see Harriet in the evening. Gloomy conversation about the misery of life, about the coming summer,

20. It's clear, I think, that Strindberg is using the word 'exteriorized' in the sense in which he seems to have understood it when he wrote: 'I am certain that the soul possesses the power of extending itself and that it does extend itself greatly during normal sleep and that finally, at death, it leaves the body and is in no way extinguished.' (*Legender*, p. 278.)

and so forth. On my way home I saw a display of fireworks over the roof-tops which put me in happier frame of mind.

[...]

Harriet Bosse's explanatory note, 1932.

During the summer of 1905 I took Lillan down to Hornbaek, a place of which I had the happiest memories. We stayed there the year we were married and I thought then that it was very beautiful. Strindberg had gone to Furusund again.

June 17th.

[...]

Saw beautiful female faces on my pillow and on the sheets; Harriet's and a nun's.

Have been aware of Harriet all day like a taste on my palate. The ring finger of my left hand has been numb today as well.

June 18th.

For no apparent reason a large piece of wood fell out of the dinner-table this morning.

(Crash.)

[...]

An affectionate letter from Harriet. She is not happy at Hornbaek.

July 8th.

[...]

On Wednesday and Thursday I had a feeling that Harriet was very unhappy. Wrote yesterday, Friday, and invited her here.

The innkeeper here at Furusund is called Swedenborg. (!)

August 1st.

Left Furusund.

Harriet Bosse's explanatory note, 1932.

In the autumn I had an engagement as a guest-artist at Stora Teatren in Gothenburg.

[. . .]

Later that autumn, when my time in Gothenburg was over, I went to Berlin on a journey of study and reconnaissance.

September 5th.

Letter from Harriet now in Gothenburg with Castegren* [. . .] She is in Inferno.

September 6th.

This morning a white canoe, without an owner, was lying in Sirishofsvik. (Cf. the white sailing-boat that lay in the same spot on June 12th, 1903.)

Strindberg to Harriet Bosse, September 13th.

Dear Friend,

[. . .]

Annmari's presence makes my life brighter,[21] but we sadly miss our 'third party'. She is no longer a baby and therefore I begin to feel that I am superfluous. My interest in life has slackened, I long to escape and have lost all desire to bind myself to life or to the living. I only want to float over what remains, to be ready to sail at a moment's notice.

In Sirishofsvik, where the white sailing boat came ashore three years ago, a white canoe has gone aground. It has been lying there for eight days and no one has tried to

---

* Victor Castegren, who produced *A Dream Play* at Svenska Teatren in 1907, but was at this time directing at Stora Teatren in Gothenburg. Harriet Bosse did not like the plays in which she was being asked to perform.

21. Anne-Marie frequently lived with her father when her mother was away from home.

steal it. I wonder if it is waiting for me, has come to fetch me?

I am ready to depart! The whole of my life has been spent in preparing for the journey!

Your

August Sg

Harriet Bosse to Strindberg, c. September 14th.
Gusten, I am so fond of you! Good-night.

Harriet

November 1st.
Walked along Strandvägen, salvoes, and flags flying, 'clean' flags.
(Day of rejoicing!)

November 6th.
Harriet returned from Gothenburg this evening.
[...]

November 7th.
Harriet and Lillan to dinner.

November 8th.
Supper with Harriet.

November 21st.
Harriet left for Berlin. Lillan staying with Inez Ahlqvist.
[...]

November 29th.
Suspense! Darkness. Do not know what is going to happen next. Can sense Harriet in Berlin; she is agitated.

December 8th.
Aware of Harriet all day. Friendly, extremely!

Strindberg to Harriet Bosse, December 8th.

Dear Harriet,

Do you think we shall ever disentangle ourselves from each other after the way in which we have entwined our lives? When you are anxious, even far away in a distant land, the heart in my breast beats as hard as if it were yours.

There are times when I feel your warm breath sweep past my cheek, and then I think you are uttering my name in a kindly spirit.

There are times too when I have you within my coat, and I am You –

[. . .]

August Sg

1906

January 1st.

Sunshine. Took flowers to Harriet and Lillan this morning. H—t (*had a bath!*) Gave H. and Lillan dinner here.

Relations with Harriet peaceful and affectonate.

January 13th, Saturday.

Spent the evening until about 10 o'clock with Harriet. She asked me to stay, but I did not.

January 14th, Sunday morning.

After a restless night woke with an impression that I was free of H—t. Made plans for absconding. At 10.30 a letter arrived from H—t. Convinced that it was a 'final letter' I opened it in some trepidation. It turned out to be an agitated love-letter! But earlier in the morning Harriet had telephoned to say that she was ill in bed and could not come to dinner. I too was ill, but I went to see H—t in the evening. She asked me to stay the night, but I left.

January 15th.

[. . .]

Spent the evening with H—t. Poisonous, gloomy, so much so that I had to leave her. H—t told me that she had had a terrifyingly infernal day; quite indescribable. [. . .]

February 21st.

After a period of distaste, darkness and disputes Harriet invited herself and Lillan to dinner. The wine-merchant had sent a bottle of Champagne by mistake, so we celebrated H—t's birthday (instead of on the 19th). Gay and bright! Lillan was sent to Inez. Alone with H—t.

February 27th.

    [...]

    Went to see Harriet this evening. Subdued; ill, décolletée, beautiful, evil, loving. She told me that yesterday evening she had intended to write me a final letter. This upset me so much that her caresses left me cold, at which she grew angry. I left in a hurry.

    Dark at home.

February 28th.

    Dark all day. Telephone call from Harriet that I did not take. Felt as if everything was over. Pitch black.

March 1st.

    Darkness and gloom until dinner-time. Once again I had the feeling that my light came from her and the child. Harriet telephoned and invited herself over for the evening. She came: light returned. I had flowers, Champagne, and 'souper'. She played. It was glorious.

March 2nd.

    At H—t's home in the evening. Lillan had a bath. All was light, warmth, and peace. There you have it!

March 5th.

    Harriet went to Finland.

Strindberg to Harriet Bosse, March 13th.

    Dear child,

    You are storming and buffeting me more than usual to-day, the 13th.

    [...]   Your
                                       August Sg

May 2nd.

    Visited Hasselbacken this morning. The bridal birdcherry is in leaf again. My wedding day was May 6th, 1901.

May 3rd.

Harriet returned from Finland.

May 5th.

Harriet, Lillan and I had dinner together at Lidingöbro.
Drove home by way of Djurgården.

September 22nd.

Night before: Death of Levertin.[22] A bright morning.
Good news from Malmö. *Miss Julie*, with August Palme performing in it, had gone well.

In the morning I walked down Strandvägen in high
spirits; continued along Hamngatan, saw Klara church and
its school – a neighbourhood where every house holds
memories – down to Vasagatan and saw Klara Primary
School, where I had once taught; passed Vasateatern where
Master Olof and *Lucky Peter* were performed; walked
up Kungsgatan – where I saw a horrible picture of myself
– turned up by Hötorget, Badstugatan and Oxtorgsgatan,
past the house where the Seippels* and then Wieselgren†
lived; along Regeringsgatan and past Jacob's School and
the house where Axel lives; down past the furniture shop
where I bought the things with which I had set up house;
but the whole time I was being drawn towards Sturepark,
towards Lillan and Harriet. I had an 'idea' that I must go to
them to give them the money for Lillan's school fees and
take some scent to Harriet. On my route I had tried to call
at a number of perfumeries, but they had all been shut. I
renewed my efforts and eventually found some French
Muguet,[23] but not the Syren (Lilac) that I was looking for.

22. Oscar Levertin, the author and critic, whom Strindberg
regarded as one of his worst enemies because of the unflattering
things Levertin had said about his works.

* S. Seippel and his family, friends of Strindberg's parents.

† Harald Wieselgren, a colleague of Strindberg's at the Royal
Library.

23. Muguet = lily of the valley.

After that I tried to find a florist and some flowers, but in vain. I climbed the stairs at No. 3 Sturepark. There I found sunshine and beauty. Harriet and Lillan were friendly and grateful.

As I walked back to Karlavägen I thought to myself: this has been like an 'Agony' or the very moment of death when the whole of one's life passes before one, and I decided to write about this morning walk, on which, in an hour and a half, I had been able to review the whole of my life till now.

When I got home I felt that life was easy and bright. Something that had been oppressing me had gone. I took time off work and fell into a holiday mood. Kind letters arrived, money too. At 2 o'clock I learned that Levertin had died (at 10 a.m.). That was the first I heard of it!

This is incomprehensible. He dies, but I pass through my 'agony'. And I wanted Harriet to have a bottle of scent 'while he stank).[24]

[...]

October 6th.

My sister Anna's wedding anniversary. Five years ago today Harriet came back to me. She had left me on August 22nd, 1901, her name-day, and the day of my father's birth.

This morning, near Sirishofsvik, I met a large muzzled dog by itself. A horse, also with a muzzle, was standing outside my door. Though he is in his grave August Bondeson stinks in my nostrils just as Levertin did when his unfavourable review of *New Swedish Destinies* appeared posthumously in *Svenska Dagbladet*. When his father died a

24. Levertin was taken ill on the night of the 21st–22nd. It is believed that he accidentally swallowed a gargle containing potassium chlorate. This may explain what was in Strindberg's mind when, in a note added later to the above entry, he wrote: 'Heard that L's body instantly began to decompose, so that he had to be buried as quickly as possible because of the stench (=perfume).'

couple of years ago, Bondeson jeered at him for having found again the faith of his childhood. Bondeson went mad, was shut up and died. We are not told whether, before that happened, he too found again the faith of his childhood. That is a thing they are careful not to mention.

Spent the evening with Harriet. A gloomy, poisonous and entirely false atmosphere. She fondled me but I remained cold. When she drew back her face changed into her Miss Hopps' face.

[. . .]

October 28th, Sunday.

Night before: Woken just before 2 o'clock by what seemed to be a hostile attack by Harriet, that gave me palpitations and a pain in my head. This is exactly what happened when she once tried to hypnotize me while I was asleep in our bedroom. This time I had dreamt that she was setting my nerves on edge (with *Gyllensköld*) and I hit her in the face. When her only retort was to cast evil, scornful glances upon me I prayed God that she might be abandoned by her family, her friends and her servants (for has not she divided me from all my people?) and that she might be 'eaten alive by worms'. Fell asleep once more, but again dreamed antagonistically, of H—t.

[. . .]

November 5th.

Have not seen Harriet since October 6th, on that occasion I withdrew, as she was expecting her suitor, Docent Castrén,* and I did not want to be her second string. I do not know whether he ever came.

---

* Gunnar Castrén, the Finnish literary historian, whom Harriet Bosse had met during her visit to Helsingfors as a guest-artist.

November 10th.

[. . .]

It is worth noting that, since I freed myself from Harriet, I can again plainly see the road to Christianity and that, in my thoughts, I have achieved reconciliation with my worst enemies such as (*G. af G., Paul, Philp, Sigurd, Wirsén*),* even with (*Levertin*). Then too, I lived as if I were preparing myself for death. It seems to me now, that all the beautiful things I wrote during my life with Harriet came about as a reaction to her wickedness and that, by re-creating her as beautiful, I sometimes managed to bring a good influence to bear on her. She said herself that she was 'the wickedest person ever born'.

November 28th.

Intensely aware of Harriet every day.

Last night I dreamed of white horses followed by brown. This made me uneasy and I tried to get away. Instead I fell under a white horse that lay down on top of me, but I crept out from under him and was saved.

This morning a cart, drawn by a large white horse, came up behind me and then crossed my path in an unpleasant fashion. When (remembering my dream) I tried to get out of its way, a cab, drawn by a brown horse, came up and brushed against me. The coachman yelled and I only just managed to avoid being run over.

[. . .]

The telephone rang this evening. I picked it up, it was Harriet. She simply wanted to talk about the production of *Sir Bengt's Wife* that Ranft wants to put on. I disapproved, and we had exactly the same conversation we had in the

* Gustav af Geijerstam, Adolf Paul, Alfred Hedenstierna (pen-name Sigurd), Carl David Wirsén. Fellow writers of whom Strindberg had fallen foul for one reason or another. Hugo von Philp Strindberg's brother-in-law.

autumn, the same subject, the same words. I gently cut it short. N.B.! I have not seen or spoken to Harriet since October 6th = 7 weeks. This conversation was conducted and broken off without the least trace of emotion. This must mean either that she is quite indifferent to me, or that our life together has been continuing as before, but secretly, and that she takes it as a matter of course.

December 14th.

Harriet came to see me after an interval that lasted since October 6th. I visited her in the evening. Everything as before; no explanations. This after over 2 months!

December 15th.

Harriet has hurt her foot.

Associating with Harriet and Lillan as before. She is like herself though not quite. Cool, untrustworthy, false!

December 23rd, Christmas Eve.

H—t and Lillan to dinner. August Lindberg arrived with presents.

Associating with Harriet and Lillan but on a false footing. She is intimate with my enemies!

December 31st.

Rupture with Harriet! Because I refused to visit her this evening.

1907

January 9th.

Remained at home this evening, instead of going to Harriet. There was light. I now believe that the darkness comes from her and I want to break free. On the occasion of our last reunion I found her stupider than before, but just as proud and wicked! Black and venomous!

[. . .]

January 10th.

Lillan telephoned this evening. She asked me to go to her. I went. Calm, peaceful, beautiful.

January 20th.

Harriet and Lillan came to dinner. Ruth* and Lillan went to see Aug. Lindberg. H—t remained behind in the Yellow Room. (Last time.)

[. . .]

March 8th.

[. . .]

Went with Lillan and Harriet to the dress-rehearsal of *Lucky Peter's Travels* this evening.

What is going to happen next?

March 9th.

Dark and austere. Fröken Kopparberg came to work in the house instead of Ebba.

March 10th, Sunday.

(Passion Sunday or Mid-Lent Sunday.) Dark, threatening, horrible. Alone, and have no news of *Lucky Peter's* fate

* Harriet Bosse's maid.

yesterday evening. I lost my appetite at dinner and a fright-ful sensation came over me x x x. This state of dejection continued until 6 o'clock. As the clock struck 6 Harriet telephoned to say that *Lucky Peter* had gone well. – What I experienced today was not a physical thing; it must cer-tainly have taken place on the 'astral plane'. It resembled what happened in August and September 1901 (when Harriet had left me). Then I had the same sensations and the same desire to commit suicide, but not so pronounced.

[. . .]

March 13th.

Harriet and Lillan have come to live with me as they are moving house.

March 15th.

Everything the same, poisonous, spiteful. She blames me, poor innocent, for all her troubles.

March 26th.

Anna has left! Alma has entered the house. Calm, clean and pleasant. Decent food for dinner. Lillan and Ruth came to visit me. Telephone call from Harriet! Have taken a dislike to strong drink in the evening.

March 27th.

Beginning to drink wormwood ale!

March 29th.

Alma has left because I complained that she spoiled the food.

March 30th.

Caretaker's wife cleans. Food fetched in. (Pig-swill.)

Horrible! Dinner with Harriet and Lillan on Easter Day in their new home. This home is so preternaturally beauti-ful, that I might very well have 'wished it together' for the two of them.

[. . .]

April 1st.

Sofi came to look after the house. Things worse than ever.

April 14th, Sunday.

Alone. Grew more light-hearted this evening. I got out the punch, which I have not tasted for fourteen days. As I raised the glass to my lips the people in the flat downstairs struck up a brilliant gallop. It cheered me up.

April 15th.

Once again I found a red feather, but in the street.

Today, at 12 o'clock (it is now 10.30), there is to be a dress rehearsal of *A Dream Play*. The odd thing is that I wrote this play after 40 days of suffering (Aug., Sept. 1901), at a time when Harriet had left me, bearing with her my last child, then unborn. Now, when it is about to be performed, I have, for 40 days, been in a depressed (black) inferno-like mood and afflicted by domestic misery.

The sun is shining. All the shutters of the tobacco-drying shed are wide open and leaning against it, white and gleaming, are four paper windows (from the forcing-frame).

A kind of calm, resigned feeling of uncertainty prevails within me. I ask myself if some catastrophe will not prevent the play's being performed, if in fact it *may* be performed. True, I have talked nicely to people; but to wish to influence Him who rules the world is presumptuous (perhaps blasphemous). The fact that I have revealed the relative nothingness of life (Buddhism), its insane contradictions, its wickedness and unruliness, may be regarded as praiseworthy, if it imbues people with resignation, and to have shown that man is relatively guiltless in a life which of itself entails guilt, is surely no bad thing ... But ...

Just had a telephone call from Harriet: 'The outcome of all this is in the hands of God.' 'I entirely agree,' I answered, 'and I doubt whether the play *may* be performed.' (I believe the Powers on High have already made up their minds about that, and also about the result of the first night – if there should ever be one.)

It feels like Sunday at this moment. I can see the white figures on the balcony of 'The Growing Castle'. During these past ... days my thoughts have been much occupied with death and the life to come. Yesterday I read Plato's *Timaeus* and *Phaedo*. Am I going to die now or soon, I wonder? At present working on *Toten-Insel*, in which I am describing the awakening after death and what follows it; but I shrink with horror from laying bare the abysmal misery of life. I recently burnt a play so honest that it made me shudder. Yet I never feel sure that I ought to flatter humanity by concealing what is vile. I should like to write of things as bright and beautiful, but I may not, I cannot. I regard it as my dreadful duty to be truthful, and life is so indescribably ugly.

The clock has just struck 11! ... (The rehearsal is at 12.)

Evening, 8 o'clock. I went to the rehearsal of *A Dream Play* and suffered intensely; had the impression that this thing ought not to be performed ... It is a presumption, probably a blasphemy (?) ... I am out of harmony and afraid (unblest).

Got no dinner. Have just eaten – at 7 o'clock – cold food fetched in a container. The Publisher has just returned my three Chamber Plays.

During these last forty days of pondering on religious matters I have read the Book of Job, telling myself, it is true, that I was no righteous man. But then I came to Chapter 22, in which Eliphaz the Temanite exposes Job thus: 'For thou hast taken pledges of thy brother for nought and stripped the naked of their clothing. Thou hast not given water to the weary to drink and thou hast withholden bread from the hungry ... Is not thy wickedness great? Neither is there any end to thine iniquities.'

So the comfort I had expected from the Book of Job came to nothing and I was left standing, deserted, at my wits' end. To what is a poor human being to cling? What is he to believe? Is he to blame if he thinks wrongly?

Yesterday I read Plato's *Timaeus* and *Phaedo* and got from them so much contradictory wisdom, that in the evening I cast aside all my devotional books and recited 'God who holds all children dear,'[25] with my whole heart. What will happen next? God help me, Amen!

Castegren came to see me this evening; dejected. Quiet night.

[. . .]

April 16th.

Read the proofs of *Black Banners*, written in 1904. Is this book a crime and should it be withdrawn? I hesitated; turned over the leaves of the Bible and came upon the Book of Jonah which tells how the prophet was forced to come forth and prophesy, even though he had tried to conceal himself.

This gave me solace. But it is a terrible book!

April 17th.

A Dream Play is being performed today. Snow fell gently this morning. Read the last chapters of the Book of Job which tell how God punished Job for his arrogance in daring to find fault with His works. Job begged for forgiveness and this was granted. Quiet and grey until 3 o'clock. Then Greta* arrived with the news that I had been nominated to receive an Honorary Doctorate in Upsala at the Linnéan Celebrations in May, and that the dress rehearsal of *A Dream Play* had been favourably reviewed. Alone at home in the evening. On the stroke of 8 the door-bell rang and a

25. *Gud som haver barnen kär.* A traditional child's prayer.
* Greta, Strindberg's second daughter by his first wife.

girl entered with a laurel wreath and three roses, sent anonymously and inscribed: 'Truth', 'Light', 'Liberation'. I immediately took it to the mask of Beethoven on the stove, as there is so much I have to thank him for. But today *children* have been haunting me. When I got outside the front door this morning the first thing I saw was a lady with a little girl, and when I returned there was a boisterous child and an old woman in front of me. This depressed me so much that I tried to hang back, but it was impossible. I had to pass them and as I did so the old woman turned threateningly to the child and said: 'Don't you dare go ringing the door-bells.' Later on at dinner-time, when I was lying in the Yellow room, they whipped a child three times in the house next door. I could hear it screaming horribly. What does all this mean? Is it tit for tat? (*A Dream Play*)? Human beings=naughty children! August Falck* came to see me.

The tobacco shed is shut, but outside it I saw a large grey goose (it was a wheel-barrow for muck).

[. . .]

'The Castle' (=The Barracks) is dark this evening. Heard the neighbour's cuckoo-clock strike! (most unusual). Used to mean horrors, but the last time all was well!

At 11 o'clock this evening Harriet, Castegren and Ranft† telephoned to say that *A Dream Play* had been a success! T.b.t.G.!

April 18th.

My mind is in a turmoil! A storm of hatred – even Harriet's, who had vowed that the play should fail – is being loosed upon me from a distance; envious hatred, inspired by its success. Falck came to see me!

---

* August Falk, the future director of Strindberg's Intimate Theatre.

† Albert Ranft, who was, among other things, the proprietor of Svenska Teatern.

Found a stone on the stairs!

Axel here this evening!

N.B! *After 40 days of fasting*, confusion and suffering of all kinds, I can see on both my hands deep scars that look as if they had been made by large nails (=stigmata!). Is this my Easter? Shall I be crucified again? As I crucified Christ? I am filled with thoughts of death and await a catastrophe!

I have now been drinking wormwood ale (=gall) for a whole month.

April 21st.

In one of the windows of my former home at 31 Banérgatan there is now a little white cutter (a toy) with all her sails set. At the rudder sits a child wearing a blue cap. (Cf: this diary on the white boats in Djurgårdsbrunnsviken). Later on I noticed inside the boat a little white-clad girl.

Harriet and Lillan to see me. Very friendly.

Schering has recently sent me Klinger's etchings of *Dead Children*. This foreshadows a child's death!

During these painful 6 weeks in which, among other things, I have been given over-cooked and filthy food, I have lamented like Job: 'Can that which hath no savour be eaten without salt? Or is there any taste in the white of an egg? . . .' Only to be answered by Ezekiel, Chapter IV: 'And thou shalt eat it as barley cakes, and thou shalt bake it in their sight with dung that cometh out of man.' (And the Lord added: 'Even thus shall the children of Israel eat their defiled bread among the Gentiles . . .' And when the prophet lamented he was granted the favour of baking with cow-dung . . .) (Prototype of the overthrow of Jerusalem.)

Cf. below the 23rd when, as I was telling Axel about this, it instantly started to thunder and lighten.

April 22nd.

A Dream Play has now been going well since last Wednesday. So in the end permission was granted, but I had to suffer until it was. I am still out of harmony, but less so than before.

[. . .]

April 23rd.

Axel here this evening. I told him that the food I had been given was so filthy that I could not eat it. (At the same time I had bestowed 2 crowns on a beggar, and for his dinner what is more.) At that very moment a flash of blue lightning shot past the dining-room window, followed immediately by a clap of thunder. This happened three times in succession!

April 24.

Ellen arrived this evening.

April 25.

My heart is somewhat lighter. Huge mountains of cloud in the north.

Harriet and Lillan to see me.

April 26th.

Darkness!

Apathetic, idle, no interest in anything, unable to work. Tried to write about Linné's System of Classification, but lost interest.

Shivering fit at dinner-table, a deathly ague, forced myself to eat. Opened the Bible at the Book of Job and came upon reproaches for having blasphemed. Wanted to read the Psalmist, but the rapping on the wall started.

After my mid-day nap I found that the thermometer on the window had been wrenched off. This thermometer, which neither of us had wanted to put up (since neither of us believed that our union would last), had been left lying about or moved from place to place and had finally ended up in a drawer. When at last Harriet departed from the house I put it up. Why had it been taken down? And who could have done it?

Have had a feeling all day that Harriet was friendly, very! (too much so).

Harriet's Benefit Performance of *A Dream Play* this evening.

[...]

May 1st.

Harriet has gone on tour. Lillan came to dinner. Cold, distant, naughty; result of Fru Möller's upbringing.

May 2nd.

My heart a little lighter! Thinking of writing Idylls and a Shepherd's song. Slept this afternoon and woke in an ecstasy, having seen again in my dreams the Dalarö of my youth, 1871.

May 9th, Ascension-day!

Letter from Harriet! – Alone all day! –

She is being tormented and complaining about it. I knew of this already, knew too *who* was tormenting her!

Strindberg to Harriet Bosse, May 12th.

Harriet,

Need I write to you? You are aware of my thoughts and my feelings as I am of yours. I already knew of what you told me in your letter and who was annoying you, though no one had said a word to me about it. I am near you when you suffer and suffer with you; but when you are happy I cannot always follow you, as life then puts you on the side of my enemies. I cannot rejoice at unwarranted success that is achieved at my expense!

I am growing accustomed to the great loneliness of the summer and no longer hope for anything from life, as everything has shown itself to be unstable, transitory, and perishable. [. . .]

I cannot bear to see your home, as it is now the haunt of beings alien to me. And yet your home is so completely beautiful that I might myself have wished it together for the two of you, you and the child. I cannot talk to you, for I have nothing to say that can be put into words. I do not long to see you, for I can see you when I will and as I will.

People and life have tried one means of parting us, but I believe we still meet, sometimes, in another place, for we are kin, you and I, and shall never cease to be so . . .

Your
Nameless One

May 14th.

Aware of Harriet in kindness and intimacy right up to noon, then she disappeared.

May 16th.

Read the last proofs of *Black Banners*. Nothing now remains, I suppose, but to drain the last Cup.

May 17th.

My brother Oskar came to supper.

May 18th, Whitsun Eve.

Harriet 'persecutes' me from morn till noon! Had a card from H——t from Lund. She seeks me in intimacy and forces herself upon me. Ill in the evening, chest, throat, stomach.

[. . .]

May 19, Whit Sunday.

[. . .]

Have a feeling that Harriet and Lillan have met.

There has been no sound from Captain M.'s flat under mine for about a month. Have heard neither the Pianola nor the Phonograph. I decided the family must be away. A few days ago someone began to play the pianola, but stopped suddenly. Ellen tells me that the couple have parted and that the husband is alone. The impression this made on me was horrible. Even in the silence I can hear the man down there suffering!

[...]

When I woke this afternoon I heard the pianola and the phonograph in the flat below. [...] But female voices as well. I thought M.'s wife and children had returned and rejoiced; but very soon I heard the sound of dancing and the gabbling of females who were certainly not members of the family. They sounded quite different, and I pictured to myself what had been a home invaded by sluts. The contrast affected me so deeply that I began to weep, so dear to me is my dream of home-life and family as something austere, strict, but purifying, sacred! (And look what life gave me!) However, the merry-making quietened down towards evening and by the following day all was silent again.

He was divorced and was now celebrating a new engagement.

It seems to be part of my fate that I may not defend myself!

As soon as I try to get people to admit that I am in the right, they say I am wrong, and call it justice!

If I were to write about my experiences of recent years and of what now oppresses me, no one would believe me. All the same I have slipped in a hint of it into *Historical Miniatures*.* This misunderstanding is so horrible and every effort to correct it proves impossible.

* Strindberg is referring here to a passage in the short story about the French Revolution, *Days of Judgement*. In it he says that Queen Marie Antoinette led a dissolute life at night and that she had an 'illicit relationship with her son'. [See *Historiska Miniatyrer*, Sam-–

When I married Bosse I got her with child immediately. But she grudged me that great honour, and out of spite she went off with her unborn child. She alleged that I had deserted our bedroom, but the truth was that she had *begged me to move*, as pregnancy had given her a dislike for my person. She returned and the child was born. The next thing was that she did not want to have more children, but did want to continue 'married life'. This resulted in distaste and disgust. First we separated, then we got a divorce. After that we came together again and I became her lover, and still am. This then is the question, in what have I failed? My reputation was restored, but is so no longer, for her lies are enduring, in spite of all there is to confute them! At 50 I was no good as a husband, but at 58 I am good enough to be a lover! It is sublime! Sublime!!!

Today, Whit Sunday, I dined alone, of course. As I sat at table in the dining-room two pigeons came and pecked insistently at the window. I gave them bread and peas which they ate, looking at me all the while through the window. When they had done, they kissed each other and flew away. It was like having a visit from Harriet and Lillan, who are far away, and reminded me of our Sunday dinners.

Swedenborg's body is to be brought home to Sweden. Read Swedenborg all today! and yesterday too! See B.

May 20th, Whit Monday.

Night before: woke to hear the clock striking 3 and simultaneously the click of an electric switch. This was followed by the slop-pail rattling first three times and then two. I was not alarmed but turned on the light and took it as a warning. Dreamt about murderers, whom I evaded. Likewise about a gold coin (in my waistcoat pocket) that multiplied itself.

---

lade Skrifter, vol. 42, pp. 316–17, as the passage in question is omitted in the English translation. M.S.]

Reading *Swedenborg*. When he visited the other planets he came to the conclusion that the Earth was the worst of them all because its inhabitants do not say what they think, or else they say things other than those they think. This is why they have governments and princes, things that are not found on the other planets, where people live solely in families, and where they cannot lie. *Swedenborg* says that the Swedish nation is on the whole worse than the others and, with the exception of the Russians and the Italians, 'the *worst* in Europe, as the Swedes do not say what they think'. Quite right!

I am well today and was able to take my morning walk.

Rupture with Ellen while at dinner as she had given me *overdone* pig-swill! She gave notice! Interesting to see what happens! (She stayed.)

May 24th.

Feeling of contact with H—t very strong in the early morning and followed me through the day, the whole of it, intensifying towards evening. In other respects a gloomy, colourless day.

It is curious that contact and harmony with H—t should give me a sensation of being drawn towards the light, even though she hates me, *on one plane*. Now and then she has a suspicion of what manner of man I am, but then evil influences are brought to bear on her from outside. She must be both a very high and a very low creature! She can be the wickedest and vilest person I have met; in a way the stupidest and the ugliest, yet at times she is the very reverse, in every respect!

May 29th.

Black Banners comes out today. Made an agreement about *A Blue Book*, on *excellent* terms. Decided to remain in town and in the flat.

[. . .]

Harriet Bosse's explanatory notes, 1932.

I had been to see Strindberg one Sunday and played the piano for him. In order to do so with greater ease I took off my engagement ring, the one Strindberg had given me set with brilliants and sapphires. I placed the ring beside me on the piano, but forgot to put it on again when I left. When I got home I telephoned to Strindberg to ask him to take care of the ring, but he replied it was not there. A thorough search was made for it; the floor was taken up, but with no result, the ring had gone. When I dined there the following Sunday we discussed the disappearance of the ring in front of the maid, who was waiting at table. She condoled with us on its loss – with rather too much animation, I thought – and quite intuitively I began to suspect her.

June 11th.

Telephone call from an unknown lady who says that Harriet's engagement ring was stolen by Ebba. It disappeared on Feb. 17th, 1906. The curious thing about it is that, just before this telephone call about the ring (it has one sapphire and two diamonds), I had been working on precious stones. A book with coloured illustrations is still lying open beside me.

June 12th.

Fru Kreüger came, bringing with her the ring. I sent it on to Harriet with a 'final letter', in which I rejected her offer of a visit!

[. . .]

June 13th.

[. . .]

Loving letter from Harriet! Heard the cuckoo-clock striking insistently this evening.

[. . .]

Harriet Bosse to Strindberg, June 13th.

How very strange about that ring –

How very strange life is as a whole –

My dear, beloved friend, yes, I still call you that. You must feel, you must know that no one has yet taken your place in my heart –

You do not ever want to see me, us, again. I understand you, and I shall respect your wishes.

We are together, all the same, and I am firmly convinced, *now*, at any rate, that even if I were sometimes to link my future with that of another man, *you* have coloured my life in such a special way that I shall never forget you.

You may think I go out and about among people to amuse myself. *Amuse* myself! Oh no! I do so in order to have something to occupy me, something to deaden myself with for, like you, I long to make an end, long for it so intensely that, if I had not our child to hold me back, I should have set myself free long ago.

I am so profoundly sad and sorrowful that I think nothing can ever make me happy again.

We are going into the country now. One must be somewhere, in one place or another and, as it will probably do my throat good, we are going to Åre again. It does not *really* matter to me where I am –

I am very fond of you – whatever may happen – I love you, perhaps because, through such deep and boundless sorrow, you have infused my life with meaning –

Farewell,

Your
Harriet

Strindberg to Harriet Bosse, July 25th.

My dear ones,

To meet only to part is more pain than pleasure, to be sure; but as we are going to live in the same town, it would be better to consort than to turn into ghost-like memories, and hardly know if we dare greet each other. – Therefore I ask if you will both dine with me on Sunday at 3 o'clock? [. . .]

Your

August Sg

July 25th.

Friendly letter from Lillan (Harriet).

[. . .]

July 29th.

Harriet and Lillan came; but Ellen departed, so we got no dinner. I myself laid out cold food at 5 o'clock. Then Ruth arrived!

August 4th. Sunday.

Ruth departed. Fröken Johansson came instead.

August 22nd.

Six years ago today (1901), on her name-day and the anniversary of my father's birth, Harriet took herself off, for no reason, bearing with her my unborn child. On the same day a fire-ball (bolide) fell in the Waggoner, close to Capella. A year ago today a comet appeared in Pegasus!

I am now reading the proofs of *A Blue Book* and feel that, with it done, my mission in life is ended. I have been permitted to say all that I have to say.

October 6th.

Anniversary of (1) Anna's wedding, (2) my unfortunate trip to Paris in 1879?,* (3) Harriet's return with my child in 1901. I went to fetch my Anne-Marie for a drive. Harriet, whom I had not seen for two months, came to see us off.

---

* Strindberg is referring here to his interrupted journey to Paris in 1879 on which he had embarked in order to avoid the love affair that he knew was developing with Siri von Essen, his first wife.

(Siri v. E., who has been in town for fourteen days, is leaving to-day.)

[. . .]

December 24, Christmas Eve.

Alone. It is hard! Harriet did ask me there, but I would not go. Aug. Lindberg came to see me. Axel Jäderin and Tor Aulin telephoned in the evening. Completely alone all day, and in the evening too!

Strindberg to Harriet Bosse, c. December 24th.

Do not let us meet, it is too painful. Now, in the seventh year of this everlasting bidding of farewell, have I not suffered enough?

As for the world in which you live, I have broken with it forever.

My child was stolen from me while still in her mother's womb. Now her mind has been stolen too . . .

[. . .]

1908

February 26th.

Lillan and I out for a drive. Contact with H—t again! from a distance.

April 3rd.

Aware of H—t this afternoon before 5 o'clock. At the same instant sound of furniture-moving overhead. I jumped up. This evening Anne-Marie came. [. . .] Later I went out with her. At the corner of Karlaplan Harriet drove up in a cab. I did not recognize her; she was small, insignificant, ugly. I greeted her as one would a stranger! Hardly saw her!

[. . .]

April 4th.

In the evening Lillan arrived with a letter from Harriet telling me she was engaged. Lillan said to W—d.* Yet H. had 'sought' me that afternoon! Shortly afterwards Lillan made out a card for me in our alphabet game: 'Unkind'. I asked her if W. was kind. She answered: 'Yes'.

The night that followed was marvellous! At about 11.30 I became conscious of H—t, but did not respond. At 3 o'clock again, and that time . . . In the morning ditto – On the very night of her engagement!!!

[. . .]

April 5th, Sunday.

In a strange mood all day. I am re-living my engagement of 7 years ago. Grew cheerful in the evening and played

* Gunnar Wingård, the actor. He and Harriet Bosse were divorced in 1911, and he died by his own hand in 1912.

376

Gounod's *Romeo*. Could feel that H—t was friendly, al-most as if we had just got engaged again!

April 7th.

Went out early in the morning. The feeling that it was Sunday was so strong that I almost believed it was. Re-membered all that was beautiful in my early days with Harriet. She is now as one dead, and therefore I only see her as beautiful, mourn and lament her as one does the dead, regret every harsh word, reproach myself for every-thing, tell myself that I was in the wrong . . .

Laid aside *A Blue Book*. Did nothing. Wept in anguish over the dead illusions of love. Were they no more than illusions, those feelings that overpowered me?

Is there no end to this? Will it last for ever? Is it seek-ing to find expression in poetry, but failing? Heard Schu-bert's *Serenade* being played this evening: 'Softly through the night is calling, love, my song to thee . . .', but I do not know where it was being played.

[. . .]

April 8th.

In a light-hearted mood all day. Paid Harriet's book-seller's bill and had the receipt sent to her. Experienced warm contact with Harriet the whole day. She sought me. I believed that she was unhappy! *Swanwhite** is being per-formed in Helsingfors this evening! Wrote a letter which I did not send.

[. . .]

Strindberg to Harriet Bosse, April 8th.

When you told me last Saturday that you were engaged, I think I almost knew it beforehand. But I could not wish you happiness, for I do not believe in it, since it does not

* In 1901 Strindberg had given *Swanwhite* to Harriet Bosse as an engagement present.

exist. About the child I felt no uneasiness, for I believe in God.

All the same I did want to bid you farewell, and now I want to thank you, in spite of everything, for everything, for those months of spring, seven years ago when, after 20 years of misery, I was permitted to see a little splendour in life. I could not bring myself to write before. I had experiences that made me hesitate. Sunday passed, Monday too, in work and calm resignation. You will have noticed that for exactly a year I have ceased to visit you, and you know why.

Then came yesterday, Tuesday! When I went out in the morning, I thought it was Sunday. The city did not look the same, nor did the flat here at home. You were dead! And then began the apotheosis of my memories. For the whole day, for twelve hours, my life was no more than a re-living of these past seven years.

Everything, everything, reproaches, pangs of conscience for all things left undone, for every harsh word, exactly as when a beloved person dies. All that was less beautiful had gone, only what was lovely stood out. [. . .]

Just one thing! Let me have Lillan when you marry! Or would you rather have me go far away?

For us to pass each other by in the street would be painful and unclean, and the child ought to be kept out of it!

Shall I go away? I think I am a disturbing influence here and I know that invisible wires stretch from this flat and transmit inaudible sound-waves, which nevertheless reach their mark . . .

Our bonds are not broken, but they must be severed . . . otherwise we shall be defiled . . . You remember how it was in our early days, when malicious alien souls, merely by the act of thinking of us, were able to project rays upon us that perturbed us, that destroyed us!

Say how you would like matters arranged, but see to it

that this does not drag us down into the murky depths, a thing I dread.

[...]

Strindberg to Harriet Bosse, April 9th.

[...]

I will not live this double life, ensnared in the erotic life of other people ... I would rather mourn you as dead than remember you as another man's wife. You are bringing disharmony into your own life too, for it is not only you and I who 'live on the astral plane'. Lightning can strike backwards or to the side, and any one of us may die; perhaps the one you would miss most.

[...]

I beg you now: Leave me in peace! In my sleep I am defenceless, as everyone is, irresponsible ... and I am ashamed afterwards. Now I think it criminal!

[...]

April 10th.

Spent the whole morning reading Harriet's and my letters. I wept with emotion, so great and beautiful did they seem. Wrote an agitated letter to Harriet and enclosed some of my letters of 1901. Contact with Harriet was very strong all day.

What I am now experiencing is so strange. Harriet and I are friends. She 'seeks' me. I eat but little, drink but little, dress myself – for whom? In the thoughts that obsess me I am, as it were, just engaged, re-living 1901, seeing Harriet as she was seven years ago, young, great, glorious, ethereal!

April 11th.

Wrote a letter to Castegren this evening asking him to put on *Swanwhite* and let Harriet and her fiancé perform in it. Left the letter unposted overnight. During the night

Harriet sought me twice with passionate intensity and I responded. This after I had experienced a feeling at 10.30 yesterday evening that Harriet was in a state of great anguish. In the morning I sent off the letter to Castegren and one to Harriet to inquire whether she would act in *Swanwhite*.

[...]

Strindberg to Harriet Bosse, April 11th.

[...]

Of one thing I am certain; I shall not survive your wedding night, not out of envy, but because of the power I have of imagining what will take place.

So be it! On that night I shall celebrate my marriage with Death! God will allow me that after all my suffering! For I must go before my true self, my immortal soul is defiled. It is no good my saying to myself: Why should he touch my woman? She is not mine in the ordinary sense, and he has the right. But she is my creation, all the same, and there is in her something of me for him to touch ... it is me he caresses, that is why I must depart!

Why will you not let me go? What do you want with my old person? Take my soul if you must, but let me go!

This will end badly!

[...]

Did you never notice that many of those who wanted to take you from me were hurt, died, lost wife and child? I did nothing to bring these things upon them, hardly dared even to wish them ill, for I knew how dangerous it was!

That is why I am so afraid of interfering with you both; for if I do I shall suffer for it!

Therefore let me go!

You may not have more than one! Two is murder, crime!

April 12th, Sunday.

Night before: It was as if I were only just married ...
And without any feeling of self-reproach. This morning I
sent flowers and a letter.

[...]

Strindberg to Harriet Bosse, April 12th.

[...]

... Nothing now remains but to ask you, as I did when
I proposed: Will you have a little child by me? And in
reply you smiled, smiled as Anne-Marie sometimes does.

Of course I knew this last Saturday night, but I had too
little self-conceit to believe it.

Will you have a little child by me, Harriet?

April 13th, Monday.

Night before. From 11.30 I held Harriet in my arms. I
'saw' her face, heard her breathing, kissed her little hand
goodnight. Then we slept until morning, just as we used to
do when we were newly married.

What is this marvel that I have been experiencing for 8
days? [...]

She becomes engaged to W., but at night she flies to me.
We live as if we were newly married, we correspond with
each other. I send flowers to her every morning. I am like
a man newly married. I eat little, have ceased to drink, dress
myself, for whom? [...] I have prayed God to deliver me, to
give me a thorn in my flesh, to smite me in the face! But he
makes no move! I am happy when she seeks me and I do
not reproach myself. What am I to make of it all?

To-day, the 13th, in the morning, I saw a whole row of
carts taking away the earth from the nursery-garden down
beside the tobacco-drying sheds and the forcing-frames. For
7 years I have watched this garden and its frames being
equipped. Now, in their 8th year, it is all over with them!

Continuous contact with H—t all evening. At 10.30 I had such violent palpitations that I had to put my hand on my heart, but when I did so I fancied it was Harriet's heart. It quietened down, then stopped. I thought she was dying, but it started to beat again, only more tranquilly. I slept. At 11.30 the feeling of anxiety returned (I believed this time that he was striking her! She told me in her letter that 'she had fought and been struck'). By 12 o'clock she was lying on my arm, calm, friendly. I was woken three times during the night and received her as my wife.

April 14th.

This morning I went out rejuvenated. Did something foolish but with the best intentions. Later this morning I wrote her a letter about all this and sent it off. Subsequently became aware of a hostile H—t. [...] Now, this evening, H—t is gone. I have no awareness of her, neither hostile nor the reverse.

[...]

Strindberg to Harriet Bosse, April 14th.

I do not know what happened last night between 10.30 and 11.30, but you two were near to bursting my heart. Your little heart beat so violently in *my* breast, that I had to lay my hand upon it, and behold it quietened down and then stopped beating, so that I thought you were dead.

But as I lay in the moonlight in the faithful blue bed, that has never thought of any woman but you, you lay upon my arm, I could see your little face, feel your breath, and in the darkness I took your little hand and kissed it and whispered as of old: 'Good night beloved, beloved wife!'

Is that what Beethoven meant by 'The Distant Beloved'? It is a truth, but I was too much of a child to grasp it before you crossed my path.

What is this thing? A higher life on a higher plane, that

only we 'Children of the Gods' are able to live! And into this life an earthworm is to be initiated, to be incorporated! No, Agnes, Indra's daughter, No! Let no profane creature enter here! Such a one must stand outside the temple!

At first I shrank back as one would from a crime! 'I will not become a dissembler,' I cried to God. I begged Him to strike me as a sign that He disapproved of me. But He did not strike me. He made the moon shine into my room, and at midnight He laid my beautiful little wife on my arm!

I may do it, I have permission! But mark well, only in the soft darkness of the night, which makes this mystery innocent! In the daytime, by the light of day, it is a sin!

And then there comes a rapping on all the walls!

[. . .]

April 15th.

Night before. H—t came again, but without perfume. Towards morning things were different. Ter.[26] At 2 and 5 o'clock (on the stroke).

After a glorious walk in Djurgården wearing only my jacket, (so warm am I), I went home. And then H—t came intensely, deliciously, as if she had only now read my letter of yesterday. This sensation remained with me until 2 o'clock, when it disappeared and for a moment I became uneasy. I ate my dinner cautiously and without schnapps. When I got up and opened the window, a whole army of White Banners was waving to me (out on Gärdet). Then I understood and was so much moved that I burst into tears. Went to my desk and opened this diary. At that instant came a scent of roses that threw me into a state of ecstasy. But when I tried to take my after-dinner rest I was so uneasy that I had to get up. I remained awake and thus missed my nap, a thing that has not happened for seven years. H—t sought me several times, but I resisted her, for I have

26. Three telepathic embraces.

'learned' that it is only allowed at night ... in the chaste hours of darkness.

Axel here in the evening; gloomy, uneasy. H—t was gone the whole time. But then night came. She reappeared, I saw her! and she slept with me all night! At 2 and 5 o'clock ...

April 16th, Maundy Thursday.

Took my morning walk in sunshine! People half smiled at me in a kindly way, as if they knew something that I did not.

I wrote a letter to H—t: 'Say one word!' (I do not even know if she is free!).

Strindberg to Harriet Bosse, April 16th.

Say one word! I know nothing, but today, in the morning, I read so much in the glances of the people I met, out in the streets, in the roads! [. . .]

Say one word! You believe, I am sure, that I know what the whole world knows, but it is not so! I do know in a certain way, intuitively, but not as the world knows! Have been told nothing!!!

April 16th, Maundy Thursday.

A dress rehearsal of *Easter* this morning. Flygare* played Harriet's role. Got home at 4.30. Tranquil, slept for an hour. Then became aware of a wicked and threatening Harriet. Anne-Marie came to see me. She was wearing a bracelet. I asked who had given it to her. Uncle W! – Oh God, what malice! Thou wicked woman! 'The wickedest ever created.' May God never call you to account for this sin!

Yet I sense her as the 'incense' of the early days of our acquaintanceship, Feb. 4th, 1901, when *Easter* was collated.

* Anna Flygare, who took the part of Eleonora in the production of *Easter* at Strindberg's Intimate Theatre in 1908.

Before that time, from the autumn of 1900, it was celery, and from myself as well.

Spent the evening alone. Played Haydn's *Seven Last Words* while they were performing *Easter* at the Intimate Theatre. Experienced contact with H—t, but fitfully. A telephone call from Falck after 10 o'clock to say that *Easter* had gone well. At 10.30 H—t began to seek me, but irresolutely, and this continued all night until 5 o'clock, when she found me, but without joy. Hatred came between us! There was no soul! And without soul (love), no joy.

[. . .]

Strindberg to Harriet Bosse, April 17th.

Yesterday, Thursday, I woke with the feeling that I was once more newly married, so begged you for one word, you will know which, the word those people would have liked to say to me, but that I only want from your lips.

I did you no ill yesterday, neither with words nor with thoughts, not even with looks!

In the evening came your answer! You sent your child to me wearing the Thrall's[27] bracelet! From that moment the child ceased to be mine! I renounced her. I renounce her! To protect her little soul from your malice, you wickedest being ever created! I will never see her again.

[. . .]

You have now sunk so low that only One, the Almighty, can raise you up from the abyss.

I did not weep yesterday, I was turned to stone! You Black Swanwhite! You took with you all my good thoughts, took them away. Now take with you everything, everything, the child too. And go!

[. . .]

27. Gunnar Wingård. A few lines later Strindberg bursts out: 'Now the child is his! from this very moment; the Earl's daughter has become the Thrall's possession, and her mother likewise!'

April 17th, Good Friday.

Wrote a letter to Harriet in which, after the business of the bracelet yesterday, I renounced the child and said farewell! It was sent off at 10 a.m. It is now 10.30. Experienced H—t as friendly, almost loving until 2 o'clock. Then a storm began, first of palpitations, then of shooting pains in the region of the stomach and a noise like Grasshoppers in my ears. (Duplicity and Sensuality, according to Swedenborg.) I assumed from this that she had only just opened my letter. Then came incense (=Harz)[28] which probably signifies malice and hatred.

[. . .]

The evening, 8.30. A misgiving is growing within me. Perhaps the bracelet was a trifle (I did not look carefully at it), a thing of no importance, that the child would not surrender and the mother had not the heart to take from her. Was the whole business a demoniacal plot to ensure that I too should suffer Good Friday? To ensure too that I should have it in me to say to her: 'He struck you!' – I almost feel as if it were. At this moment I am experiencing Harriet as friendly! – But why not? It was love that inspired us. We love each other! And it was not done in malice. But on Good Friday we had to live through this evil thing.

[. . .]

April 18th, Easter Saturday.

Night before: At 11.30 she sought me, kindly, lovingly, x x x x. 3 o'clock ditto; 7 o'clock ditto. Six times! – News of *Easter.* It went well yesterday. Saw my portrait and that of a dark young girl in Strandvägen. I bought the latter ... Sent Anne-Marie an Easter card. – Experienced H—t first friendly, then indifferent, at times with palpitations.

... In the afternoon I was warned at 5 o'clock by a din from the courtyard. Heeded the warning and got up ...

28. The German for rosin.

Later on H——t, by turns neutral, hostile or friendly . . .

At about 9 o'clock (she was at that moment playing *vis-à-vis* W. in *Elga* at Svenska Teatren) she came to me like roses in my mouth. I sensed that she was already longing to come home and rest. At about 11 o'clock she came, lovingly, with fire and roses . . .

At 2 o'clock I had a most extraordinary experience. [A sort of dragging sensation began in the small of my back and proceeded downwards through my pelvis on the opposite side. I assumed from this that Harriet was about to start her period. This was confirmed later on by the fact that she only sought me shyly and without delight. We wrestled amiably until the morning, when I was victorious.][29]

Strindberg to Harriet Bosse, April 18th.

After a Good Friday – about which you know – when everything was one huge, distressing mockery, the evening came. I fell into a calmer mood, someone whispered in my ear: 'That unoffending bracelet was a worthless toy, of which no one wanted to deprive the child. It was no great treasure.' There I was, humbled, again, but I could hardly bring myself to wish that the ordeal we had passed through had never been. It was necessary, or at least beneficial.

Was it so about the bracelet?

In any case I sent you a 1,000 prayers for forgiveness and do so still, even if it was not so, but that a demon had spoken ill of me, as I believed. Of me! who can never be other than faithful to you in my heart, if not always in my words!

My one question, which you have perhaps misunderstood, is this: Are you free? It is a matter of life and death to me, for I will not live as a criminal. Why do you not answer? I implore you, send me your answer!

[. . .]

29. The paragraph between square brackets was not included in the Swedish edition of the book.

Last night you sought me like fire and roses, roses in my mouth. Every morning, when the sun rises, I feel a need to give you something! But my hand is so clumsy, my gifts always a mistake, giving pain where only good is intended ...

Whisper me a wish, great or small, preferably great! I want to make a sacrifice, take something of value from myself to bestow on you in exchange for the joy you give me by loving me, the joy that only spiritual love can give! You understand!

But above all: Answer! Are you free?

[...]

April 19th, Easter Day.

H—t kind, loving, giving me roses in my mouth, all the morning until 2 o'clock. – H—t must have been having her period 6th to 12th when she did not come. She sought me again on the night of the 12th with ardour. Yesterday evening, when she knew her period was approaching, she sought me like a taste or a fragrance in my mouth, as of roses or fruits. Then I asked myself: Can the abode of demons smell of roses? Surely not! Swedenborg says that when good spirits draw near there is a scent of flowers.

[...]

Every time I have achieved mental reconciliation with Harriet I have reproached myself, even to the verge of despair, for all the evil things I have thought or spoken or written about her. But subsequently, when I have reflected upon the matter in a calmer mood, it has struck me that I have, as it were, 'written away' her malice, put it on a piece of paper and let it float away on the wind. For, after every outburst she has, as it were, been cleansed, been more careful what she said, particularly in the matter of faulty accusations. She has refrained from insolence, wickedness and quarrels; she has grown calmer. That means that no harm was done! It means that by writing it away I also rid her of her malice.

At 10 o'clock in the evening, H—t returned, gentle, fragrant.

April 20th.
[...]
This evening she came again, like roses, loving and full of longing. Night came; she slept on my arm, but did not desire me until towards morning, then x x x.
[...]

April 21st.
The whole morning, solely as roses. Later she disappeared! In the evening she returned, but went again. At night apathetic and calm until the morning, when she sought me x x x.

April 22nd.
A delicious Harriet with me as I worked for the whole of the morning and afternoon. At dinner I ate meat and drank wine. My strength returned after 18 days and nights of fasting and abstinence and I thanked God. Had the feeling or awareness that Harriet was with the Möllers and that they were advising her to re-marry me and have a child. She put up a fight! This evening from 8 o'clock she has been stretching and squeezing me as if she were inside me or wanted to fling herself upon me ...
[...]

April 23rd.
[...]
A heavy day, spent in idleness. Slept much. H—t away, but towards evening could feel her stretching me below the chest.

Went to bed, grew calmer. No contact with H—t during

the night. I sought her but did not find her until 5 o'clock,
x x.

April 24th.

A glorious morning. H—t was with me all forenoon,
gentle, loving, like flowers in my mouth! Now I believe
that she is free and that we are united! But no, she disappeared in the evening when Axel came and although I received a summons to go to bed at 10 o'clock, she was not
there to meet me.

Slept and experienced faithlessness. Had bad dreams but
was left in peace until morning when she sought me with
passion but without love. I responded x x x.

April 25th.

The morning bright, pleasant. She was with me in love
for the whole forenoon while I worked. Then the photographs of *Swanwhite* arrived from Helsingfors. I sent them
on to H—t and also the title-page, previously overlooked,
of the manuscript of *Swanwhite* that belongs to her. It
must have been 3.30 before she received them.

Neutral until the evening, then gone. She sought me
but without love and only towards morning with any fire.
But she was cold, there is hatred between us!

April 26th.

[...]

Last night H—t was gone and I did not seek her. She
sought me, but not in love and therefore I did not respond
until about 5 o'clock in the morning, and then up to 6.30.

April 27th.

Bought and sent roses to 'Anne-Marie'. I was aware of
it when H—t received them, she 'exhaled fragrance'. After
that she was kind and loving right up to 3 o'clock and on to
6, when she became uneasy and gave me palpitations. She

was suffering (from W.) and was not being unfriendly to me. Now, at 7 o'clock, she is calmer (W. is acting this evening).

Here is another of the things that happened during these wonderful 23 days of suffering and delight. When I saw the photograph of the dark-haired lady who resembled Harriet in Strandvägen, I bought it and wanted to get it framed. That morning I went to a certain frame-maker, but he was shut. I continued along the street, saw another shop and marched in. There I encountered an old fellow who had cheated me shamelessly two years before and whom I had hated ever since. On that morning I was in a conciliatory mood, so said: 'Well, I never intended to come here again, but here I am!' – Even here I had to become reconciled. The old fellow grunted, and that was that.

This evening I looked out of the window. The whole sky was overcast and in the north-west horrible smoke was pouring from the chimney of the Sports Hall, though above it I could detect an orange glow left by the sunset. The smoke was fighting the light and the light won. It turned into a long streak and then widened out towards the north, while the smoke subsided and came to an end.

April 28th.

Harriet all day: seeking me lovingly, quietly, sorrowfully. Drank wine in the evening; slept heavily. Did not wake until 3 o'clock when she began to seek me. At about 5 o'clock we met x x x.

Note: It seemed to me that she woke as I was being woken, and with palpitations, which I then got. (H—t has complained of being woken up at night by palpitations and anxiety. Incubus, those that she herself has roused to life and activity.) This evening *Elga* is being performed for the last time.

I experienced the feeling that H—t had been set free.

April 29th.

[...]

Had Harriet strongly, at times tempestuously the whole forenoon. After that, towards evening, she disappeared.

At night she sought me several times, but I did not respond. Finally, at 5 o'clock x x x, when she came to me, submissive and loving. Afterwards she thanked me with a fragrance!

April 30th.

[...]

(This business with Harriet. At times she seems to seek me in her sleep. When I wake and respond, she wakes up and withdraws. This makes it appear as if when unconscious (sleeping) she wants to possess me, but when conscious does not!)

Harriet with me the whole morning as I worked, but in the afternoon she disappeared. In the evening, anxiety and faithlessness. At night, cold. I sought her but she only responded with palpitations, as if she lay weeping. Not until morning did she seek me, and then I received her x x x.

May 1st.

Harriet amorous all day, especially in the afternoon. At about 6–7 she sought me and tried to take me by storm. Telephone call from Castegren about *Swanwhite* at the Opera. Presumably H——t is studying the part.

At night she sought me, eagerly, imperiously, but I said no!... Whereupon she withdrew, in anger.

May 2nd.

H——t gone! Her love as I experienced it today is nothing but pure deception. *He* probably threw her over yesterday, and in desperation she flung herself at me. It would be best if I could rescue the child and we were out of all this. She cannot change her nature. I cannot be the saviour of one who is made only of lies, treachery, malice, and lust! Lust and hate!

Towards evening she sought me in love. Castegren came to talk about *Swanwhite*, which they are going to perform. He told me that Bosse has asked that Kåge should be the Prince. (Not W. therefore.) This must mean that she has finished with W.! I was pleased, of course. When Castegren had gone I drank wine and played the overture to *Romeo*. Was aware of H—t storming me and expected her at night. However, at about 10 o'clock I was overcome by intense drowsiness and at about 10.30 I fell asleep. Woke at 11.30 to a moment of jubilant embrace x x x x. Was woken again at 5 and 6.30. This was the greatest of our unions, it was wedlock! And on this same day she published the banns of her marriage to W.!!!

May 3rd, Sunday.

H—t amorous all day until noon when I wrote and sent off a letter about this intimate relationship of ours. Silence followed! It is now 5.45.

[. . .]

Strindberg to Harriet Bosse, May 3rd.

[. . .]

I have your soul now in a little Japanese box on my desk. In this box lie all your letters, a ring with many smaller rings attached (one is lost), your bridal crown and veil, the gold pen, – Grant that I may write more lovely things with it! Beloved! – and two little lavender bags from Denmark (1901), one red and one green, joined by an inextricable knot.

The most beautiful letters are those of 1904 (when we got our divorce). I am reading one in which you respond to the news of my application for a divorce by a cry of anguish and of defeated love! It reads like a cry of woe to high heaven and I roar in pain!

My bride of seven years ago! And now another's, and yet not!

Can you loosen this bond? Can you? I cannot!

[. . .]

After fourteen days of negotiation with Ranft about your *Swanwhite*, he went away yesterday without giving me an answer. We can do nothing unless he accepts the play.

Do you demand that I should abandon this favourable opportunity and wait for you? You know that I can wait, but you have so much and I have so little! There is a chance that I may be able to get *Swanwhite* performed at Dramaten. Only a chance, mark you! Falck will always be willing to put it on – Ranft knows that – and with a little child of seventeen,[30] who is like you, can smile as you do, but is melancholy. She is well educated, of good family. Would you not, if necessary, adopt her as your pupil, your spiritual child, since you refuse to have one of the earthly variety? In that way you would still be acting, but through her.

I cannot understand why you will not let your talent breed, and why you are so unwilling to see offspring of your strong, unusual soul. The common run of people can give life to ordinary children, but only Children of the Gods can give birth to beings within human souls.

I sometimes wonder if there will not emerge from our super-natural marriage small beings of a spiritual nature. Something must surely come of a union like ours, in which tremendous spiritual forces meet and merge.

30. Fanny Falkner, whom Strindberg had seen playing the part of a page in *Sir Bengt's* Wife at the Intimate Theatre. Thanks to him she was given the title role in *Swanwhite* at the same theatre in October 1908. She was his last love, and in 1909 they were engaged for twenty-four hours.

At times I believe that you will have another child by me, though I do not know how. And it will be born in love and will become a power on the earth, not of great estate, but a power in word and deed. I have a fancy that a little soul is waiting to make parents of us again, and I believe I have seen her little face on a white sheet, at night, in the moonlight.

I want to take this opportunity to inform you of something, so that, if it should occur, you will not be alarmed. I have read in 'a book' that there is such a thing as false pregnancy, which has all the symptoms of real pregnancy, but is without any reality. I wonder if we may not expect something of the kind? I have also read, but still doubt its truth, that an actual immaculate conception can take place, that is to say telepathically! What should we believe then? What would the world say?

Whatever happens I shall learn of it through my own sensations for the soul of your body is in mine. [. . .]

I know of your every emotion. Know when you are happy, when someone is tormenting you (then a nail is struck into my heart), and when He is angry with me, I have shooting pains below my breast.

May 3rd, cont.

A tranquil evening. H—t seems to be spending it at home with Lillan.

However, when I went to bed at 10 o'clock she was lying there waiting for me x x x. Again at 5 o'clock x x x. Last at 6.30, but then she was satisfied.

May 4th.

H—t had not answered my letter. It is a month now since she got engaged. In the forenoon she sought me, but angrily, hostilely. At 12.30 aggressively, not in love, only in desire. I sent off a letter at dinner-time. In the evening came her answer! See what follows! Auto-deception! W. is going to Gothenburg this evening. She says she is getting married in June. It is a lie! He will not have her!

[...]

She got my second letter while at the theatre, but cannot have read it before 10.30. – I fell asleep, was sought by H—t at 3.30, but in her sleep, and she retreated when I responded. She sought me again and at 6.30 we found each other in love. This after my sharply worded letter of yesterday! It might have been a whipping! She must love being whipped!

Strindberg to Harriet Bosse, c. May 4th.

You have not answered my direct question about *Swanwhite*. If you have outgrown her, or are tired of her, tell me. I do not like the idea of Ranft's having the play. It was only for your sake that I offered it to him. Herod's daughter is more in your line today, is she not? I shall regard your silence, if it continues, to mean you do not care, and shall request the return of the play. [...]

I think the time has now come for me to escape from your net. There is only one way, but it never fails! You have recently tried this method, but unsuccessfully. I shall be successful!

Harriet Bosse to Strindberg, May 4th.

No, I did not answer you – I told you in my letter that all contact between us *must* cease –

I belong to another man, am going to marry him in June. Put yourself in his place. What would you not suffer –

You demand the return of *Swanwhite*. You should never take back what you have given –

However, here it is, to be performed, if you want, either at Dramaten or at the Intimate Theatre. I relinquish it without bitterness. I can only rejoice that such a lovely thing should have been written, whoever interprets these thoughts of yours from the stage in future –

May 5th.

Sent off another letter, equally sharp and ruthless, and which she must have read just now, at 10 o'clock. She is storming me so that I am almost suffocated, but she is seeking me too, erotically.

[. . .]

This morning I received a letter of which every word was untrue. I tore it to bits!

At 4 o'clock she stormed me with palpitations, so that I was almost suffocated. She must have read my last letter. I slept until 5 o'clock. Then she sought me erotically. Curious creature! And the whole of this evening while acting in *Elga* she has been with me.

Night: 11 o'clock. Could feel that she was seeking me, but was unable to reach me. I was, as it were, shielded from contact. Slept until 4 o'clock, when she came x x x, and again at six-thirty. But she was in a selfish mood and went away when she was satisfied, could not be bothered to wait for me. I suppose that her period must have come on towards morning.

May 6th.

My last letter, unopened, was returned by post. All the better, for it was cruel! Thereupon I burned the last 3 letters, which were evil. They swelled up, formed shapes and finally 2 hearts!

[. . .]

Now, at 11 a.m. she is with me erotically as I work.

A telegram from Ranft to say he will accept *Swanwhite*. I telegraphed the news to H——t and reminded her that today is the anniversary of our wedding . . . After doing so I slept and dreamed about W. . . . Then Falck arrived and told me Harriet's banns had been published on Sunday the 3rd. And

I had not known of it! ! ! My mind is now at a standstill! Is she literally two persons? And do I possess one? The better one? That would seem to be the case, for when we meet or write we hate each other. Is this possible? (She must be two independent persons who are unaware of each other for, when I talk or write to her of this life we live together unconsciously, she keeps silent, makes no response, knows nothing about it, or will not know.)

Axel here in the evening; gloomy. – I did not know what to make of H—t this evening. She sought me at 4 a.m. and at 6.30 x x x. She had sought me at 12 o'clock, but had not been able to reach me!

May 7th.

H—t lived with me from morning till dinner time in love and eros. While under this influence I wrote to Falck and asked him to find out if she was expecting a child. I offered, if that is the case, to take her to Switzerland until the child is born, and then there would be no necessity for her to marry. – Now, at 5 p.m. she has tried to take me by storm, erotically. I was just about to yield when there came a sharp, purposeful bang from above, followed by the moving of furniture.

In the evening I sent her *Huon de Bordeaux** with a dedication.

H—t fairly friendly during the evening. At night I was woken at 1 o'clock by an unusual sensation. She was mournful and submissive and kissed me but would not have me. Nevertheless at 5 o'clock she came and after I had kissed her x. Later she sought me, but without joy or ardour.

* A medieval French heroic poem about the Fairy King, Oberon. Strindberg sent a Swedish translation of this poem to Harriet Bosse with the following dedication: 'Give me more beautiful things to write about, Swanwhite, gave me a new golden pen, Chrysaetos.'

May 8th.

Overcast, gloomy, H——t mournful, yet seeking me at times, erotically but submissively. H——t with me all day in love and eros, storming me without pause. The same in the evening. Then I sent her a glorious rhododendron, in full bloom, like the one I gave her after Lillan's birth. I reckoned that she would see it when she got back from the theatre tonight.

I went to bed at 10 o'clock when H——t stormed me with palpitations. I fell asleep, but was roused at 11.45, when H——t gave me palpitations. On top of that I developed a pain in my abdomen (the spot corresponding to her 'Athanor').* After a while she sought me ardently and I responded x. She came again at about 4 o'clock x x. What does all this mean? Are the two of them playing an insolent game with me? Have not the banns been published? Yet she is with me night and day. When does she have time to think of him?

[. . .]

May 10th, Rogation Sunday.

Walked along Gref Magnigatan, past the door of No.12, where H——t lived when she was my fiancée. It has a pane of glass through which we used to kiss goodnight. I wondered whether, after 7 years, the marks of our lips would still be there. They were; and there too was a marvellously beautiful drawing of an Angel with a child on her arm, floating in the air, and behind her a man who might be me. What can this signify?

It is 11 o'clock. I am aware of H——t in a loving mood. I

---

* Really a digestive furnace used by alchemists, here womb. Writing about the womb in *A Blue Book* Strindberg says: 'It resembles the alchemist's Athanor, in which were distilled the Philosopher's Stone, gold, the Elixir of Life, and the homunculus.'

am reading the text for the day and praying to God on her behalf. 'Help us, Oh Lord, for we are undone!'

H—t is seeking me in love and eros, but I am not responding. I write, I read the Bible, I pray, I weep. Viewed from one angle things look threatening (she weeps), from another hopeful (but lamentable). What is it that I hope for? That Lillan may escape having a stepfather! But for the rest, what? I do not believe in any happiness with H—t. She cannot change her nature! I beg God to deliver me from this tunic of Nessus.

Ate scarcely anything at dinner. Wept and prayed to be allowed to die! Then came a shower of rain. Great white clouds appeared in the N.E., followed by a splendid rainbow. I slept tranquilly!

This telepathic state of affairs (marriage, which has also been a fact) began before our engagement, when Harriet, in a manner which I cannot explain, sought me at night. I was awakened, even as I slept, and experienced the illusion that she lay beside me, that I held her in my arms and possessed her and had possessed her before I proposed. But then I did not think of it (when I proposed that is). Since then it has manifested itself every time we have been parted. Distance does not exist for us. She has sought me from Paris and Vienna, and we have come together as man and wife. It can never cease!

Drank wine in the evening; it gave me courage and the life I am living seemed to me unworthy. I determined to break out of it, even felt that I was on the way to freeing myself. Fell asleep! Slept until 3.30 when she woke me though she did not receive me until about 5, and then briefly and ardently. After that she would not have me. Beforehand she had played with me and kissed me too, submissively, in the way she did just once before, but not quite the same.

[...]

May 11th.

H—t friendly and loving all forenoon, erotic at times, but briefly. I think she is having her period! In the morning I walked round Rosendahl where I had not been for months. It seemed to me that Harriet had been deposited there on the ground and that she now rose up. I found her again and fell into a state of ecstasy and wept and called to her. The fact is, that for seven summers I have walked there thinking about her, caressing her remembered image, weaving stories about her. That is why she was deposited there!

N.B.! Harriet and I got engaged on March 5th, 1901; but before that time I had possessed her at *night*, telepathically from January 13th, 9 times in all; Jan. 13th and 26th, Feb. 12th, 18th, 20th, 21st, 22nd, 25th, and 27th. During that time she came to visit me in the daytime looking just as innocent as before and behaving as if nothing had happened. It is very strange. Does she know nothing about her nocturnal adventures and her visits to me?

H—t loving the whole day and towards the evening erotic. I think her period started on the 6th and comes to an end today. I have now written and proposed but have not sent the letter!

[. . .]

May 12th.

[. . .]

Went up to Hasselbacken to look at our Bird-Cherry — now bursting into leaf outside the room where our wedding-feast was held — and to break off a twig. (Cf. the May 6ths in various parts of this diary, on which I took the first green twig from this tree.) A waiter was standing on the bank as if he were expecting me. He followed me with his eyes and walked towards the tree. Another waiter was sitting on a bench right opposite the tree, as if he were guarding it. Two more men appeared and also a waitress who said: 'What is going on here?' In a word, the tree seemed to be under guard and I was not to be permitted to break off a twig. But the tree was in full leaf and had sent up a quantity of suckers! What can that mean?

Last autumn, when Harriet returned from Jämtland and came to see me, she suddenly said: 'We are married! you know' – She meant of course that we had lived (telepathically) as man and wife for the whole summer and for long before it!

H—t mournful but erotic all day. Drank wine with my dinner and punch in the evening.

I felt too weak to go on suffering today, so went back to wine and punch. I suppose that things must run their course. My 40 days will have run theirs on the 16th. Nearly fell out of a cab and got killed this morning, I was so weak!

Fell asleep at 10.30. Then H—t stormed me with fearful palpitations, as if she had received a piece of evil news, or as if someone were teasing and tormenting her. Was woken about 2 o'clock with palpitations, but was forced to seek her out myself in eros. She was mournful and unwilling. At about 4 o'clock she came herself and I took her by storm until 5 o'clock x x x. Woke again at about 6 in a violently erethistic state. Wanted to take her in my arms then and there, but was instantly disarmed. This suggests that, during my sleep, she is within my body, but when I wake she withdraws, for otherwise this sudden retreat on my part is inexplicable. Such a thing usually takes time, but this happened in an instant. It used to be the same in our conjugal life when she sought me and offered herself; but as soon as I came to her I was deprived of my arms by her 'Athanor', which seemed to possess an individuality of its own.

[...]

I wrote to Anne-Marie in the evening, offering her my

services! But I burnt the letter this morning thinking: H—t shall say the first word this time.

[. . .]

May 13th.

[. . .]

Towards noon I 'heard' Harriet's heart pounding in anguish. I thought she was dying I sent her a card with a few words of comfort and offered her my help. After two hours I received the following sphinx-like answer. What in fact does her letter say? Nothing! A few words, words! 'Wish me happiness! I believe in happiness. The banns have been published twice!' What is this? Nothing!

Fell asleep. She sought me ardently, but I was shielded, as it were, from within. Against my will there was something that put up resistance and drove her back. This happened repeatedly until morning, when she got her way and I took her in my arms. She literally drank me and departed in a swoon.

Strindberg to Harriet Bosse, May 13th.

My dearly beloved little friend!

Your little heart throbs all day!

You are unhappy and seem to be calling to me.

Say one word! Just one! I promise to answer kindly! I shall help you out of all this! There is nothing I would not do for you, for the two of you!

Say one single word! August Strindberg

Harriet Bosse to Strindberg, May 13th.

I told you not to write – True – my heart throbs – all day – but only because I am overwrought – because I have worked too hard this year –

The banns have already been published twice –

Wish me every happiness – I believe – in happiness –

Harriet

Strindberg to Harriet Bosse, May 14th.

You are beginning to believe in happiness! That is what I have done during these wonderful six weeks! But your two last letters have deprived me of my faith in it.

Write one more!

Strindberg to Harriet Bosse, May 14th.

Three times have I written and then burnt these words, that come from the depths of my heart:

Wilt thou be my wedded wife,
In the eyes of God, the law and the world,
For better or for worse,
In faithful love,
Now and for evermore?
Must this too be burnt?
Yes? or No?

But you must be free, so that you can receive into your womb a blessed and longed-for child, receive it in my arms, those arms that I have never opened, not even in thought, for any woman! but you ever since I saw you.

[. . .]

May 14th.

Wrote a postcard to H—t this morning. No answer! Wrote again at noon and proposed! No answer! Only naïve eroticism!

This evening the growing castle was illuminated and I saw a red tuft rising up out of the sun. No answer to my letter other than erotic advances. I was cheerful all evening; drank punch and played *Faust*. Fell asleep. Woke at 3.30 and sought Harriet, but she was gone. I could not reach her. However, on the stroke of 5 I experienced within my body a sensation as though her matrix were moving slowly downwards, and when it got down my desire was kindled and hers too, at the very same moment, so that embraces in love and eros followed. Her matrix really seems to be an independent being, possessed periodically by desire, at 2 and 5 a.m. Her little athanor seems to love my counterpart, which is as childish as her own. But H—t's acts independently of her will and is filled with desire at certain specific times! This means that it loves me against its owner's will. At 5 o'clock in the morning it descends and wants love. At other times it is no good trying, nothing comes of it. If only one had known this seven years ago! H—t sought me at 6.30 too and I responded, but something disturbed her. Probably the child woke up.

May 15th.

Sofia. Harriet's name-day.

Sent H—t another card this morning telling her that the flat under mine is vacant. I was out for a walk at the time she received my note, and could sense that it had made a good impression. This sensation remained with me until 11.30. No answer has come. Only the feeling that she is seeking me in eros. I am calm, have a feeling that my fate has been decided! It would be ideal if she and Lillan lived in the flat below. I think it is going to happen! We shall see!

No answer! An endlessly long evening.

Fell asleep! Was not woken until 5.30, but by that time the spell she casts was lifted. I thanked God and rose feeling well. Saved.

Strindberg to Harriet Bosse, May 15th.

To Let (immediately).

No. 40³ Karlavägen, (*third*) floor.

Four rooms and kitchen, etc.

No rent need be paid!

Harriet Bosse's explanatory notes, 1932.

I cannot describe how I suffered during this time, when I knew that Strindberg thought of me daily, hourly, and lived with me in his imagination. I wanted to cut myself off from all contact with Strindberg and begged him not to write to me, but it was no good.

[. . .]

I never saw Strindberg again after the spring of 1908. My daughter continued to visit him right up to a few months before his death.

May 16th.

[. . .]

Fell asleep at 10.30; had imagined I was cold and had pulled another blanket round me like a shawl. I was expecting H—t, of course, for she had sought me out in the evening and misled me . . . During the course of the evening I had sent her a letter containing an explicitly worded proposal of marriage, and with it a photograph: Hartman: Man and Woman, so I was expecting to be woken at 11.30 when she returned from the theatre and had time to read the letter. I did not wake until 2.30 and then became aware that she had been attacking me since 2 o'clock, but the blanket had protected me. She continued her onslaught but without success. I fell asleep again, woke just before 5 and sought her. She responded but without success. Not until the clock in the dining-room struck the first chime of 5 did we meet and then what a wedding it was! x x Ditto 6.30 after which she sank back into the void and disappeared!

[. . .]

May 17th (Norway's Seventeenth).

[. . .]

At 12 o'clock a letter arrived from her fiancé W., now in Gothenburg. He is threatening to shoot me if I continue to 'persecute' H—t. Wrote a lot of nonsense about how I had wrecked her youth, and the like. My letter of yesterday to H—t was also returned unopened. (H—t must have received a letter from W. at the same time that I did, for she gave me palpitations for a whole hour, during which time I experienced her as loving and erotic, which I still do at 2.30.)

In the paper-shop in Strandvägen this morning I saw two portraits of H—t that were so horribly ugly and evil (devilishly) that I grew frightened and prayed God to deliver me! It was terrible! – She is playing with us both, but most of all with W. She loves me body and soul! (See this diary.) But her evil self would willingly murder me!

This will certainly end in tragedy!

[. . .]

I know that in gatherings, in trams, in the street in broad daylight, she has had contact with me. We are indeed grown together as one being, and yet we may not live together. There is no place here for W!, and yet the banns were published for the 3rd time today! What can this be? For the whole of today, since the stroke of 5 this morning, we have lived as one; the same heart-beats, the same sufferings, the same fears! Now she is at the theatre, acting before the public, but she is with me! Talking to me. Never can we part!

H—t really shows more delicacy by not wanting to correspond with me. Our relationship is so fragile that it cannot endure words, neither spoken nor written words. And I have a clumsy hand. (Ungeschickt Hand.)

Drank much wine at supper; slept heavily and did not wake until about 3 o'clock. H—t sought but in vain. Fell asleep and woke at 6.45 when I got up, saved! That is to say slept through 5 o'clock. T.b.t.G. At about 10 o'clock, before I fell asleep, H—t had attacked me so violently that I thought she was dying! After that too she sought me in Eros and love, but I was shielded.

May 18th.

[. . .]

Axel here to supper. Beethoven, but without enthusiasm. The night that followed was terrible. I woke at 1.30 to find H—t stretching my Epigastrium* so that I had to get up. I waited until the stroke of 2 when she stormed me in eros, but I resisted and fell asleep about 3. Was woken again at 5.30 and was again attacked, but stood firm!

Got up saved.

May 19th.

H—t sought me this morning in true love, at last, and innocently, like a rose. When that scent came to me, about dinner-time, I responded. After dinner I sought her out, and went into the attack when she tried to escape me. We embraced again in eros, as before x. And all this evening, while acting in the theatre, she had been with me, erotically, naïvely.

This morning a man came up to me in Djurgården and sold me a brooch: an anchor with a red stone and a white pearl. (Anchor=Hope.)

White banners are waving on Gärdet. The Growing Castle is illuminated by the evening sun.

Went to bed at 9.30. Was woken at 1.30 but with a feeling of aversion. Fell asleep and was woken at 5.30, but nothing came of it as H—t was cold and sceptical. Saved.

May 20th.

H—t is seeking ineffectively. I have been reading the offensively intimate interview with H—t in D.N.† Also read her announcement about her honeymoon trip and the one about *Swanwhite*.

---

* The part of the abdomen immediately above the stomach, the pit of the stomach.

† The daily paper *Dagens Nyheter* interviewed Harriet Bosse on 20 May 1908 on the topical subject of actresses' extravagance in the matter of stage costume.

I drank at dinner, drank until 5 o'clock[31] and eradicated her by destroying a heap of photographs!

She is furious with me. I burnt them up in a stove, all the pictures of her out of the Green Room.* [. . .] At 9 o'clock I wanted to go to bed, but I was so dangerously attacked by – hatred = electric currents, that I did not dare to lie down. It streamed upon me from above, from below and my chest was squeezed together. Thought: You are trying to kill me . . . Fell asleep. Did not wake until 4.45. On the stroke of 5 H—t sought me; but I got up from the bed!

I put up a struggle and begged God for help. I walked to and fro, not daring to lie down. But I was driven to it against my will, and when she came to my arms I had no feeling of regret, only love of infinite happiness. In our repeated embraces that threatened never to end x x x x, it seemed to me that she shared my feelings. We could hardly bring ourselves to part . . . What am I to believe now? That she is mine, that I shall regain her and that this is the will of Providence? Or shall I die? By my own hand, in order to escape this life of sin and crime with W. through H—t.

May 21st.

Harriet accompanied me in Eros on the whole of my early morning walk . . . I went out again and bought a revolver.

Am preparing myself for death. At this moment, 10 o'clock, she is with me in love and eros.

Received a letter from W. that I burnt unopened. – It is now between 11 and 1. H—t is seeking me in a way I do not understand, but which produces in me a mania for suicide.

31. Strindberg always had his dinner punctually at 3 o'clock.
* The sitting-room at 4 Karlavägen which was decorated and furnished in green.

Praying to God for advice and help. The house is as quiet as if there were a dead body in it! A terrible morning, filled with thoughts of suicide. Spent it in anguish of mind and prayers to God. Falck came and stayed to dinner. Slept peacefully until 5.30.

H—t is sometimes afflicted by suicidal mania. Is it she who is passing on to me this deadly anxiety, or is it W.?'

Axel here; it calmed me! Slept well all night, though H—t repeatedly assaulted me in Eros. Got up saved!

[. . .]

May 22nd.

Went out strong. H—t sought me mournfully as if she had lost me. She remained loving for the rest of the morning.

Found a scrap of paper saying *Pax* (Peace). Met a cart carrying Palms (Victory and *Peace*). Heard a shot and rumbling noise like thunder from Djurgården in the south-west. Thought of Gbg[32] in the S.W.

There was a sound in my right ear this morning like the moaning of a dying person! (W.) Felt that I was getting better all day and worked with enthusiasm and hope, accompanied by H—t's love and eros to which I did not respond. There is a Benefit Performance for her today. Roses were sent to me from two sources. Axel here. We drank wine and he played Beethoven. It gave me a feeling of joy and I went to bed. At 10.30 H—t stormed me but I fell asleep. At 11.30 I was half awakened by H—t, who offered herself to me, but I was shielded and fell asleep again. She sought me all night but I resisted her. Finally on the stroke of 6 she found me. x x in love, but mournfully and without ardour. Made up my mind to go to Stocksund! Bought portmanteaus!

[. . .]

32. Gotherburg.

May 23rd, Desideria.

Gloomy! Prayed God to let me die! Now I am bound to her again.

Gloomy all day. Weep, and pray for release. I pray God to help me out of this; pray for W. too, who perhaps suffers most.

Falck here. Axel here. Went to bed at 9.30. Slept right through in spite of the fact that she stormed me in eros. Woke saved.

[. . .]

May 24th, Sunday.

A heavy morning, wept mostly. Axel came. Nils Andersson* came. I went to the station with him in a barouche. When I got home at 7.30 I wept for my child, who I could feel was longing for me too. Then Harriet came to me in love, and this time I indicated that I had not abandoned her. She responded by giving me roses in my mouth! Fell asleep. Was woken at 12 o'clock and embraced her in endless love x x x. When she was married . . . She sought me later at 5 o'clock and at 6.30, but was not allowed to have her way.

[. . .]

May 25th, Monday.

On this, the very day of her marriage, Harriet dogs my steps in eros! Found a postcard this morning with a picture of two sailors beside a sentry-box and underneath the words: Corps de garde! That means *you* are protected against his attempts on your life! On certain occasions during the past 7 years I have met sailors in Djurgården, and have instinctively turned back at the sight of them. I felt they were a warning. It seemed to me today that the reason for this was made clear to me. – In Banérgatan, outside

* One of Strindberg's friends from his time in Lund. He was Clerk to the Justices and later Mayor of Lund.

the house in which I once lived, I found two objects that looked like cartridges, joined together by iron wire.

I asked a workman if they were dynamite. He looked at them, took a pair of pliers (!) out of his pocket, and cut the wire. I asked a guardsman. He thought it was the battery of an electric bell. I took the objects home and joined the piece of wire together again. Wrote, grew drowsy, slept. Had lunch. Then H—t called to me. I went into our yellow room! She welcomed me and we embraced 6 times! ... though she is now married to W.

After dinner she was gone, not to be found.

At 6 o'clock came a telephone call from Falck who told me that Harriet and W. were married yesterday! (May 24th.) What am I to make of this? ... For the whole of today I have been in a good mood, almost a happy one! Can anyone explain this?

Axel here this evening. I went to bed at 10 o'clock to avoid visitors. But then something happened between me and H—t that put me on the rack. I prayed to God from the depths of my soul that I might henceforth be delivered from living this life which is now adultery. Slept with my prayer book on my breast and prayed to God, even in my sleep, that he would take my soul. Was woken at 1.30 by my heart that was heavy as a stone, and because I was being squeezed together below my chest. Read the Bible and prayed ... Two o'clock came, and with it the irresistible, like a friendly summons. Harriet was in my arms and received me with delight. I felt no self-reproach, only joy and happiness. Later on she sought me again, twice, but we were no longer permitted to meet! – Then came the morning, bringing with it self-reproach and despair.

May 26th.

Self-reproach, despair. I pray God to let me die rather than live in sin, for now she is married. It is 9.30 a.m. and she is seeking me in eros! though married.

Harriet persecuted me erotically all morning and finally I was forced to embrace her or burn up (even though she is married to W!.) – Despair and shame followed! I called upon God to let me die rather than go on living in sin!

Some days ago Axel told me of a dream he had had. He was conducting a small choir. Harriet was on one side of it and I on the other. Axel was conducting with a silver table-spoon. What can this mean? That H—t and I are to be reunited? A silver table-spoon ? (A christening present?) Is it possible that this will end as with Job? With three daughters, Jemima (= Day), Kezia (= Fragrance), Karen-Happuch (= Power and splendour overthrown). Is it possible? No!

Every day and every hour I pray God to let me die, but he has hidden himself from me! I believe that no human being has ever suffered as I suffer!

H—t pursues me, but I elude her. I lay down for my after-dinner nap in the parlour.

[. . .]

At noon I wrote two more farewell letters, one to H—t and one to Axel, as I was intending to shoot myself before evening!

Drank a lot of wine. Slept saved!

May 27th.

Night before: Slept shielded from H—t's onslaught. T.B. t.G.

Towards morning I began to feel I was being liberated from H—t. It was as if many small knotted strings were being untied in my trunk; first in the nerves of my spine, then in my spleen, my liver, my lungs, my heart, my stomach and the small of my back. I felt blessedly delivered from tension ... I got up, washed my whole body, put on clean linen and went out. The whole of Strandvägen was beflagged: saw a flag with a black cross, but it was blue. Saw some dry paint spilt on the road; red and green! – While I was having my coffee two erotic pigeons settled on the sill outside the dining-room window and gazed at me. When I got out into the street these same pigeons came and coquetted just in front of my feet. It is now 9 o'clock. *A New Blue Book* is just coming out! White flags are waving on Gärdet!

[...]

Wept half the day for Lillan (Children's Day). H—t seeks me in Love and eros, but I respond only in love. Ate no dinner. Things looked somewhat brighter in the evening and I played the piano. H—t sought me in eros all night. I fought back, came near to falling, but was saved.

May 28th.

Woke with a new idea: H—t has simply entered into a pact with W. 'in order to have companionship' (which is what she said herself in her first letter). He has rented a room from her in the new flat. He gets engaged to her, and the following night she is with me. He gets married, goes away, and that night she celebrates a wedding with me. Is theirs a platonic relationship? Spiritual marriage without rapport? A disgraceful pact? A Eunuch's Marriage? Perhaps this is the secret! But I have been given a hint that she was not really properly married (when she went to parson Fries's house), but that she was 'bound' in some way by a betrothal, or that nothing at all happened there! I met Fries one morning recently and he looked very sly.

Wept all morning! Resisted H—t's attacks! But after dinner I took her in my arms, rather than burn up! – No self-reproaches, only happiness and release from melancholy and the desire to kill myself. – Abstemiousness has produced suicidal mania before, has always done so! (Aug., Sept. 1901?) Now I believe that things are as they should be. We shall see ...

A terrible evening even though H—t was with me in eros. Slept through the night, shielded! Got up saved.

May 29th.

Terrible morning! Wept so much that my soul almost fled from my body. But H—t was with me in eros, shyly, mournfully. I was forced to embrace her in order not to take my own life ... She responded by giving me roses in my mouth. Is this a sin? Why am I not warned? I have begged God to kill me if this is a sin.

H—t seeks me all day in Eros!

Axel here in the evening. I went to bed in a new frame of mind. At about 2 o'clock I woke and sought H—t, but did not find her. At about 6 she sought me, but I was shielded! Got up saved.

May 30th.

Wrote to Fröken Falkner. She came to see me! ... H—t pursued me this morning and insisted that I must embrace her.

[...]

In a light-hearted frame of mind this evening. Is their marriage about to break up? I am sure that something must have occurred in Gbg. Drank Punch. Played the piano!

Slept peacefully, but only after vain, mournful seeking. Got up saved!

May 31st, Sunday.

H—t is seeking me in infinite love, mournful, despairing. All must be over between her and W.!

Alex and Aulin here for the evening, bringing Bach.

Beethoven until 3 o'clock, when the sun rose. The atmosphere was good, but heavy-laden. At 5 o'clock I was woken by H—t who seemed to want to kill me or take me by force. I was saved, got up, went out!

[...]

June 1st.

H—t seeking me mournfully all morning. When I responded she stormed me with such violence that I had to embrace her several times and she received me without reservation or doubt, and in great and infinite love. And today her husband, W., is coming back!

At about dinner-time I was attacked by the most violent palpitations and shooting pains in my abdomen. I thought that H—t must have received a telegram to say he had run away, or something of the sort, and that she was ill with hysterics. I was in pain all afternoon, but H—t, who seemed to have gone to bed, pursued me in eros, as if she were keeping jealous guard over me. What has happened today? The theatre in both Gbg and Sthlm[33] closed yesterday. *He*, W., ought then to return today, or has he already arrived?

What is to happen to me will probably be decided tomorrow. The revolver is ready loaded!

I dreaded the night, prayed to God for deliverance and put the revolver beside my bed. Was sought by H—t in eros towards morning, but she disappeared. Got up saved!

June 2nd.

They must have just met. H—t is gone! But at about 11 a.m. she sought me in eros, shyly. I responded! Where is *she* now? In Gbg or here? Where is *he*?

This is the critical day! —

H—t sought me, but sadly, as if she only wanted to find out if I was still there! When I took her seriously she drew back. I think she must be lying ill, here, in Stockholm! —

33. Stockholm.

Tor Aulin was here between 5.30 and 7.30. H—t sought me the whole time, sometimes she stormed me ... Went to bed at 10 o'clock. H—t was waiting for me and I embraced her several times in endless love! – The same later on, at 5 o'clock, but without joy. What is this? Where is she? Is she married? How can there be room for me?

June 3rd.

H—t is now seeking me at my desk, in eros, ceaselessly, the whole day! At times I am in despair! Albert Wiekman* and Fröken Falkner came to see me. Ate scarcely any dinner! A horrible evening. – Thunder! – Called upon God: 'My God, my God, why hast thou forsaken me?' This evening Blake's *Book of Job* gave me comfort.

H—t sought me during the night at 2 and 5 o'clock in great love, and I responded!

June 4th.

[...]

H—t seeking me all this morning, in endless love and eros, giving me roses in my mouth. Things are a little better today. Have a feeling that the crisis is approaching! It is just 2 months since April 4th. (The engagement!) I drank a lot in the evening, went to bed at 11 o'clock and slept until morning in spite of H—t's repeated attacks. Got up saved.

June 5th.

[...]

God help me now so that I may free myself!!!

Having made up my mind to free myself I intended to spend a peaceful night in sleep. Was woken, however, at 5 o'clock and, after H—t had shown her delight and surprise at finding me again, we met, irresistibly, in endless love. – First I saw her face and then that of a little smiling child!

* A Baptist Minister and pacifist agitator, known as the Peace General.

June 6th, Whit Saturday.

All this morning as I work H——t pursues me with her naïve eroticism. I am aware of her with every breath I draw! But at about 10 o'clock she stormed me with such violence that my epigastrium was nearly shot to pieces ... She is in my mouth like a fragrance. – Where is she? Lying ill? Where? She does not leave me for an instant! ... I know nothing about the journey she made last Monday. (On that very evening, at about 6 o'clock, I possessed her!)

I ate and drank a lot at supper. Slept through the night. Got up saved!

June 7th, Whit Sunday.

In the early morning H——t was gone. But at about 10 o'clock she stormed me so that my epigastrium was nearly shot to pieces! Does that mean that he is beating her? These shooting sensations occur in the morning and in the afternoon!

I have been hearing a steamer today, from morning till noon!

Terrible day! Went to bed in the afternoon and met H——t in love. She called to me! She must be lying ill in bed.

Slept right through the night! Got up saved, though H——t sought me at 5 o'clock, but in vain.

June 8th, Whit Monday.

I had shooting pains in my epigastrium from 9.30 to 11.30. H——t sought me in eros, but weakly, mournfully, as if she were ill.

I was obliged to embrace her in the morning and in the afternoon, on the last occasion in love, after which she followed me, in love only, all evening. My heart rejoiced, I felt as if she had now made up her mind to choose me and that she had parted from W. I drank, and I played for her until 12 o'clock. But at 11 o'clock something must have happened for she assailed me with palpitations, as if someone was tormenting her. – I slept all night in spite of H—t's attacks. Got up saved.

This was an infinitely dismal Whitsun, but I worked hard at *A Blue Book*.

[. . .]

June 9th.

H—t is seeking me in love and eros, but I do not respond to eros, for it is her soul I want to meet. – At about 10 o'clock I could feel her in my epigastrium, shooting me to pieces, and I had to lie down and sleep. I wonder if she has another stomach ulcer that torments her in the morning and the evening; or is she pregnant?

When I was reading (Matter)* on Swedenborg yesterday, I began to wonder whether H—t is conscious of our life together, or whether the personality I embrace is a 'double' about whom she knows nothing, a phantom.

Matter tells us that one day, as Swedenborg sat writing, Cuno came in. Swedenborg proceeded to tell him that recently, in the spirit world, he had encountered the deceased King and also the still *living* Queen. Cuno asked him if a living person could visit the spirit world. S. answered that it was not the Queen herself, but her habitual spirit (esprit familier;[34] is that the same as spiritus familiaris?). S. said he had even encountered himself and Professor Ernesti in the spirit world.

This cannot be the explanation in H—t's case. Last autumn, when she returned after being away in the country for two months, she said quite openly: 'We are married, you know.' (She meant and admitted that for the whole summer we had lived together like married people, tele-

* A French theologian who published a biography of Swedenborg in 1863.

34. Strindberg was quoting here from the French translation through which he had first become acquainted with Swedenborg.

pathically, and with a joyousness that was never vouch-
safed us when we were actually in each other's company.)
And then again, after she got engaged, she wrote saying
that W. 'suffers because we are in rapport, he feels instinctively that we are'. That is a clear admission. And
when we were newly married she told me too how she
managed to seek me out during our engagement! She lay
and 'thought herself' into my dwelling ... – Yesterday
afternoon I saw her face clearly on my pillow. It was probably her astral body!

Fröken Falkner came; told me that Harriet is living at
Grand Hotel, here in Stockholm. Made no mention of W.
What can that mean?

H—t feels *abstracted*, almost unfriendly. She seeks me,
it is true, but I seem to be shielded, or she withdraws. At
about 6 o'clock I experienced the most fearful tension in
my epigastrium: 10 o'clock in the morning and 6 o'clock
in the evening! What can it be? I slept it off this morning.
Yesterday evening I embraced H—t and that caused it to
subside. It is inexplicable!

The night: H—t tormented me all night but I resisted
her for I experienced her as *false* and *hostile*. Fell for the
temptation at about 7 o'clock, but it brought me no joy.

[...]
June 10th.

H—t seeks me in eros. On the stroke of 10 a.m., the tension in my epigastrium was such that I got up and went
to lie down. 12 o'clock x x x.

By dinner-time suicidal mania had come upon me.

At 5.30 the tension in my epigastrium began and lasted
until 6.30. (It is *not* hysterical mereorism,* nor is it colic.)
My awareness of it is connected with H—t (she feels
friendly, like roses in my mouth) she wants me to embrace

---

* Hysterical mereorism is a nervous condition of the intestines.

her, but I do not want to abuse eros, or her. Today H—t was at Vetterö with Lillan!

A terrible evening. Went to bed at 10 o'clock. H—t sought me naïvely all night, but I was shielded. A little dog howled almost all night.

Read the last part of *A Blue Book* in the evening. Felt that my life was over!

[...]

June 11th.

Got up ill and returned to bed. Lay ill. Received a letter and flowers from Lillan. H—t had addressed the envelope. [...]

In the evening came a telephone call from Fru W. (Bosse). I went to take it, but the telephone rang off, gently, not in malice. I went back to bed and had H—t's palpitations. H—t seeks me all night, but I am shielded.

June 12th.

Got up while the bed was made. Lay down again! Suffered such frightful tension and was so much sought by H—t that I was forced to embrace her! After that I got up well, gave my body a thorough wash down, drank some milk and put on my clothes.

Have now settled down to work, but H—t is with me in eros and love. What is the meaning of all this?

H—t gave me shooting pains all night. The pain in my ventricle [35] was excruciating but I did not fall, even though I knew I should be free of it if I embraced her (in my thoughts).

'How then can I do this great wickedness and sin against God?[36]

[...]

35. An obsolete word for stomach in man or quadrupeds.
36. Genesis xxxxix: 9.

June 13th.

H—t torments me so much that I think I shall die of it. At this moment, 10 a.m., it is unendurable, but I will die rather than fall. Now, when I resist her and refuse to accept her in eros she seeks me like roses in my mouth.

I wonder if she has a stomach ulcer (as she had last year), and I am in pain because of it? Or is she pregnant and suffering periodically from the explosive movements of the foetus? (10 a.m. and 6 p.m.) (Or an abortion or a miscarriage?) God let me die rather than fall into sin. From now onwards I shall do my best to resist her in earnest, even if I have to die for it! Up to now I have not known how to act, have thought things were meant to be as they are, since the temptation was irresistible and God gave me no help. 10.30 a.m. My pain is at its height: even my heart is affected! – I lay down to sleep, it calmed me. (Reading: Christian Science.) When I woke I looked out of the dining-room window. A piece of white paper with something written on it was being carried by the wind, outwards, upwards, never came down, disappeared. A letter? The little dog howled (Anne-Marie). Worked on *A Blue Book*! Read Christian Science. Ate no dinner. Slept peacefully! Reading Christian Science. The sky is dark! I feel as if my last hour had come! The moment of suicide approaches! But that would appear hardly necessary as I am dying of hunger. My loathing for food has increased so rapidly that I have lost an incredible amount of weight. In 12 days I shall be dead as only 3/5 of my body is left now. Falck came. Told me the reason they could not go away was that W. had no money. Are living at 6 Grefgatan.

At 5.30 the excruciating tension in my epigastrium began!

After 60 years of torture I pray God that I may depart from this life! The little joy there was in it was illusory or false! My work was the only thing worth while, but that in part was wasted, or useless, or harmful.

Wife, child, home, all a mockery!

The only thing that gave me an illusion of happiness was wine! That is why I drank! It also mitigated the torment of being alive. It made my sluggish mind alert and intelligent! At times, in my youth, it stilled my hunger!

In my *Blue Book* I have been able to build and plant on the fire-ravaged sites, to set things right, to make amends. Now I have nothing more to say.

Women too gave me great, though specious, happiness which, however, immediately evaporated, and revealed itself for what it was. The first two left no memories, only active abhorrence. The last had qualities from a higher sphere, but mixed with much that was evil and ugly. All the same I remember her often as very beautiful though most of her was false! When my children were small they gave me the purest delight, but that did not last long!

Friends? They are among life's compromises! One cannot be quite alone! But since people all have conflicting interests they cannot be friends, may not be! Everything one does cuts across somebody's interest. Nils Andersson was my most faithful friend, and I his, perhaps most of all because we were not pursuing the same career!

A fairly quiet evening. I had a feeling that H—t must be with Lillan at Vettersö. All the same she sought me in eros, and I indicated that I was still with her; expected that she would come at night. She woke me at 12 o'clock, but I was shielded. Slept until morning, even though she sought me erotically. Got up saved. I had in fact intended to respond to her in eros, in order to be quit of my shooting pains and suicidal thoughts, for it is her hysterics that torture me, but I was not given leave. The little dog howled frightfully, but the noise it made sounded as if there were two of them. Mother and child?

[. . .]

June 14th.

Got up in a state of disharmony. In my book of devotions I got chastised for defending sin. At 9 o'clock my epigastrium was attacked so violently that I had to go to bed. Slept until getting on for 11 and was then calm. Read the text for the day and was again chastised. – But I cannot really feel guilty, for when H—t assaults me in my sleep I am defenceless and irresponsible, and in our embraces there is chaste love, as between husband and wife! She is 'my wife', isn't she? It makes me well and happy and, in the hell in which she now lives, she seems to find support in my love. Indeed, I sometimes believe that I shall save her from W.; save her for Lillan (not for myself).

[...]

About 1 p.m. the shooting pains began again. For a time I resisted temptation, but then I noticed that H—t was seeking me. I gave her to understand that I was still with her, and things became quieter. She felt friendly and loving (at that moment, about 2 o'clock, came a salute of guns); I had found her again, like roses in my mouth, palpitations and eros. What can have happened now? Is it she who stretches me? And with such strength? I seem doomed to love her or die!

[...]

Ate just a little at dinner. Slept tranquilly. No tension at 6 o'clock, but at about 8 it began. I sat down at the piano. H—t sought me out. I sat down at my desk. H—t was there too. And no sooner do I respond to her than the tension begins to ease. So it is caused by her onslaughts.

A terrible evening filled with suicidal mania! (Fru Carlén the portress came in for a chat. About Klemming!)[37] Later

37. Gustav Edvard Klemming, d. 1893. Librarian of the Royal Library in Stockholm at the time Strindberg was working there as an assistant, 1874–82. He was an ardent spiritualist and Swedenborgian and appears to have been a sort of father-figure to Strindberg. 'He

on, as I sat at my desk, H—t came, friendly, loving. I went to bed at 10 o'clock. As soon as H—t began to attack me I embraced her in order to get some peace. – Got peace and fell asleep. Was woken at 12 o'clock and was so squeezed until 5 o'clock that I thought I should die. The pain that came up from my stomach was like two swords penetrating my lungs. I could not bring myself to abuse H—t, but then I was made aware of the infernal hatred by a nauseating odour, like that of madness, as if she were trying to murder me by some of her wiles. On the stroke of 5, the time when I am usually called to her arms, the tension ceased.

June 15th.

Walked out to Djurgården. On the stroke of nine, while still there, the sensation of tension in my epigastrium, rising towards my chest, came on; but it only lasted for half an hour.

Worked all day and was spared further sensations of tension, probably because I maintained vague contact with H—t. All was quiet until 6.30, when I began to suffer frightful tension in my chest and stomach. Took a whisky, but did not enjoy it. Sat down to my desk. H—t was there and shot me to pieces. I went into the Yellow Room and took her in my arms x x x. Then things calmed down! – Is this what she wants of me? What then does her 'husband' mean to her? She is my wife, isn't she? If so, all is as it should be!

[. . .]

Night came. H—t attacked me with shooting pains, but I immediately put out my hand and stroked her and things grew quieter. Was woken at 3 and 5 o'clock, but avoided

---

seemed to be omniscient yet just, mild yet annihilating like the Almighty,' Strindberg said of him in *Genvägar* (*Short Cuts*), and he would have felt it to be no accident that the portress came in to talk about him at this crisis in his life.

pain by caressing her. She could not receive me (period, or prolapse, inversion?).[38]

June 16th.

Went for a walk this morning. At 8.30 the shooting pain began. I tried to calm it by responding. It helped to some extent, but not completely. The pain lasted until 11 o'clock. I slept for an hour.

My state is unendurable, but there is no need for me to take my own life as I shall die of this shooting pain that threatens my heart. What it is I do not know!

At about 1 o'clock, when the shooting pains came on, I drank cognac with wormwood. Fröken Falkner came and played Mendlessohn to me.

Had soup for dinner. Slept! tranquilly. Drank all evening and ate. Drank until 12 o'clock when I went to bed. Slept until the morning, tranquilly, even though I was aware of H—t's erotic but unloving assaults (which appear to be my shooting pains). She wants to keep me to herself, out of hatred. She wants to deprive me of my strength, so that I cannot re-marry, as she fears I may. Or is it that she wants to inveigle me into her infernal schemes? . . .

June 17th.

Went for a walk in Djurgården. At 9 o'clock she attacked me with shooting pains. When I got home I was aware of her in my mouth, like madness, elemental evil, hatred, witch-craft, like a taste from hell of brass and corpses. She sought me at my desk, erotically, but I did not respond! – Slept! – At about 1 o'clock she gave me more shooting pains and I took wormwood. Now, as I write, she is seeking me eroti-

38. In another part of the diary he writes: 'In the early days of our marriage I used to be pushed out at the very moment of climax, exactly as if her uterus were driving me back. She suffered both from "prolapsus uteri" and "inversio vaginae". This is what I had to put up with.'

cally, with shooting pains. So it is she! What does she want with me when she has a husband?

Terrible day and evening! Hatred!

A hard night; was tortured by pain from 2 o'clock until 5.30.

June 18th.

Ate hardly anything this morning. Took a walk in Djurgården. Both life and nature are black. At 8.30 the pain came on again, but when I caressed H——t, quite lightly, so that she knew I was there, it stopped. This is how I got through the morning until 11 o'clock, when I was forced to embrace her and thus escape further torture.

Grew more cheerful.

[...]

From 10 o'clock the night was tranquil, free from pain because I calmed H——t by stroking her gently. She could not receive my embraces. She must certainly be ill.

June 19th.

Out in Djurgården. Slight tension at about 8.30, but it slackened when I intimated I was there. Slept a lot. Ate little. A hard night!

June 21st. Sunday.

[...]

A terrible day!

A terrible night! Was tortured for five hours! Dreamt of H——t, modest, beautiful, like she was the time she knotted my cravat and afterwards kissed my lips as if I were her child. Dreamt too of a grey hen who came rubbing against me, wanting to be stroked. She was afraid of me, thought I was dangerous, but I stroked her and then she flew up and settled on the roosting-bar or shelf in the hen-house.

June 22nd, June 23rd, Midsummer Eve, June 24th, Midsummer Day.

Terrible days! So terrible that I shall no longer describe them! I shall only pray to God to let me die, and by dying escape from this horrible physical and spiritual agony!

A doctor has been called!*

Stayed at 40 Karlavägen until the 11th.

July 11th.

Moved to 85 IV Drottninggatan.

---

*On the same day, 24 June 1908, Strindberg wrote to his publisher, Karl Otto Bonnier: 'I am sure that I have cancer of the stomach. I am in pain for twelve hours out of the 24, and shall cease, little by little, to eat or sleep.' The shooting pains in his epigastrium, so often mentioned in his diary at this time, and which he himself associated with Harriet Bosse's telepathic visits, were probably the first symptoms of cancer, and a forewarning of the illness from which he died four years later.

APPENDIX: AN OUTLINE OF STRINDBERG'S LIFE AND WORK

August Strindberg was born in Stockholm in 1849 and died there in 1912. He was an enormously prolific writer, interested in everything, and there is hardly a field of literary activity to which he did not make some contribution. John Landquist's edition of his collected works numbers 55 volumes.

Strindberg's first major work, the play *Master Olof* written in 1872, did not win recognition until 1881, and his real literary break-through was achieved with a novel, *The Red Room* (1879).

In 1877 he married the would-be actress, Siri von Essen, and in the '80s wrote many more plays, among them the naturalistic dramas, of which *The Father*, *Miss Julie* and *Creditors* are perhaps the best known.

In 1891 he was divorced from Siri von Essen, and in 1892 lack of recognition in Sweden drove him to Berlin where he met his second wife, the young Austrian journalist Frida Uhl, whom he married in 1893. After a brief visit to England they went to Germany and France and parted in 1894.

Strindberg now entered upon a new phase, known as his Inferno period, a time of mental and spiritual ferment and readjustment, described in two autobiographical works, *Inferno* and *Legends* (1897–8). During this period he eschewed belles-lettres and, under the influence of the French alchemists and occultists, devoted himself instead to scientific or pseudo-scientific studies and writings.

In 1898, after he had regained his equilibrium and was settled for a time in Lund, came first *To Damascus*, Part I; the story in dramatic and symbolic form of his second marriage and Inferno crisis, interwoven with reminiscences from both earlier and later periods; followed in the same year by *To Damascus*, Part II, and then, in 1899, by a flood of historical plays. His standing as a dramatist was now greatly improved and with his return to Stockholm came more plays, among them *Easter*, *The Dance of Death*, and *To Damascus*, Part III.

In 1900 he met, and in 1901 he married the gifted young Norwegian actress Harriet Bosse and, under the influence of his love for her, he wrote the fairy-tale play *Swanwhite* (1901), followed in the same year, during a period of anger and disillusionment with Harriet, by *Queen Christina*. In 1901 he also wrote the remarkable expressionistic drama *A Dream Play*.

Writing was the breath of life to Strindberg, and even after his marriage to Harriet Bosse had broken down and in days of dark despair he continued to produce both plays and prose works. In 1907 he and the young actor August Falck succeeded in starting the Intimate Theatre, especially for the performance of Strindberg's plays, and for this he wrote the four Chamber Plays, *Storm*, *After the Fire*, *The Ghost Sonata* and *The Pelican*. His last play, *The Great Highway*, was written in 1909. Sequels to his *Blue Book* and philological and polemical writings occupied his last years.

M. S.